ENEMIES
WITH A COMMON GOAL—
SURVIVAL!

Harvey Ardman's powerhouse novel of human
beings thrust against their will into the furious
arena of international power politics . . . com-
rades-in-espionage caught in a maelstrom of
hatred between countries and men, relentlessly
propelled toward an explosive climax of violence,
desperation, and death!

"A STUNNING INTERNATIONAL ESPIONAGE
ADVENTURE . . . One deadly intrigue after another. Hooked on page one, I stayed hooked to the
gut-wracking end. Ardman is a master craftsman!"

LELAND COOLEY
Bestselling Author of
THE ART COLONY and *CALIFORNIA*

"AN IMAGINATIVE CRAFTSMAN . . . HE BEARS
COMPARISON WITH THE BEST . . . Here he al-
ters the familiar espionage elements into patterns
as unpredictable as those wave-forms at the Hall of
Mirrors in the Tivoli Gardens where the most sus-
penseful scenes in the book take place . . . A well-
made novel with much going for it!"

PUBLISHERS WEEKLY

HARVEY ARDMAN
ENDGAME

AVON
PUBLISHERS OF BARD, CAMELOT, DISCUS, EQUINOX AND FLARE BOOKS

ENDGAME is an original publication of Avon Books.
This work has never before appeared in any form.

AVON BOOKS
A division of
The Hearst Corporation
959 Eighth Avenue
New York, New York 10019

First Avon Printing, June, 1975.

AVON TRADEMARK REG. U.S. PAT. OFF. AND
FOREIGN COUNTRIES, REGISTERED TRADEMARK—
MARCA REGISTRADA, HECHO EN CHICAGO, U.S.A.

Printed in the U.S.A.

To Perri and Lauren.

MAY 11

Prologue

The blue Volkswagen bus labeled "Chin Lee—Hand Laundry" slowly lurched over the uneven cobblestones at the foot of Damrak street, crossed the canal bridge that linked Amsterdam's ornate, multi-gabled Central Station with the rest of the city, and cautiously drove into the *Stationsplein*—a paved, treeless plaza that served as a parking lot and drop-off point. It hesitated a bit at the station's main entrance, as if reconnoitering, then pulled into an unobtrusive parking spot about a hundred yards away, its motor left running.

A few moments later, a young Oriental on a moped— a noisy little motorbike—repeated the Volkswagen's route. But he found a parking spot at the other end of the station, closer to the freight dock than the passenger entrance.

Before another minute had passed, another Oriental—a compactly built fellow in his early twenties— sauntered out of the station's main entrance carrying a denim duffel bag and a small grey Samsonite two-suiter. He dumped both at the curb, plopped down on the duffel bag, opened a battered copy of *Europe on Five Dollars a Day* and began whistling "Oh, What a Beautiful Morning." He glanced at neither the Volkswagen bus nor the man on the moped.

It was about six-thirty in the morning. The sun was up, but most of Amsterdam was still asleep. It would be at least an hour until bicycles, cars and mopeds did battle in the city streets as they transported their owners to work once more. At this hour, anyhow, Amsterdam was placid. Even the opaque canal waters seemed to flow more slowly, an impression that might have been caused by an unusual paucity of floating debris. That would change within the month, though, as the flood tide of tourists began, bringing with it a flood tide of empty yellow Kodak boxes, Kleenexes, Hershey bar wrappers and cigarette butts.

Amsterdam Central Station was also relatively quiet, or at least as quiet as a major European railroad station ever gets. Seven taxis of assorted colors were lined up at the curb in front of the station, apparently waiting for the first train of the day from The Hague, each of them hoping to bag a diplomat. Five of the drivers were dozing, one was working a crossword puzzle and the last—a thin blond man with watery blue eyes—was leaning on his cab door, tossing bits of stale bread to a trio of mangy pigeons.

At the other end of the station, a small van was parked at the loading dock. Two men in striped overalls were stacking cardboard cartons marked *damesverband*—sanitary napkins—onto dollies. Occasionally one of them made an obscene remark and the other laughed loudly.

In front of the station, a portly man in his middle fifties walked wearily to a shuttered-up newsstand, unlocked the door, pulled in a twine-tied package of morning papers and began cutting it open. As he worked, a little old man dragged a snack cart into position a few yards away and began setting out a row of cellophane-wrapped donuts.

The unmarked silver-colored armored car lumbered through downtown Amsterdam's nearly empty streets at close to its top speed—40 mph. Though it wasn't much bigger than a delivery van, the vehicle was built more like a tank. It was protected top and bottom and on all sides by three inches of carbon-steel plating. The front windows—actually, they weren't much more than slits—were heavy, bullet-proof glass. The side windows and rear portholes were four-inch quartz glass, impervious to handgun projectiles.

Today, the vehicle was manned by four men: a driver, two guards, and, in command, Sergeant Rudolph Von Hahn, formerly of Interpol. The two guards sat in back, each at a porthole. They were armed with Browning Automatic Rifles. Each carried two hand grenades. Sergeant Von Hahn and the driver were in the front compartment, which was separated from the rear by an armored partition. A standard NATO heavy machine gun sat between them in a special mount, its muzzle poking through a hole just below the windshield.

Sergeant Von Hahn peered once more at his wristwatch. It was 6:31. "How far?" he asked the driver.

The driver glanced at a street sign. "Another four minutes," he said.

Von Hahn nodded. "Good." He made no attempt to engage the driver in conversation. The man wasn't a talker. He hadn't volunteered a word since the trip began, and, when questioned, answered as briefly as possible. Von Hahn wasn't comfortable with men of this sort, but he supposed they had their place.

So far, Von Hahn thought, everything was going exactly according to schedule. They'd left The Hague vaults at 6:00 exactly, encountered no traffic, no unusual problems, nothing out of the ordinary. The elaborate precautions—as usual—would be nothing more than wasted effort. That didn't disturb him, though. The precautions were a kind of ritual, a ceremony. They imposed a comforting order on everything.

The armored car paused at a changing light at the corner of Oudezijds Kolk and Geldersekade—at the Schrieerstoren (the Tower of Tears)—continued over the Singel Canal and headed toward Central Station.

Von Hahn leaned forward, looking through the slitlike front windshield. "The freight dock is to the left," he told the driver. "There's a small van there. Do you see it?"

9

The driver hesitated momentarily as he scanned the *stationsplein*. "Yes," he said. "I see it." He tugged on the wheel and the van slowly turned left.

As the armored car approached the freight loading dock, the newsdealer stood up, folded his knife, and stepped out of his kiosk. The Volkswagen bus and the moped pulled out of their parking places and headed toward each other. The young man who'd been sitting on his duffel bag rose to his feet, picked up his suitcase and clicked open the latches, holding the case shut with his thumb. The old man at the snack cart cocked his head in curiosity, evidently surprised by the sudden burst of activity.

The Volkswagen bus and the moped passed each other almost exactly in front of the main station entrance, the little motorbike putt-putting directly for the armored car now, the Volkswagen toward the loading dock.

"Hey!" Von Hahn shouted.

"I see him," the driver said calmly, steering abruptly to the right.

The evasive maneuver would have worked if the moped operator was merely being careless. As it was, he was an excellent driver, particularly chosen for this mission. He altered his course slightly to compensate for the armored van's attempt to avoid a collision.

"That bastard's aiming at us!" Von Hahn shouted once more.

"You're sure?" the driver asked. It was his first question of the trip.

There was no need to answer. At the last possible instant, the moped driver flung himself from his little machine, struck the pavement with a gymnastic bound, rolled over three times and leaped to his feet. The moped smashed into the armored car's right rear wheel at perhaps 30 mph, shattering itself into a thousand pieces—and instantly disabling what was obviously its prey.

Minus a wheel, the armored vehicle ground to a quick halt, its steel undercarriage sending a shower of sparks in all directions, the metal screeching hideously against the paving blocks.

Then, for a moment, there was silence.

The young Oriental at the station entrance now opened his suitcase and took out a steel tube two feet long and about five inches in diameter. He reached back into his suitcase, took out a tiny rocket, inserted it into the tube, pointed the contraption at the rear doors of the armored car, and pressed the firing button.

There was a soft *whoosh,* then, almost immediately, a tremendous bang as the shell hit its mark. A small round hole suddenly appeared in the armored car's left rear door. Then, a moment later, there was a muffled explosion. Both doors blew open. Dense black smoke poured out of the doorway. After a second or two, a uniformed guard appeared where the doors had been, BAR in hand. He fell to the pavement, lifeless.

By now, the dozing taxi drivers were awake and staring. The one who'd been feeding the pigeons had hopped into his cab and was slowly backing up. The pigeons were winging their way west. The newsdealer, who'd been unfastening a shutter, now closed it and retreated inside his kiosk, where he was joined by the snack-cart man.

The Oriental who'd fired the rocket and the one who'd run his moped into the armored car were now running toward it, both brandishing machine pistols.

"Are you all right?" Von Hahn asked the driver.

"So far," the driver replied.

"Then help me with this thing."

Together, they pulled the machine gun from its mooring and reversed it, so that it faced rearward into the main compartment, through a firing port evidently designed for exactly these circumstances.

"See anything?" Von Hahn asked.

"Just smoke."

Outside, the two Orientals had reached the van. They peered cautiously inside. Then one clambered aboard.

"Something's moving in there," Von Hahn said.

"He's not ours," the driver observed.

Von Hahn squeezed the machine gun's trigger

briefly. A dozen shots rattled back into the main compartment, at least half striking the man who'd just climbed aboard. The force of the slugs propelled him backward out of the van and onto the pavement. He stumbled for a few yards, then fell, his arms and legs oddly tangled.

His companion gazed at him for just a moment, then ran back to his suitcase. Once more, he loaded the steel tube.

"Let's get out of here," said Von Hahn, who'd been watching through a side port.

"Right."

The sergeant opened the door on the van's far side and dropped to the ground. The driver followed a moment later. Shortly, the armored car was shaken by a second shell, which blew out its front and side windows.

Satisfied that the danger was past, the man who'd fired the rocket launcher ran once more toward the armored vehicle. He hopped up inside the still-smoking main compartment. No sooner had he disappeared into the smoke than Von Hahn came around back, his handgun drawn. He fired twice into the haze, then climbed up himself. Moments later, he dropped the dead Oriental out of the door.

Now the Volkswagen bus left its post at the loading dock and started for the armored vehicle, guns firing from both side windows. It never reached its destination. The cab that had been backing up had now freed itself of the taxi line. With screeching tires, it accelerated across the *stationsplein*. It struck the Volkswagen bus just behind the passenger door. For a moment, the Volkswagen teetered on its two outside wheels, then, with a crash, fell on its side. One rear wheel continued to spin.

For a time, the only noise in the place was the echo of the crash. Then there was the rasp of metal against metal as the bus's side door slid open. Three more Orientals hopped out, all of them wearing black pajamas and carrying pistols and hand grenades.

Two were picked off almost immediately by the men

who'd been stacking the sanitary napkins. At the first sign of trouble, each had ripped open a carton and pulled out a rifle.

The remaining Oriental pulled the firing pin from a grenade and hurled it in the general direction of the armored vehicle. It fell short, rolling up against the snack cart. Then, it exploded, sending a shower of burning donuts, cold cereal and milk-carton fragments fifty feet into the air. For a few moments, it rained breakfast food. The Oriental was trying to pull a second grenade out of his jacket when he, too, was picked off by one of the freight handlers.

Then nothing moved.

Shortly, the newsdealer left his kiosk and walked toward Sergeant Von Hahn, who was standing near the armored van.

"I think that ends the excitement, sergeant," he said. "How are the guards?"

"I'm afraid one is dead, Mr. Jelle. The other man is still in there, knocked out by the explosion, I think. How many of them did we get?"

"I counted five," said Mr. Jelle. He stuck his thumbs in his vest pockets—revealing a small black pistol tucked in his waistband—and surveyed the scene.

"Do you think we have anything more to worry about?"

"Of course. There's always something more to worry about. But maybe not today."

In the distance, there was the sound of approaching sirens. "Did someone call the police?" Von Hahn asked.

Jelle chuckled. "We've had two auto accidents, three explosions, and any number of gunshots, sergeant. If that isn't enough to interest the police, I'd think they were all on vacation."

As Jelle and Von Hahn talked, the rear door of the Volkswagen bus slowly inched open. Yet another lithe Oriental slipped out and slid behind the armored car. By this time, the men on the loading dock had ceased their vigilance. The taxi driver—if that's what he was—was fully engaged in trying to pry open his door.

Jelle and Von Hahn were not in a position to see the man.

Suddenly, he darted between them, raised both hands, uttered a piercing karate cry, and, in a flash, kicked Von Hahn once with each leg. The stolid officer crumpled to the ground. Then the Oriental turned to Jelle.

"*Hiiyaaa!*" he cried.

Jelle raised his eyebrows, as if offended. He took one step backward. The Oriental grinned wickedly. Jelle pulled the small pistol from his waistband and squeezed the trigger once. There was a tiny pop, a cap gun-like sound. The Oriental looked at Jelle in astonishment, then fell over backward in a single, smooth motion. He hit the pavement hard and never moved again.

Jelle hurried to Von Hahn. "Are you all right, sergeant?"

Von Hahn was on his knees, coughing. "Yes, sir," he said, struggling for breath. "I think so, sir." He got to his feet and brushed himself off. "Sorry I let that one get by."

"No matter."

"No, sir. Not with the way you handled him."

Jelle smiled and shrugged.

Now the first of the police cars arrived, its siren blaring, its light flashing ominously. It screeched to a stop, and no less than four officers piled out and ran toward the scene.

At the other end of the station, a second armored van—smaller and older than the first—pulled into the *stationsplein* and backed up to the loading dock. The doors quickly swung open and three large wooden crates were taken from the vehicle and wheeled away.

"So much for that," said Jelle.

"Yes, sir," Von Hahn replied.

"You get on the train, sergeant. I'll be with you in a moment, after I speak to these gentlemen."

"Yes, sir," Von Hahn said brightly. He turned and walked briskly toward the station.

MAY 12
DAY ONE

Chapter One

The task was impossible, actually and theoretically. Still, it would be interesting to try. Maybe there was one last miracle left in him.

Yaakov Ben-Ezra smiled as he realized, finally, that this time it was curiosity that motivated him, not patriotism. Had it always been that way? No matter.

He paused on the cobblestone street in front of the *Rund Tarn*. It was comforting to be home again. But was Copenhagen his home? When he was younger, he had no such doubts.

Ben-Ezra took a deep breath of the crisp Scandinavian air. For a moment, he felt nothing. Then there was the pain. It was like an old friend by now, reminding him that he was alive. Another breath, and it passed.

He walked down the street, feeling the throbbing in his calf again. How the high command of the *Mossad*—the Central Bureau of Intelligence and Security—must have argued about him. The old men had probably contended that he was too old; the incompetent questioned his abilities; the lambs doubted his courage; the sickly, his health.

Yaakov Ben-Ezra stopped at the corner of Krystalgade and Peter Hvitfeldts Straede. The Svenska Quality

Porno Shop was in view. He almost reached for a cigarette, then remembered he'd find none.

"You cannot resist it, can you, Yaakov," General Nachman had said, so sure of the answer he'd made the question into a statement.

Some men put on a show appearing noncommittal immediately after they've made up their minds with finality, and Ben-Ezra was one of these. He'd shrugged. "I think it's a job for a younger man. Give it to one of your go-go boys."

Nachman hadn't been fooled. "It would be a fitting climax to your career, my friend. Don't pretend to me that you're not interested. Remember, you're talking to an old, old friend who knows you very well."

It was true. Ben-Ezra had always harbored the notion that he was an artist. And, like every artist, he'd always hoped to paint one surpassing picture before he put the brushes away for good.

He walked halfway down the block, ostensibly looking into shop windows. No one was paying the least attention to him, he noted almost unconsciously.

It wasn't the situation that was so bad. God knows, he'd threaded his way through worse. It was the competition. Egyptians, Russians, Dutch, Americans, maybe even Chinese. True, most of them were kibitzers. But who can play at top form with a roomful of kibitzers?

Ben-Ezra casually entered the porno shop. The small bell at the top of the door tinkled in response. Inside, a young American couple was excitedly shuffling through a stack of *Color Climax* magazines. They were like children in a lollipop factory. He felt a small glow of paternalism.

They'd insisted Miriam go back with him to help—his own daughter. He knew he wouldn't be comfortable with her, but he managed to stay silent, for her sake and his. Intellectually, at least, he admired their judgment. She had just the right mixture of softness and hardness. She was blonde and blue-eyed, thanks to her Nordic mother. And though she wasn't all that experienced, she'd shown she could handle herself well, which wasn't so surprising, considering her teacher—himself.

Ben-Ezra checked his watch. Miriam would be back at any moment. He grew impatient for the young American couple to leave. Finally, they did, buying so much that the apple-cheeked salesgirl had to use two plastic shopping bags to package it all.

The doorbell tinkled again as they left, and the salesgirl smiled at Ben-Ezra. He gave a little shove on a row of bookshelves, and they opened up, like a door. On the other side, another shove put the bookshelves back into place. Ben-Ezra flipped on the light switch and looked around. There was a fine layer of dust over everything—the scratched-up wooden desk, the squat little safe, the desk chair with the cracked green leather upholstery, the two wooden side chairs. Even the overhead fixture seemed dimmer than before. But then, he'd been away for almost a month, being briefed, rushed through a beginner's course in nuclear physics.

There was a time when Ben-Ezra wanted to do everything himself, from beginning to end—locate the quarry, figure out a plan of attack, parry the defense, if any, and bring the mission to a successful conclusion. Now he preferred to let others handle the preliminaries, even the major maneuvers. Openings and middle-games bored him, sapped his energies. He was best in the endgame.

Ben-Ezra sat down heavily in the leather desk chair and checked his watch once more. Miriam should be back soon and the game begun. This afternoon, Borgmann would arrive in Copenhagen. Then there was a chance. Ben-Ezra edited the thought: there was no chance—not really—but he couldn't do more. He would play out the game—though for the first time in his life there seemed to be only one possibility, not two.

The bookcase creaked and Ben-Ezra looked up sharply. Miriam "Shazar" stepped into the inner office. She was in her late twenties and quite pretty, in a healthy-looking, outdoorsy way. She was dressed, as usual, in a bulky ski sweater and light blue corduroy pants. She and Ben-Ezra had argued about that outfit.

He'd called it unseemly and she'd called him old-fashioned. "My clothing makes me look like a college student," she'd said. "What better disguise could there be?" Ben-Ezra had yielded, with no notable grace.

His eyebrows rose and stayed up. "Well?"

"I was at the railroad station when the train pulled in," Miriam said. "It was heavily guarded, just as we'd thought. But EURATOM security took three packages from it, not one. They put each one in a separate armored van and the vans drove off in different directions. There was no way I could follow all three of them, Yaakov."

There it was again, that first-name business. The *sabras* respected no one.

"Miriam, I sense you have more bad news for me."

"I saw Suliman Ferrara at the station, watching the train. I don't think he took any special note of me."

"Ah. Black moves. Pawn to King four."

"Yaakov, I don't think I can stand another one of those portentous chess analogies. This is life, you know, not an Ingmar Bergman movie. We expected the Arabs and they're here."

"And so what else is new?" Ben-Ezra snapped back. "Well, let's see where we stand now. We have no idea where those boxes went. We don't even know for sure that they're still in Copenhagen. Whatever opportunity we had to take a bead on them is gone. And now Ferrara is on the scene. He's not an experienced espionage agent, Miriam, but from what we know of him, he's extraordinarily able and intelligent."

The girl sat down in one of the side chairs, bravado gone for the moment, her eyes refusing to meet Ben-Ezra's.

The old man gazed at his daughter and his anger drained away. In moments like these, he saw the little girl, not the woman—if he let himself. He saw past the wall she'd put up to protect herself against the world, to the wounded child she once had been—and still was, underneath it all.

Miriam had never really recovered from her mother's death. Ben-Ezra knew that now. She'd seemed to weather it easily enough—at least he'd seen it that way, in his own grief. He'd told himself that small children don't have deep emotional attachments, as do adults. And he'd thought it was just as well.

So he'd felt free to leave her with friends and relatives, to resume his career, to spend long months away from her. Now, seeing the result, he blamed himself for his blindness.

After her mother died, Miriam had never had another really close relationship with anyone. Her wall protected her from unhappiness well enough. She was safe from the loss of a friend or a relative, or even a father. But her wall also kept her from trusting, from committing herself to someone else. It allowed her one kind of intimacy—the trivial kind—while preventing her from experiencing the other variety, the only one that mattered. He'd tried a dozen times to repair the damage and failed. Even time hadn't helped—it had been nearly twenty-five years since Karen had died.

Still, he hoped.

Ben-Ezra looked at his watch again, then speaking more gently now, broke the silence. "Frederick should be here in an hour or so."

Miriam brightened. She hadn't seen Frederick Borgmann since she was a little girl, but the name still brought a warm feeling with it.

"With Frederick's help," Ben-Ezra went on, "anything is possible. After all, this is his homeland. An old acquaintance renewed, a small favor here and there and we're back in business."

"Yaakov, stop patronizing me." Miriam had regained her composure. "Even if we can convince him to help us—which is unlikely—that may not be enough. And, we have an impossible task—you said so yourself."

"I was exaggerating. I always exaggerate, Miriam. You know that," Ben-Ezra said. His tone was that of a man trying to be convincing.

"And what about the difficulty of convincing Frederick to help? Was that an exaggeration, too? I remem-

19

ber what he said about that when he was in Israel years ago."

Ben-Ezra was surprised. "You do? That was so long ago. But it doesn't matter. The situation has changed. Now we're talking about the very survival of Israel."

"We're always talking about the very survival of Israel. Have you ever undertaken a mission where less was at stake? It's a broken record already."

"If patriotism isn't enough, maybe friendship will be," Ben-Ezra said, half to himself, half in response to Miriam. "But that's my department, young lady."

"And no trespassing, eh?"

Ben-Ezra made no response. He was tired. The pain was back when he breathed. It was enough that the whole thing was impossible. Did he also have to contend with an equal thirty years his junior, female, and his own daughter besides?

Chapter Two

Borgmann squinted into the sun. It was morning and he was awake. He tried to stretch, but he'd yet to find the economy-class chair that could comfortably accommodate his six feet two inches, and this one was no exception.

He stood up, half-crouching under the seat lights and reached up into the luggage rack, feeling around for his suit jacket. Finding it, he pulled it free and plopped back down. He pulled a pair of horn-rim glasses from the breast pocket of his jacket and slipped them on.

All in all, Borgmann felt lousy. He hadn't slept all that well. He was annoyed by the stubble on his face and by that greasy, unwashed feeling. He felt cramped in his seat and he had to go to the bathroom badly. Once more, he wondered why he'd decided to go.

True, Dr. Kastner hadn't objected when he'd asked for time off. Borgmann had come prepared with a variety of arguments—that he hadn't had a vacation in nearly two years, that he was at a natural stopping point in his work, that the conference might have professional value. None of them had been needed.

"Take a week," Dr. Kastner said. "Take two. When you come back, your design will be machined into hard metal, ready to be tested. Unless I miss my guess, you've done it this time."

"That's what the computer says. Still, I'm anxious to see the pilot plant start up. If the pilot design works, we'll have breeder reactors in commercial operation three years ahead of schedule. Think of what that will do to the energy crisis."

"Thanks to you, Frederick."

"Thanks to everybody at Argonne. It just shows you what we can do if we're given a practical problem—instead of being assigned to verify one esoteric theory or another."

Kastner grinned. "I can't wait to see how Washington would react. When would you say we'll be ready to show it to the AEC?"

"Ten days after we run definitive tests. But count me out of that party."

"Why?"

"You know how I feel about that Washington crew. And they don't like me much, either. Let Hoffman show off the gadget. After all, it's his creation, too."

Kastner considered the thought. "Whatever you say, Frederick. Now go home and get packed. I don't want to see you around here for at least a week."

Borgmann yawned and stretched. He glanced out of the airplane window again, just in time to watch a spectacular cirrocumulus formation glide by. In seven days, the lab would demonstrate the viability of his new design—there was no question of it. Fifteen separate computer simulations had removed the few doubts he'd had. It was the culmination of seven years' work on breeder reactors. Now, perhaps, he would turn to fusion power. Maybe what he'd learned at Los Alamos could also benefit mankind.

"Pretty hard to sleep in a plane, isn't it?" asked the man beside him, speaking just loud enough to be heard over the noise of the jet engines.

Borgmann regarded him hostilely. Either he had forgotten the man, after seeing him last night, which was exceptionally unlikely, or the man had switched into that seat after he'd dozed off. There was something familiar about him, Borgmann decided, but it was an old memory, not a fresh one.

"Yeah," Borgmann replied, mouthing the appropriate cliché, "especially for someone my size."

He managed a smile while his mind flipped through

image after image, trying to pin down the familiar elements. The man was five or ten years older than he—about fifty-two—burr-headed, greying at the temples, dressed in country gentleman's attire—tweedy jacket, leather elbow patches, pipe in the pocket and the like. Borgmann's mental card file suddenly stopped rotating. A wave of anger swept over him. This could be no accident.

"And you, Mr. Stabile, how did you sleep?" Borgmann waited for a reaction.

There was only the slightest widening of the eyes. The man had admirable control. "Pardon me?"

"I said, did you sleep well, Stabile?"

"I think you're confusing me with someone else, fella. Name's Fowler. I work for Pepsi International." The plane jounced slightly as it hit a patch of turbulent air.

Borgmann was enjoying himself, despite his earlier bout with anger. "No confusion here," he said. "You're Gary Stabile, CIA Security."

"CIA?" the man asked, doing a fine job of appearing astonished. "That's silly."

"Come on, Stabile. I not only know who you are but also why you're sitting here beside me."

"This is really a case of mistaken identity," Borgmann's seatmate insisted. "I'm sure we've never met before."

"Well, it has been a long time. Eniwetok, 1952. The H-bomb project. You were a 'security aide,' I believe they called it, for foreign-born personnel."

The man looked at Borgmann as if he were weighing another protest. Then he gave up. "You have a remarkable memory, Professor Borgmann."

Borgmann ignored Stabile's remark. He'd heard that phrase a thousand times in his life, more or less. "And now you're going to be my baby-sitter in Copenhagen, right?" The plane jolted again.

"I suppose you wouldn't believe me if I said it's just a coincidence that we're on this plane together."

"Hardly."

Stabile bit his lips reflectively. He glanced up to see if

23

the no-smoking sign was lit. It wasn't. He slipped the dark briar out of his jacket pocket, stuffed it with tobacco from a small yellow plastic pouch, and lit up. "You're right, of course."

"Why, after all these years, is anyone at CIA security interested in me? All my secrets are seventeen years out of date."

Stabile smiled amiably, taking a small puff on his pipe. It gurgled disreputably. "Frankly, we're not interested in you, exactly. It's just that you may be involved in something that's caught our attention."

"I'm not involved in anything," Borgmann replied. "I'm just going to listen in at the annual EURATOM conference. I'm an invited guest, you know."

Stabile took another puff and grinned like a leprechaun. "You'd be surprised what we know."

The tall physicist looked at his seatmate with annoyance. "Stabile," he said coolly, "I think it's about time the government stopped prying into my personal life. Whatever you think you may know, let me assure you, it's of no interest to anyone but me."

Stabile puffed away, unperturbed. "Including that request from Yaakov Ben-Ezra?"

Borgmann felt his face flush. In spite of himself, he knew his surprise showed.

Stabile's pipe went out and he went through great ceremony putting in more tobacco, packing it down with a pipe tool, and relighting it. "Here you are, flying to Copenhagen, about to participate in the EURATOM conference, and all at Ben-Ezra's request." There was a friendly, slightly ironic twinkle in his eye.

The note. They must have intercepted the note. Thank God the meeting place and the passwords were written in that private code he and Ben-Ezra had put together long ago. "You've got it backward," Borgmann said. "When I knew I was going to the conference, I wrote him. He's an old friend, and it was a chance to renew our ties." And now, for the first time, Borgmann realized the real request implicit in Ben-Ezra's message.

"Good morning, ladies and gentlemen. This is the captain speaking." His English was practically perfect.

24

"We shall be landing at Kastrup Airport in approximately forty-five minutes. The ground temperature in Copenhagen this morning is 20 degrees Celsius, 68 degrees Fahrenheit. Let me take this opportunity to wish you a pleasant stay. We hope to see you again soon on SAS."

A stewardess, dark-haired and shapely, paused at Borgmann's row and handed out hot towels. Borgmann took off his glasses and wiped his face. It was a considerate touch, and it improved his mood considerably.

"Listen, Professor Borgmann," Stabile said, his tone carefully apologetic, "It may be that we've gotten our wires crossed back at Foggy Bottom. That happens from time to time, you know. If so, I hope you'll forgive this intrusion. I'm just doing my job."

Borgmann let the remark echo between them without comment. His mind had translated it into another familiar phrase: I was only a good German.

The stewardess had returned, with trays of juice and rolls. Borgmann pushed the button on the back of the seat in front of him to release the meal tray. It opened—then collapsed.

"Oh," the stewardess said, dismayed. "I'm so sorry, sir." She looked around for a vacant seat Borgmann could shift to. There was none.

"No problem," Borgmann said. He reached awkwardly into his pocket and pulled out a multi-bladed red Swiss army knife. With a thumbnail, he flipped out the screwdriver blade. He tinkered with the meal tray frame, then raised the tray to its proper position. It stayed. "I'll take that juice now," he said with a smile.

"Always prepared, aren't you," Stabile said, amused.

"It's my Boy Scout training," Borgmann replied coldly.

They ate their snacks in silence, Borgmann involving himself in a newspaper he'd brought from Chicago.

The news was familiar enough. Kosygin was traveling once more to Damascus, this time to see the new Syrian leader and renew his support. A Concorde SST had crash-landed at Johannesburg, South Africa—six dead, fourteen injured. The Secretary of the Interior had announced that oil shale production would top 100,000 barrels a day for the first time, by June first. The president had vehemently denied he'd had anything to do with the firing of George Allen, former coach of the Washington Redskins. The Association of Potato Farmers predicted a fifteen per cent price rise by year end, blamed it on increased fertilizer costs. Doctors at Houston reported that Szlodnik Lopati, the man with the artificial heart, was doing well as he entered his second postoperative week. Police officials said they were unable to explain how four huge glass panels on the seventy-third floor of the John Hancock Building had been shattered the previous night, apparently from the outside. The mayor told reporters that the meter maid strike, now in its third day, had not affected police ticketing policies. The Chicago Bears announced that they'd signed Jesus Ramirez, the famous Brazilian soccer player, to kick field goals during their next season.

Borgmann started flipping through the paper, looking for any mention of Argonne National Laboratory, as was his habit. After a half-hour or so, the plane began to descend. "Listen," Stabile said, trying once more to be friendly, "you enjoy yourself in Copenhagen. I won't be bothering you again."

"Flying back right away?" Borgmann asked.

The no-smoking sign lit up and Stabile snuffed out his pipe. "No, not right away. Thought I'd stay in Copenhagen a few days. On the expense account, you know. Beautiful city, I hear. But then, you'd know that better than I."

"Yes." The word was intended to end the conversation, and it did just that. Borgmann folded his paper and looked around the cabin, trying to forget about Stabile. It was his first time on a 747 and, he decided, he liked it. It was more like being in a movie theater than on an airplane.

As he glanced at the passengers, an eight-year-old boy came running down the aisle nearest him. As he arrived at Borgmann's row, the boy stopped, jumped up and down on the floor with all his weight. Then he did it again.

A stewardess appeared out of nowhere. "I'm sorry, young man," she said. "You'd better return to your seat. We'll be landing soon."

"It doesn't go down," the boy told the stewardess.

"Beg pardon?"

"I jumped with all my might and it didn't go down, not even an inch."

"What?"

"Watch. You'll see." The boy jumped again, then looked at the stewardess in triumph. "There."

"Very impressive." The stewardess smiled a plastic smile. Borgmann couldn't tell if she were amused or annoyed. "Now would you please return to your seat?"

"Yes, ma'am."

A few seconds later, the seat-belt sign lit up. Borgmann fastened his belt and closed his eyes. Exactly what awaited him in Copenhagen, he could not be sure. He looked out the window. In the distance, he could see the city, shimmering in the sun. It seemed unreal, as if it were only an exceptionally detailed miniature.

Borgmann had been too busy to anticipate this moment. Now, it caught him off guard. He was nearly overwhelmed by a rush of emotion, by a thousand unsorted memories. Below him was his home, the city of his birth and of his childhood. The plane dipped lower. He began to catch glimpses of familiar buildings. At the same time, he began to see that much of this city was new to him.

Ben-Ezra was down there somewhere, waiting for him, wanting something from him. He hoped against hope that he'd be able to agree. There'd been no question of not answering Ben-Ezra's summons—he owed the man that much and more.

He tried to concentrate on Copenhagen, but despite his best efforts, Borgmann thought back to the time he'd last seen Ben-Ezra, in Chicago in 1965, at Ruthie's funeral. Even now, he did not know how his old friend had found out about the auto accident. Borgmann was standing there, surrounded by his friends, listening to the eulogy, wondering why he continued to breathe, why his heart continued to beat, when his old friend suddenly appeared at his elbow, unasked, unexpected, but very welcome.

Ben-Ezra's presence in no way made up for Ruthie's death. How can a man accept the loss of a woman who shared not only his life, but his thoughts? Yet, Ben-Ezra did help to close the door in such a way to preserve the memories and, as much as possible, bypass the pain.

Borgmann saw the lights of Kastrup Airport up ahead of the plane now. A few moments later, the giant plane jounced heavily as its sixteen wheels made contact with the tarmac.

Shortly, Borgmann, Stabile and 173 other passengers paraded up a long modern corridor to the baggage claim area. The American agent, Borgmann noted with some pleasure, dropped far back into the pack, giving every sign of having no further interest in him. Perhaps that talk on the plane had been enough.

At the baggage carousel, Borgmann quickly spotted his single piece of luggage, handed his check to the porter, and walked back through the terminal to the taxi stand.

He was pleased with what he saw. Kastrup was just as modern and efficient as O'Hare Field. Yet it radiated a warmth and friendliness that clearly showed its Danish origins. Outside, he quickly found a taxi. "Kong Frederik Hotel?"

The driver motioned him inside and they drove off.

Another taxi from the line moved into place. No sooner had Borgmann's cab driven off than Gary Stabile stepped through the airport's front door. He entered the taxi, pipeless for the moment and, if the expression on his face was any indication, inordinately pleased with himself.

Chapter Three

For the fourth time in the last half hour, Suliman Ferrara went to the grimy front window of the small flat, opened it, and peered out. And, for the fourth time, all he saw was a few small children playing on apartment house steps, a streetwalker or two, back from an early trip to the grocery store, and a dirty grey dog sniffing around the garbage cans.

He craned his head to look down the street. Four blocks away, the massive bulk of the Copenhagen Central Railroad Station loomed up, its magnificence making the apartment building seem even seedier.

Ferrara glanced at his watch. Past eleven now and there were no Palestinians in sight. The PLO (Palestinian Liberation Organization), and PFLP (the Popular Front for the Liberation of Palestine)—even *Fatah*—had sent no one—at least not yet. Perhaps Arafat was right after all. Perhaps the promises meant nothing when they required cooperation from the Palestinians. Once more, he realized how ridiculous the venture was, on its face.

Ferrara pulled the window shut and resumed his pacing, his mind reviewing the data like a computer. His conclusions had not altered between Beirut and Copenhagen. The task was still just about impossible. And without help, it would be silly to attempt it.

He let his mind drift away from the immediate problem. This had become a habit, and a useful one. So often, Ferrara had found the answer to a difficulty when he turned his mind away from it. His unconscious mind, he sometimes thought, was more rational than his conscious mind.

This was not the first time he had confronted an impossible situation. In 1962, when he returned from America, a Yale law degree in his pocket, his troubles had been even worse. Like his native Lebanon, Ferrara was half Christian, half Moslem. His father was an Italian immigrant, Guiseppe Ferrara; his mother, Riska Sarami, was the daughter of a minor bureaucrat who, years earlier, had lived in Jerusalem. The Maronite Christians, the class to which he might naturally have belonged, since that was the group his father had adopted, distrusted him because of his Arab blood. He could not find a place in government since each position, by tradition, was reserved for either a Christian or a Moslem, in an elaborate system of checks and balances. There were no places for men of mixed blood. Neither could he make common cause with the Moslem merchants. His skin was olive, but his sandy hair, grey eyes and Western education made it certain he would never be accepted as an Arab.

Barred from the bureaucracy, excluded from commerce, out of place in his homeland, Ferrara left Beirut and went hitchhiking through Lebanon for a while, searching for a *modus vivendi*. He ended up in ancient Baalbek, amidst the ruins of Greek and Roman temples.

At the dawn of recorded history, Baalbek had been the site of a Phoenician temple honoring the god Baal. Then it became a Canaanite settlement. Centuries later, it was conquered by Alexander the Great, who renamed it Heliopolis, City of the Sun. Alexander was followed, eventually, by the Romans, who took Baal for their own and renamed him Jupiter Heliopolitanus. Each of these peoples, in turn, built temples and monuments here. The Romans were succeeded by the Byzantine Christians, who erected a church in honor of Saint Barbara. Later, the Arabs built a large mosque and school. This was converted into a citadel, which suffered raids from both the Crusaders and the Mongols.

At Baalbek, Ferrara felt he had come to the center

of all things. Here was the history of mankind at a single site, a record of men, their wars, and the gods to whom they had prayed. Dropped off at the city's outskirts, he slowly walked toward its epicenter, the great Temple of Jupiter, now in ruins.

Since he had last been in Baalbek, as a child, the archaeologists had reconstructed much of the temple's former splendor—without actually rebuilding it. Ferrara emptied his mind of thought as much as possible and headed through the propylaea toward the sanctuary. The first time he had seen the Temple of Jupiter, he felt he was trespassing in the house of the gods. Now, he heard the echoes of men long dead.

This time, he was surprised at how Western the temple looked, not only in form, but also in decoration. It seemed as though the huge stone blocks, the columns and their Corinthian capitals, the architectural devices and classical ornaments had been made in Rome, labeled and packed for export, shipped to Baalbek and reassembled like jigsaw puzzles. Ferrara had seen nearly identical—but smaller—structures in Italy. He walked through the hexagonal forecourt, into the great court of sacrifice. Here the parallel with Western architecture broke down. Though the court was surrounded by the remains of a Corinthian colonnade, the Western world had no counterpart to the altar, which stood eighteen meters high, facing the entrance to the temple. This structure resounded with Semitic tradition. It was here that Baal had been worshipped. The Romans had merely built a temple around the shrine.

The last time Ferrara was here, a Byzantine basilica had occupied the great court. To his pleasure, it had been removed by the archaeologists. He stood at the altar a moment. Just beneath his level of consciousness, he felt some nagging thought. He let it surface. There was something here for him—a kind of answer. That was it: the clue to his new course was here, in Baalbek, if only he were alert enough to see it and wise enough to interpret it.

Ferrara luxuriated in the thought for a few moments, allowing himself to believe he was about to be saved.

Then he dismissed it all as childish nonsense. He didn't believe in mysticism. The voice of the gods, or of men long departed, called neither to him nor to anyone else. There was no key here, no solution to his problem. Still. . . .

He walked on, past the altar, past its smaller companion, between two ornamental pools, toward the high platform of the temple. Sixty years after the birth of Christ, the Romans had built this place. In that day, fifty-four yellow stone columns, each twenty meters high, topped with a magnificent, imposing entablature of six additonal meters, surrounded the high platform. Now, to his left, six remained, a reminder of past grandeur.

Years ago, when Lebanon was French, a writer had said, "If the columns of Baalbek disappeared, there would be less beauty in the world and less poetry in the skies of Lebanon." Ferrara contemplated the columns, silhouetted against the clear blue sky. For a time, he was lost in the majesty of ancient days.

Past the columns, he could see the smaller Temple of Bacchus, complete except for its roof, part of the peristyle and the altar. He let his eye follow the delicate decorations carved into the stone. The scrollwork was astonishingly intricate, filled with a sculptor's visions of imaginary ferns and fabulous animals.

Ferrara left the Temple of Jupiter and headed back toward the street. He had seen no signs. He had been given no answer. Nearby sat three enormous stone blocks—each of them nineteen or twenty meters long. They'd been intended for a terrace which was to surround the giant temple. The terrace had never been completed. Conceivably, he thought, this is how his life would end, incomplete, unrealized.

He found himself heading toward the quarry from which the stone blocks had come. There, half-buried in the sand, was the largest single piece of stone ever worked—a perfect rectangle twenty-three meters long, dwarfing the building blocks of the pyramids, making the Stonehenge rocks of Britain seem like scale models. At one end, the colossal block had been raised and propped up by smaller stones, as if the builders had taken the first step toward moving it into position near the temple.

Ferrara climbed up on top of the block and walked across its slanting surface toward the center. For no particular reason, he thought of his days at Yale, where such things were studied in books. What would his fellow students have said if they could have walked on this stone, as he did now? He smiled as he thought of them, the young Americans who tried to put everything into numbers, or, failing that, make comparisons. They would have taken one look at this stone and said it was one-quarter the length of a football field.

He sat down on the edge of the stone and dangled his legs, kicking the side. In the dim past, a single man had come up with the idea for the Temple of Jupiter. Somehow, he had raised legions of workers, who had translated his idea into stone, leaving an imprint on history that did credit to both the designer and the builders.

That was worth thinking about. He, too, wished to make an imprint on history, to make his name known and his power felt. He too wished to have legions of followers. Yet there seemed no way even to find himself a place in society.

As he sat there, grimly contemplating his future, a gaggle of tourists—mostly Americans and West Germans—walked toward the quarry, oohing and aahing over the very stone on which Ferrara was perched. Several lifted their cameras. Ferrara started to scramble down, but a chubby American woman in her fifties, her ample chest crisscrossed with cameras of every shape and size, motioned him to stay.

"Who would know how big the stone is without someone sitting on it?" she said. "You just go ahead and stay there. You don't mind if we take your picture, do you?"

He sat down once more. Now, he knew, his likeness would be forever preserved in some box of slides in a dusty closet in Chicago or Detroit or Denver. It was a cheap sort of immortality, but then he merited nothing more.

The chubby lady took several pictures, switching cameras and lenses deftly. Then she made a mistake. In her eagerness to use the camera hanging from her left shoulder, she removed the one hanging from her right shoulder and put it down on a rock at her feet. While she was composing her next shot, a small Arab urchin—he couldn't have been ten years old—snatched the camera, like a frog snatching a fly with its tongue.

Before the tourist lady even realized her burden had been lightened, the little boy was off and running. Ferrara followed it all, with a bemused smile. The lady snapped off a couple of shots, then looked for the other camera. It took her several valuable seconds to realize she hadn't merely misplaced it.

By this time, the little thief was several hundred yards away. His furtive scrambling now had a joy to it—he was beyond her reach. The prize was his. But it wasn't. Even as he turned back to see that the camera's original owner had no chance of catching him, two older boys stepped from behind a yellowed stone pillar.

They grabbed the boy before he even knew they were there. One pulled both of the thief's hands behind his back; the other lifted the camera from his grasp. For an instant, Ferrara thought the older boys would return the camera to the lady, perhaps with the thought of getting a reward. But that wasn't what they had in mind. Once they were in possession of the camera, they fled even faster than had the original thief.

It was a funny scene, but also a sad one. There was no honor among thieves after all, even young ones. For a few moments, the tourist lady complained vigorously to the guide, a man in a bus driver's uniform. He listened politely, reminded her that he'd said to watch for thieves, and told her there was nothing to do now, except to report it to the police.

Then the group of tourists began to move toward the Temple of Jupiter, every last one of them holding onto their cameras for dear life. Ferrara idly wondered how many times such a scene had been enacted at this very spot.

He was alone again now, but, in his mind's eye, he was watching the immediate past again and again, as if it were a movie. Was there something here he had missed?

In a flash, it came to him. Here was a way out of his dilemma. He would become a thief. But not an ordinary thief. It was a crowded profession in Beirut in 1962, and he had no intention of becoming one of many. Instead, Ferrara would steal from other thieves—as the older boys had stolen from the younger. And perhaps that was the sign he had awaited.

The more he thought about it, the more convinced he was that he had found the answer. There was a moment in every theft when the perpetrator had eluded immediate capture, when he was euphoric with success, a moment when natural caution was suspended. That was when he would strike.

Ferrara climbed down from the stone. The time for dawdling was over. He was ready to pursue his future. With the confidence born of a knotty problem solved, he easily attached himself to the tourist party. When they left the Baalbek ruins for the return trip to Beirut, he was aboard their bus, having been welcomed by the guide, who was only too anxious to share his duties with someone—anyone—else.

While he charmed the foreigners and told them stories of the Lebanese shepherds, Ferrara's mind was ablaze with plans and ideas. There were, he decided, two possible routes to his goal: he must either keep an eye on some valuables, then waylay the thief when they were stolen, or he must keep an eye on some thieves, and waylay them immediately after they pulled off a job.

The first alternative was obviously impractical. Who could know which bank, which collection of jewelry, which payroll, was next on some thief's list? Besides, there was no way he could hang around such valuables without attracting unwelcome attention—except by joining the police force. Many policemen, he guessed, stole from thieves. But that meant sharing the booty with his fellow officers. Anyway, he could not picture himself in the police force.

The second alternative seemed best. It should be easy to follow a thief, allow him to do his job, then relieve him of the proceeds. An inept thief could even be aided, if necessary, so long as he didn't know he was being helped. The trouble with this alternative was that Ferrara knew no criminals. He hadn't any contacts in the underworld, nor did he know anyone who did. Of course, there was a simple way to acquire the necessary knowledge. He wasted no time.

On October 19, 1962, three days after he'd returned from Baalbek, Suliman Ferrara tossed a brick through the window of a big jewelry store at the intersection of George Picot and Weygand streets. He was arrested approximately thirty seconds later, while stuffing Accutron watches into his pockets. Because it was a first offense—and a pathetically inept one at that—he was sentenced to thirty days in Beirut central prison. It was the only time in his life he was ever to be kept behind bars.

On November 17, after serving just twenty days of his sentence, Ferrara was released from jail—on the grounds of good behavior. During that twenty days, he had compiled a definitive list of the best and most experienced thieves in the country, together with their habits, targets, and methods of operation. It had been even easier than he had imagined. Certain of his fellow prisoners, charmed by the inadequacy of his technique, had taken him under their wings and taught him what they thought he needed to know. They peppered their teachings with examples from the masters. Ferrara acted the eager student, eliciting a score of names with a question or two. At night, he would transcribe the information into a notebook, pretending to be writing letters to a girlfriend.

On January 15, 1963, he bagged his first victim— Mohammed el Kaddar. El Kaddar was a second-story man. His specialty was hotels. Once or twice a month, he would climb up the balconies at four in the morning, slide open a glass door and relieve some tourist of his cash and jewelry. January was hardly a month for

36

tourists in Beirut—it was too cold—but one hotel was still nearly full: the Hotel Phoenicia, the best in town.

Ferrara awoke at about five-thirty on the afternoon of the fourteenth, after a full day's sleep, got himself a good meal, saw an American movie on the Avenue des Français—a John Wayne Western—then took up his position in a doorway across from el Kaddar's apartment, repeating his pattern of the last week. He knew that the man was bound to undertake a caper in the next few days and he was quite content to wait.

As it happened, the waiting was over. At about two-thirty in the morning, he heard el Kaddar unlock his front door. Ferrara doubled over in his doorway, acting the role of a sleeping bum. El Kaddar, dressed as a TV repairman and carrying a small satchel, never even glanced his way.

The thief walked purposefully toward the Hotel Phoenicia, only a few blocks away, and Ferrara followed at a respectable distance. The last thing he wanted to do was alert the man. On the other hand, he had to be sure el Kaddar had completed his task.

Ferrara followed the thief to the hotel and watched him walk through the parking lot to the rear of the building. Then he cautiously took the same route himself. By the time he'd gotten to the back, el Kaddar had apparently vanished. Then Ferrara remembered what he'd heard of the man's technique. He peered upward, struggling to see something on a balcony, though the night was moonless and dark.

Through the corner of his eye, he caught a hint of motion about three stories up. He looked over just in time to see el Kaddar slide open a patio door and disappear inside. About ten minutes later, he reappeared, climbed upward again, and once more vanished. Ferrara watched admiringly.

A half hour later, el Kaddar, his satchel bulging, was back on the ground, walking briskly back to his apartment. As the thief bent to unlock his door, Ferrara hit him once on the back of the head with a rock and relieved him of his satchel.

For the next ten months, Beirut's criminal population

experienced a crime wave all its own. By that time, Ferrara had accumulated nearly three quarters of a million dollars in currency and gems. He'd also accumulated the ugliest, toughest gang of enemies any man could ever want. Fortunately, despite their best efforts, they'd been unable to discover his identity.

Ferrara now undertook step two of his master plan. He spent a fair portion of his ill-gotten gain to buy himself a nifty little private army. Then he told the underworld just who their nemesis was and announced that the intramural crime wave was over—that the thieves were free to operate, unmolested, so long as they contributed thirty percent of their take to him.

There was grumbling for a time, especially among the older men. One fellow, a safecracker, even tried to assassinate Ferrara. His failure was fatal. If they had banded together, the rest of the thieves might have dismembered Ferrara's little army, not to mention Ferrara himself. But thieves are a notoriously disorganized lot. They accepted their new master, however reluctantly.

As Ferrara's treasury grew—and with it, his strength—he began to provide various services to his clients which eventually drew their enthusiastic support. He imported fine burglary tools from Europe and America. He set up a bail bond service and hired two full-time criminal lawyers. In time, he was able to purchase the chief justice of the Appellate Court. As his influence spread, he set up his own intelligence service, tracing the movements of wealthy tourists. His clients were encouraged to use these services, so long as they paid their dues. The two or three who refused to pay were discouraged from practicing their profession, one dying as a result.

By June 1965, Suliman Ferrara was by far the most powerful man in Beirut's underworld. He ran a businesslike operation, kept good books, made sure his clients were happy, and accumulated sizable capital, most of which he sent to Switzerland, as old-age insurance.

Though he had started with thieves and robbers, Ferrara soon numbered several espionage agents among his clients. This was a natural turn of events. His own little intelligence agency had grown steadily, and it had come to his attention that international secrets often commanded a good price in Beirut.

At first he was totally apolitical, interested in no causes but his own. He didn't care whom his clients stole from, who exchanged secrets with whom—so long as he received his royalties.

But when his father died in late 1965, his mother set out to awaken his political conscience. She told him again and again of the Palestinians' plight, of their exile from their homeland. Eventually, aware that he was growing powerful and that his power could be harnessed to her cause, she introduced him to various Palestinian leaders. The message sank in slowly, but, in time, his mother's interests and those of the Palestinians became his.

In 1967 Ferrara's intelligence network informed him of the coming war more than a month before it took place. He communicated his knowledge to both the Christian president of Lebanon and the Moslem premier. Though both had found his services useful in the past, they chose not to believe him—or not to act on what he'd told them. When the war came, Lebanon stayed out of it.

Thinking back on it, Ferrara felt the fury rise within him once more. Arabs died—Egyptians, Jordanians, Syrians and, most of all, Palestinians—while the Lebanese Army contented itself with war games near the Israeli border. If only they had acted together—all of the Arab nations—there would no longer be an Israel in their midst to plague them. The Palestinians could have returned to their homeland.

The 1973 war was an even deeper disappointment. Egypt, Syria, Jordan, Iraq, Saudi Arabia and the rest had acted in concert. They even used the "oil weapon" effectively. But Lebanon did nothing. As if that weren't enough, each Arab nation went its own way when it came to fighting for recognition of the Palestinian state. That's why the settlement talks turned out the way they did.

There was only one solution to the problem: The Palestinians had to achieve power of their own. As he saw his mother's people ignored by the rest of the Arabs, Ferrara pledged himself to a new goal. He would do his utmost to build Palestinian unity and strength, with or without the help of the Arab nations. He would be the rational man who channeled Palestinian passion into an effective force.

The mission that had brought him to Copenhagen was his first opportunity to realize that goal. It was preposterously difficult, but if it succeeded it could weld the Palestinian splinters into a single sturdy tree, so that they could finish the task Egypt and Syria had started.

The sound of barking dogs brought Ferrara's mind back to the present. He walked over to the window and looked out again. Nothing. It was a dreadful, depressing sign. A few more hours and the opportunity would slip away, probably forever. The problem was quickly becoming academic. Israel probably had agents on the scene. There was that girl at the station this morning watching the guarded train. She seemed a bit too alert, a bit too collegiate, a little too Nordic-looking to be real. And Ferrara was by himself. What chance was there for him, especially without help of any kind?

Suddenly Ferrara grinned broadly. It was incredible that he hadn't seen the answer earlier, hilarious in a way. Once more, he would steal from the thieves. No one was better at this than he.

Now Ferrara was back on comfortable, familiar ground. He knew where he must concentrate his efforts. All he had to do was to watch the Israeli team. Only one question remained in Ferrara's mind: had he read the Israeli intentions correctly? Did they plan to make a serious attempt? Every instinct told him that they did.

There was a muffled knock at the door.

"Ferrara, are you in there?" It was a hoarse whisper, but the Lebanese recognized the voice and felt a wave of disgust pass through him.

"Come in, Abdul," he said, his voice filled with resignation.

"I'm so sorry, Suliman. Please forgive me."

Suliman Ferrara's visitor was a short, thin, black-haired man with a hawklike nose and watery black eyes. He wore a badly pressed business suit, complete with white shirt and curled collar points. He shook Ferrara's hand limply.

"First, I could not find the address," he said. "I do not know Copenhagen. It is large, like Cairo, but all of the street names are foreign to me. Then, when I did find it, there were no parking spaces. Please forgive my lateness."

Ferrara sighed. "I forgive you, Abdul. Let's waste no more time on apologies."

Abdul bowed slightly, apologetically. "Of course. I'm sorry. I'm at your service."

Suliman Ferrara gazed at the man for a moment. Of all the people *Fatah* could have sent to help, why did they choose Abdul Amer, a recognized incompetent? Was the barrel really that empty?

"Any message from *Fatah*?"

Abdul drew himself up. "Yes, sir. I'm to inform you that Arafat has positive information that Jacob Ezra is in Copenhagen."

"They said Jacob Ezra? Was that the name? Could Arafat have meant Yaakov Ben-Ezra?"

"That was it. They wouldn't let me write it down."

Ferrara swallowed down an insulting remark. For the next four days, he'd have to work with this man. A moron. *Fatah* has sent me a moron, he thought, and asked me to work a miracle. And against Ben-Ezra. Was life just a situation comedy?

"I see. Well, Ben-Ezra is a tough man, Abdul."

"Yes?"

"Yes. Do you know the details of our mission?"

"They said you'd tell me."

Ferrara nodded. Ask your mother, dear. Wasn't anyone willing to take on responsibility anymore?

"You see, Abdul, the plans for a device that can cheaply refine uranium for atomic bombs arrived in Copenhagen this morning. . . ."

41

Chapter Four

Gary Stabile perched himself on the office windowsill and looked out at Copenhagen harbor. It was a bright, beautiful day and the sunlight pouring through the windowpane added to the elegant coziness of the office.

Stabile was basking not only in the sun, but also in that comfortable inner glow one has when all plans are proceeding on schedule and one's enemies seem doomed.

He pulled his pipe out, lit it, then turned to the other man in the room, Jack Salter, an eager-looking fellow in his late twenties, with bushy brown hair, wire-framed glasses and a bright, wide tie. Salter was sitting behind a large handsome mahogany desk.

"Well, Jack," Stabile said, his voice gentle and fatherly, "how do you see it? After all, this is really your bailiwick."

Salter tilted back in his desk chair and glanced reflectively at the ceiling. "Frankly," he said, "I don't think we have anything to worry about."

"How so?"

"Well, to begin with, the Israelis don't have much of a chance, with Borgmann's help or without it. And if they do manage the theft, they'll have to deal with the Palestinians. They have an agent here, don't they?"

"Yes. A man named Ferrara. Washington told me where to find him," Stabile said.

"Besides, the Russians are in town and they're not about to let any Mideastern power get hold of those plans."

Stabile raised an eyebrow slightly. "You're sure about the Russians?"

"Got a coded teletype from Washington last night. They say a KGB man will be at the conference tomorrow morning. They also believe we may have a GRU man on our hands."

"Anyone we know?"

"Haven't a clue. Washington didn't send any details."

"Typical. But it doesn't matter."

"That's my thinking, too. All we have to do is sit tight and let them all make trouble for each other. Then we go in and pick up the pieces."

Stabile nodded. "That's the assignment all right, Jack. Now what's your plan?"

"Plan?"

"Yes. I mean, what steps have you taken to make sure that this little drama will take place as written? All the participants might not be reading from the same script, you know."

Salter hesitated. "I assumed things would pretty well take care of themselves."

"Assumed?" Stabile was chiding the man. "Didn't the Foggy Bottom school teach you not to use that word?"

Salter flushed. "Of course. What I meant is that such things usually work out by themselves, in my experience. Besides, the rule is to interfere as little as possible."

Stabile puffed on his pipe. "As little as possible," he agreed, "but that doesn't mean not at all. Sometimes the actors need just a touch of direction."

The student waited patiently for the professor to confer the benefits of his wisdom.

Stabile slid off the windowsill and plopped down in a large burgundy-colored leather club chair that seemed to suit him perfectly. "First," he said, "we must be sure all the members of the cast get acquainted. That's one of the most common flaws in your average spy movie, by the way. The good guys and the bad guys always make contact through some sort of coincidence. In real life, many operatives spend months—even years—without seeing anyone from the opposition."

Salter nodded. As usual, the professor was long-winded and his knowledge consisted mostly of platitudes. But it was politic to show respect. Besides, Stabile was an old-timer, and to get to be an old-timer in this business, you had to be pretty smart.

"Second," Stabile continued, "we have to be in the wings at all times. You never can tell when one player or another will need prompting."

Salter nodded again, as if he were carefully noting the master's words. He waited for more, but apparently the lesson was over. It was now up to the student to ask questions.

"What's the first step, Gary?"

Stabile took another puff on his pipe. "Get me a sheet of that Russian watermarked paper and a Russian-made envelope."

Salter scurried to the supply cabinet to obey, while Stabile searched his pockets for a pen, finally settling on the old, corroded Esterbrook in the desk set.

Salter brought the paper and Stabile started to write on it. The pen was dry. Stabile sighed. "Three hundred thousand dollars worth of electronic monitoring equipment and teletypes, an arsenal full of handguns, a cabinet loaded with exotic gadgets, and no ink in the pen. I'm surprised at you, Jack. You know how important the little things are. They can be the difference—remember that."

"I know, Gary. I'm sorry." Salter found a bottle of ink and Stabile filled the pen carefully. Then he printed a message on the greyish paper: "Pay close attention to the man Borgmann. He is at the Kong Frederik." He let the paper dry, then handed it to Salter.

"You know what to do with this, don't you?"

Salter nodded soberly. "Give me Ferrara's address."

Stabile scribbled the address on a small slip of paper and handed it to Salter. He took it eagerly, stuffing it in a jacket pocket and left the office without further conversation.

From the window, Stabile watched the young man

44

hurry down the street. Salter was a fairly bright fellow, Stabile allowed, even if he was still a bit damp behind the ears.

When Salter was out of sight, Stabile slipped into his own coat and went down to the street. He stood there awhile, admiring the quaint buildings of Nyhavn, the old sailors' quarter. It had changed very little over the years, which was one reason he liked it so much. And no part of Copenhagen was less like the United States, another reason for his admiration.

The place held memories for him. He'd spent eighteen months here after the war, digging Nazis out of the woodwork. It had been an easy job. The Germans were very conspicuous. He and the other members of the OSS team rounded up nearly two hundred of them and sent them back by sealed train. There were few Danish Nazis. The Danes just didn't take to that sort of thinking. Most local Nazis were caught by Danish authorities, thrown into jail and the key tossed away—all before Stabile or another OSS operative could get to them.

His main trouble in those days was the Russians. They, too, had agents on the scene, ostensibly to see that all Nazi influence was expunged from the little country, actually, to replace it with their own if possible. But the Danes didn't take to that philosophy either, despite their socialistic convictions. The Communists were able to recruit only the customary small number of intellectuals.

It was good in those days, when Stalin was in command. You didn't need a scorecard to tell the good guys from the bad guys. And the Russian agents were solid professionals—not fruitcakes, like so many of the Nazis. Like their CIA counterparts, they killed only when necessary.

Stabile looked out toward the waters of the Sound. He'd spent hours doing just that in 1946, searching for a conning tower, with a Russian agent barely fifty yards away, disguised as a fruit peddler, doing the same thing. The company was convinced that Martin Bormann had managed to squirrel away a Type XXI

45

schnorchel-equipped U-boat and would shortly make a dash for freedom.

The submarine had come—anyhow, *a* submarine had come, on a moonless night in September. And about five hundred yards off the coast, it had exploded, while he and the Russian agent watched. Either it had hit a mine or it had been torpedoed. Stabile never knew the truth of the matter. The next day, frogmen went down to view the wreckage. Their report only deepened the mystery: no bodies were found aboard. Stabile sighed. He didn't like unresolved endings.

Back home, he'd questioned the boys at the Pentagon. The best he was able to get out of them was a grin, a shrug and some wise remark about asking the Kremlin. He never liked those smug desk-jockeys.

Evidently, they'd liked him, though. Or at least, they recognized his talents. That's why they put him in charge of the team that went looking for SS treasure at the bottom of Lake Schwerin, near Lübeck. Now there was nothing unresolved about *that* ending.

Stabile recalled the pleasure he'd felt when the slimy, mud-crusted steel box broke water, pulled by the protesting winch on a two-and-a-half-ton Army truck. It had taken the acetylene torch operator just twenty minutes to open it up and reveal pile after pile of new American twenty-dollar bills. That little mission had done wonders for his career. Among other things, it had gotten him a very cushy stateside assignment that included a couple of trips to the South Pacific.

Now it was fun and games again in Europe. Well, Copenhagen was a nice place to come back to. It was long on good food and creature comforts, short on hippies and protesters.

Stabile tapped his pipe against the building's stone stoop, knocking out the dead ashes. Then, he methodically refilled it. An empty cab cruised by and he flagged it down.

"Kong Frederik Hotel, please."

Chapter Five

Frederick Borgmann stood at the Kong Frederik Hotel registration desk.

"*Jeg har besilt vaerelse til idag,*" he told the clerk. The man smiled and nodded, and consulted a list in front of him.

"*Ja,*" the clerk said brightly, "*Vaer sa venlig at skrive Dem ind i hotellets bog.*"

He handed Borgmann a pen and Borgmann signed his name on the register. Then the clerk banged the bell on his desk and a bellhop quickly appeared, picking up Borgmann's bags.

"*Er den nogen breve eller besked til mig?*" Borgmann asked the man behind the desk.

The clerk turned and checked the mail boxes. "Borgmann, Borgmann, Borgmann," he whispered to himself. "*Nej,*" he said, with a small shrug.

Borgmann nodded. "*Tak.*" He followed the bellhop toward the elevator.

Originally he had intended to meet Ben-Ezra at the designated spot immediately after checking into his hotel. Now he wasn't so sure. Stabile or some other CIA type might well be watching him. If he went to Ben-Ezra now, he might give his friend away. Yet that note had reverberated with urgency.

In the end, there was no choice. Borgmann opened his suitcase, hung up his clothing, shaved, showered, and changed into something casual. At least he could make sure he wasn't followed. He was certain he was alert enough to manage that.

Forty-five minutes after he'd arrived, Borgmann left his room and locked it. Then, he remembered a trick he'd read about. He pulled a hair from his head and placed it carefully in the keyhole. At least he'd know if anyone searched his room in his absence.

When the elevator doors opened at the lobby, Borgmann took a quick look around. No one seemed to be the least bit interested in him. He walked through the lobby briskly, but not so briskly, he thought, that he'd attract attention. Then, he headed in the direction opposite from the address Ben-Ezra had written in code, darting down alleys, turning corners quickly, disappearing momentarily into the shops. That ought to shake off any tails, he thought.

Ten minutes later—his long legs served him well— Borgmann arrived at the designated address: the Svenska Quality Porno Shop, just three blocks from Copenhagen's glittering Strøget, the main shopping street. A porno shop? It didn't seem right. He checked the address again. There was no mistake.

Borgmann took one last look up and down the street. The coast, he was sure, was clear. He slipped into the shop with a speed and grace surprising for a man of his size.

An instant later, Stabile rounded the corner, riding a bicycle, his whole frame shuddering as the bike bumped over the cobblestones. He was wearing a beret, large black-framed sunglasses and a nylon golfing jacket, looking just like a native. Or, at any rate, nothing like Gary Stabile. He pedaled slowly up the street, puffing as he went, nonchalantly glancing into the shops as he passed them by. About mid-block, he began to slow down. Anyone watching would have thought he was tiring. After all, the street was on a slight hill.

Stabile passed the Svenska Quality Porno Shop at about walking speed, glanced in as he glided by, stood up on the pedals and picked up speed. His face wore a small, self-satisfied expression, the look of a man who'd told his wife how the mystery movie would end, and, to her annoyance, had it exactly right.

Inside the shop, Borgmann looked around, trying to settle his eyes on something nonpornographic—which wasn't easy. He hadn't been in Denmark since long before the liberalization and he wasn't comfortable with the rack after rack of erotic picture magazines he now confronted.

Was Ben-Ezra really in here somewhere? He checked the address again. There was no mistake. Then he remembered the question Ben-Ezra's message had instructed him to ask of the person he found at this address. There was only one person in view—a female salesclerk, who was smiling at him courteously. He took a step toward her.

Suddenly, the bell at the top of the door tinkled. Borgmann grabbed the nearest magazine, a copy of something called *Girl Chaser,* with a picture of two young blondes and a collie on the cover. He opened it and practically buried his face in it, keeping his back to the door.

A young couple had walked into the shop, holding hands and giggling as they looked through piles of books and magazines on a small counter near the cash register. At the sound of giggling, Borgmann glanced quickly backward. Then, he began to relax again.

The young couple must have stayed in the shop nearly twenty minutes, during which time Borgmann browsed through more dirty pictures than he'd seen in his entire lifetime. He pretended to be intent on studying what was available, on selecting only what was to his taste. He even collected a small stack of magazines—his choices, evidently.

The young couple finally left, still giggling, with a bag full of magazines and films. But before Borgmann could ask the clerk the coded question, the entry bell tinkled once more, to announce the entry not of another couple, but of a trio. It consisted of a pretty, well-shaped dark-haired, green-eyed girl in her early twenties who was wearing tight blue jeans, a snug white T-shirt labeled "Carlsberg" that did little to disguise her bralessness, and neither shoes nor sandais; a model-slender blonde a year or two older with deep

49

blue eyes, the tawny sort of skin that seems perpetually tanned, and sweet, almost angelic features that in any other setting would have been prima facie evidence of innocence, wearing a suede skirt that permitted all who wished a splendid view of her lithe, lightly muscled legs, all the way to her upper thighs; and a tall, casually attired fellow in his late thirties, a man with pleasingly regular features, his hair greying attractively at the temples. The two girls were holding hands and the man, standing behind them, had an arm around the waist of each.

It took Borgmann only a few seconds to understand just what sort of a relationship this threesome had. And, when he realized their bond, his reaction was midway between amusement and shock. He wasn't a prude. He and Ruth had had a very active sex life, greatly abetted by the odd, irregular hours he kept at work. And many a woman had warmed his bed in these last few years—but always one at a time. If ever there was a monogamous man, it was he.

Yet the trio who entered the porno shop seemed happy enough. The members were openly affectionate to each other and he could detect no sign of jealousy between the women, which wasn't all that surprising, considering that in addition to sharing a man, they also had each other.

The puzzlement was why this *ménage à trois* had found it necessary to visit a porno shop. What pictured scenes could they buy here that they couldn't act out for each other? Borgmann found himself a rack of paperback books and made a pretense of browsing through them—while watching the trio approach the clerk.

He couldn't quite hear what it was they were asking for, but he could see that they were pointing to a long glass case that hung on the wall, over the clerk's head. The girls were giggling with delight. The clerk smiled her courteous, clerkly smile, opened the case and withdrew a number of pinkish rubber devices, some with elastic straps.

Now Borgmann understood.

The girls examined each of the gadgets carefully, comparing shape and size, firmness and texture, passing them back and forth, grinning at each other mischievously. Behind them, the man watched benevolently. His hands had slipped down from their waists and were now lightly resting on their buttocks. This caused both girls to press back against him and against each other. Either they were unaware that Borgmann was watching—or they were quite aware of it.

Finally, they made their selections—one object perhaps a foot long, obviously ambidexterous, another a little more than half that size that contained a little motor. The man bent forward and whispered something to the clerk, who nodded understandingly and gift-wrapped each gadget separately. The dark-haired girl picked up the longer box and, with eyes twinkling gaily, presented it to the blonde—who accepted it with a gracious little kiss of thanks. Then the blonde presented the other package to the dark-haired girl, who took it tenderly and with obvious appreciation.

As the threesome headed out of the store, still intertwined, the dark-haired girl caught Borgmann's eye. Her expression conveyed a "don't you wish you were he" message. Borgmann did his best to send back a "seems nice, but it's not for me" reply but she'd looked away too quickly to get it.

The bell tinkled once more. Now the shop was empty. It was time to get back to business. Borgmann quickly approached the clerk.

"I'm looking for some Spanish films," he said.

The girl tilted her head, puzzled. "Spanish films? But there are no Spanish films."

"There must be," Borgmann said, surprised and disturbed at her response. "My friend tells me you carry the best Spanish films in town."

"Oh," the girl said, the light dawning, "*Spanish* films. Of course."

She led him to the row of bookshelves separating the salesroom from Ben-Ezra's little office. "Push," she said, indicating where. Borgmann did as he was told and the bookshelf-door swung open, rubbing noisily against the floor.

"Hello, Frederick Borgmann."

The physicist found himself face-to-face with Yaakov Ben-Ezra. For an instant, he was shocked at Ben-Ezra's appearance. It had been seven years since Borgmann had seen the man, and time had not been kind. The sandy hair was grey now, and thinning. The smile lines had been joined by frown lines. The tan was rich and deep, as Borgmann had remembered it, but now it seemed as though it were makeup, covering translucent paleness. Only the eyes were completely unchanged, warm and brown, with a slightly ironic glint.

"Yaakov," Borgmann said softly, grasping the man's hand. The handshake was the same, strong and lingering. Handshakes were important to Borgmann. He felt they revealed a great deal, since they were about the only physical contact that occurred between most people. "You're looking well," he said firmly.

Ben-Ezra did not contest the remark. "And you," he said, "the years have healed you."

"I've been busy," Borgmann said. "Working mostly in nuclear power-plant research. But you must know all that."

"I've kept an eye on you," Ben-Ezra admitted. "I've felt responsible for you, somehow."

"I appreciate that," Borgmann said. "But you could have turned your attention elsewhere. My life is placid and uneventful."

"Your life—yes. Too much so, I think. But your work is hardly uneventful. I understand you've made major breakthroughs in breeder power plant design."

"My God, Yaakov," Borgmann said, amazed, "is there anything you don't know?"

"Too much, Frederick. Too much." He moved aside slightly and Miriam stepped forward. "Frederick," Ben-Ezra said, "I want you to meet Miriam Shazar. She's my assistant." They'd agreed not to tell him of their relationship—at least not yet. The "Shazar"

52

Miriam had chosen herself years ago in honor of the then President of Israel, Zalman Shazar.

There was another handshake. Borgmann was impressed by the girl's directness and intrigued by her smile, which seemed a bit broader than a first meeting really called for. She was very pretty, but there was something about her beyond her appearance that he found appealing.

"Thank you for coming, Frederick," Ben-Ezra said.

"You knew I would. But I wasn't sure this was the right place. Your office—I didn't expect—"

"The pornography shop?" Ben-Ezra laughed. "A perfect blind, I think. All sorts of people can enter without suspicion. We can send and receive a great deal of international mail without arousing special interest from the Danish postal authorities. The Russians are such prudes this is the last place they'd look for anyone. It did not make you uncomfortable, I hope."

"No," Borgmann said, "not really."

"You know," Ben-Ezra went on, "I have a favor to ask."

"I know."

Ben-Ezra was suddenly very alert. "How?"

"There was an American CIA agent on the plane. He accused me of coming here to help you. He didn't say what you wanted me to help you with, but I know it must have something to do with atomic weapons."

Yaakov and Miriam exchanged glances.

"And what did you tell him?" Ben-Ezra asked his friend.

"I said I was just seeing you to renew our friendship—which is true. You know I cannot help you—at least not in any project where my knowledge could be useful."

"Frederick, Frederick," Ben-Ezra said softly, shaking his head, unwilling to acknowledge Borgmann's refusal. "We must have your help. Israel's survival depends on it."

Miriam coughed a phony cough and was rewarded with a dirty look from Ben-Ezra.

"I understand," Borgmann replied gently. "But you

53

know I will not do anything to increase the number of atomic weapons in the world."

"Frederick," Ben-Ezra said, his voice still soft, "we do not intend to build any more bombs."

"Any more?"

"We already have three. And, to build them, we had to forgo adding one graduate school to the university."

For a moment, Borgmann's thoughts flashed back to 1954, when he'd received another summons from Ben-Ezra. It had been just as mysterious as this call to Copenhagen—except that he'd been asked to come to Tel Aviv as soon as possible.

Borgmann had been happy to go. He'd been happy to see Ben-Ezra once more, after more than a decade. But he hadn't been happy at the reason for the summons. Acting on behalf of David Ben-Gurion, Ben-Ezra offered him the weapons development job at Israel's new atomic research center in the desert, near Dinora.

If the same offer had been made two or three years earlier, Borgmann might have accepted it. But by 1954, he'd seen the awesome destructive power of the hydrogen bomb and foresworn weapons work, despite the pressures put on him by Edward Teller and others he'd worked with.

For two weeks, the Israelis tried to convince him. Ben-Ezra, the scientists, even Ben-Gurion on one occasion, talked to him night after night. In a thousand ways, they told him that Israel's survival depended on his acceptance. Again and again he told them that mankind's survival might depend on his refusal. In a thousand ways, they showed him that he was a part of Israel, wherever he might live. He could not deny that argument, but he turned it against them, saying that his vision of Israel did not include atomic weapons.

It was the kind of confrontation that brought men closer together, rather than dividing them. Though they disagreed, Borgmann and Ben-Ezra grew to respect each other even more, with each meeting.

Borgmann did more in Tel Aviv than debate with Ben-Ezra and the others. He joined Ben-Ezra's family and social circle. And he met Ruth Ben-Zvi, his Ruthie. How completely unprepared for that he'd been. They fell in love in a matter of days, like two people who seemed to know each other even before they met. He delayed his return to Chicago again and again—until he could take her with him. No one could have known how fleeting that love was to be.

And now Ben-Ezra had summoned him again. He was once more asking for help. But why?

"I don't understand, Yaakov. If you already have the bombs, what do you want with me? How can I help you?"

"What are three A-bombs against Russia? If we dare to use even one—against Cairo, let's say—Israel wouldn't last twenty-four hours. You remember Russia's threats in the last war when Israeli troops surrounded that Egyptian Army near the Great Bitter Lake, don't you?"

"I'm confused, Yaakov," Borgmann said. "You tell me Israel already has atomic bombs, but that they are useless. You insist Israel won't build any more bombs, yet you implore me to help with some mission you haven't even described."

"We're attempting a bluff, Frederick. We want Russia to think we can make as many A-bombs as we like. We've even gone to the trouble of designing and building prototype missiles that could carry A-bombs into Russian territory. Perhaps, if they think we are truly dangerous, they will leave us alone and back away from the Arabs a bit."

"How do you intend to convince them Israel can build A-bombs in quantity?" Borgmann asked, still puzzled.

"We hope to steal the gas centrifuge plans, Frederick," Ben-Ezra replied. "You know of the gas centrifuge?"

Borgmann smiled humorlessly. "Of course. It can make unlimited quantities of cheap, enriched uranium to supply power plants."

"Or to make bombs."

"Yes, or to make bombs." Borgmann had the look of

a man who was beginning to fit some puzzle pieces together without being pleased at the result.

"Those plans are now in Copenhagen," Ben-Ezra said, ignoring his friend's expression. "We need your help to find them and to separate the genuine blueprints from the decoys. Once we have the plans—and Russia knows that we do—we can make the bluff work."

There was a long silence in the small room as Borgmann thought over Ben-Ezra's words and Ben-Ezra waited for his reaction.

"Israel would be more secure if it actually built the bombs, wouldn't it, Yaakov?" Frederick said at last.

Ben-Ezra shrugged. "Perhaps. But it would cost us too much, Frederick. It would cost us another school. It would cost us a million acres of land reclaimed from the desert. And then there's the defense debt. If we chose to build the bombs, we would be choosing to be an arsenal, not a country. In that case, I would rather there were no Israel."

"How can you be sure the bombs would not be built?"

"I tell you they would not be built. We would spend our energies convincing Russia they existed, even though they did not."

Borgmann nodded. He had known Ben-Ezra since Copenhagen's darkest days, since 1943, and never once had the man lied to him.

"Will you help us, Frederick?" Miriam interrupted the give-and-take between the two men. Ben-Ezra was clearly annoyed at the sound of her voice, but Borgmann seemed charmed.

"Even if I wanted to, I couldn't help, Miriam. I'm just a guest at the EURATOM conference. I don't know where the plans are. I'm not on the technical committee, so I'll never even get to see them."

"You have friends here, Frederick. You know people in the scientific community," Ben-Ezra said. "Perhaps through one of them the plans might be located."

"Perhaps," Frederick said, not at all convinced.

"We know that at least three sets of plans have been

delivered to Copenhagen," Miriam interjected. "There may be as many as seven. We need a nuclear physicist to spot the phonies. Would you be able to do that?"

"Possibly," Borgmann said, doubtful.

"Will you help us, Frederick?" Ben-Ezra asked.

Borgmann gazed at his friend. There was no way he could refuse Ben-Ezra, not this time. Perhaps he'd known that from the start. Besides, he wasn't really being asked to take part in weapons work.

"I've trusted you before, Yaakov," Borgmann said slowly. "How can I not trust you now?"

It took a moment for Borgmann's meaning to sink in, but when it did, both Yaakov Ben-Ezra and Miriam Shazar broke into broad smiles.

"We have one difficulty I haven't mentioned, Frederick," Ben-Ezra said. "In four days, when the conference ends, the plans will be removed from Copenhagen and returned to their vaults in The Hague. Those vaults, I'm afraid, are impregnable."

"Then this is our only chance at them," Borgmann said reflectively.

"Yes."

"Can it be done?"

Ben-Ezra smiled. "There are two possibilities. Either we never get within a hundred yards of the plans, or we find them and take possession. God knows which is more likely."

Borgmann snorted. "Finding the plans is our first problem then, isn't it? I'm intrigued by problems."

"If you'll allow me," Ben-Ezra said, "let me make a suggestion. Make inquiries of your friends at the EUR-ATOM conference, by all means, but do it very carefully. Let your interest seem mild. And be wary of any bogus conference delegates. We already know the Americans and the Arabs are interested. There are bound to be Russians, too, and God knows who else."

"I'll do my best."

Ben-Ezra was more than satisfied. "You see Miriam," he said, "Frederick is the perfect operative. He even listens to suggestions."

The Israeli agent knelt for a few moments at the office safe, twiddling the dial. Then, he turned the handle and the safe door swung open. He withdrew a small grey metal file box. "Here," he said handing it to his daughter. "This is a file of Danish Jews we can count on—names, addresses, occupations, phone numbers, and past services. Somewhere among them, I hope, is someone who can help us."

Miriam nodded and started looking through the cards. After a moment, she stopped. "Code key?"

For a moment, Ben-Ezra was flustered. He patted his pockets, looking for something. Then, he took a small card from his inside jacket pocket and handed it to her. She continued working with the files.

"Frederick," Ben-Ezra said, "it is nearly dinnertime. I have work to do tonight and so does Miriam. I suspect you wish to say hello to your city again. Will you be at the conference tomorrow morning?"

"Yes."

"Good. And Miriam will check out our helpers then, too. Shall we meet here around noon tomorrow?"

"That's fine," Borgmann said. He shook Ben-Ezra's hand once more—and Miriam's—then left, via the bookcase door.

For a moment, until they heard the bell over the porno shop tinkle, Yaakov Ben-Ezra and Miriam Shazar were silent.

"Congratulations," the girl finally said, sarcasm in her voice.

"He will help us," Ben-Ezra said defensively. "He agreed."

"You lie so well."

"Lie?" Ben-Ezra was angry. "I haven't lied."

"About never making more bombs—was that the truth?" It was an accusation, not a question.

"So far as I know," Ben-Ezra said. "That's what they tell me. But I expect to have something to say about it, you know."

"You really believe that, don't you?"

"Yes, Miriam, I do. And don't tell me otherwise. Allow an old man his conceits."

Miriam sighed. "And what about the danger? There

was no mention of that. You know that if the Russians get on to him, he won't live out these next four days."

"He understands that. Besides, I plan to take steps to protect him."

Miriam looked at Yaakov Ben-Ezra, her eyes full of doubt and discomfort. She said nothing.

She wanted to take it all back, both the words and the tone of voice. She wanted to tell him that she trusted him, that she cared for him. Such words never came easy to her, however, even in the midst of a romance. Saying them to her father was simply impossible. Had it always been that way? Would it be that way forever?

Chapter Six

Outside the Svenska Quality Porno Shop, Frederick Borgmann, for the first time since he had arrived, permitted himself to look at his surroundings, to gaze at the little shops on the narrow cobblestone streets, to smile at the ruddy Danish faces of the passersby, to breathe deeply of the clean, clear Scandinavian air.

The memories came flooding back into his mind, a jumble of vivid images of the city in which he had grown up, the city he had not seen since 1943. Tonight, he decided, he would deal with those memories. He would put them to rest, once and for all, by confronting them head on.

He walked slowly up the Strøget—Copenhagen's famous shopping street. Though many of the shops he had known in his youth were gone, the avenue was still a glamorous outdoor arcade, the prettiest street in downtown Copenhagen, perhaps in any Western capital. The stores hadn't closed yet, and the sidewalks were jammed with tourists, mostly Germans and Americans. He could still recognize the difference.

As Borgmann approached Radhuspladsen and Town Hall, he began to realize how much his Copenhagen had changed. There were skyscrapers in the heart of the city and neon signs almost wherever he looked. Modern buildings abounded. The years had been good to Copenhagen. She had prospered.

Borgmann's long legs carried him down Vesterbrogade, past the Tivoli. If anything, it was more brightly lit than he remembered. Waves of young Danes, intermingled with tourists, were heading toward the amusement park's main entrance. For an instant, Borgmann almost yielded to the temptation to step inside and end his confrontation. But he walked on, along main thoroughfares and down side streets, through good neighborhoods and bad, past more fancy shops, more porno outlets, past a long line of sleazy bars behind the railroad station.

Finally Borgmann began to feel hungry. He circled back through the city, toward his boyhood hangout, Oscar Davidsen's, on Vesterbrogade, adjoining the artificial lakes. Though it was a cool night, he chose to sit on the outside terrace, overlooking the city.

As he waited for service, he gradually remembered his last meal at the place. It had been with Maj Hartling, his boyhood sweetheart. He saw her again in his mind's eye, with her long sweep of auburn hair, glowing cheeks and athletically trim figure. Then, the memory began to fade. He'd tried to hold it too long.

"Yes sir, may I help you?" the waitress said. How American I must look, Borgmann thought—she speaks to me in English.

"May I see the menu?"

The girl handed him the famous Davidsen menu, a narrow strip of paper nearly a yard long, listing 178 different *smørrebrød*—sandwiches. Borgmann made his selection and told the girl.

"Anything else?"

He shook his head. *"Tak, ikke mere."*

The girl broke out into a smile. She realized her error.

Borgmann heard laughter to his left. He looked over to see a young couple holding hands and was once more transported back into his memories. The faces had changed, but not the actions.

After a few moments, the waitress brought him his sandwich.

"Kan jeg fa en flaske Tuborg lager?"

He was rewarded with another bright smile. *"Ja,"* the girl said, and again disappeared for a moment. She soon returned with the beer.

Borgmann watched the young people while he ate. Before long, he began to feel at home. Despite the changes, Copenhagen was an integral part of him. But there were more memories to confront.

After a while, Borgmann finished, rose, paid the bill and left the restaurant, walking resolutely toward the next memory. In ten minutes, he stood in front of the Copenhagen Synagogue, an imposing structure sheathed in rose-colored limestone, with a stained-glass Star of David mounted above its huge oak doors. He tried the handle—with no success. There was a large, worn, brass knocker on one of the doors. Borgmann lifted it twice and let it fall. After a moment, the door swung halfway open.

"Yes?" the caretaker said. "Can I help you?"

Again, he had been taken for an American. He decided to take advantage of it. "I have only a few hours," he said. "Could I see the sanctuary?"

The man seemed reluctant.

"Please," Borgmann said. "It is important to me."

The caretaker relented and opened the door the rest of the way. "I'm almost finished cleaning," he said. "I'll be locking up in fifteen or twenty minutes."

"Don't worry. I'll be gone by then."

"Good," the caretaker said. "The sanctuary is that way."

Borgmann walked down the hall, into the main chamber. The oak benches were still there, prayerbooks in the racks on the back of each bench. He turned around and looked toward the balcony, where the women sat, then toward the altar, where the Torah was kept. It all seemed the same. Perhaps the carpeting was new. For a change, he did not remember.

He took a seat on the aisle and looked toward the altar, thinking back to the morning of September 30, 1943. It was a Friday morning, the day before Rosh Hashana. Yet Rabbi Marcus Melchior had urgently summoned his entire congregation. Borgmann had come with his mother and father.

He remembered how strange it had been when

Rabbi Marcus walked out, not wearing his rabbinical robes. Even now, he could recall the ominous atmosphere that seemed to sweep through the sanctuary at that instant.

"There will be no service this morning," Rabbi Melchior had said. "Instead, I have important news to tell you. Last night I received word that tomorrow the Germans plan to raid Jewish homes throughout Copenhagen to arrest all the Danish Jews for shipment to concentration camps. You must leave the synagogue now and contact relatives, friends and neighbors you know are Jewish and tell them what I have told you. You must do this immediately, within the next few minutes, so that two or three hours from now, everyone will know what is happening. By nightfall tonight we must all be in hiding."

There had been silence for a moment, then the assembled congregation dispersed. "So," Borgmann's father had said, "the other shoe has fallen. For three years, the Nazis have occupied Denmark. We could not expect them to be benevolent forever. With what has happened in Africa and Russia, they must put on a strong front."

"This is not the time for discussion, Eduard," his mother had said. "We have much to do."

Borgmann sat for a moment, remembering. Then he rose and walked toward the front door. The caretaker was carrying a large trash basket. "Leaving now?"

"Yes. Thank you for letting me see it."

"Oh, it's a beautiful church," the caretaker said. "I like to show it off every chance I get."

Borgmann strode down the street, toward Dagmarhus, toward Mogens Staffeldt's bookstore, his thoughts still immersed in the memories of 1943. Even though his shop was directly across the street from Gestapo headquarters, Staffeldt had offered it as a hiding place and a way station. The Jewish leaders agreed. It would be their "purloined letter." For the first two weeks in October 1943, that store—and the Dahlgaard residence—had been the only home Borgmann had.

Dagmarhus, Borgmann saw, when he turned a corner, had changed dramatically over the years. It was rundown now. There was another of those ubiquitous porno shops on the corner. He walked up the block. What had once been the headquarters of the feared Gestapo was now a half-empty warehouse. Across the street, the building that had once housed Mogens Staffeldt's bookstore was now occupied by a clothing shop.

Borgmann looked into the window. Twenty-nine years ago, Jacob Kaplan had walked into that bookshop and asked for a copy of Kaj Munk's poems. For some reason, Borgmann had been on the sales floor at the time. He'd heard the introductions and explanations.

Jacob Kaplan had told Staffeldt that he was a member of *Shai*, a secret Jewish intelligence group organized by the *Haganah* in Palestine. A few of its members were now in Europe, their mission to save as many Jews from the concentration camps as possible.

In the days that followed, Jacob Kaplan was literally everywhere, setting up escape routes across the sound, to Sweden, hiring fishing boats, selecting and provisioning hiding places, personally transporting to them the aged and infirm. He was one of the guiding forces in the great effort to save the eight thousand Danish Jews, a man of remarkable energy and intelligence.

But there were others. Borgmann remembered his teacher, Niels Bohr, the greatest physicist of his day, with the possible exception of his friend, Albert Einstein. Bohr was not Jewish, but he was an outspoken anti-Nazi.

On the night of September 30, with Kaplan's help, Borgmann later discovered, Bohr was smuggled into Sweden by boat. There, he was met by Frederick Lindemann, Churchill's personal science advisor. Lindemann wanted to fly Bohr directly to London so that he could continue his work, but Bohr refused to go. It made Borgmann smile to remember it. It was so typical of the man. His philosophy was more important to him than his science.

Bohr told the Swedish government he would not leave the country until they guaranteed refuge to all the Danish Jews able to reach Swedish shores. In fact, he'd said he wouldn't go to London until Sweden's assurances were announced on the front pages of their leading newspapers and broadcast to Denmark by radio.

After forty-eight hours of debate within the Swedish government—after all, such an offer would be a dangerous slap in the face of the Nazis—the announcement was made. Every night thereafter, for nearly three weeks, the sound was filled with fishing boats ferrying Jews to the safety of Sweden.

Almost from the first, Kaplan had befriended young Borgmann. He was sent on many a mission, to warn Jews whose hiding places had been compromised by Nazi informers, to bring them food and clothing, to serve as a translator for Kaplan as he tried to convince Danish fishermen to risk everything to take a few Jews to Sweden.

After he'd been working with Jacob Kaplan for about a week, the agent took him aside. "I understand Professor Bohr thinks highly of you," he'd said.

The conversation embarrassed Borgmann. "I am his student."

"He has asked that you and your parents be smuggled to Sweden as soon as possible. He wants you to join him in London."

"I'd rather stay and help. There's plenty of time."

Borgmann remembered how Kaplan had ignored his protests. "I've arranged for two boats, one tonight, one tomorrow night. I don't know which will have the room. Be ready."

"I want to stay and help you."

"I am sorry, my young friend. We each serve in our own way. From what Bohr says about you, you can best serve us by joining him."

"But I am just a student."

"A prodigy. That's what Bohr calls you. We will not argue, Frederick."

The scene was still fresh in Borgmann's mind. He

even remembered what he had done immediately afterward. He'd raced back to the house of his friend and classmate Bent Dahlgaard, where he'd been hiding.

"A prodigy!" Borgmann had told Dahlgaard in breathless delight. "The professor called me a prodigy!"

"Well, you are the best student in the class, Frederick."

"But we are so close, Bent, so very close. If it were not for this trick memory of mine, you would beat me on every examination."

"Perhaps," Dahlgaard had said, brushing his straight blond hair back across his forehead in a characteristic gesture. "But that no longer matters. Professor Bohr wants you to join him, and we both know you must. When will you be leaving?"

"Tonight, I think."

"From the fishing wharf near Langelinie?"

It was the most frequently used departure point. "Yes."

"I'll pray for you, my friend," Dahlgaard had said.

The scenes played themselves back in Borgmann's mind, like movies, as he stood in front of what used to be Mogens Staffeldt's bookstore. There was just one memory left to confront. He knew he had been avoiding it.

Borgmann walked on, back past Town Hall Square, along the tiny, museum-studded Slotshomen, by the huge, granite Christiansborg Palace, toward Nyhavn. His step quickened. When Borgmann was a boy, when there were no troubles in the world and no tragic endings, he often spent his free afternoons at Nyhavn, watching the ships go by, laughing at the drunken sailors who lurched from bar to bar.

Years ago, a red-haired sailor with a huge green and blue anchor tattooed on his forearm had befriended him and taken him into a bar for his first drink. Now he needed another. He walked into a place called the Skipper Kroen and took a spot at the bar.

"*Akvavit,*" he told the bartender. The man nodded, reached into a little refrigerator against the wall for a

66

tall green bottle and carefully poured out a thimble-sized glass of the pale liquid.

Borgmann took it, tilted it against his lips, and drained it in a swallow. He felt the chill as the liquid poured into him. There was a slight caraway flavor. *Alborg Taffel*, he said to himself, automatically identifying the brand. He smiled wryly. Nearly thirty years and he could still tell which *snaps* he was drinking.

After one more, he left a pile of *kroner* on the bar and walked out. He backtracked to the dignified Kongens Nytorv Square, where Scandinavia's largest department store, Magasin du Nord, stood in grandmotherly solidity. When the Langelinie bus came, he hopped aboard.

It was dark now. Despite the street lights, there were few people on the pathway to the shore, where Langelinie—"The Little Mermaid"—stood. Borgmann found himself a little grassy spot, sat down, and looked out at the statue, now nothing more than a dark silhouette.

Of all the memories, this one was the most painful. Just a few yards from this spot, he'd said good-bye to his parents. At the last moment, he'd decided to wait one more day. A kiss, a quick hug from each, and they'd sailed off, along with six other university faculty members, headed for the safety of Sweden.

They never arrived. Jacob Kaplan later told him that their boat had been intercepted by a Nazi patrol. It was a tragic misfortune. Eduard and Margriet Borgmann were among the 472 Danish Jews captured by the Germans and taken to concentration camps. They were never heard from again.

Borgmann looked out at the sound and listened to the gentle lapping of the water at the shore. He thought of his mother and father and tried to make a final peace with the memory.

He wondered how many of those who had escaped to Sweden eventually made their way back. He wondered if Rabbi Melchior had returned. He wondered what had happened to his best friend, Bent Dahlgaard, to his teen-age girlfriend, Maj Hartling. For just a moment he considered trying to look them up, to see if

67

any of his old friends were listed in the telephone directory. Then he dropped the idea. It was too long ago for that.

Finally, Borgmann thought of Jacob Kaplan. He, at least returned—older, worn, using a different name, but moved by the same dedication.

Chapter Seven

It had taken Suliman Ferrara the better part of two hours to explain the situation to Abdul Amer. The man had an IQ in the low double figures, as the banks might say. Praise Allah, Ferrara thought, he did not have to explain everything to the man—especially his motives. Amer would never have understood just how much the centrifuge could mean to the Palestinians, to the eventual recapture of all of Palestine.

Nothing—not four different wars, four different cease-fires, nor any number of Palestinian "National Conferences"—had managed to unite the Palestinians. Whenever one group seemed on the verge of secure political power, another would send out its terrorists and upset everything. So nearly a million and a half Palestinian refugees still wallowed in poverty in the countries that surrounded Israel, kept from starvation only by UNRWA—the United National Relief and Works Agency. Another million lived in Israel itself, or in the lands the Jews had grabbed, especially the Gaza Strip. Together, the Palestinians outnumbered the Israelis. Given the means and the unity, they could retake Palestine by themselves, without help from Egypt, Syria, Libya, Jordan or Iraq—help that always had strings attached. And the centrifuge could give them both the means and the unity.

"Suliman, please forgive me," Amer said. "I have not eaten."

"I see," Ferrara said. He knew what was coming.

"I saw a small restaurant on the corner as I was looking for a parking place."

"Yes."

"Please pardon me for suggesting it, but could we perhaps have lunch there?"

"You go, Abdul. Eat as quickly as you can and return."

"But you, Suliman—do you not want to eat?"

"I have to wait here. Others are expected."

"You must eat, Suliman."

Ferrara sighed. "Bring me a sandwich."

"What kind?"

His eyes narrowed. "Any kind, Abdul. Just make it fast."

"Yes, Suliman. Of course. You can trust me."

"Go!"

Amer scurried from the room like a frightened chicken. Now Ferrara was once more alone with his thoughts. He could wait another hour. If no one else had arrived by then, he would have to take Amer and do the best he could.

Once more, he thought of the centrifuge. He had known of it for about six months now. And even that had been a matter of luck. He had been having lunch with an old Yale colleague, Monef el Kadoumi, at the Saad one December afternoon. Over *kebbeh* and *mouloukiea*—lamb and chicken—his friend, now a physics professor at American University in Beirut, had been telling him about the latest developments in nuclear technology.

"I fear for the world, Suliman," el Kadoumi said.

"Yes. So do we all." He observed the beautiful women as they sauntered by the outdoor cafe, and they returned his interest.

"No, I'm talking about something specific. Soon the day will be upon us when any nation can have atomic weapons."

"Nuclear proliferation. I have read about it. But what of the technically backward nations, the poor countries?"

"That's what scares me, Suliman. The Europeans

have developed a new device, something called a gas centrifuge. They claim it is not terribly expensive nor terribly difficult to build. And once it is in operation, it can produce very cheap bomb-quality uranium."

"Ah, Monef, what would the Europeans want with the bomb? Half of them are protected by the Russians, the other half by the Americans. What would they do with enriched uranium?"

"Oh, they don't talk of building bombs. They plan to use the uranium for nuclear energy—electrical power."

"And yet you think, my friend, that this device could give many nations the ability to build atomic bombs?" Ferrara was skeptical.

"Certainly," Monef said. "It's just a matter of getting hold of the centrifuge plans. They're secret and closely guarded, I expect. But secrets have a way of becoming known."

Ferrara now tried to recall the exact moment when the idea occurred to him—that here might be the opportunity he sought. He wanted to remember exactly how it had felt, exactly what his thoughts were.

Instead, he remembered, to his amused dismay, that at that moment two women had taken the table next to theirs and that he had almost immediately established eye contact with the prettier one, a slender, dark-haired Christian girl with light grey eyes. They continued to glance at one another from time to time while he and Monef talked of world-shaking ideas.

"Tell me, Monef," Ferrara said, now questioning his friend more closely, "wouldn't it take a highly industrial nation and a large community of scientists to build these devices—even granting that they had the blueprints?"

"Not at all, Suliman. We could even do it here in Beirut, if we wanted to. Our university scientists have plenty of technical skill and knowledge. And our best metalworkers are more than equal to the job. The same is true for most countries, even small ones. Fortunately, most countries don't have access to uranium ore."

Ferrara looked away from the pretty girl, angry with himself. He'd been figuring out whether the Palestinians might build such machines and he'd forgotten the most important element—uranium ore. "So," he said, forcing a smile, "we couldn't make enriched uranium in Lebanon after all, eh?"

Monef glanced toward the next table, having seen Ferrara look there repeatedly. He caught Ferrara's eye, pursed his lips, and nodded appreciatively. Then he fumbled a bit, trying to regain the thread of conversation. "In Lebanon? It would be easy here. Few people realize it, but between them, Syria and Egypt have more uranium and thorium oxide than any other single country in the world. They control nearly a third of the total known worldwide supply."

Now despite his efforts to control himself, to be the strictly rational man, Ferrara abruptly sat up in his chair, tense and excited. Monef was flirting, though, and he didn't notice. "Well," Ferrara said, "that *is* surprising. I wonder why that isn't commonly known."

"The scientific community knows it well enough," Monef answered.

Ferrara let the conversation grow quiet. He needed time to think. He had to ask the proper questions without raising any suspicion on Monef's part. His friend was an Arab, it was true, but a man committed to the West. They'd talked about the Palestinians in the past, and Monef had made it clear he despised their guerrilla tactics.

"This gas centrifuge, Monef," Ferrara said, his interest carefully casual, "do you really think the plans will become public?"

"Public?" Monef was amused. "Not likely. I imagine they're under the tightest security imaginable now—somewhere in The Hague, I believe. But the British, the Dutch, and the Germans intend to use the centrifuge to promote European political unity. I understand they're going to try to interest the Scandinavians in joining them.

"The idea is to build a string of centrifuges throughout Europe and create a massive power grid. Such a thing could make Europe as economically powerful as the United States. If this is to be done, the plans must

72

be shown to the Scandinavians. Then, the security may not be so tight."

"I see," Ferrara said. "Well, if you want my opinion, I don't think anything will come of the whole thing except electrical power. No one is interested in building bombs today. Nuclear war is unthinkable. Economic power is what everyone wants."

"Perhaps you are right," el Kadoumi said. "I sincerely hope so."

Within three days, Ferrara's organization had been able to verify every detail of el Kadoumi's remarks. There was such a machine as the gas centrifuge, and it did what el Kadoumi said it did. Furthermore, centrifuge plans would be shown to the Scandinavians in a few months, in Copenhagen. With every new piece of information, Ferrara's excitement grew. Could the centrifuge be that *deus ex machina* for which every Palestinian had prayed?

Ferrara lost the train of thought for a moment. He was not in Beirut, but in Copenhagen. The question was not if the centrifuge plans were important to the Palestinians, but if he could get them. Once more he went to the apartment window. He stared at the street for several minutes, trying to create the men he sought, by force of will. But there was no one. More and more, it looked as if he'd have to make the attempt with only Abdul Amer's help. After all the difficulties he'd already transcended, it would be the purest sort of irony to see the mission scuttled by Palestinian disunity.

It wasn't that he hadn't anticipated the problem, Ferrara thought bitterly. He'd done everything humanly possible to overcome it. From the first, he'd realized that he'd need help to steal the plans. That meant getting cooperation from every Palestinian organization lest one sabotage the other. His own associates were useless for this job. He'd only realized that stealing the plans brought him only halfway to his goal. Once he returned with them, he'd have to make sure they were put in the hands of the right people. His choices were bewildering: the PLO, the PFLP, the DPFLP, the Palestine Liberation Army, the *Sa'iqa*—or *Fatah*. It wasn't a matter of favoring one splinter group over the others so much as choosing the one most likely to unite them all in the effort to build the machines. Anything less than total cooperation, Ferrara was sure, meant failure. Could he trust the PLO's current preeminence.

He had struggled with the decision for days, but the answer hadn't presented itself to him. Finally he realized that he could never make a rational choice in the cacophony of Beirut, where the splinter groups constantly contended at the top of their lungs. He decided once more to retreat to Baalbek. It was early February. The place would be almost completely free of tourists.

He left just after breakfast one day, this time driving the eighty-six kilometers from Beirut to Baalbek in his silver-grey Citroën-Maserati, one of seven in all of Lebanon—a far cry from the young hitchhiker who'd made the trip more than a dozen years earlier. He sped up the Beirut-Damascus highway, shooting past the mountain resorts of Aley, Bhamdoun and Sofar. Behind him, he knew, lay Beirut and beyond it, the sea, in striking vista. But, except for an occasional glance through his rear-view mirror, he ignored the sight. There were other things on his mind.

About an hour out of Beirut, Ferrara's sleek sports car sliced through Dahr el Baidar Pass, the highest point of the drive. A few seconds later, he was on the plain of the Beka'a. Now the descent began. The road dropped sharply, to Chataura, at the foot of the mountain, past hotels and restaurants. Then it branched off to the left, toward Baalbek. Ferrara expertly negotiated the turn, hardly slowing.

If he had continued straight, he would have ended up in Damascus before the day was out. Instead he headed north, toward Zahleh, passing the Ksara vineyards on his way. He stopped at Zahleh and lunched on frogs' legs at one of the restaurants that flanked the Bardawni River as it rushed down the mountain and through the town. At Rayak, the road turned left again. Now the countryside took on a different character. The rich farmlands stretched for miles, bordered by blue grey snow-capped mountains. Ferrara could almost feel the presence of the ancient city some twenty-five kilometers ahead.

Twenty minutes later, he saw it, a forest of yellow stone ruins on the plain, surrounded by surprisingly lush green trees. He parked his car near the Great Temple of Jupiter, the same temple at which he'd found his life's direction, more than a decade ago. Then he submerged himself once more in the majesty of ancient days.

But those were not the days for which he yearned. Even then, two thousand years ago, the Middle East was a battleground for the world's major powers. What Ferrara wanted was a Palestinian nation that was co-equal with those powers. And not just a West Bank sliver. What he dreamed of was the end of Israel and the establishment of an Arab Palestine, won not with the oil weapon, which the Saudis and the Egyptians had used only for their own ends, but with the very weapons by which the great powers held sway.

He sat on the floor of the temple, near the gigantic altar, hoping for another message, another sign. His mother would have had him reason it out, weigh one factor against another, write out a checklist of pros and cons. Nonetheless, Ferrara knew this was not a problem he could solve with logic. He had come to Baalbek not only because it offered peace and quiet, but also because he hoped that the ancient gods might deign to magnify his intuition.

The difficulty in getting the centrifuge plans resolved itself into a conundrum: He could unify the Palestinians with the centrifuge. But the plans could only be obtained if the Palestinians were unified to begin with.

He let his mind drift away from the problem and gazed at the stones on the temple floor. How perfectly they were fit together, how straight their edges. He raised his eyes, to the magnificent edifice above. It had been built as an offering to the gods, though it turned out to be an offering to posterity.

Ferrara, too, wanted to make an offering to posterity—but how presumptuous that seemed, here at Baalbek. He wanted to make Palestine once again Arab.

Possibly, he would succeed, only to have his success wiped out a century from now, by twenty-first century Roman legions. That was fatalism, though, the curse of the Arab people. His mother had warned him against it time and time again. Fatalism was the seedbed of defeat, she'd said. It siphoned away passions and becalmed the brain.

Like the man who had designed the Temple of Jupiter, Ferrara recognized that he, too, must call upon other men to bring his plans to fruition. In the end, he must trust another man to help him. But which man? He got up and walked out of the temple, toward his car. In the distance, he could see the mountains, composed of pale streaks of purple, yellow and pink, a rainbow of water colors.

One man's name intruded itself into his thoughts: Arafat—Yassir Arafat, long-time leader of *Fatah*, and the designated representative of the Palestinian people. Arafat had serious drawbacks and Ferrara knew them all. The worst: he had failed to unify the Palestinians, though he'd had more than twenty years to accomplish the task. Even his current political position was hardly a guarantee. Who else was there, though? Habash had little power. Hawatmah owed ideological debts to both Russia and China. Shukeiri had shown his incompetence.

Ferrara drove back to Beirut, his mind made up. He would approach Arafat. That didn't mean that the whole thing was settled, though. It wasn't enough to give Arafat the plans. That wouldn't unify the Palestinians. He had to get the man to agree to cooperate with the other organizations, and they with him, both in getting the plans and building the centrifuges.

And that was just the beginning. When—and if—Arafat agreed, Ferrara had to visit the other groups and persuade them to work with Arafat while subordinating themselves to Arafat. It was no simple task.

If everybody said yes, every group would participate, in stage one, a team of men—one from each of the major splinter groups—would work together in Copenhagen to obtain the plans. In stage two, a second team, again representing every group, would work together to provide the raw and finished materials necessary for centrifuge construction.

As for the uranium ore, that was the least of their problems. Arafat would first ask Syria. If Syria refused, he'd ask Egypt. If Egypt refused—well, Ferrara would take over then. It would be like smuggling any other commodity into the country—heroin, for example.

Once more, Suliman Ferrara looked out toward the streets of Copenhagen through his apartment window. And where was the help he had been promised? What excuses would they offer, all of them? He looked at his watch. Another fifteen or twenty minutes; then he'd have to make his move.

Making contact with Arafat hadn't been difficult, not with Ferrara's underworld connections and his acquaintances among the Palestinians. At ten o'clock one morning, he'd been picked up by a surly looking Palestinian in a Land Rover. They drove in almost total silence for the better part of three hours, into Southern Syria. Then the Arab blindfolded him. When they finally stopped, Ferrara guessed they were about sixty-four kilometers from Damascus. His blindfold was taken off.

In front of him, he saw two large buildings on a stony plain a short distance from some hills. About a hundred men in camouflage uniforms and rubber boots were running in closed formation, some of them stripped to the waist. Some were carrying Kalashnikov rifles of either Russian or Chinese origin. A few years earlier, Ferrara himself had occasion to use a Kalashnikov. It was a good weapon.

Once more he was blindfolded. Evidently, he thought, they've shown me what they want me to see. He couldn't decide whether he'd witnessed a stage production or actual military training. At any rate, there was another car trip—this one about fifteen minutes long. Then the blindfold was removed once more.

The memory was still vivid. Ferrara had been escorted into a large cave, furnished with tables, chairs and even a telephone—which rang incessantly. Was that part of the production, too? A Kalashnikov lay on a table, in plain view. It was surprising, considering Arafat's status in Syria.

There was a wait of several minutes, then Ferrara was told that Arafat would not be able to see him after all, that he would have to be content with a deputy, Abu Ammar. Ferrara made no objection. He knew that Abu Ammar was Arafat's code name.

"Ammar" turned out to be a surprisingly short man—five feet four inches at the most—built like a ripe pear. He was wearing army fatigues, grey suede sneakers, dark glasses and a five-day growth of beard. The handshake consisted of two quick, businesslike jerks.

"Have a seat, Monsieur Ferrara," Arafat said, pointing to the cave's battered wooden chairs.

Ferrara sat down and looked around further. The cave was filled with *fedayeen*. "Ammar," evidently, followed his gaze. He motioned his men to leave, which they all did—reluctantly.

"Well, *Monsieur* Ferrara. *Fatah* has heard a great deal about you over the years. But we have never met you before. You have never given us any aid. Now we understand you are promising great things, things that you cannot discuss with anyone but our leader."

"That's true, sir," Ferrara said. "But I am confident you will relay my message to him."

"Ammar" smiled slightly without parting his lips. They understood one another. "Go ahead, *Monsieur* Ferrara. I will do my best to inform him of what you say."

By the time Ferrara had finished outlining his proposal, there was a new glint in Arafat's eye. And he was no longer interested in keeping up the phony identity pretense.

"I take it on faith that what you tell me is true."

"It is true."

"And you think you can steal the plans?"

"If anyone can, I can."

"It is all reasonable—except for one thing."

"Yes?"

"The part about unifying the Palestinians."

Ferrara felt his pulse leap. "That is the key element," he said.

"You don't know what you're asking, *monsieur,*" Arafat said. "The Palestinians have had nearly three decades to unite, and they have not. Whenever I try to do something, terrorists from one group or another interfere. You would have thought that all Arabs would have united in 1948. They did not. The 1956 war offered another opportunity, which we declined. After the 1967 and 1973 wars, the message was clearer than ever: the only way for us to return to our homeland was to forget our petty differences."

"I never said it would be easy."

"Easy? Hah! It is harder than ever now. I must deal with leftists and rightists, Marxists and Maoists. We've been kicked out of Jordan—those of us who survived Black September. Lebanon—your home, I believe—would do the same to us if it could. Egypt tolerates us barely, in the smallest numbers. Syria offers us a home, but watches us carefully. Libya and Iraq say they are with us, but to this day, I do not trust their motives."

"If you have the centrifuge," Ferrara said, "they will come to you. You will have the power to win the allegiance not only of the Palestinians, but possibly also of the Arab nations surrounding Israel."

Ferrara remembered, with a chill, the look with which Arafat had greeted that remark. For pure cynicism and doubt, he'd never seen anything like it, before or since.

"Perhaps, *Monsieur* Ferrara, perhaps. Or perhaps you are a Don Quixote."

Arafat ended up agreeing to supply some help—one experienced operative. If Ferrara had known, at that time, that the *Fatah* operative would turn out to be Abdul Amer, he mused, he might have saved himself that drive into Syria.

As it was, that trip was only the start of his effort to arouse the Palestinians. In the weeks that followed, Ferrara visited six other Palestinian partisan groups, each time suffering through blindfolds, secret rides and hidden headquarters. In Lebanon, Syria and Jordan, he told his story again and again, never completely convincing the partisan leaders, never gaining anything more than halfhearted promises of support. He even talked to the Soviet military attaché in Damascus, who was pleasant but impossibly vague.

Ferrara went ahead with his plans despite lack of partisan enthusiasm. He took his inspiration, instead, from rank-and-file Palestinians, from those who lived by the tens of thousands in refugee camps throughout the Middle East. Unlike their leaders, the refugees shared a common goal: they all prayed for the moment when they could return to their lands and homes in Palestine.

After each trip, he returned to Beirut, only to be confronted by the refugees. Colonies of them surrounded the Lebanese captial, crowded into shacks and hovels, living in huts built from wooden crates, occupying caves in the rocky mountain coast. They might have settled down, here and elsewhere. They might have blended with the local populace. But the Palestinians had a dream, a dream of return. Permanent settlement would have dulled that vision.

Ferrara lived with the diplomats, in Raouche, in a white high-rise overlooking the Pigeon Rocks. It was elegant, sophisticated. Jaguars and Mercedes-Benzes parked outside of his building. Smart parties were held on the balconies facing the Mediterranean. Ferrara often went to them; he blended in well, with his American-accented English and London-cut clothing. Diplomats' wives found him attractive and he returned the feeling. It was a relationship of both convenience and pleasure.

Situated at the juncture of East and West, Beirut was destined to be a sophisticated city. Given the oil-rich lands of Arabia and the gold they brought into Lebanese banking houses on Weygand Street, Beirut was also destined to be a decadent city. No upper class anywhere in the world was richer than Beirut's. No upper class knew better how to spend its money to maximum effect in the world of finance, speculating on the value of the dollar, or any other likely currency or on gold itself—all on a vast scale. No upper class knew better how to make its leisure luxurious, playing *chemin de fer* or *baccarat* at the Casino du Liban; watching the showgirls at the Kit Kat; showing off Parisian styles at sidewalk cafes on the Rue el Hamra.

Part of Beirut, anyway, was glamorous, with grand boulevards reminiscent of Paris—for, after all, it was the French who built modern Lebanon. Ferrara was at home here. His wealth had given him entry. But he was also at home in the other part of Beirut, near Place des Canons, where Arabs—who lived so deep in poverty they didn't know how poor they were—bought and sold life's necessities in Oriental *souks*. Uptown, he was the ambassador from the underworld, a man of mystery and excitement, whom hostesses fought over. Downtown, in the *souks,* he was a sultan.

The rich and the poor of Beirut would never join the Palestinians against Israel, at least not *en masse.* The poor had no real argument with the Israelis. The rich wanted to be left alone, so that they could concentrate on increasing their fortunes. In 1967 and 1973, Ferrara knew, they had influenced the Lebanese government to hold back. As a result his was the only nation that had not challenged the Zionists, despite the thousands of Palestinian refugees who lived there.

Yet it had not always been that way. Three thousand years ago, the direct ancestors of the Lebanese—the Phoenicians, the Canaanites and the Moabites—led by King Mesha, had done battle with the Hebrews of Palestine. The rhetoric that followed that war was bitterly amusing today. In the National Archaeological Museum in Beirut, in the alcove called the Gallery of the Alphabet, there was a stele dating from the tenth century B.C., the Stele Mesha. In sharp, angular letters—actually the first syllabic alphabet, the ancestor of all Western and many Eastern languages—Mesha had recorded the result of the war. As a boy, after the 1948 war with Israel, Ferrara and his classmates had been encouraged to memorize the words. He knew them still:

"I am Mesha, King of Moab ... Johoram, the King of Israel has humbled Moab for many years ... But I triumphed over him and over his house, while Israel hath perished forever."

It sounded just like Arafat, or at least the public Arafat.

Only after Ferrara went to Yale did he come across what the Israelites had written about the same war, in the Second Book of Kings:

"The Israelites rose up and smote the Moabites so that they fled before them; but they went forward smiting the Moabites even in their own country. And they beat down the cities, and on every green piece of land cast every man his stone and filled it, and they stopped all the wells of water and felled all the good trees."

And that sounded like Moshe Dayan—arrogant, certainly, but accurate. . . .

The doorknob rattled and Ferrara looked up with a start. It was almost as if he'd been asleep. "Who's there?" He felt like praying.

"It is me, Suliman, Abdul."

Ferrara opened the door. The Arab walked in and handed him a little bag.

"How much do I owe you?" Ferrara asked.

"Not a piaster," Amer said proudly. "*Fatah* will pay for this."

Ferrara managed to say nothing.

"I have been thinking about our situation, Suliman," Amer said. "There's one thing that bothers me."

Ferrara gazed at this poor excuse for a man. "Yes, Abdul. What is it that bothers you? Tell me."

"How do we get the plans?"

Suliman Ferrara smiled. He felt benevolent, almost fatherlike. "We don't, Abdul. The Israelis get them. We steal them from the Israelis."

At first, the Arab was confused. Then a grin slowly broke over his face, like the rising sun, revealing a rotted upper-front tooth. Ferrara tried not to look at it. "I understand, Suliman. It is a magnificent idea. An idea worthy of a true Arab."

82

Ferrara had heard that phrase before—a true Arab. Perhaps that was one reason he could not get them to cooperate. Would he ever be totally trusted? He sighed.

"Of course, Abdul, it is not so simple as it sounds. We first have to locate the Israeli team."

Amer nodded. "How do we do that?"

"Your leader Arafat has contacted his friends here in the Soviet Consulate. . . ." He let his voice drift off. Amer need not be told this part of the plan. Besides, it was only a hope at this point. As soon as the Palestinian team was all here, he'd send men out all over the city.

Ferrara just happened to be gazing at the apartment's front door when it happened—an envelope came sliding under the doorsill. He was on his feet instantly. He covered the distance between his chair and the door in less than three steps. Still, when he flung the door open, there was no one in view. He ran out of the apartment, onto the street. At least twenty people were within ten yards of the apartment house door. The envelope could have come from anyone of them.

Ferrara walked back into the flat, picking up the envelope as he entered.

"What happened?" Amer asked, mystified.

Ferrara showed him the envelope. "Someone slipped this under our door."

"But who?. . . ."

"We'll know that in a moment, I hope," Ferrara said, opening the envelope and removing the note inside. He read it silently and snorted to himself. Then he held it up to the light.

"What does it say?"

"Well, my friend, someone has anticipated our needs. We've been instructed to watch a man named Borgmann. He's supposed to be staying at the Kong Frederik."

Ferrara handed the envelope and the note to Abdul Amer. The Arab looked at it carefully, on both sides.

"Hold it up to the light, Abdul."

Amer bent down and held the paper close to the bulb in the cracked, dusty table lamp. There was a watermark, but he could not read it. The words were in the Cyrillic alphabet. Finally he understood.

"It's Russian," he said, excited. "This paper was made in Russia."

"Exactly," said Ferrara. "Arafat's friend in the Soviet Consulate, no doubt. He knows we're here and he's helping us."

"It does seem that way."

"But why not contact us directly. And why not tell us more about this man Borgmann?"

Ferrara shrugged. "The KGB is even more inscrutable than the Chinese."

"What if it's a trick? What if the Israelis are trying to trap us?"

"That doesn't seem likely. Would you go out of your way to tell your enemies you're in the neighborhood, Abdul?"

The Arab scratched his ear. "No, I guess not."

"Besides, it's the only lead we have at the moment, my friend."

Amer nodded. He was still worried about the note. It was just too convenient. It had arrived at too nearly the exactly perfect moment. But he knew better than to press the point with Ferrara. When superiors placed their faith in a single idea, it was unhealthy to offer a serious challenge.

"What do we do now?" Amer asked his tall, handsome colleague.

"It's what *you* do, Abdul."

"Yes?"

"I want you to go to the Hafnia."

"Now, Suliman? It's almost dinnertime. Borgmann wouldn't be there now."

Ferrara considered the question for a moment. "Yes, you're right. Have dinner. Spend the evening as you wish."

"Suliman, I hesitate to ask this, but. . . ."

"Yes? Go on, Abdul."

"I hope you won't think I'm taking advantage. . . ."

"What is it, man?"

"The newspapers—they speak of sex shows. . . ."

84

Ferrara smiled. So Amer was more than a lump after all. Underneath all that apologetic sadness, there was a man. Or at least a male.

"What are you asking me, Abdul?"

"I was wondering if I might be permitted to attend one of the shows. I've heard that they actually have intercourse, right in front of your eyes. I would love to see such a thing. . . ."

"The night is yours, Abdul. Do with it what you will."

"Then you do not object?"

"That's what I just said, didn't I?"

"Yes, of course. But I don't want you to think I'm taking advantage."

"I think you should go, Abdul. You'll enjoy telling about it at the campfire, when you get back."

Abdul considered the thought. "Yes," he said, grinning. "The soldiers don't know about such things. They only dream and boast foolishly."

"Typical soldiers."

"Yes."

"Do me one favor, will you Abdul?"

"Of course. Anything you ask, Suliman."

"When I see you again, don't tell me anything about this evening."

"Yes, Suliman, certainly." The Arab was puzzled but obedient.

"One more thing. Do not get into any trouble. And be in the lobby of the Hafnia by—oh—seven-thirty tomorrow morning. Find Borgmann. Stay with him—by car, if necessary."

"That is my specialty, Suliman. I am an excellent driver."

"Good. I suspect Borgmann is involved with the Israelis, somehow. No doubt, there is some sort of secret meeting place where they all gather. Find it and report back to me."

"And you, Suliman? What will you be doing?"

"There's no special reason for me to tell you, Abdul. But because I know you are the sort of man who cannot bear to have his curiosity frustrated, I will say this:

I will be waiting for more help, which I expect momentarily, and I will be arranging for our departure."

"We're leaving?"

"Soon, Abdul. In a day or two, I suspect."

Back at his room at Hotel Helgoland, Abdul Amer nervously leafed through the small "Sex Guide" folder he'd bought at a porno shop near Ferrara's apartment. He guessed that tonight would be his only free night, his only opportunity to take advantage of what made Copenhagen so different from anywhere else he'd been. He wanted desperately not to waste his chance.

What Amer was doing was trying to determine—from the ads alone—which of Copenhagen's many live sex shows would be least likely to disappoint. In the end, he settled for the one with the biggest, blackest advertisement: the Private Club, on Herluf Trollesgade.

According to the ad in the Sex Guide, the Private Club offered advanced striptease, pornographic pictures with sound, lesbian love, intercourse, a sex-lottery, drinks (at popular prices), lots of naughty girls, and dancing in beautiful intimate rooms. The price, said the ad, was 99 *kroner* for "non-keyclub spectators."

Amer grabbed his money conversion scale, anxious to see if he could afford the tariff. The price worked out to £ 45 Lebanese pounds—about $16.50, American. This was nearly a quarter of his weekly expense money. It would mean skimpy meals and much penny-pinching. But, Amer decided, it was worth it. He could eat when he got home.

Amer was in front of the Private Club by 7:45. He didn't want to miss a minute of the action. Herluf Trollesgade turned out to be a nice, stodgy, tree-lined street filled mostly with warehouses and small apartment buildings. The Private Club was housed in a nondescript grey building. Half a dozen lighted globes distinguished it from the other buidings on the block.

The Arab walked through the archway that led to the club's entrance and pushed what appeared to be a doorbell. There was no sound. Instead, a small bulb lit up over the door—and probably inside too. After a few moments, the door opened and a greasy-looking man in a blue suit motioned Amer inside.

"That will be 120 *kroner*—in advance," the man said.

Amer gaped at him. "But the ad said 99 *kroner*."

"Oh, yes," said the man. "That was last year's price."

"The price has gone up?"

"Yes."

Amer did some furious mental arithmetic. If he entered now, he'd be spending more than a third of his weekly expenses in a single shot. If he didn't, he might be missing the opportunity of a lifetime.

"Are you coming in?"

"Ah, yes, of course."

Amer paid and the man offered him a ledger to sign.

"You want me to write my name?"

"Yes, sir. It's Danish law. You're becoming a member of a private club, you understand." The man was smiling faintly.

"Of course," said Amer. He scribbled something on the paper in illegible Arabic, proud of himself for disguising his identity. No one in the world could ever trace that signature, he was sure. Then he stepped inside.

To his right was a twenty-five-seat movie theater, behind some heavy red velour drapes. The screen flickered with an out-of-focus pornographic film. Directly ahead of him was a bar. To his left was an archway rigged with flashing lights and lit by a small neon sign that blinked on and off. The sign said "sex show."

Amer turned back to the man who had admitted him. "When does the sex show begin?"

"In about twenty minutes," the man said. "You may go in now, if you wish."

Amer wished.

Past the archway, he found a room about the size of an average living room, lined with a single row of foam lounges. To his great pleasure, he had arrived first. That meant he had the pick of the seats.

For the next half hour, he sat waiting for the action, entertained only by the Danish equivalent of Muzak and by the occasional arrival of other spectators. By about 8:45, the room was full, populated by an assortment of European, American and Japanese tourists. Most of the audience was male, though one American had brought his wife and there were two Japanese women in the group of Orientals.

Then the lights began to dim. Amer felt his heartbeat soar. His shirt was long ago soaked with perspiration. For an instant, the room was dark. Then, a single spotlight flashed on, illuminating an attractive brunette about twenty-five years old, wearing a long white gown, standing in the middle of the floor.

"Good evening, ladies and gentlemen," she said, her English perfect. Then she repeated her welcome in Danish, Swedish, and German. "I am your mistress of ceremonies," she went on, a distinct sparkle in her eyes. "We're a bit shorthanded this evening, so you may see me participating in the show in other capacities also." She looked around the room, smiling. "I see we have some Oriental visitors. Sorry I cannot greet you in your language."

One of the Japanese tourists called out the words for "good evening" and the pretty brunette repeated them and said them to the Oriental part of her audience. Then, she looked directly at Amer.

"And you sir. If I am not mistaken, you are from the Middle East. Yes?"

Amer's heart was pounding in his chest. His hands felt clammy. "Yes."

"Whereabouts?"

"Oh, all over," he said nervously.

"And how might I say good evening to you?"

"Salaam," he told her.

"Then salaam it is. And peace to you all. I hope you all take off your ties and jackets and relax. There's no need to be formal. You are here to have fun. So am I. Now, ladies and gentlemen, on with the show."

For a moment, the lights went out. Then the music began—sensuous, insinuating, pseudo-Oriental music. When the lights went on again, three beautiful "harem" girls were dancing to the music, clad only in diaphanous veils, every one of them at least reasonably attractive.

Because of the size and shape of the room, no member of the audience was more than three feet from one of the dancing girls. Amer, sitting in the middle of the row, could have reached out and touched one, a fact which was giving him palpitations.

Dancing around the room, the girls came closer and closer to the audience. Finally, one of them pointed to one of the veils that made up her skirt and motioned to the Japanese man sitting in front of her. He understood. He reached for the veil and pulled it away from the elastic strip that held it in place. The girl let him keep his prize, then she danced on to another spectator, who removed another veil. The other two girls did the same.

Finally, it was Amer's turn. The prettiest of the harem girls—a statuesque blonde—had stopped in front of him, wearing no more than a garter belt and a flimsy piece of gauze that might, with charity, have been called a bra. She gestured at him teasingly. She wanted him to remove her bra.

Sweating, hands shaking, Amer stood up to do just that. He gathered his courage together and reached around behind the girl, looking for the clasp. She pushed herself into him and rubbed her body against him. It was almost more than he could stand.

Finally, his fumbling fingers found the clasp and undid it. The girl shook herself loose from the scrap of underwear, leaving it dangling in his hands. Then she danced away.

Soon, all three dancers were stark naked. Their bodies glistened with perspiration as the tempo of the music increased again and again and their dance became increasingly frantic. The music hit its peak—as did the girls—then both began to slow. The movements of the dancers became more and more languorous. They began to move about the room to retrieve their garments—indicating to the men who held them that the person who had done the undressing was now to do the dressing.

Amer gazed at the two bits of triangular gauze connected by a thin cord that he held in his hand. He noticed how an elastic string went around back and how the clasp fastened. Then, he began to think of how he might have to touch the girl to get the garment back in place. And he began to get excited.

When the blonde girl shimmied to a stop in front of him, Amer eagerly sprang from his chair and began to wrap the bra around her. But she did nothing to help. In fact, she laughed and squirmed away. Once more Amer tried to fasten the garment. She got loose again.

Then, suddenly, she wasn't fighting him. She pressed close again and Amer felt her flesh against his fingers. He fumbled with the bra clasp, boldly taking the opportunity to touch the girl's cool, smooth breasts again and again. Finally, the garment was in place. The girl danced away. Amer sat down, pleased with himself. He'd shown he wasn't so clumsy after all. More than that, he'd shown that he could be sexually aggressive, if he wanted to.

What followed the dancing girls were a series of acts that, in all, comprised the most exciting experience of Abdul Amer's entire life. First, there was a beautiful red-headed strip-teaser who did an act with a dining room chair (and before she was finished, had relations with it). Then, there was a little playlet, which featured "Mrs. Van Gelt" and her "maid," Yvette. In it, the lady—actually a good-looking brunette of about twenty-five—took a bath, while her maid—Amer's blonde dancer, in costume—helped relieve the frustrations caused by Mr. Van Gelt's absence. Abdul was fascinated by both acts, and he could feel his own desires intensifying. But he waited impatiently for the next part of the show, which featured a bare stage, populated only by a strong, well-built young man and an equally attractive young woman. They held the rapt attention of the audience for the best part of a half hour, contorting themselves into sensuous positions that the Arab had never even considered, much less experienced. He found it necessary to adjust his pants slightly.

At this point, the man and woman having exhausted each other—while only arousing the audience, the lights went out once more. When they went on again, the dancing girls had returned, this time in grass skirts. This time, there were six of them. They were swaying in time to Hawaiian music.

Amer found this anything but promising. He was soon proved spectacularly incorrect. One of the girls— the one whose bra he'd removed and put back on— stood directly in front of him. She smiled charmingly and motioned for him to stand. He stood. Then, he looked around the room. He was the only member of the audience standing. And the other dancing girls were headed his way. What was happening here?

The girl in front of him put out her hands and took his. Allah be praised, Amer said to himself. She wants me to *dance!* He tried to pull loose from her grasp, to sit down again and retreat into the shadows, but it was too late. Instead, he let himself be led into the center of the small stage, where he soon found himself surrounded by the Hawaiian dancers, all of whom were pressing against him shamelessly and touching him intimately.

It was an overdose of stimulation. Amer soon forgot about the audience. He stopped wondering what they must be thinking. He surrendered to the tender, touching fingers and soft bodies around him. The arousal he'd felt during the rest of the show was back, multiplied upon itself.

As he stood there, helpless, quivering with excitement, the girls continued to fondle him. Soon, he found himself gently pushed backward, onto a couch that had evidently been put on the stage for this purpose. Once he was prone, a dozen feminine hands began to disrobe him—or, rather, depants him. One girl worked on his left shoe, another on his right, still another on his belt and another on his zipper. Two others tugged on his pants legs. The rest petted and poked at him, or pushed their bodies into his face.

It had been a shock when first he felt fingers where he had never before felt any but his own. He'd been simultaneously mortified and electrified. Now he was flabbergasted to feel lips and tongues on that same place, many lips, many tongues. Was this how Farouk

91

had been serviced? Was this how a sultan felt? What was revolution, or even justice, when compared to sex?

Amer closed his eyes and let the sensations sweep over him. There was no thought now of where he was, or who watched. There was no thought at all, only feeling.

His eyes fluttered open briefly. One of the dancing girls now straddled him, her legs opened wide. Amer looked up the twin columns, to their source. Nothing so mundane as panties impeded his view.

The parts he saw above beckoned to some part of his instincts with which he was formerly unacquainted. He strained upward, to touch and tongue, but the prize was beyond his reach. He redoubled his efforts, straining his back mightily—and still he failed. He tried again, coming close this time.

Then, all at once, he could think only of his own body. The battle for self-control was over. There was no going back now. With a low, guttural groan—he'd never made such a sound before—he let loose, firing his gun half a dozen times before he ran out of ammunition. The hands and tongues and lips pulled away.

Amer roused himself and looked at his clothing. He was a mess. He forced himself to look at the audience. They returned his gaze with nervous titters. There was a scattering of applause. He was nearly overcome by humiliation. He stood, pulled up his sticky pants with one hand and hobbled back to his seat. Across the room, the dancers had found another favorite—a man in a ten-gallon hat who'd obviously spent too much time at the bar. All eyes were on the new performance.

Later, as he walked back toward his hotel, Amer realized that he'd have plenty to tell his colleagues. All he had to do was change a detail or two. His only problem was credibility. Would his friends believe that, in the end, the girls had chosen him, from the entire audience? On reflection, he was sure they would. The entire story was too incredible to be false.

While Amer was at the sex show and Borgmann struggled with his memories, Jack Salter and Gary Stabile had a quiet gourmet dinner at the Fiskehusets restaurant, facing the docks across the street from Copenhagen's fisherwomen peddlers.

At first, Salter wasn't sure whether this dinner was intended to be a pleasurable evening between colleagues or a business meal, where the supervisor would instruct his subordinate. His doubts vanished shortly after the waiter delivered his lobster salad and Stabile's filet of sole steamed in white wine.

"Well," said Stabile expansively, taking a bite, "I think we've given the Arabs the clue they needed. Now we have to rouse the Israelis."

"What do you mean?" Salter asked. He tasted his lobster salad. It did not disappoint him.

Stabile smiled condescendingly and Salter prepared for the worst. "Those Jews are smart," he said, still chewing. "You have to give them that. But they're only human. At any rate, they have to be told that the Arabs are on their trail."

"Maybe they already know. It would be logical," Salter said.

"They may have guessed, but I doubt they know for sure. You have to remember that Israel doesn't have our resources, Jack. Simply can't afford them, you know."

Why was it that whenever he was around this man, Salter felt like a high school senior? He knew his own capabilities, after all. He was a good man. He'd received several commendations from Washington. But when Stabile showed up, he felt as though he was back at the bottom of the class.

"What do you propose, Gary?"

"Violence."

"Violence?"

"Yes. What kind of weapons do you have in the office arms cabinet?"

"The standard stuff—pistols, plastic explosives, a submachine gun."

"I see. Do you have a Soviet-made pistol?"

"As a matter of fact, yes. Arrived a couple of

months ago. I believe every field office has been issued one." Salter took a sip of wine. Just a touch too sweet, he thought.

"So, they finally got around to it," Stabile said. "I've been suggesting it for years." He popped another piece of sole into his mouth.

Salter watched him, trying to unravel the man's train of thought. That proved impossible. "Why use a Russian pistol, Gary?" he finally asked. "Don't you want the Israelis to be worrying about Arab agents?"

"Of course, my boy, of course. But the Arabs might easily have Russian weapons."

"Even so—"

"If they're not sure who's shooting at them, so much the better."

"But—"

"Confusion, my boy. It's one of our best weapons."

"Yes. I see." But he didn't, not really.

That settled, more or less, the dinner became somewhat more social. Stabile repeated some old Washington gossip, and Salter asked about other agents he'd worked with. By the end of the evening, the warm glow of camaraderie had settled over both of them.

Meanwhile, Miriam Shazar spent most of the evening in the back office of the porno shop, alone, pouring through the card file Ben-Ezra had given her. There were more than fifteen hundred names, in all. By midnight, she had found only five real possibilities: Hershel Brombek, director of undergraduate studies at the Bohr Institute; Rose Homburg, professor of nuclear chemistry; Erich Lemberg, associate professor of theoretical physics; Herman Cohen, director of Institute food services; and Hildegaard Ludstein, one of the Institute charwomen. The last two, she felt, were long shots.

When she realized this was as long as her list would be, she glanced at her watch, hoping against hope that she could start contacting them tonight, but it was too late. Well, then, she'd begin first thing the next morning.

MAY 13
DAY TWO

Chapter Eight

Borgmann slept well that night, partly because the hair in the keyhole hadn't been disturbed. He awoke with a sense of challenge and excitement. Once more he was on a mission for Jacob Kaplan.

The tall physicist caught a cab outside of the Kong Frederik and arrived at the Niels Bohr Institute for Nuclear Research just before nine o'clock. He paid no attention whatever to the small grey Fiat that had followed him from the hotel.

Borgmann had heard about the Institute, seen pictures of it. Still, he was impressed. It was a complex of modern buildings—laboratories, high-domed reactors, classrooms and auditoriums. It was a great pity that Bohr couldn't have lived to see what he had inspired.

For a while, Borgmann stood on the steps of the Assembly Hall, where the conference was to be held, watching limousine after limousine pull up, disgorge its payload of dignitaries, and glide away. Then, between limousines, a yellow cab stopped at the curb and Gary Stabile stepped out, sucking on a pipe as usual.

"Good morning, Professor Borgmann," he said with a smile. "Looking forward to the conference?"

"Very much," Borgmann said, unable to hide his annoyance. He couldn't understand what Stabile was doing here. Surely the man wasn't going to try to brazen his way into the Assembly Hall!

"I'm here as an aide to the American ambassador," Stabile said, as if he'd been reading Borgmann's mind. "At least, that's my official title." He winked broadly, waved his hand, and trotted up the stairs, looking as though he owned the place.

Borgmann watched him disappear into the Assembly Hall and decided it was time for him to join the party.

Inside the building, there were two reception desks, one for "guests," and one for "delegates." Borgmann decided he'd be considered a guest. Sure enough, there was a blue badge with his name on it. A pretty, dark-haired girl handed him a program booklet and directed him toward the auditorium.

The place was crowded now. About half the people were wearing blue "guest" badges, and most of the rest had green "delegate" badges. Men outnumbered women by perhaps ten to one. Here and there, Borgmann saw a familiar face, someone he'd met at a previous international conference at one time or another.

He took a seat near the back of the auditorium, leafed through his program booklet and waited for the proceedings to begin. After a while, a small, fragile-looking, grey-haired man ascended to the podium. He pounded his gavel twice and the room grew quiet.

According to Borgmann's program, this man, the honorary chairman of the conference, was Christian Kampmann. The man was familiar, but Borgmann couldn't quite place the face. He gazed at the man on the podium as he listened to his memory. It was Professor Kampmann, the same man who had taught him basic physics nearly thirty years ago. What a thrill it was to see him still alive, in a position of honor.

"Ladies and gentlemen," Professor Kampmann began, speaking only slightly accented English. "It is my privilege to welcome you to this special EURATOM conference. As you know, we have gathered to discuss the merits of the gas centrifuge process for making enriched uranium. Our friends, the British, the Dutch, and the Germans, believe that this is the best and least expensive way to make fuel-quality uranium for nuclear power plants. They have invited the Scandinavian countries to join them in both the centrifuge project and in a giant European power grid. This conference will deal with both questions, in technical, economic, and political meetings."

The old man paused and took a sip of water. Borgmann had to admire him. He laid it right on the line—no euphemisms, no meaningless chatter.

"I would like to take this occasion," Professor Kampmann continued, "to welcome our guests and delegates, on behalf of the staff of the Niels Bohr Institute for Nuclear Research. All guests are welcome to attend any of the open meetings they wish. For obvious reasons, however, only delegates will be permitted at closed sessions.

"I would also like to take this occasion to thank Britain, the Netherlands, and Germany for giving the Scandinavian countries the opportunity to join with them in this great project. If what we have been told proves true, the gas centrifuge will be able to provide Europe with all the electricity it could possibly use for the next fifty years. It will allow us to produce more energy and at a lower cost than either the Soviet Union or the United States. As you can see, my hopes for the project are high. But all aspects must be considered."

The welcoming speeches went on for quite a while. After Kampmann, there was Danish Minister for Foreign Affairs, Søren Hansen, then the German delegate, Rudolph Krause, then the British delegate, Henry Faversham and finally the Dutch delegate, Gerta Shroeder.

Borgmann spent the time leafing through his program, looking for familiar names. All guests, delegates and host dignitaries had been listed. One listing brought him up short—the Finnish delegate, Arne Torngren. He'd never heard of Torngren, which didn't mean anything much. But he was astonished to find that Finland had sent a representative. The Finns had never before attended any international conference dealing with atomic energy, to Borgmann's knowledge. This really wasn't surprising. Finland had preserved its independence and neutrality only by obeying Russia's every whim. And one of those whims had been that Finland not show the slightest interest in Western scientific endeavors, especially nuclear ones. What was surprising was that they'd sent a delegate this time. Borgmann was intrigued.

Then, he started looking through the list of host dignitaries. Perhaps he would find a name he knew amongst them—an old teacher, or a classmate. After a brief scan, his glance fastened on one name, which might just as well have been printed in bold type, considering the impact it had on him. The line read "Delegate from Denmark—Dr. Bent Dahlgaard."

Borgmann looked wildly around the audience. His old school chum, his best friend from the old days, was here somewhere. And in a position of importance. He searched among the faces. Then, after a while, he gave it up. Even if he had looked directly at Bent, he realized, he might not have recognized him.

Borgmann stared backward, toward the podium. Dr. Kampmann—of course! He'd reintroduce himself to the old man, then ask him to point out Dahlgaard. About fifteen minutes later, Borgmann had his opportunity. The conference recessed for a coffee break. When it resumed, in twenty minutes or so, the delegates would go to separate study sessions.

He threaded his way through the milling delegates, toward the podium.

"Dr. Kampmann," he called, "Dr. Kampmann."

The old gentleman turned toward Borgmann. "Yes?"

"You probably don't remember me, Dr. Kampmann, but I am Frederick Borgmann. I was your student once, during the war."

Kampmann looked at him with an odd intensity. "Borgmann?" He seemed to be talking to himself. "Borgmann?" He was almost on the verge of remembering.

"It was a long time ago," Borgmann said. "I was also Professor Bohr's student."

"Ah! Borgmann!" Professor Kampmann said, his eyes alight. "The boy with the memory. Of course I

98

remember you. How are you? You are a delegate here?"

"A guest. From America. I went there with Professor Bohr in 1944. We worked together at Los Alamos."

"I see," said Professor Kampmann. Suddenly there was a distinct chill in the air. Borgmann had felt it before. Los Alamos meant the bomb.

"I've been working on nuclear power plants since the middle 1950s," Borgmann explained, but Kampmann's expression did not change.

"Good to see you, Dr. Borgmann," the old professor said. He started to turn away.

"Wait, Dr. Kampmann. I have one small favor to ask."

The old man seemed a trifle impatient. "Yes?"

"According to my program, Bent Dahlgaard is here. He was my best boyhood friend. Could you point him out to me? It has been many years."

"Of course." Kampmann glanced around the room. "There," he said finally, indicating a small group of men. "The blond gentleman in the grey suit."

Borgmann looked at Dahlgaard. By the time he turned back to thank Professor Kampmann, the old man had wandered away.

Borgmann headed toward Dahlgaard, wondering if he would have recognized his friend by himself. Over the years, he saw, Dahlgaard had filled out. He was an impressive-looking man now, about six feet tall, perhaps 180 pounds, stylishly dressed, his blond hair combed back evenly over his head, his red "host" badge sitting on his lapel like an ornament. He was the center of attention at the moment, speaking animatedly with three other men, two delegates and a guest, according to their badges. Borgmann edged toward them through the crowd, finally joining the group.

Dahlgaard accepted Borgmann's presence as if it were the most natural thing in the world. He barely gave him a glance, just went on talking.

"For me," he was saying, "the most important thing about the centrifuge is that the Americans and the Russians have ignored it. They're still making enriched uranium in their gaseous diffusion plants. It's a far more expensive process, but they spent billions to make those plants and they can't very well shut them down now. So the centrifuge will put us in an enviable competitive position."

"I wonder how the Americans feel about that," one of the other delegates said with a smile.

"Well, let's ask one," Dahlgaard said pleasantly, looking directly at Borgmann. "You're an American, aren't you, sir?" he asked, peering at Borgmann's badge.

Abruptly, his eyes snapped up, meeting Borgmann's gaze directly. "Frederick?" he said wonderingly. "Could it be? Is it really you?"

Borgmann broke out into a broad grin. "Yes, Bent," he said, "I am the same Frederick Borgmann."

They reached for each other's hands simultaneously, then embraced, European-style. Both faces glowed with pleasure.

"I'd heard you were in the United States with Niels Bohr," Dahlgaard said, his voice ringing with excitement. "Then I lost track of you."

"I had no idea where you were. I didn't even know for sure that you were alive until I saw your name listed in the program."

"Frederick, Frederick, I can hardly believe it's really you. You've changed so much over the years. But not for the worse."

"We've both changed, Bent. It has been a long time, you know, a very long time."

"But what is time among friends, eh, Frederick?"

Borgmann just smiled, his eyes a bit damp. "Nothing, nothing at all," he managed to say.

"You are married? You have a family?"

"I was married," Borgmann said. "My wife died in an auto accident—but that was nearly seven years ago. No family."

"I'm sorry," Dahlgaard said. He looped his arm around Borgmann's shoulders. "I'm married. We have two daughters."

"That's wonderful, Bent."

"You know the girl I married, Frederick—Maj Hartling."

Borgmann was simultaneously surprised and delighted. "Maj? How wonderful for you both. You are treating her well, I hope." There was a note of mock sternness in his voice.

Dahlgaard laughed. "We are happy," he said.

"Good, very good."

From the podium, Borgmann heard the sound of the gavel pounding again and again.

"Ladies and gentlemen," Professor Kampmann was saying, "it is time for the study sessions to begin."

Dahlgaard looked at his watch. "I have urgent business," he said. "But you must come to dinner tonight. Will you?"

"Of course."

Dahlgaard scribbled an address on a small slip of paper and pressed it into Borgmann's hand. "Seven o'clock?" he asked.

"That will be fine."

"I'm really looking forward to it, Frederick. It will be like old times, eh?"

"Yes," Borgmann said, "yes, it will."

The two men clasped hands once more and Dahlgaard hurried off. The handshake was firm, unyielding. Borgmann was surprised how good it made him feel to see his old friend again. Then, he remembered he had other business here. As the guests and delegates began to return to their seats, or filter toward side rooms for individual study sessions, Borgmann scanned the green badges, hoping to spot Arne Torngren, the Finnish delegate. This time he failed to locate the man he was seeking.

There was another hour of speeches by Danish scientists, EURATOM officials, and various ambassadors, mostly directed at the conference guests, most of them stressing international cooperation or other platitudes. Borgmann barely managed to stay awake until the next coffee break.

Then, all at once, it seemed, the meeting recessed and the delegates again began milling around, talking to each other, trotting off to the men's room, sipping coffee. Dahlgaard was nowhere to be seen, but Borgmann shortly found himself standing next to someone else of interest—Torngren, the man from Finland.

The Finnish delegate—if that's what he was—had joined a small group of other guests and delegates and was apparently listening to the conversation. He was about forty, tall, stocky and balding. His skin was very fair and densely freckled. His fingers were thick and the backs of his broad hands were profusely covered with reddish blond hair. Borgmann took a spot beside him.

This time, the conversation concerned the technical aspects of the gas centrifuge. And, as he listened, Borgmann realized it would be reasonably easy to discover if Torngren was a phony. Even if the man had been carefully briefed about the centrifuge, he'd still have enormous gaps in his knowledge.

"The one thing I cannot believe," said a tall, grey-haired man of aristocratic bearing, whose badge identified him as a Dr. Søren Thorwaldsen, a delegate from Denmark, "is that the centrifuges spin so fast that the uranium is subject to forces approaching one million times that of gravity."

"Anything stubstantially slower than that and it might take years to separate the uranium-238 from the U-235," said a corpulent man in a brown plaid suit, his head bald and egg-shaped. His badge listed him as Dr. Bertel Lindeborg, delegate from Sweden. He spoke as though his words had been memorized long in advance.

"But how can the centrifuge spin so fast without burning itself up?" asked Dr. Thorwaldsen. The whole subject seemed new to him.

"The mechanism spins like a top, on a steel needle," Borgmann put in. "And it's suspended from the top by magnets. That keeps it from falling over. It's the same principle that the German physicist used in the 1940s. The man with the funny name—you remember." Borgmann turned to Torngren, the Finn, as if he expected the man to supply the name.

The big man's reddish eyebrows knit for a moment,

in a combination of concentration and consternation. "I do not remember," he finally said, his English barely intelligible. He was gazing directly at Borgmann.

"Zippe," said Dr. Lindeborg. He looked at Torngren, puzzled. "All the current designs are derived from the Zippe model."

"Of course, of course," Torngren said, attempting to cover. "I could never remember that name."

Borgmann listened politely as the conversation went on. No one who'd ever taken a college physics course could ever have forgotten Zippe's name. It was his work that had almost given the Nazis a shot at beating the Americans to the atomic bomb. Among scientists, Zippe was nearly as well known as Bohr, Szilard, Teller, or Fermi.

There was no doubt of it. Torngren was a ringer. A Russian agent, most likely, Borgmann thought. He glanced at his watch. In an hour he'd see Ben-Ezra again, and he'd have some news for him.

"Excuse me," said Dr. Lindeborg, "are you the Borgmann who's been working on the breeder reactor?"

"Why, yes," Borgmann said, surprised. "How did you know my specialty?"

Lindeborg stammered for a moment. "Why, ah, I'm not sure. Must have read it somewhere."

"I see," Borgmann said, on guard. He'd only published one paper on the subject and that was six years ago. It was extremely unlikely that this man had read it. He must have come by his knowledge some other way. Was the place full of agents?

"What do you think of the breeder reactor's future— in light of the centrifuge?" Lindeborg went on, keeping the conversation going.

"Hard to say," Borgmann said. He sought the appropriate cliché, as usual. "Only time will tell."

"Yes," said Lindeborg. "That's what I think, too."

Once more the gavel sounded, and the delegates and guests began to head for the meeting rooms. Borgmann walked back to his seat, unaware of Arne Torngren's steady, hostile gaze. But he did see Dr. Lindeborg scribble a note in a little notebook. And Dr. Thorwaldsen seemed to be watching him with unusual interest. It was all very odd.

As Borgmann took his seat, he reviewed the conversation. Had he stumbled into a nest of agents? Torngren was obviously a phony. Lindeborg knew more than he should have, or so it seemed. Thorwaldsen seemed lost in a fog.

Thinking back, Borgmann recalled hearing of Dr. Lindeborg. He'd been involved with isotopes or with atomic structure. For once, Borgmann couldn't remember the details. But the man seemed legitimate enough. Could he actually have remembered reading about Borgmann's work in breeder reactors? Unlikely—but possible.

As for Thorwaldsen, he seemed a parody of the absentminded professor. Either he was what he appeared to be or he was far cleverer than he seemed, a man playing a role. Borgmann couldn't make up his mind.

Torngren gave him no trouble, however. Everything about the man was wrong. Not only was his knowledge deficient, he seemed out of place and uncomfortable at the conference. Then there was the Finland-Russia angle.

Borgmann decided to tell Ben-Ezra about Torngren. As for the other two—well, he'd ask Dahlgaard about them.

Chapter Nine

As usual, Miriam Shazar was up early. After a quick breakfast, she drove her little green Saab 97 to the Bohr Institute for Nuclear Research, beating Borgmann by about a half hour. She went into a side door, missing most of the arriving delegates and guests. No one disturbed her as she entered; she looked more like a student than most students.

It took Miriam about three minutes to locate the wall directory. To her surprise, neither Hershel Brombeck nor Rose Homburg were listed. The first name on her list that also appeared on the directory was that of Erich Lemberg. He held forth in room 3107. Miriam hurried to his room.

Professor Lemberg, it turned out, was a thin, nervous little man in his late fifties, dark bushy eyebrows providing a comic contrast with a balding dome.

"Professor Lemberg?" Miriam addressed the man in English, outside his classroom door.

"Yes?" he said, annoyed at the interruption. "Make it fast. My class starts in two minutes."

"I have come at the request of Jacob Kaplan." Miriam paused, to let the name sink in.

Lemberg looked at her curiously at first, unable to place the name. Then, as he remembered, a flicker of fear crossed his face. "I don't know any Jacob Kaplan," he said, backing away.

"Jacob Kaplan has a favor to ask. He says it is your duty to grant it, if it is within your power."

Lemberg sighed and stopped. "All right," he said. "What is it?"

"We need to know where the plans to the gas centrifuge are located."

Lemberg's eyes bugged out in astonishment. "And you've come to me for this information?"

"We are approaching several people—Danish Jews, all of them."

"I know nothing. I teach theoretical physics to graduate students. I barely know the principles of the gas centrifuge. I've never seen the plans. I'm not even attending the conference."

"It's important that we locate the plans. Have you any way of finding out where they are?"

"No," Lemberg insisted. "I am a teacher, nothing more. I know only other teachers and students. The conference board is an entirely separate group. They're mostly from the laboratory. I have no contact with the laboratory."

Miriam nodded. "What about Hershel Brombeck and Rose Homberg?"

"Hershel died last year," Lemberg said. "Rose remarried. She's living in France, I believe."

"Can you direct me to anyone else who could help?" Miriam asked persistently. Suddenly, three of her five possibilities were dead ends.

The hallway was swirling with students now. Classes were plainly about to begin. "No," Professor Lemberg said slowly, as if he'd given the matter more than adequate consideration. "I am sorry."

"I see."

"I would help if I could."

"So you say." She wasn't about to let him off easily.

"Please give my best to Jacob Kaplan."

"Your best is not good enough," Miriam said. She turned without another word and walked off. The man was telling the truth; she was sure of that. Still, if he had known something, he might have tried to hide it. Miriam had only contempt for such men.

The next person on the list was Herman Cohen, the Institute's director of food services. Miriam took the elevator to the basement, where the cafeteria was located.

Herman Cohen was a tubby man, with a bullet-shaped head and thick, stubby arms, which he waved around a lot in constant impatience. He was wearing what at one time must have been a white apron.

"Mr. Cohen?"

"No vendors, no vendors," he said in heavily accented English, waving her away.

"I'm not a vendor."

"No students, no students. We open at eleven-thirty, not a moment before. Out, out, out."

"Mr. Cohen, I come from Jacob Kaplan."

"No," he said, after a moment's pause. Now there was terror in his eyes. "Not more trouble. Not again. We're so happy now."

"No trouble, Mr. Cohen," Miriam reassured him. "The Nazis are gone. Forever, I hope. Now Jacob Kaplan needs a favor."

"Yes," said the fat little man, "anything." He looked at Miriam with the willing gaze of a three-year-old. What she would ask, he would do.

"You know the gas centrifuge?"

He shrugged. "I have heard of it."

"We need the plans."

Mr. Cohen smiled sadly. "Then I cannot help you. This is my only domain," he said, waving a pudgy arm around the cafeteria. "This and the vending machines on each floor. I know nothing of any plans."

"I see. Well, have you noticed anything unusual going on in the building?"

He thought for a moment. "The conference," he finally said, "everyone has been preparing for the conference. They have us making gallons and gallons of coffee."

"Anything else?"

"No."

"Do you know anyone who might help me?"

"I know the cooks and the busboys and the vendors. They cannot help, I fear."

"No, I suppose not. But thank you."

107

Miriam was worried now. Not a whisper of the plans. Would it all depend on Frederick? If so, she feared they were lost.

She looked once more at the list. A charwoman, Hildegaard Ludstein. It was worth a try. Miriam turned back toward Mr. Cohen. "Do you know where I might find Mrs. Ludstein?"

"Mrs. Ludstein? Never heard of her."

"Hildegaard Ludstein."

"Oh, Hilde. Try the mop room. Second floor, end of the hall. But I don't think she'll be able to help. I'll bet she's never even heard of the gas centrifuge."

Miriam took the elevator to the second floor and headed down the hallway. The classroom doors were closed now. Here and there, she could hear a teacher's voice droning away. Ahead of her, there was a small, dingy room with an open door. The mop room. A woman was inside, changing the head on a mop. She was sixty, perhaps, stout and strong, a peasant woman.

"Mrs. Ludstein?"

"Ja?"

"Taler De engelsk?"

"Ja, a little."

"I have come from Jacob Kaplan, Mrs. Ludstein." She paused and waited for the inevitable reaction.

The old woman's eyebrows rose. She tilted her head in disbelief. *"Nej.* I do not believe you. He cannot be alive yet, still?"

"He is very much alive, Mrs. Ludstein. And he asks your help."

"My help?" There was a big grin on the charwoman's face, as if she'd just been paid a handsome but outrageous compliment.

"We need to know something about the Institute."

"Ja, the Institute. *Hvard?* What?"

"Something has been hidden here, and Jacob Kaplan needs to find it. Blueprints, plans. Do you understand?"

"Ja."

"We're looking for the hiding place. Can you help us?"

The woman rested her chin on the mop handle and thought for a moment. "A safe, you mean?"

"Perhaps. But it would be a new one, a very large one."

"No. There is no such thing here."

"Then perhaps a new set of locks on some private room."

"No."

Miriam was getting desperate. It would not be pleasant to return to Ben-Ezra empty-handed. "Well, has anything at all changed about the Institute, any new construction, new doors or anything of the sort?"

"No. Nothing is new here. Except the cable."

"The cable?"

"*Ja.* The television cable they installed last week leading to the conference room. So much drilling, so much broken plaster. I spent a whole evening cleaning up the mess."

"Was it a big cable, Mrs. Ludstein?"

"*Ja, ja.*" She made a circle with her thumb and forefinger. "This big, bigger even."

"Could you show me where it is?"

"Ja, if you want. It is not blueprints. It is a cable."

"That's all right. I'd still like to see it."

Miriam followed the woman down the hallway, into a stairwell. "There," the charwoman said pointing, "it comes out there."

Miriam looked up. A thick grey cable poked down from the ceiling and disappeared into a hole in the wall. "Where does the cable go, Mrs. Ludstein?"

"I don't know. Outside the building. I only know inside the building."

"Do you know why they'd install a TV cable here."

"For the sets. Mechanics, they brought sets, three of them."

"When they installed the cable?"

"*Ja.*"

"Thank you," Miriam said, her mind racing. "You've been a very great help. But, for the sake of Jacob Kaplan, please say nothing about this."

"No one can make me talk," the old woman said. Miriam believed her.

Chapter Ten

Yaakov Ben-Ezra sat sipping coffee in the K.A.R. restaurant near the railway station. He'd managed to get one of the tables near the wall of windows that overlooked the street and he was watching the Danes as they walked, pedaled and drove to work. This restaurant wasn't particularly close to the small furnished room in which he was staying, nor to his office in the porno shop. But having breakfast here was a longstanding habit, established in the days just after the war. The place had sentimental memories for him. He had eaten there with his wife, Karen.

By now, Ben-Ezra thought, Borgmann would be at the conference. Miriam would be talking to whatever likely prospects she'd found in the card file. Soon he would know if there was any real chance to accomplish the mission. There was little for him to do now, except send the cablegram. That he would do on the way to his office.

The coffee, as usual, was black. And it was accompanied, also as usual, by a piece of pastry. One, he hoped, would nullify the other. Behind him, Ben-Ezra could hear the clink of silver and the low buzz of conversation. The restaurant was full now. In a half hour or so, it would empty out. In front of him, the bustle seemed to continue out onto the street. He watched the faces go by. Few peoples, he told himself for the umpteenth time, are as good-looking as the Danes, few people as pleasant and friendly.

Ben-Ezra's thoughts drifted back, to his first impressions of the country. Initially, he hadn't wanted to come here. He'd wanted to take the training he'd received at the hands of the *Haganah* and the British back to his native Poland to fight the Nazis directly. He'd yearned to blow up troop trains, the railroad link to Auschwitz, or perhaps, a gas chamber. But the British, who controlled Palestine, would not permit that, for reasons of their own. So, he begged the man at *Shai*, as the *Haganah* Secret Police was then called, for an espionage assignment, also somewhere in Poland. This too the British forbade. Finally, in August 1943, he had been sent to Denmark, possibly to keep him quiet. It had been the right place for him, even then—an oasis of civilization in a desert of barbarians. The Nazis, though they controlled the country militarily, held it loosely, to demonstrate their benevolence to the world.

Ben-Ezra had fallen in love with Denmark almost at once. The countryside was charming, the people handsome—but it was more than that. In so many societies, there is a repressed anger—one group of people anxious to do ill to another, or the entire country in conflict with a neighbor. There was none of that in Denmark. The people seemed to want nothing other than to live their lives with full satisfaction, at no one's expense.

Over the years, Ben-Ezra had idealized the place. He knew that. It was partly because he'd been introduced to Denmark in the fall of 1943, when the entire country selflessly did its best to save its Jewish citizens. But the initial impression had lasted through the years. Perhaps Karen had something to do with that. How ironic it was that she should leave tranquil Denmark for tumultuous Israel, how she should escape the Nazis only to die at the hands of the Egyptians.

It was a painful memory. He could not pursue it. He thought of better things, of the problem at hand.

"More coffee, sir?"

Ben-Ezra looked up at the smiling waitress. They were all pretty here, even the ugly ones. "Yes," he said, returning her smile. "Why not?"

He watched her pour. Her arm was strong and

111

tanned. How was it, with such a short summer, so little sun and such fair skins that Danes always seemed to be tanned? He'd never been able to figure it out.

But back to the problem. The gas centrifuge plans. The bomb. He had told Borgmann the truth about that, so far as he'd known it, but was it really the truth? There were two possibilities: either Nachman was leveling with him, as an old friend and colleague, or Nachman was lying, since this time the stakes were high enough to sacrifice a friendship. He had listened to the man with all of his senses alert, but he could not be sure. Nachman was always good that way. Perhaps that's why he was the head of the organization now, and Ben-Ezra was still an operative. A respected operative, certainly, one of the most valued—but only that.

"We must have the centrifuge plans," Nachman had said. "There are two reasons. First, we have to worry about the Arab nations. With Western help, several are building their own atomic research facilities, as you know. And it's not because they're interested in supplementing their oil supplies with nuclear power; you can be sure of that. We have to do anything we can do to make them think they'll never be able to catch us in atomic weapons development, anything we can do to discourage their research projects.

"Second, we have to worry about the Palestinians. Imagine what would happen if a terrorist group got hold of the centrifuge plans and an adequate supply of uranium ore. Well, we have information that Palestinians are trying to do just that. We must keep those plans from them at any cost. If we fail, the price could be the destruction of Israel and most of its inhabitants."

"And you lay all this responsibility at my feet?" Ben-Ezra said.

"Not all of it, no. We have men well placed in Egypt, Syria, Iraq and Jordan. You know some of them, I imagine. We have men in the major guerrilla organizations. But as for the plans themselves—that I leave to you. No one is better at such things."

Ben-Ezra smiled at the memory. How often he had heard Nachman say those words. He took another sip of coffee and watched a long-legged, big-breasted Danish girl pedal past the restaurant on her bicycle. He appreciated the girl on an aesthetic level. The days when other thoughts might have occurred to him were, alas, long past.

When was the first time Nachman had given him an assignment? Ben-Ezra considered the question. It must have been before the UN vote establishing the State of Israel, sometime in early spring, 1948, when Isser Harrel commanded the *Shin Beth*. He remembered now—it involved the *Lino*.

Somehow, Nachman found out that the Czech government had agreed to sell sizeable quantities of arms to Syria—six thousand rifles, eight million rounds of ammunition, thousands of hand grenades and other explosives. The arms were shipped to Yugoslavia, where they were loaded into a small Italian vessel, the *Lino*. From the port of Fiume, the ship was to sail to Beirut. The arms would then be transported by land to Syria.

It was at this point that Ben-Ezra got Nachman's cable, he remembered. There was a breakneck dash across Europe by train. But when he reached Fiume, the *Lino* was already under way. Luck was with us that time, Ben-Ezra thought. He took another sip of coffee. Luck is always with us, it seems, or maybe God actually is on our side. The *Lino* ran into rough weather in the Adriatic and put in at Molfetta, in southern Italy. This time, Ben-Ezra caught up with it.

Ben-Ezra permitted himself a small smile. Somehow the *Lino* never made it to Beirut. Somehow it sank, in shallow water. Somehow the arms it carried found their way into the hands of *Haganah* units—just as the first Arab-Israeli war began. Even now, he felt good about it.

Ben-Ezra took another sip of coffee. The older I get, he thought, the more of this stuff I drink. Could I function without it?

The waitress reappeared with a coffeepot. She looked at him with an eyebrow raised, asking a question without words. He nodded and she poured. Ben Ezra checked his watch. He mentally calculated the time difference between Copenhagen and Tel Aviv. It would be another twenty minutes or so before he could send the wire. Even then, he'd be cursed for awakening someone.

And then there was the "Italian Opera" affair, a few months later, in the midst of the '48 war. In his wildest dreams, Ben-Ezra had never thought he would find himself owning a munitions plant, especially one that supplied artillery shells and land mines to the Egyptians. It was another idea from Nachman. And it was also Nachman's idea to stuff the shells and mines with sawdust instead of gunpowder, or to alter them so they exploded en route, or in the barrels of the guns that were to fire them.

For a moment, Ben-Ezra pulled away from the memories. Why, he wondered, was he reviewing his career at this moment? Did he have a premonition of some sort? He snorted and dismissed the thought. That was nonsense, that kind of thing. He enjoyed remembering, that's all there was to it. And he often turned to such memories when the problems of the present seemed insoluble.

Ben-Ezra took another sip of coffee, popped a sliver of sweet roll into his mouth, and let his memory wander on. The Mirage engine affair—now, that gave him particular pleasure. After the 1967 war, France refused to sell Israel any spare parts for the French-built Mirage jet fighters that formed an important part of the Israeli Air Force. The engines began to wear out, and more and more of the fast, versatile jets had to be grounded.

Ben-Ezra had been on leave when Nachman called him back to Tel Aviv, to Defense Headquarters. There, the intelligence chief explained the problem.

"Do you want me to steal the parts?" Ben-Ezra asked, when he finished.

"No. You could only steal so many, and soon we would need more," Nachman replied. "Stealing them a second time would be difficult indeed."

"What then?"

"We want you to 'obtain' the engineering drawings.

Our factories can make the parts if we have the specifications."

"Couldn't you take them from existing parts?"

"That would take at least six months. And then we could never be sure about the precision of our measurements."

Ben-Ezra had accepted the mission. Soon he was on the way to Switzerland.

Dassault, the French plans-maker, had licensed the Sulzer engine factory in Winterthur to make Atar 90 engines for the Mirage 3s France had supplied the Swiss Air Force. Ben-Ezra had little trouble getting a job at Sulzer. It took him just two weeks to make the necessary contact. One Alfred Frauenknecht, it turned out, was in charge of putting the engine blueprints on microfilm, then destroying them. It had taken a strong appeal to the man's conscience—and $200,000 in cash—but Frauenknecht ended up turning twenty cartons of blueprints over to Ben-Ezra. It was a short drive from Winterthur to West Germany. From there, the plans were flown directly to Tel Aviv.

Later, Ben-Ezra had returned to enjoy his leave. One morning Nachman called.

"Not again, Nachman," Ben-Ezra protested. "Give me my days of rest. I want to spend time with my daughter."

"Wait a minute. I have no assignment for you," Nachman told him. "But I just thought you might be amused to know what we've done with those plans."

"Yes?"

"The parts for the engine are now being made at the Beth Shemesh factory near Jerusalem."

"So?"

"So, the Beth Shemesh factory is half-owned by a French company. Turbomeca. Imagine how the French owners must feel."

"I understand, Nachman. For you, it is not enough to win. You must also make the loser look foolish."

"It's the sadist in me, Yaakov. You understand."

"Of course I understand."

Ben-Ezra glanced at his watch, his thoughts flickering back from the old days. He took another sip of coffee. The K.A.R. restaurant was nearly empty now. It was time to send the wire. In a way, getting the centrifuge plans was like stealing those jet engine plans. Except in the case of the engine plans, there were no airtight security measures in effect, no phalanx of vulture-like agents waiting for you to slip up.

Even the French gunboat affair was not directly comparable. But it was another memory worth recalling. They gave him confidence, these memories. They made him feel a bit younger than he was.

Ben-Ezra rose, paid the check and walked out. He loved Copenhagen's cobblestone streets. He loved the huge stone palaces, Christianborg and the others. Every year or so, he'd join the tourists and gawk at the ornate paintings in Christianborg. He'd even wear those funny soft slippers the palace tourist authorities insisted on, to protect and polish the marble floors.

He strolled toward the RCA cable office. Now what was that memory he'd been on the verge of recalling? Oh yes, the gunboats. Israel had ordered twelve of the 147-foot, 40-knot vessels from France before the embargo that followed the '67 war. Seven of the boats were turned over to the Israeli Navy before France halted arms shipments to the Mideast.

"We must have the rest," Nachman told him. "Egypt's navy now far outclasses ours, you know. They have twelve submarines to our three, six destroyers to our one, twenty missile boats and thirty torpedo boats. The difference could make it difficult for us to protect our coast."

"But what good would five more gunboats do us?" Ben-Ezra asked.

"We intend to equip them with the Gabriel."

Ben-Ezra had heard of the missile, but he knew little about it. "What about *their* missile boats?"

"They carry Soviet cruise missiles that have a relatively high trajectory. We can detect them with radar in time to shoot them down. The Gabriel, which we designed and built ourselves, hugs the water. It can't be spotted until it's too late."

And so, Ben-Ezra went off to swipe some gunboats. First, through the Israeli consulate in Paris, he arranged that Israel notify France that it surrendered all claim to the ships. Second, he set up a phony shipping firm, a Panama-based Norwegian concern he named Starboat and Weill. Starboat and Weill came to the French government and concluded a deal for the remaining gunboats, without difficulty.

In December 1969, Israeli crews were secretly transported to France. And on Christmas Eve, having been cleared through customs, the five vessels started their powerful engines, slipped out of Cherbourg harbor and into the English Channel. They were flying Norwegian flags, and were presumably bound for Oslo. Actually, of course, they were on the way to Israel, some three thousand miles away.

Later, the news reports said that the team had been headed by a certain "Commander Ezra." Nachman, amused by this, even supplied the press with a bogus picture of the clever Navy commander.

Yes, Ben-Ezra thought, there were many triumphs to remember, to savor, up to and including the '73 war. But now he had been asked to supply another. Only then could younger men take over. He spotted the cable office and walked in.

Chapter Eleven

The first thing Jack Salter felt that morning was the throbbing in his head. There had been too much wine last night. At least *he* had had too much. Somehow, Stabile had managed to nurse a single glass throughout the evening.

All at once, Salter remembered the plans they'd made. He leaped out of bed and darted into the living room of his apartment. Last night Stabile had decided to sleep on the hide-a-bed instead of going back to his hotel. Now he was gone.

Salter squinted and tried to make out the numbers on the wall clock. It was nearly nine-thirty. He felt the rush of panic one gets after oversleeping on the day of an important engagement, then he got hold of himself. There was plenty of time, so long as he went about his business.

About a half hour later, Salter unlocked the door of the Nyhaven office. He hung up his coat, then fiddled with the combination lock on the arms cabinet. It opened on the first try, which was a good sign. Contrary to his own impulses, Salter obeyed Stabile's orders and selected the Russian pistol, an obvious copy of a German Luger. He pulled out a clip, checked the cartridges and pushed it home. The "Company" provided shoulder holsters for such occasions and Salter strapped one on. It felt entirely comfortable. Salter enjoyed assignments like this one. There was no ambiguity about them, just simple orders to be carried out exactly. And he was fully capable of carrying out his orders. He was an excellent shot. In fact, marksmanship had been among his strongest points at Foggy Bottom.

Salter shoved the gun into his shoulder holster, buttoned his sport jacket, slipped on a pale grey raincoat and took one last look at the file photo of Yaakov Ben-Ezra. Then he headed toward the office door. Just before he opened it, a thought occurred to him. He needed some kind of cover, in the event of trouble. It needn't be elaborate, just something to throw any casual observer off the trail. He grabbed a copy of *Scandinavia on Five Dollars a Day* from the bookshelf and stuck it under his arm.

Downstairs, he got into the "Company" Volvo, the one with the untraceable license plates, and drove toward the appointed address—the Svenska Quality Porno Shop. There, he parked and waited. Stabile had warned Salter that he might have a long wait, but that didn't bother him. He was good at waiting.

Scientific conferences never end at the appointed time. The one which Frederick Borgmann was attending at the Niels Bohr Institute was hardly an exception to the rule. Yet there was no gracious way for him to depart before the session broke.

When it did, finally, Borgmann rushed out of the building and hailed the first available cab. What Ben-Ezra could do with his information about Torngren, he didn't know. But the man had accomplished miracles with less, in days past.

What Borgmann didn't notice, as he rushed out of the Institute, was a small grey Fiat, the same car that had followed him from his hotel. Of course, even if he had looked at the vehicle carefully, he would have seen nothing to arouse his interest. Inside was a small, nondescript figure with a swarthy complexion, wearing a wrinkled business suit. It was Abdul Amer.

If Borgmann had waited just five minutes, he would have seen Miriam Shazar come hurrying out of another door, hopping into her Saab and heading off in the same direction in which he had gone. Miriam also had information. She couldn't be sure, at this point, just what that cable installation meant. It had to be significant, though. Ben-Ezra would know what to do. He always seemed to know.

Moments earlier, Yaakov Ben-Ezra had left the cable office and headed toward his little hideaway at Svenska Quality Porno Shop. There were, he thought, two possibilities—as usual. Either Frederick or Miriam had come up with something—or they hadn't. If they had, there were two more possibilities—that he would find some way to get the plans or that he wouldn't. If they hadn't . . . well he'd deal with that problem if he had to.

In his Volvo, Jack Salter scanned Peter Hvifeldts Straede in both directions. He used his rear-view mrror to check the street behind him and covered the front through his windshield. It had been a boring morning. He'd had the car radio on, but that didn't keep him much company, since he spoke only a few phrases of Danish. Then, Salter saw his quarry—a man in his late fifties, perhaps, about five foot ten, weighing about 170 pounds, balding, with sandy hair. It was Yaakov Ben-Ezra. The photograph Salter had looked at earlier was obviously dated, but there could be no mistake.

Salter slipped his gun out of his holster and steadied it against the ledge of the car window. He noted with pleasure that, aside from Ben-Ezra, the street was free of pedestrians.

Ben-Ezra walked slowly toward the porno shop. So this, Salter thought, with just a trace of contempt, was the famous Yaakov Ben-Ezra Stabile had mentioned. He wasn't impressive. Far from it. He walked slowly. There was no visible determination, no special alertness. Perhaps once he had been in good physical condition. Now, he carried a bit of a potbelly. Salter couldn't picture the man passing through the vigorous trials of the Foggy Bottom "school." If this was the best Israel had to offer, perhaps its intelligence service deserved a good deal less respect than the big powers tended to give it.

Ben-Ezra strolled up the street, looking now and

then in store windows, pausing once to tie his shoe, glancing momentarily at a man in the parked Volvo without any sign of suspicion.

Salter had pulled his sleeve over the end of his pistol, to hide it from exactly the sort of casual scanning Ben-Ezra had given him. He waited as the Israeli approached the porno shop, his nerves and muscles taut. Salter was determined to wait for the perfect moment. Among other things, he wanted to show Stabile that he could carry out instructions to the letter.

Ben-Ezra reached the porno shop, paused, looked in the window and shook his head. How the world had changed since he was young. Salter aimed carefully and slowly squeezed the trigger. There was a sharp crack, and Ben-Ezra dropped to the pavement. Salter aimed again, carefully, and squeezed off another shot. There was another sharp crack and a small signboard some three inches from Ben-Ezra's nose was blasted into splinters.

Salter started the car and was underway not five seconds after he had fired the second shot. He was delighted with himself. Let Stabile try to find fault with him this time, he thought to himself fiercely. Just let him try.

Salter's pale blue Volvo had barely turned the corner, onto Krystalgade, when Frederick Borgmann's cab entered Peter Hvifeldts Straede, heading toward the Svenska Quality Porno Shop. Borgmann saw Ben-Ezra lying on the sidewalk, leaped out of his cab, and ran to him.

"Yaakov, Yaakov—are you all right?"

Ben-Ezra propped himself up on one elbow. He smiled wanly. "I haven't quite finished taking inventory," he said, "but all of my parts seem present and accounted for."

Borgmann did his best to return his friend's smile. He wasn't satisfied with the result. "What happened?"

Ben-Ezra slowly got to his feet. "Nothing unusual, really. Someone fired two shots at me."

"Nothing unusual!"

"In your line of work, it would be a shocking occurrence. In mine—well, to use an American expression, if I had a nickel for every time this had happened to me, I'd be rich."

Up the street from the porno shop, the small grey Fiat that had been following Borgmann slowed, stopped and parked. Its occupant was close enough to see everything, without attracting attention.

"Yaakov," Borgmann said with feeling, "I just thank God whoever was shooting at you missed."

"Missed?" Ben-Ezra said, as if he were only mildly interested in the subject. "Who said they missed?"

It was then that Borgmann said the blood on Ben-Ezra's left arm, near the shoulder.

"My God, you're wounded!"

Ben-Ezra casually examined his arm. *"Wounded* is far too grandiose a word, Frederick. *Injured* is better, or *scratched.* The bullet just creased the flesh. I have a box of bandages and some iodine inside."

"Listen, Yaakov, let me take you to the hospital."

Ben-Ezra chuckled. "The hospital? For this? Come inside with me. If you must play nursemaid, you can help me bandage it."

Borgmann opened his mouth to object, then thought better of it. One rarely won arguments with Yaakov Ben-Ezra. "Do you at least know who fired the shots, Yaakov?"

"Ah," said Ben-Ezra. "I'm glad you reminded me. Let's see if we can find one of the bullets. All I can tell you about the man who shot at me is that he was driving a pale blue Volvo 122S. The bullets might tell us more."

Ben-Ezra knelt down and started searching the front of the shop for bullet holes.

"But the wound—"

"It can wait a few minutes, Frederick. At the rate my heart beats these days, it would be a week before I bled to death."

They had just started to examine the shop facade when Miriam Shazar drove up in her Saab. She ran toward them, evidently sensing trouble. Borgmann, for one, was very glad to see her.

"Yaakov's been shot and wounded," he said.

Ben-Ezra looked up at the girl. "Very slightly, Miriam, very slightly."

"Is the bullet still in you?" There was fear in her voice.

"It creased my upper arm. I think it's embedded somewhere in the storefront."

"Was Frederick with you when it happened?"

"He arrived a few moments afterward."

The girl took a deep breath. "Well, at least he was not the target."

The three of them studied the front of the small porno shop. Borgmann found the hole. "Look, Yaakov."

"Yes," Ben-Ezra said. "That's it. Now we have to find a way to extract the bullet."

"Leave that to me," Borgmann said. He took his Swiss army knife out of his pocket and started to enlarge the hole.

"Try to damage the slug as little as possible," Ben-Ezra instructed.

After a few minutes of digging, Borgmann handed the flattened lump of lead to Ben-Ezra. "Now can we go inside and bandage your arm?"

"If you insist."

The trio entered the shop and found the young female clerk cowering behind the counter. "Are you all right?" she asked, voice quivering. "Was anybody hurt?"

"Just a scratch," Borgmann told her, parodying Ben-Ezra's attitude of unconcern. "Happens all the time." Ben-Ezra gazed at his friend with a raised eyebrow and just the faint trace of a smile.

The girl swallowed down her fear.

"It's all right, my dear," Ben-Ezra told her, touching her arm to reassure her.

Borgmann pushed open the concealed door. He, Ben-Ezra, and Miriam entered the hidden office, Miriam shutting the door behind her. She went immediately to a closet, where she rummaged around for a first-aid kit. Ben-Ezra sat down heavily on the desk chair. He seemed a bit tired.

"Take off your jacket," Miriam commanded, sure of her role now. "And roll up your sleeve."

Ben-Ezra did as he was told, after first placing the slug on the desktop, so he could examine it while he was being tended. The girl opened a bottle of iodine and let some of the brown fluid soak into a cotton ball.

"This may sting," she said.

She applied the cotton ball to the wound, a shallow gouge perhaps two inches long. Ben-Ezra winced, but did not stop studying the bullet. He picked it up with his other hand and held it close to his eyes.

"It's a nine-millimeter," Ben-Ezra said, turning the slug over in his fingers. "About the most powerful and destructive cartridge you can buy commercially. Many police departments use them."

"You're not saying that the police shot at you, are you, Yaakov?" Borgmann asked, horrified.

"Ah, Frederick. We both have a lot to learn. I am a total idiot when it comes to nuclear physics. And, when it comes to espionage, you—"

"It probably came from a Luger," Miriam said. "Either a German gun or a Russian copy."

"It had a jacketed soft point," Ben-Ezra told the girl. "Russian standard issue."

"Perhaps," Miriam said.

"All I can say is that I'm glad whoever fired at you wasn't much of a shot."

Ben-Ezra leaned back in his chair and thought a moment. "Well," he said, finally, "there are two possibilities: either the man was a bad shot, or he was an excellent shot."

"But he missed you," Borgmann said, confused.

"Perhaps he meant to. Perhaps he meant to wound me slightly. Perhaps he meant me to study the bullet, just as I am now doing."

"For what possible purpose?"

"Many Arab espionage units are supplied with Soviet-made handguns," Miriam told Borgmann. "Either

124

Yaakov's attacker was an Arab, or he was trying to make us think he was one."

Borgmann gazed at the pretty blonde girl. For an instant, she sounded just like Yaakov. But her expression betrayed her cool tone. She was clearly worried.

"The more I hear about this, the more confused I get," Borgmann said. "Who would want you to think the Arabs were shooting at you?"

Ben-Ezra shrugged. The gesture was so characteristic that the man making it could have been identified by anyone who knew him at a distance of a hundred yards or more, from behind. "Perhaps someone who wants to divert our attention from the centrifuge plans. Russians, Chinese, Americans—who knows?"

Stabile's face flashed into Borgmann's thoughts for an instant. The CIA agent couldn't possibly have done this. He was at the conference this morning. Or had he shown up simply to divert suspicion from himself, while another CIA henchman did the dirty work? Or had he left early? Nothing ever was what it seemed to be in this business. Borgmann felt himself far beyond his depth.

"But let us ignore the diversion," Ben-Ezra was saying. "What do you have to report?"

Now Borgmann remembered what his job had been. "I think I may have spotted a phony delegate to the conference—a Finn."

Ben-Ezra was pleased. "Very good, Frederick. What makes you think he's phony?"

"Well, Finland never sends delegates to that sort of conference. And when I talked to the man, he had some suspicious gaps in his knowledge of centrifuges."

"You're sure?" Ben-Ezra asked.

"Absolutely. He didn't even know the name of the scientist who came up with the centrifuge principle."

Ben-Ezra nodded slowly. "I see. Very possibly he is a KGB man, someone to be watched very closely. I hope you didn't give him the impression you were questioning him—or testing him." There was just a trace of concern in Ben-Ezra's voice.

"No, no," Borgmann assured him. "It was all very low-key."

The Israeli took it in silently. "I'm not sure what use this information will be, Frederick. But it is good to know who our enemies are. Anything else to report?"

"I have my suspicions about a couple of others at the conference—but nothing definite yet."

For a moment, Ben-Ezra seemed about to pursue the subject. Then something else occurred to him. "What about the plans? Any news? Can anyone you know tell us where they are?"

"There's a chance, anyhow. An old friend of mine is the Danish delegate. A man named Bent Dahlgaard. I'm having dinner at his house tonight. If he knows anything, I'm sure he'll tell me."

Ben-Ezra weighed Borgmann's words. "Can we trust this man, Frederick?"

Borgmann's answer was quick and unequivocal. "Absolutely. It's true that I haven't seen him for many years, but we went through a great deal together, with the Nazis."

"Dahlgaard, Dahlgaard," Ben-Ezra mused, trying to remember. "Yes. I recall the name. Your friend and schoolmate. Didn't you hide at his house?"

"I don't know how you remembered that, Yaakov, but you're right."

"You're the man with the memory, Frederick, not me." The Israeli smiled at his younger friend. "But about Dahlgaard: don't tell him any more than he needs to know. Too much knowledge could be dangerous for him."

"Of course, Yaakov. I understand."

"And you, young lady," Ben-Ezra said, his mood obviously good. "What have you discovered?"

Miriam shot Ben-Ezra a look that would have withered a lesser man. Evidently she was not pleased to be called "young lady."

"Did you find out anything?" Ben-Ezra asked again.

"Perhaps," she said. She spoke slowly, to punish him. "A charwoman told me that some physical alterations had been made in the conference rooms."

Now Ben-Ezra was totally alert. "Yes," he said impatiently. "Go on."

"It seems as if a television cable has been brought in from somewhere outside the building. It leads to three television sets recently installed in the conference room."

"Yes? Go on."

"That's all I could find out."

"Do you have any theories, Miriam?" he asked.

"Only one: that the plans are not actually in the Institute, that they'll be televised to the closed sessions."

Ben-Ezra glanced at Borgmann. "Possible?"

Borgmann shrugged. "I don't see why not. If the TV sets are equipped with enlarging projection screens, it might be the best way for a group of people to study the plans."

Ben-Ezra suddenly stood up. He rolled down his sleeve and put on his jacket. There was a hole where the bullet had hit, and a bloodstain. The Israeli agent started pacing the room, his steps quick, nervous, almost mechanical.

Borgmann watched him in awe. It was almost as if the man's thinking processes were visible. As abruptly as he had begun, Ben-Ezra stopped pacing.

"I think we have found the flaw in our opponent's defenses," he announced. "The king has been inadequately protected. They've forgotten to castle. All we have to do is to exploit the weakness."

Miriam coughed. A cold look from Ben-Ezra prevented her from making another sarcastic remark about his chess analogies.

"What do you mean, Yaakov?" Borgmann asked, puzzled.

Miriam smiled slyly, but Ben-Ezra refused to look at her.

"We have to trace the cable. Where it ends is where we will find the plans, I think."

"That may not be easy, Yaakov. I know a bit about coaxial cable, from the H-bomb telemetry. That cable probably disappears into an underground network. Only an expert could trace it to its source."

"Then we will find an expert," Ben-Ezra said calmly.

He went to the safe and once more withdrew the grey metal file box that contained the names of most of Copenhagen's Jewish citizens.

"You see," he told Borgmann, as he opened the file box, "many think that Israel can't afford a large espionage network. In fact, we have sixteen million agents all over the world, some of them in very high places indeed."

"Half of which would refuse to help, if asked," Miriam put in.

"So?" Ben-Ezra said, annoyed, "so we have only eight million. Does that make me a liar?"

"And almost all of them amateurs, reluctant amateurs."

"They make up in zeal what they lack in experience." Ben-Ezra flipped through the cards, after consulting the code key. "Television, television. Here—write this down."

Miriam found a little notepad on the desk.

"Alfred Wurtzelbach, 101 Istegade—"

"Yes. Any more?"

"That's it," Ben-Ezra said.

"It's not much," Miriam said. "Does the man have anything to do with cable installation?"

"No. He owns a TV repair shop, according to the card. Maybe he'll have a friend who can answer our questions."

"That sounds like a long shot," Miriam answered curtly.

Borgmann looked at her, puzzled. There was a definite antagonism between Ben-Ezra and Miriam Shazar and it disturbed him. There was also a great deal of affection and respect. It was altogether an odd relationship, full of subsurface nuances. Something was going on here that Borgmann did not understand; yet there was no way to clear matters up with a simple question or two. He decided not to go further with the thought—for a while.

"A long shot, it may be," Ben-Ezra conceded testily, "but it's the only shot we have at the moment. I want you to go to the man, Miriam. Find out what you can."

The blonde girl agreed.

"Maybe I should accompany her, Yaakov," Borgmann said. "I have nothing else useful to do this afternoon and perhaps my knowledge will be valuable here."

Ben-Ezra thought a moment. He looked at the two of them, Borgmann and the girl. "Yes," he said. "Why not? Besides, I have business of my own."

"Be careful, Ben-Ezra," said Miriam, softly and unexpectedly.

"Are you worried about me?" Ben-Ezra asked. There was a teasing note to his question.

"Of course," she said. Then she smiled warmly and added, "We could never complete the mission if you got hurt."

"Oh. You're worried about the mission."

"Yes. That's my main concern. Isn't it yours?"

"Naturally."

The exchange seemed to come to an end. "Are we ready to go?" Borgmann asked Miriam.

She turned toward him. There was just the slightest twinkle in her eyes. "Certainly," she said. "Knight to Bishop seven, or something."

Ben-Ezra shook his head in exasperation, without any real anger. He had new problems to worry about now and these already occupied his mind. There was the matter of the shooting. This was the third time he'd been shot at in the last year.

Borgmann checked a peephole to make sure the store was empty, then pushed the bookshelf-door open. He and Miriam walked out onto the street.

"We can take my car," she said. "I'll drive."

Borgmann took his place in the passenger seat without protest. Behind the little green Saab, perhaps half a block down the street, Abdul Amer started up his grey Fiat.

Chapter Twelve

Miriam shoved the key into the ignition and the little car roared to life. She glanced at Borgmann for an instant, then looked quickly away when she found that he'd been looking at her.

She put the car in gear and drove down the street. Frederick doesn't remember me, she thought. But it would be asking too much of even his memory for that. After all, it had been almost twenty—and she'd been just ten years old. Time had changed her a great deal.

It had not, she reflected with pleasure, had much of an effect on Frederick. He was tall and slender, his chin strong, his grey eyes deep-set and clear. Except for the light sprinkling of grey hairs and glasses, the man almost exactly matched the image she'd carried in her memory all these years. And all the affectionate feelings she'd had for Frederick—dormant for all these years—were back again, with a new note: Miriam was no longer a ten-year-old girl, but a grown woman.

"Do you know the way?" Borgmann asked.

"Yes," she said. She could find nothing else to add though she wanted very much to engage Frederick in conversation, to know him better and to have him know something of her.

Miriam glanced into the rear-view mirror. The only car in view was a small grey Fiat. She turned onto Voldgade Street, a broad avenue lined with squat, matronly buildings. The Fiat followed.

"I'm worried about the TV repairman," Borgmann said. He, too, seemed anxious to make conversation.

"Why?"

"Well, I'm just not sure he'll know anything about the installation of a coaxial cable at the Institute."

"He should have friends who do."

"Perhaps. But many of these repairmen are small, isolated operators."

Miriam shrugged. "It's our best hope at the moment."

The little Saab crossed Glydenlovesgade, just where that street became Hans Christian Andersen Boulevard. This was the center of the city, with the elegant hotels and restaurants and the hordes of tourists. It was still early, though. Peak tourist season was at least two months away. Ahead of them now was the stately Radhus—town hall—with its tower and famous clock. Miriam turned once more, onto Vesterbrogade. There, to their left, was the Tivoli, Copenhagen's jewellike downtown amusement park. Miriam saw it from the corner of her eye and for a moment found herself wishing she and Frederick were headed there for a day on the Ferris wheel that had *Around the World in 80 Days*–type balloons with cabin seats, or on board the merry-go-round that carried Viking ships, not horses.

She glanced once more into the rear-view mirror. The little grey Fiat was still there. She'd made three turns now, and the Fiat had imitated each. Were they being followed? It would not be long before she found out.

Miriam stopped at a traffic light at the corner of Bernstorffsgade and Vesterbrogade, across from the International Hotel and SAS Building.

The grey Fiat pulled up behind her.

"I'll be damned," she said softly, looking into the rear-view mirror.

"Pardon me?" Borgmann said, confused.

"We seem to have company, Frederick—no, don't turn around. We're being followed."

Borgmann couldn't believe it. "But who would know who we are? No one followed me, I'm sure of it."

"Well, someone obviously has us spotted."

131

"Perhaps it's the person who shot at Yaakov," Borgmann suggested.

"No, I think not. All Yaakov could tell us about him was that he drove a pale blue Volvo. The man behind us is in a light grey Fiat."

She squinted into the mirror and patted her hair, as if she were putting a lock or two back in place.

"What's more," she continued, "I know who it is."

Borgmann looked at the young girl in astonishment. "How is that possible? Is he one of us?"

Miriam laughed. "Hardly. He's a Palestinian, a man named Amer. Abdul Amer, I believe."

"A Palestinian," Borgmann said, trying to digest the fact.

The light changed and Miriam drove the little Saab through the intersection. "He's nothing to worry about, really. He's one of Arafat's hatchet men. He tried to infiltrate the Israeli Army just before the 1973 war."

"How in the world do you know that?"

Miriam shrugged and laughed again. "To be honest, Frederick, this isn't my first assignment."

"No," Borgmann said. "I didn't imagine it was. Did he manage to get into the army?"

"Of course," said Miriam, accelerating slightly. "The Israeli Army has never been known to refuse a volunteer. We put him on one of the patrols that secured the southern part of the Sinai Desert. Even gave him some responsibility."

"I have a feeling you're putting me on."

"Not at all. Amer was put in charge of digging latrines. He proved to be quite satisfactory, I understand. And then, after the truce, he disappeared one night."

Borgmann chuckled. "What do we do about him now?" he asked. "I don't think we really need an escort today."

The girl took a deep breath, then grinned. "I suppose you're right. Well, hang on—"

The green Saab suddenly accelerated, shooting out of the intersection, past the International Hotel. After a moment's lag, the grey Fiat followed. Miriam pushed the car up to about fifty kilometers, then eased back on the accelerator. Borgmann looked at her curiously.

"No quick turns, squealing tires or hundred-mile-an-hour chases?" he asked.

"Not at the moment," she said. She pointed in front of them. There was a small light blue car with signs all over its back end, a highway patrol car. A huge speedometer about the size of a school wall-clock was mounted where the rear window of any normal car would be.

"You could always turn onto another street," Borgmann offered.

She weighed the suggestion. "I have another idea," she said. "Should be more fun."

They continued down Vesterbrogade for what seemed to be a couple of miles, heading toward the edge of the city's central section. The shops became smaller, the apartment houses more frequent.

Borgmann bent toward Miriam, looking into the rear-view mirror. The grey Fiat was still there, as if they were towing it. "Where are we going?"

"I was thinking we might visit the zoo."

Borgmann was delighted with the idea. "The zoo? I haven't been there since I was ten. I wish we had the time."

"We won't be there long, I suspect."

In front of them, the patrol car turned off, onto Plantanvej. The Saab and the Fiat stopped for a light. Immediately ahead, a blue-and-white number 28 bus had pulled over to discharge and take on passengers. The light changed to green. For a moment, the bus hesitated. And in that moment, Miriam snaked the Saab around it, putting the bus between her car and Amer's.

Borgmann turned around now. "I don't think we've lost him yet," he said.

"No. He's still there. But we've lengthened the rope a bit, haven't we?"

From the tone of her voice, one might have gathered that she was playing hide-and-seek with a friend, instead of trying to shake an Arab spy. Borgmann was reassured by it. He joined the banter easily.

"There's another bus ahead—a number 41. Shall we try for two?"

"Why not?"

Miriam jammed the accelerator to the floor for an instant, gave the steering wheel a quick jerk, zipped around the bus—which had already left its stop and was lumbering down the street—and jabbed the brakes lightly. The caravan now had four vehicles; the Saab, the two buses, then the Fiat.

"Think he can still see us?" Borgmann asked.

"He's practically riding the center line," Miriam answered. "We haven't lost him yet."

"You say 'yet' as though you haven't a doubt you'll lose him."

"Give me another ten minutes. Then you can judge for yourself."

The little caravan rolled up a hill. A few hundred yards away, to the right, through the chestnut trees, Borgmann could see the magnificent Fredericksberg gardens and the palace the royal family had once used as a summer house. Then, suddenly, the zoo was beside them. Miriam wrenched the steering wheel and the Saab twisted its way into the parking lot, leaving the two buses and the grey Fiat somewhere behind.

Frederick peered out at the window, torn between looking back for the Fiat and looking ahead at the zoo. Already, he could make out the Chinese pagoda version of the Eiffel Tower. When was the last time he had ridden up it—with Bent? With Maj? With his father?

Now the Saab snapped around, toward the parking lot exit. A faded old burgundy Humber Super Snipe unexpectedly appeared in the lane, headed right at the Saab. Miriam rammed her foot against the brake and the Saab came to an abrupt stop. Without hesitating, she threw it into reverse and started backing out of the exit lane.

"Where's the Fiat? Did we lose him?"

"I don't see it," Miriam said. She twisted the wheel and the Saab heeled over, toward the other exit lane. Its speed: nearly seventy kilometers an hour. As it whipped down the lane, a little brown Opel began to pull out of its parking place. Miriam laid her hand on the horn until the Opel retreated, terrified.

The Saab shot out of the parking lot, made a sharp right down Fasanvej and kept up speed, zipping by the back of Fredericksberg Park at well above the posted limit.

Borgmann leaned against the car door for a few moments and watched the young blonde put the car through its paces. Her movements were birdlike and darting, her judgment certain, her confidence unbounded.

"Oh for God's sake," Miriam said in disgust. "He's back."

"I don't believe it!"

"Look for yourself."

Borgman gazed over his shoulder. The grey Fiat was directly behind them now. How in the world had it followed them through the zoo parking lot?

"I think he picked us up after we turned," Miriam said. "If only I'd have turned left instead of right—"

"I'm sure we'll manage to shake him."

"Look!"

About a block ahead of them, Borgmann saw, a pair of trolley tracks cut across the road. And heading toward the crossing was a yellow-orange trolley car.

"Can we make it?" Miriam asked.

She didn't wait for an answer. The Saab leaped forward as she jammed the accelerator pedal to the floor. For an instant, Borgmann was sure the trolley would smash into them. As it was, they cleared the track with about two seconds to spare before the trolley glided by, its bell clanging wildly.

Behind them, they heard the screech of brakes, the squeal of protesting tires and, finally, the tearing crash of fenders and headlights against steel.

"My God!" Borgmann said, awed, "you racked him up!"

"Not quite, I'm afraid," Miriam said.

Borgmann stared through the back window. The little Fiat, bruised and disheveled now, had swerved around the trolley—which had stopped dead after the crash—and was still coming after them. The crash had penalized it less than ten yards.

"That Amer fellow—he acts more like a tank driver than a latrine digger."

"He's not bad," Miriam said grudgingly. "But that was just the beginner's course."

She whipped the car around a corner, drawing a dirty look from a bicycle-mounted grandmother.

"If I'm not mistaken," Borgmann said, "that's a hospital, to our left."

"Yes. Fredericksberg Hospital. You thinking of dropping in?"

"Not voluntarily."

Miriam pulled on the wheel once more and the Saab squealed around another corner. It was headed directly for the S-train track again. But there was no train in sight this time. A few seconds after the Saab rounded the corner, the Fiat appeared, game but limping a bit.

"Look back there, Frederick. Is the Fiat steaming? I think I see something coming out of the radiator."

Borgmann studied the car behind them as Miriam navigated. It might have been steam—he couldn't be sure. "Can't tell."

"Well, we'll find out soon enough."

The Saab jounced over the S-train track and continued on. Borgmann continued to gaze out of the rear window. There was a little cloud of steam above the hood. "I think you were right, Miriam. Maybe the radiator was punctured when he hit the trolley."

"Probably so."

"But he can still follow us for a couple of miles before the engine overheats and seizes."

"I know. I have to think of something else."

Borgmann looked through the windshield, trying to come up with a suggestion on his own. And he found what he was looking for. "Shall we try that?" he asked, pointing to a large, multi-story municipal parking garage.

"I think you have a flair for these things, Frederick," Miriam said with a smile. She gave the steering wheel a flick, and jabbed the brakes. The Saab obeyed instantly, darting into the garage and up the ramp.

"He's in the garage," Borgmann said, watching through the back window.

"That's perfect," Miriam said. "We'll use up what water is left in his radiator in a couple of minutes, then we'll be on our way."

The parking ramp was one of those narrow, sharply curving lanes that seemed modeled after medieval paintings of the Tower of Babel. Miriam flogged the Saab upward like a race driver, until its tires were squealing, and its engine panting.

"I can't see him," Borgmann reported.

"He's still behind us. I can hear his fender rattling."

At the fifth level, the ramp turned into a plateau and the plateau into a parking floor. Miriam ignored it, spinning the car around and starting down the exit ramp, which curled around the parking garage parallel to and visible from the entrance ramp they'd just ascended.

At the third level, they came up to the grey Fiat, which was still chugging up the entrance ramp, steam pouring out from under the hood in huge white clouds. Just as they drew even with it, the Fiat let loose a loud cough and stopped dead. Miriam slowed down and opened the window.

"Want me to send a tow truck, Abdul?"

The swarthy Arab glared at Frederick and Miriam with venom and banged a hand against the steering wheel. He swore at them with feeling.

"No? Well, whatever you say." Miriam responded, as if he'd replied to her. She rolled down the window and hit the accelerator again. The car darted out of the garage entrance, followed by a fat, ill-dressed garageman, his beady eyes red with rage, his voice raised in fury. "Stop!" he yelled. "Stop, *tyven!*"

Miriam drove on. "What did he say?"

"I think he said 'stop, thief!' or something like that," Frederick answered, amused.

Three blocks later, the small green Saab 97 screeched to a stop. Miriam Shazar and Frederick Borgmann just sat there a moment, both of them vibrating, their pulses beating wildly from the chase. They looked at each other and grinned.

"You drive rather well," Borgmann said, purposely understating it.

Miriam shrugged, in mock self-deprecation. "The Tel Aviv police wouldn't agree with you."

"You've had some accidents?"

"No, no accidents. But plenty of speeding tickets."

"They'd give you a speeding ticket while you were on an assignment?"

"Oh, no," Miriam said, with an elfin expression. "When I'm on an assignment, it seems, the police never notice me. It's when I'm racing out to the beach or when I'm trying to make a tennis date when I'm late."

"Police are the same all over."

"Yes."

They looked at each other and laughed once more. "Where do you suppose Amer is?"

"I wouldn't be surprised if he was still somewhere in that parking garage."

It was an amusing thought and Borgmann smiled again. His pulse rate was nearing normal now, though there were still beads of sweat on his forehead. The girl beside him, though, seemed entirely in control of herself. He was very impressed with her. More than that, he liked her. She was resourceful, determined and—there was no other word for it—courageous. But underneath it all, there was a subtle softness. Borgmann allowed himself a long glance. He felt good, looking at her. The wispy blonde hairs on her neck, her grey green eyes, the taut firmness of her body made her very attractive indeed. It had been a long time since he looked at a girl this way. The feelings evoked memories long forgotten, but not at all unpleasant.

"How far are we from the TV repair shop?" he asked.

Miriam's eyebrows rose. "How far?" she said. "Look there."

She pointed across the street. There was a small shop, street number 101 Istegade. A faded painted

138

sign said, simply, "Alfred Wurtzelbach; *Fjernsyn reparero*"—television repair.

"Shall we?" she said.

"We shall."

They got out of the car and headed toward Wurtzelbach's shop. There was no grey Fiat anywhere in view.

Wurtzelbach, it turned out, was a short, slender man in his late fifties or early sixties. His face was grey, his glasses thick. He looked as though he might break if jostled. As Miriam and Frederick walked into his shop, he looked up at them without expression, blinking.

"Yes," he said, his voice almost too low to be heard, "can I do something for you?"

Again, Borgmann noted, he had been addressed in English. What could he do to change his appearance so he'd look like a Dane? Did he really want to?

"Mr. Wurtzelbach?" Miriam asked politely.

"Yes," the man said. He appeared impatient. "I am Mr. Wurtzelbach."

"I have come from Jacob Kaplan."

Borgmann looked at Miriam in surprise. He had not heard that name uttered in more than twenty-five years. Why had she used it now? How did she know it?

"Jacob Kaplan?" The name seemed to mean nothing to Wurtzelbach.

"Yes. Perhaps you remember him from the war."

Behind the thick glasses, the old man's eyes slowly widened. "Jacob Kaplan—but that was so long ago—"

Borgmann watched with interest. How would he have reacted to that name today, if it had come out of the blue like this? He couldn't even guess. The repairman had responded with a combination of fear and wonder.

"Yes," Miriam said, almost gently, "the same Jacob Kaplan."

The old man stood erect. He looked at Borgmann, as if for confirmation. Borgmann nodded slowly.

"You do not come to tell me of more trouble, do you?" Wurtzelbach said in his soft voice.

"No. Those days are over—forever, we hope," Miriam replied. "Jacob Kaplan helped you then?"

Borgmann thought he saw a bit of moistness behind the lenses.

"He saved my life. He saved my son and my daughter."

Miriam nodded. "And now he needs your help."

To Borgmann's surprise, the repairman seemed to straighten up even further. He seemed younger, stronger. He walked around from behind the counter, apparently ready to follow wherever Miriam might lead.

"I will do whatever he says."

"We need information, Mr. Wurtzelbach," Borgmann said, deciding to play an active role. "We need to trace some newly installed coaxial cable."

The old repairman's eyebrows knit. "But why?"

"To aid Israel," Miriam put in. "I cannot tell you more."

Wurtzelbach gazed at her for at least ten seconds. "That is enough," he finally said.

"All we know of this cable is that, at one end, it leads into the Niels Bohr Institute. It evidently serves two or three receivers there, in a closed-circuit setup."

Wurtzelbach listened. There was a glimmer of understanding in his eyes now, Borgman thought. Perhaps he did not guess the exact details, but the Institute could mean only one thing, so far as Israel was concerned—atomic research of some sort. "I don't work with cable," he said slowly. "I work only with sets. I repair them. Here, in the shop."

"We realize that, Mr. Wurtzelbach," Borgmann said. "We hoped you might know someone."

Wurtzelbach chewed on a dry upper lip and thought. Borgmann glanced around the shop. It was small and dingy. There were a few TV sets on the bench. He wondered how anyone could survive at this business.

"I don't know anyone who installs such cables," the old man said.

Miriam and Frederick looked at one another. So the chase through Copenhagen had led them to this dead end?

"But there is a man at the broadcasting station who might know someone."

"Can you call him?" Miriam asked quickly.

"Will he tell you?" asked Borgmann simultaneously.

"Perhaps. If I ask the question the right way." Mr. Wurtzelbach sounded as if he had joined a conspiracy. "I must be careful not to arouse his suspicions."

Frederick and Miriam exchanged barely perceptible smiles. Meanwhile, the old man flipped through the Copenhagen telephone book. He found a number and dialed the phone.

"God dag, Karl. Den er Alfred. Ja, Alfred Wurtzelbach . . ."

Miriam caught Borgmann's attention and frowned. Well, he thought, so she doesn't understand Danish. He listened to Wurtzelbach's side of the phone conversation for a moment. "He's asking his friend who in Copenhagen installs coaxial cable."

"Ja," Wurtzelbach said, writing down a name on a pad. *"Nogen mere? Ja."* He wrote down another couple of names. *"Tak, Karl, tak. Farvel."*

Wurtzelbach hung up. "He gave me three names. One, he says, is the outfit that handles most of the coaxial cable work in Copenhagen. The second does the best job."

"What about the third name?" Miriam asked.

"That's one of Karl's friends," Wurtzelbach said with a twinkle. "Which should I try first?"

"The biggest," Miriam said.

"The best," Borgmann, in counterpoint.

"The best," Miriam said, correcting herself.

"The biggest," Borgmann said, at the same time, for the same reason.

Wurtzelbach cocked his head in curiosity. "I'll try Ørsteds first." He looked through the telephone directory, spotted a number and dialed.

Once more, Miriam waited for Frederick to translate the conversation.

"He's asking about a new coaxial cable at the Bohr Institute," Borgmann said, listening with one ear. "Says it's causing interference on a set in the student dormitory."

"Why did he say that?"

141

Borgmann shushed the girl with a finger to his lips. He listened to Wurtzelbach. "They seem to be protesting. He is saying, 'Doesn't that new cable go right under the dormitory?' They seem to be disagreeing. 'I was sure I saw new line there.' Wurtzelbach is saying. They're arguing. 'Well, where does it go, then?' Wurtzelbach asked them."

"Tivoli?" Wurtzelback said, speaking into the phone receiver in a tone of astonishment. *"Jeg forstar ikke."*

"He says he doesn't understand," Borgmann told Miriam.

"Hvorfor?"

"Why?" Borgmann translated.

"Ja. Jeg forstar. Tak. Mange tak. Farvel." Wurtzelbach hung up. He looked at Borgmann and Miriam Shazar. "The man said that the cable went directly to the Tivoli—no detours, no subsidiary cables."

"The Tivoli?" Borgmann asked.

"That's right," Wurtzelbach said.

"But why?"

"That he wouldn't tell me. Said it involved some sort of secret underground installation there. But he wouldn't tell me any more."

Borgmann managed to appear calm. "I see."

Miriam vigorously shook the old man's hand. "Thank you, Mr. Wurtzelbach. I think we found out what we needed to know."

"It will help Jacob Kaplan?" Wurtzelbach said anxiously.

"It will help Jacob Kaplan and many of his friends."

Wurtzelbach's eyes turned damp and he smiled. "If I can help in any other way—"

"Yes," Miriam said gently. "I understand."

Borgmann shook hands with the man and he and Miriam left the shop. Miriam paused at the door and looked up and down the street with some care.

"No one," she told Borgmann.

They walked toward the car. "What happens now?"

"I go back to Ben-Ezra and tell him what we have found out," Miriam said brightly. "And you—didn't you say you were dining at an old friend's house?"

Borgmann looked at his watch. "By God, you're right. I'd better get going. It's all the way across town."

"I'd be happy to drive you down," Miriam said. But she seemed hesitant, as if worried that she might be refused.

Borgmann paused. "No," he finally said. "I'll take a cab. I'm going in another direction. Besides, I suspect Yaakov will be eager to hear what you've discovered."

"Yes," Miriam said, impersonal now. "You're right, of course."

She climbed into the green Saab.

"I should be back at the hotel by eleven or so tonight," Borgmann told her. "Call me and I'll tell you what I've found out—if anything."

"Okay."

He watched Miriam drive off. It hadn't been easy to resist riding with her. But he had to keep his mind on his task.

Chapter Thirteen

It was a long car ride to Bent Dahlgaard's house, but a beautiful one, along Vejen Strand, beside the sound, up toward Skodsborg. The evening sun shimmered on the waters. Eleven miles away, Borgmann remembered, was Sweden. Eleven miles away was freedom—or at least, so it had been those many years ago, when the Nazis had decided to add Denmark to their collection of nations.

This was a part of Copenhagen that Borgmann did not vividly recall. It was the wealthy section. Here the merchants, the doctors and the lawyers lived in their large, beautiful houses overlooking the sea, from which they could watch freighters glide by during the day, or hear foghorns at night. In those few days of real heat, in July, their wives and daughters could walk across the road, down to the white sand beach and sunbathe, perhaps even wade in the perpetually chilly waters.

The homes here were few when Borgmann was a boy. Now there were many. The country was richer and more crowded. If Dahlgaard lived here, he must be doing well—very well.

Borgmann checked his watch. *"Hvor laenge varer turnen?"* He asked the cabbie.

"Tyve minutter," the man said. He seemed disinclined to converse.

Borgmann let his thoughts drift toward his friend, Bent. So Bent had married Maj. Did he feel jealous? Borgmann contemplated the question. There was a twinge, perhaps, but it had to do with the past, not the present. Had they always liked each other, he wondered—even when he and Maj were seeing one another? No, he decided, that was not the case. He imagined how it must have happened: When he'd left Copenhagen, Maj and Bent had naturally been thrown together. They'd provided companionship for each other, and the companionship had turned into love. And how could he be jealous of that?

In fact, he was not. He was warmed by it. After he escaped, he had written to them—both of them, but his letters had gone unanswered. That wasn't surprising, in view of the war and turmoil that prevailed at the time. He'd very likely written things that the Nazis felt had to be censored.

What he felt was just a trace of nervousness, a natural sort of emotion for a man about to see a former lover after many years. And he and Maj *had* been lovers. It had started out as play and ended up as something far more serious. He could recall the details if he wanted to, but he'd always resisted examining such memories.

Perhaps now was the time to face them. Soon he would see a Maj far different from the image he carried around in his mind. This one would be in her early forties, married, with children, the flush of youth long past, perhaps the beauty too. Despite himself, Borgmann remembered the beauty—the eyes, so large and clear, the skin so soft, the body like a single flawless piece of milk glass.

He remembered the first time he'd seen her naked. It was the sort of memory no man forgets easily. It was on a Sunday afternoon, in the basement of her parents' house. They'd gone off somewhere, leaving Maj and Frederick alone, to talk, to play games, to be together. He'd often wondered if they hadn't been providing an opportunity for something else, to let their daughter grow up a bit that day. If so, it was remarkable how much they trusted him, at his age.

They started to talk, as children—and lovers—do. But words soon turned into kisses, and kisses to embraces. Even now, he could recall the softness of her

145

body and his own excitement. They had not done this so often that the feelings and emotions were familiar.

After a bit, Maj got up. Frederick soon saw why. Light from the afternoon sun was flooding into the room, through the basement windows. Maj took cushions and pillows and blocked off the windows, and the light grew dim. How typically romantic of her. And how typically romantic of him to love her for it.

She returned to the couch and to his arms. Now, with the room darkened, their necking took on a new urgency. Their talk became whispers, then ceased altogether. They saw each other only in silhouette. The sensation of touch prevailed.

Borgmann remembered. He'd fumbled with the buttons on her blouse. After a moment, she smiled at him gently, pulled back and undid them herself. She let him slide the blouse from her shoulders, only to have her catch his hands and move them to her breasts.

He didn't know what to do, how to touch her, how to please her. He was simultaneously drunk and terrified. Then he realized he must take off her bra. He reached behind her and once again found that his fingers wouldn't work together. She helped.

Then, she tugged on his shirt and soon it too was off.

Now, they hugged again, skin to skin. He felt her breasts against him, soft and warm. Then they kissed. It was as if he had submerged himself in a rainbow. Suddenly, there was no air in the room.

The kisses were long and deep now. He alternated between being lost in the pure sensation of them and being detached, looking at himself and Maj, telling himself how significant this all was.

The undressing continued, each helping the other, until they were both without clothing. Then, they lay together on the couch, their bodies touching at all points.

Only once did conversation intrude.

"Maj—" He started, full of doubt, anxious to see if she shared it.

"Shhh," she said, not wanting to hear it.

And then they made love, if children could do such

a thing. It was far from perfect. He barely knew what to do. She was so frightened, beneath it all, that she could do no more than receive him. Yet, in the basement's darkness, they joined each other, as if sharing a fantasy.

They lay together long after it was over, not knowing whether they'd ever be able to talk to each other again. Maj broke the silence. "Hello," she said. He returned the greeting.

Slowly, they separated, until only their hands were touching. Despite the blocked-off windows, he could see her. "I never knew you looked that way," he said.

She laughed. "Would you like to see me better?"

"Of course."

They both got up, went to the windows and started pulling down the pillows. For a moment, she stood for him, naked and giggling, and let him look at her until his eyes were filled to overflowing. Then she threw a pillow at him. He threw it back.

They dueled with pillows, first at long range, then close up. Finally, her ammunition exhausted, Maj pushed and tickled and hit at him with her small hands, until he was forced to put his arms around her again.

They kissed again, playfully. Then, it was no longer a game.

How foolish I am, he thought, to wallow in these childhood memories. So much had happened since then. If I must retreat into memory, I could think about Ruth. Those were the best days. As for Maj—we were both children at the time, and what could there be between children?

Borgmann looked out of the taxi window. It was dusk now. The sun was setting behind the big houses that overlooked the sound. An hour or so ahead was Elsinore. Would he have time to see it this trip? He couldn't even guess.

"*Der en den,*" the cabbie said. He'd pulled up in front of a starkly modern structure that seemed to be composed mainly of wooden-planked balconies supported by fieldstone pillars.

"Hvor meget bliver det?" Borgmann said, taking his wallet out.

"Fem og tyve kroner, tyve øre," the driver said.

Borgmann handed him the money and got out. He looked at the house for a long moment. It was magnificent. It appeared to blend into the landscape, as if it had grown there. Its wooden balconies stretched out toward the sea in what seemed almost to be an expression of yearning. The lot was wooded—beech trees guarded the house from the elements or from the eyes of strangers. Bent was obviously doing well indeed. Borgmann was impressed.

There was a long series of flagstone steps leading up a vine-covered hill to the front door. He took them two at a time. At the top, he lifted the huge brass knocker on the massive dark oak door and let it fall. Then he waited. After a few moments, the door swung open. Bent Dahlgaard, now wearing an open-necked polo shirt and looking very expansive, invited him in.

"Welcome to my home, Frederick," he said warmly. "I can't tell you how much pleasure it gives me to say those words."

"And I can't tell you how much pleasure it gives me to be here," Borgmann replied, with equal warmth.

He stepped onto the slate floor of the entry way and glanced up at the ultramodern stainless steel chandelier above him. The walls and the ceilings were in wood of varying shades.

Dahlgaard watched him for a moment, smiling. "Nothing like the old days, eh, Frederick?"

"You have a beautiful home, Bent. Things have clearly gone well for you."

Dahlgaard responded modestly. "Well enough."

A flight of stairs—wooden beams, actually—led up into the living room. At the top of the stairs, Borgmann saw a familiar figure.

"Maj."

"Hello Frederick."

He bounded up the stairs and kissed her on the cheek. The softness of her skin almost overwhelmed him, as it had a hundred times before. Sensations, smells and feelings came rushing back to him from the distant past.

Then he stepped back and looked at her.

The shape and size were the same, but this was not the Maj Hartling he had known. And it was not just a matter of age. The lines in her face were deep. There were shadows under her eyes. Though her skin retained its softness, its healthy glow had been replaced by an ashen paleness. Even her auburn hair was mixed with grey. If Borgmann had seen this woman walking down the street and had been asked to guess her age, he might have said that she was in her middle fifties. All that was left of the girl that once was were those luminous eyes—and even they looked worried, as if they had too often looked back at something that was inexorably gaining.

In his mind's eye, Borgmann conjured up a vision of the Maj he had known as a boy. It was involuntary, he couldn't have stopped himself if he'd wanted to. And he superimposed that image over the Maj Hartling who now stood in front of him. If he concentrated, he saw only the young girl. If he relaxed, the girl aged in front of his eyes. He wanted nothing more than to destroy the memory that had surfaced from so long ago so that he could look at this woman without a rush of pain and sympathy.

"I would have recognized you anywhere, Maj," he said, hoping his expression could sustain his words.

She answered him with a small, sad smile. "You look stronger and more handsome than ever, Frederick. We women—well, we do not age so well."

"Nonsense, Maj," he heard himself saying. "You're a splendid figure of a woman. And how wonderful it is to see you again!" The effort to sound sincere took almost every ounce of his control. "But why are we speaking in English?"

"The children, Frederick," Bent said. "English is taught in all the schools now, and we are helping them to learn by speaking only that language in our home."

Borgmann looked up behind Maj, into the living room, toward a huge square limestone fireplace. Two young girls huddled beside it, one perhaps twelve, the other about nine.

"Come, girls, meet your Uncle Frederick," Maj said. Her voice was as musical as ever.

The girls hesitantly stepped out from beside the fireplace and walked toward their mother. "Is he really our uncle?" said the younger one, a fragile blonde with pigtails.

"No, not really. But he is an old, old friend," Maj told her gently.

"Frederick knew us both before we were married—when we were still in the *gymnasium*."

The girls looked at Borgmann with interest, possibly awe. The older one, he thought, would be a beauty. She had her mother's looks—or, at least, the looks her mother once had—the auburn hair, the dark eyes.

"Frederick," Bent said, indicating the older girl, "this is Erika." The girl offered him a small, tentative smile and curtsied. Borgmann was charmed by her. "And this," Bent went on, "this is Margriet." The fragile blonde turned out to be not so fragile. She boldly extended a hand. Borgmann took it and they shook firmly, as if agreeing on some business transaction.

"I'm very pleased to meet you both," Borgmann said. "You are both very pretty young ladies."

Erika, surprisingly, was taken aback by his remark. She blushed, then hurried out of the room.

"Did I say something wrong?" Borgmann asked Bent, concerned.

"Erika is very sensitive," said Margriet, sounding like a child psychologist. "She's just entering puberty."

"Oh," Borgmann said, returning the remark as seriously as it had been given. "I didn't realize that." He glanced at Bent, who was smiling broadly, then at Maj, who was looking toward the living room with concern, trying to make eye contact with her eldest.

"Yes," Margriet went on, "Pretty soon I will be at that age."

"Will you be sensitive?" Borgmann asked.

"Perhaps."

"Go to your sister, Margriet. Tell her Uncle Frederick was just trying to be nice," Maj said.

"Yes, you should leave us now," said Bent. "It's time for the adults to talk."

The girl skipped off and the three adults headed into the living room. It was a warm, beautiful, spacious room, with a beamed cathedral ceiling, a thick light-colored rug on the random-planked floor and a collection of stainless steel, glass and leather furniture that would have been at home in any futuristic science fiction movie.

"Sit," Maj said. "Let me bring some *snaps*."

"Oh, damn," Borgmann said suddenly. "I knew I forgot something. I meant to bring a bottle of Bronums or Porsenaps."

"Frederick, you didn't have to bring a gift. Your presence is more than enough."

Borgmann was disarmed. "How can I reply to that, Bent?"

"Just enjoy yourself and feel at home in our house."

Maj disappeared for a few moments, then returned with an elegant teak tray that held a small crystal flask and three delicate glasses. She filled them, offering the first to Frederick.

"Let me propose a toast," said Bent. "To Frederick and to the pleasure of seeing him once more."

They raised their glasses. "And to old memories," Maj added. She exchanged glances with her husband.

"And to a friendship renewed," said Borgmann.

They each emptied their glasses. Then, for a moment, there was silence—of the awkward variety.

"You must tell us—"

"I'm interested in knowing—"

"What do you do—"

They'd all spoken at once. The laughter that followed eased the tension slightly.

"It is a bit awkward, after so many years," Maj said.

"Nonsense," said Bent, acting the hail-fellow-well-met. "It's as if we'd parted yesterday. Tell me, Frederick, what are you doing now?"

"I'm at Argonne National Laboratory, near Chicago," Borgmann replied. "I'm working on the breeder reactor project. We hope to produce electric power very cheaply, and without any significant pollution."

"Oh, I see," Dahlgaard said, genuinely interested. "The last time I heard about you, you were at Los Alamos."

"I haven't worked on bomb projects since the middle fifties," Borgmann said. He felt defensive about the entire subject.

"I understand, Frederick. I meant no criticism. It may even turn out that developing the H-bomb was a service to the world. We do not seem quite so anxious to destroy ourselves now that we have the means."

Borgmann considered a reply for a moment. He didn't think it completely appropriate to say thank you.

"And you, Bent? Obviously, you are successful."

Dahlgaard brushed back his blond hair self-consciously. "I stayed with the University," he said. "Then, when the Bohr Institute was founded, I joined the physics department as professor of nuclear physics. I was head of the department for about a decade before I joined private industry. Danfoss hired me to head up their nuclear power research program."

"Then you are very involved with the centrifuge?" Borgmann asked.

"Oh, yes, indeed," Dahlgaard replied with a smile. "I was one of the moving forces in arranging for the conference. If Scandinavia gets involved with the project—and I confidently expect that it will—I hope Danfoss will play a major role in producing the necessary equipment."

"So much business talk," Maj said, in half-serious complaint. "What about your personal life, Frederick. Are you married? Do you have children?"

Borgmann glanced over at Maj. It still hurt him to look at her. "Married?" he said. "No, not any more. I was married for a few years, but my wife died back in the mid-sixties in a car accident. We never had any children."

"I'm sorry to hear that, Frederick," said Bent sympathetically.

"It was a long time ago, Bent."

"What was her name, Frederick?" Maj asked.

"Ruth."

The awkward silence reasserted itself.

Maj rose. "Gentlemen, you'll have to excuse me—dinner, you understand."

"Of course," Borgmann said. He watched her walk from the room. Then he was alone with Bent.

"Well," Bent said cheerfully. "She looks good, doesn't she?"

"Very."

"You're not jealous, are you?"

"A bit."

Dahlgaard laughed. "You had your chance, you know."

"That's true," Borgmann said. "Tell me, how did it happen—you and Maj?"

"It was all your fault," Bent said with a smile. "When you left, neither of us had anyone to turn to but each other."

"I thought it was something like that."

"Those were bad days for all of us, Frederick," Dahlgaard said. "Even after you left. They took reprisals, you know."

"I read about it. I always felt guilty, somehow."

"There was no cause for that, Frederick. What we did, for the Jews in our midst, we did out of our hearts—" He let the sentence trail off.

"I understand, Bent. Believe me."

"And the only guilt anyone can feel belongs to us, for those of you who did not escape."

"Yes." The reference was to Borgmann's mother and father. For a moment, it hung heavily in the air.

"But these are better days, eh, Frederick?"

"So much better that they almost make me forget the past, Bent."

They each took a sip of their *snaps*. It was starting to get maudlin, Borgmann thought. There was no way to get out of it now, though. Besides, he had an errand.

"How is it you happen to be here in Denmark, Frederick? I can't imagine two less related approaches to

153

nuclear electric power than the breeder reactor and the gas centrifuge."

"I'm here as an observer, Bent. But there's more to it than that—"

At that moment, Maj walked back into the room. "Dinner is ready, gentlemen." They both rose to follow her. How was it, Borgmann wondered, that Bent looked so well and Maj looked so bad? Was this somehow a reflection of their personal relationship? Or was there something more here?

The dining room was a smaller version of the living room—another beamed cathedral ceiling, walls of Philippine mahogany and a carpet so thick that you could close your eyes and imagine you were walking on mink. The smell of food was overwhelming.

"Wait," Borgmann said, sniffing, "don't tell me— *flaeskesteg med rødkal.*"

"Right," Maj said, genuinely surprised. "I thought you might not get much roast pork in America."

"Especially not with red cabbage," Borgmann said, agreeing. "I don't think I've had this dish since I left Denmark." He sat down.

"I'm astonished that you remembered the smell," Maj said, taking her seat.

"Astonished at Frederick's memory?" Dahlgaard said, chiding his wife. "I can't imagine how that could ever surprise you."

"Oh, yes," Maj said slowly. "That photographic memory. I forgot."

"I don't think I shall ever forget," Dahlgaard said with a chuckle. "Every time there was a test, we both studied like mad. I got ninety-nine, Frederick got one-hundred. It was uncanny."

"If it weren't for that trick memory of mine, you would have been number one in the class," Borgmann said. "And I'm not being generous; you know that." He cut into his roast pork.

"Perhaps," Dahlgaard said. "And if I'd have been first, maybe I would have been the one to work with Bohr at Los Alamos." He took a bite of his food.

Borgmann looked at his friend in surprise.

154

"Of course," Dahlgaard said, finishing a mouthful, "it all turned out all right in the end, didn't it?" He waved a fork around, more or less pointing to the house and to Maj.

Borgmann smiled. "I'd say you did all right for yourself." For an instant, he'd thought he was treading on thin ice.

"It was all meant to be this way, yes?" Dahlgaard said, his manner offhand and charming.

"It seems that way to me," Borgmann replied. He took another bite of the roast pork.

"More *snaps*?" Maj asked.

Borgmann turned toward her. There were those eyes again, and that split second when memory superimposed itself over reality. "Yes, please," he said. "Where did the kids go, Maj? I was hoping to get to know them better."

"They ate earlier. I told them they could talk with you more after dinner."

Borgmann reached for the lazy Susan in the middle of the table. It was loaded with cheeses—Danablu, Esrom, Samsø and Maribo, one for every taste. He cut himself a triangular piece of the blue-veined Danablu, anticipating its sharp flavor.

"Do you know what I've made you for dessert?"

"I haven't any idea."

"Guess."

Memory flared up again for an instant. There was just a flash of the girl, playful, always ready for fun.

"Riz à l'amande?"

Maj smiled. For a moment, she seemed almost happy. "Close—but, no, not pudding. Guess again."

"Pandekaer sma pandekager?"

"Oh, I'm sure you can get pancakes in the United States. Give up?"

Borgmann laughed. "Okay, you win."

"Bondepige med slør."

It was as if she had put the taste in his mouth—dark rye bread-crumbs, applesauce, cream and sugar. "My mother used to make that for me, Maj."

Her reply was surprisingly gentle. "I know, Frederick. I remember."

Now the tension was gone entirely. The rest of the dinner was easy and conversational. Borgmann felt he was getting to know his old friends again. What pleased him more than anything else was that he still liked them, both of them. It had been thirty years, but the basis for good feelings between them survived.

As the meal was coming to an end, Borgmann saw the girls standing in the doorway. It was astonishing how much the older one, Erika, resembled her mother, when she'd been a girl.

"Girls," Bent said sternly, "didn't I tell you that we could all visit in the living room *after* dinner?"

"But, Daddy," Margriet said, "we're getting so bored, waiting."

"Why don't you two go in there," Maj suggested. "I'll serve coffee in the living room."

Borgmann followed his old friend.

"Are you going to play the piano for Uncle Frederick?" Dahlgaard asked Erika.

She nodded nervously. Borgmann had the feeling all this had been rehearsed before his arrival. The girl sat down on the upholstered bench of a magnificent contemporary rosewood piano. A sheet of music was already in place.

Borgmann took his place on a long, low couch covered in fawn-colored leather. Margriet, the scamp, sat across from him in a chair that had been constructed from black leather belting and chromed steel pipes. She just gazed at him as if he were a member of an unfamiliar animal species.

At that moment, Maj entered. This time, the teakwood tray carried a coffeepot, a creamer, some sugar and three coffee cups and saucers. "Well," she said to Erika as she gently put the tray on the thick glass table in front of the couch, "aren't you going to play?"

"I was just waiting for you, Mommy," the girl said, petulantly.

She scanned the sheet music and started in. Borgmann poured himself a cup of coffee and stirred in two teaspoonsful of sugar. Soon, the sound of Chopin's *Marche Militaire* was floating through the room. It was played competently, if a trifle mechanically. When the girl finished, Borgmann put his coffee down and applauded appreciatively.

Erika smiled nervously in response, slid off the wooden bench and curtsied as if she'd been giving a recital—and wasn't that the case?

"The *Minute Waltz*," Dahlgaard said, prompting, "why don't you play the *Minute Waltz* next."

Borgmann saw a sudden flash of fear in the girl's eyes. "I'm still practising that, Papa," he protested. "It's not perfect yet."

"I enjoy many things that aren't quite perfect," Borgmann said. He felt sorry for the girl though he didn't know why.

"What about a polonaise, then," Dahlgaard said. Superficially, his suggestion sounded pleasant enough—but there was a slight edge to his voice.

Erika appeared ready to protest once more, but she changed her mind, sat down and began to play. This time, things didn't go so well. In about the middle of the piece, she dropped a note. And then another. And then another. She started over, making even more errors on the second pass. Finally, she crashed both fists into the keyboard, jumped up from the bench and ran out of the living room, her sobs increasing in volume with every step.

Borgmann rose and headed in the direction she'd gone, but Maj stopped him. "Let me," she said.

"High-strung, isn't she?" Margriet commented. "I used to play the violin, but I quit."

"She wanted so much to be perfect for you," Dahlgaard said. "I feel bad for her."

"If it were daytime we could go over to the riding stable and I could show you how well I ride a horse," Margriet said.

"I'm sure you're a very good rider," Borgmann told the girl. "Too bad I can't see you. But I'd like you even if you didn't ride. Same with your sister. I don't care how she plays the piano. Would you tell her that for me?"

"Now?"

"Well, maybe it would be good for her to hear it now, while she's upset."

Margriet groaned, dragged herself out of her chair and reluctantly left the room.

"I meant what I said, Bent," Borgmann said. "I think both of your children are charming."

"Thank you," Dahlgaard said. "Margriet is really amazing, you know. So much self-confidence. She's a real mischief maker."

"And very pretty—like Erika."

"Yes, Erika. She's a bit of a problem. Very nervous child. I sometimes worry about her."

"Well, you know, children—especially young girls about to enter adolescence—"

"She never got over it when her mother—ah—got sick."

"Maj?"

"She had a breakdown a few years ago, Frederick. It was after her mother died. But she's made a marvelous recovery, don't you think? You remember her before—before everything. Isn't she just the same?"

Borgmann squirmed in his seat. "Well, she's older. But it's the same Maj, there's no doubt of that."

Maj reappeared in the room. "I'm going to clean up the kitchen. The girls are getting ready for bed. Do you think I could leave you two by yourselves for a few minutes."

Borgmann managed a chuckle. "Oh," he said, "we've been known to get on all right from time to time." He watched her as she left the room, measuring her mental state in his mind. A nervous breakdown—yes, that would explain it.

Both men took sips of coffee. There was an almost palpable feeling of awkwardness. Borgmann decided to end it by doing his errand. The direct way was the best way.

"Bent, I haven't been entirely candid with you about why I've come to the conference."

Dahlgaard looked at him with innocent surprise. "No? What do you mean, Frederick?"

"I'm here at the request of an old friend, Bent. Jacob Kaplan."

Dahlgaard's mouth dropped open. "Kaplan? But I thought . . ."

"That he was dead? Or back in Israel? It would be natural to think that."

"But why in the world has Kaplan returned to Copenhagen?"

"He's still trying to save the Jews, Bent. You remember what he did for the Danish Jews when the Nazis decided to round them up."

"Of course I remember. I helped; you know that."

"Yes, you did, Bent; you couldn't have done more." Borgmann's voice was passionately sincere.

Dahlgaard seemed lost in thought. "I assume he's still working for Israel," he said finally.

"Yes."

"But what is it in Copenhagen that could interest—" Dahlgaard stopped in mid-sentence. He seemed suddenly to realize what the conversation was all about. "The centrifuge plans, Frederick. Israel wants them?"

"Yes."

"And you've come to help him get the plans?"

"At first, I just came to see him, at his request. I intended to refuse. But he's convinced me they'd just be used to bluff."

Dahlgaard brushed his blond hair back over his head. "And now you want something of me. Is that why you're here tonight?"

"I'm here tonight because you invited me, Bent. I'm here to see you and Maj. I'm here to see if a friendship that has been dormant as long as ours can be revived." Borgmann spoke quickly, with anger. His face, he knew, was flushed.

"I believe you, Frederick," Dahlgaard said, holding up a hand.

"If all I wanted to do was use you, I could have asked your help this morning—at the conference."

"Of course. Forgive me." Dahlgaard looked at Borgmann, his pale blue eyes clear and kind. "If you cannot ask an old friend for help, whom can you ask?"

"And I can't tell you what it's meant to me to see you and Maj once more. It's as if all the loose ends in my life have finally been tied together again."

"I understand, Frederick. I feel the same way."

Each of the men took another sip of coffee. It was the only method at hand to break the flow of conversation.

"Come on, Erika," Margriet said.

Borgmann looked over at the living room door. Both girls were in bathrobes and pajamas. The younger sister was trying to convince the older sister to enter.

"You *have* to say good night, Erika."

Margriet stepped into the room. Her older sister followed her hesitantly.

"Good night, Uncle Frederick," Margriet said with a tomboyish grin. "It's been a pleasure to meet you and I hope you come again soon."

"Good night, Uncle Frederick," Erika said. Her eyes were red.

"Doesn't an uncle get a good-night kiss?" Borgmann asked.

Both girls walked over to him. Margriet gave him a hug and a loud, wet kiss on the cheek. Erika presented her cheek for his peck.

"I hope I see you both again soon," Frederick said. "I want you both to know that though I am not really your uncle, I feel as if I were." He looked at Erika and smiled. "And don't worry about your piano playing, young lady. I think you showed a great deal of promise."

"Thank you."

"Thank you, Uncle Frederick," he coached.

"Thank you, Uncle Frederick."

"Good. Now give me a smile."

Erika did just that.

"You're a beautiful girl, Erika. The next years will be good ones for you, you'll see."

"Thank you, Uncle Frederick."

Both girls turned and walked out of the living room.

Borgmann watched them, especially Erika. He'd rarely felt this helpless.

"You're good with them, Frederick," Dahlgaard said. "I wish you could see them more often."

"Well, perhaps I will."

"Frederick, you wanted my help. What can I do for you? I will help in whatever way I can."

"I need to locate the centrifuge plans, Bent."

"I see."

"Do you know where they are?"

"I only know they've been carefully hidden. I believe they're going to be shown to the technical sessions by closed-circuit television."

"Can you find out where they are?"

"I can try, Frederick."

"There isn't much time."

"I know. I understand the plans will be returned to The Hague within three days."

"We have two full days to find the plans, Bent."

"I will ask those who know."

"Thank you, Bent."

The two men shook hands vigorously.

"Bent, there is one other matter."

"Certainly, Frederick. What?"

"There are three delegates to the convention I would like to ask you about: Torngren, the fellow from Finland; Lindeborg—from Sweden, I believe; and Thorwaldsen. I am not sure they are legitimate delegates. Perhaps they would give me trouble."

Dahlgaard laughed. "Thorwaldsen? Trouble? He is a harmless old man. I've known him for years. He couldn't find the men's room without help. As for Torngren, I do not know him. Your guess is as good as mine. I do know Lindeborg. He's been at dozens of these meetings. What bothers you about him?"

"I'm not sure I can put my finger on it. He just seemed to know more about me than he should."

Dahlgaard considered this for a moment. "I have nothing to say against the man, Frederick. He is not my favorite person, but I've never heard a whisper that he might be some kind of agent. Still, I say you should follow your instincts. Keep your distance from him."

Borgmann agreed. But he was not completely satisfied. He was ready to dismiss his suspicions about Thorwaldsen, but he still wanted to know more about Lindeborg.

"Ah, I see the two of you are getting along well," said Maj, smiling as she returned from the kitchen.

"Like old friends should," said Bent, bantering with her.

An hour later, Frederick was on his way back to the Kong Frederik. It had been an evening of many different emotions, too many to absorb all at once. Most important, Bent had agreed to help. That might make all the difference.

Chapter Fourteen

There was a knock on the glass door. Lieutenant Colonel Yevgeny Borsilov looked up, startled. He closed the file folder on his desk. For the last three hours, every knock had rattled his nerves.

"Enter."

A young messenger came into the room and dropped a sheaf of decoded telegrams on his desk. With the door open, the noise of the teletypes was almost deafening. And yet it had only been eighteen months since Borsilov had been sitting out there with the others, watching the machines, making decisions about which division chief should see which message.

"Anything of special interest in there?" he asked the messenger. It was his habit to ask such a question. From his own experience, no one was more sensitive to important or unusual messages than the teletype man. His own sensitivity had been an important factor in his promotion when the Scandinavian desk had become vacant.

"There is something mildly interesting from Copenhagen."

"Oh. Agent cover name?"

"Torngren, I believe."

Borsilov felt his pulse leap. "Good. Thank you, Fyodor. Dismissed."

Borsilov waited until the door had closed. He opened the file folder slowly, his hands trembling slightly. The first thirteen messages were routine—agents checking in, reporting programs in progress, accepting assignments, asking for funds and the like. The fourteenth stood out like a red flag. Borsilov held it in his strong, thick fingers and read it:

ATTN KGB LENINGRAD INU SECTION SCAN-DINAVIAN DESK:
COVER POSSIBLY BLOWN BY BOGUS CON-FERENCE DELEGATE FREDERICK BORG-MANN. MY BEST GUESS HE IS CIA. RE-QUEST PERMISSION TO ELIMINATE. HAVE LEAD ON PLANS.

TORNGREN (S. #14547)

There it was—Borgmann—the name he'd been asked to look for. He swallowed hard and read through the message again.

For eleven years, Yevgeny Borsilov had been an efficient deskman at the Leningrad KGB headquarters. He had started out as an orderly, little more than a valet and errand boy, and had progressed slowly but surely up the ladder. Now he was chief of the Scandinavian desk. It wasn't a terribly sensitive job, really, but that might come later. There were whispers that he was being seasoned for a post at the African desk, once Voshkod was eased out. From there, depending on his success or failure, he might go anywhere.

Of course, that was the key phrase—success or failure. In the KGB's foreign section, the INU, the successful men moved up the ladder and the failures simply vanished, no one knew where. No one inquired where. What's more, the risks increased as a man attained higher and higher levels of power. Here results were more critical, failures more conspicuous.

And in the highest jobs, another risk presented itself: politics. At that level, a man had to commit himself, not simply to the agency or to his job, but to some larger political figure. If he chose badly, his career was bound to be foreshortened.

Borsilov had not quite reached that level. He had committed himself only to his job and to his agency. He was a tireless worker. There was, perhaps, no brilliance in his work, but there was competence, unfailing competence. There was also loyalty, to his country and his co-workers. Borsilov wasn't the idealogue some men on his level professed to be, but then he was not driven by higher political ambitions. He wanted only to do his job, to progress modestly, to provide security for his three children, now entering their teens, and for his beloved wife, Marina, a lovely blonde who made him the envy of his co-workers.

Now, for the first time in his life, Borsilov was faced with a choice between two loyalties—between his immediate family and his larger family, between his country and another, between his motherland and his homeland. Years ago he had been told that someday he might be called upon to make this choice. But the passing of time had led him to forget.

Holding the telegram from Torngren, he could feel the sweat gather under his arms and start to drip. His pulse was high. His blood pressure was high. His eyebrow was starting to twitch.

What would happen if he ordered Torngren to go ahead? Borgmann would die and Israel would be somehow injured.

What would happen if he altered Torngren's message—just enough to throw suspicion on the man, so that the Agency would get rid of him?

Now that might be the best alternative. There'd be no way to blame Borsilov—the only contradictory witness would be dead. Message boys, he knew from experience, would never remember exact translation texts. The originals were shredded immediately after translation to prevent the codes from being compromised.

It all came down to this: Borsilov had to choose between Borgmann and Torngren. He knew Torngren only slightly and didn't much care for the man. He knew Borgmann not at all. But he did know what each represented.

Borsilov unbuttoned his uniform collar. Why was it, he wondered, that he was required to wear a uniform in a desk job like this?

Once more, he read the decoded telegram. The quandary did not resolve itself easily.

How strange and unexpected it all had been. During his lunch hour, he'd collided with a man in the park, excused himself, and found himself with a note in his hand. He had tried to catch the man in the crowds, but that had proved impossible. And then he'd read the note.

"PROTECT BORGMANN IN COPENHAGEN," it had said. It was signed with the code agreed on, years back, a simple Hebrew *heh,* a letter of the alphabet. Borsilov had walked quickly to a public toilet, ripped the paper into the tiniest shreds he could manage with his thick fingers and flushed it into the Gulf of Finland. But he could not erase what he had read from his mind.

There was no way he could know how long it had been since the message had originated in Copenhagen. Most likely, the message had been sent only hours earlier, relayed by cable to Israel, then, most likely, by shortwave radio to Leningrad. That meant his name was on a file card somewhere in Tel Aviv, his job responsibilities duly noted, updated, no doubt, as he was promoted. Since he had never relayed this information to Israel himself, that meant, in turn, that there must be others in this network, people intimately acquainted with the KGB but loyal to Israel. It was both impressive and frightening. He wondered, almost idly, whether that network would ever function to protect him, whether he would ever need it.

There was another knock at his glass door.

"Enter."

The messenger came in with another sheaf of decoded telegrams.

"Anything especially noteworthy in this batch?" Borsilov asked, almost without interest.

"Nothing much. There's one in there about U.S. Army deserters in Sweden you might want to look at."

Borsilov nodded. "Thanks."

The messenger turned and left the room, closing the door behind him.

And still the decision was not made.

Once more, Borsilov read through Torngren's telegram. An idea occurred to him. There was the sentence that read "My best guess he is CIA." What if he were to simply alter "CIA" to "GRU"? That would give the next sentence—"Request permission to eliminate"—an entirely different meaning.

All he'd have to do then was to turn the decoded telegram over to the GRU representative down the hall. From then on, matters would be out of his hands. No, he took back the thought. The GRU might check its records to see if Borgmann was one of its own. And of course he wasn't. They'd certainly ask questions then.

Borsilov felt stymied. Gradually, though, a solution occurred to him. He would simply eliminate the name *Frederick Borgmann*. Chances were very, very good that the GRU had a man at the conference. He could find out informally, from the GRU representative.

Borsilov left his office, walking into the clattering teletype room. He tore a few pages from a pad of decoding forms that sat on a supply table, then returned to his office. After a brief search for a ballpoint pen, he wrote out a new message. It read:

ATTN KGB LENINGRAD INU SECTION SCANDINAVIAN DESK:
COVER POSSIBLY BLOWN BY BOGUS CONFERENCE DELEGATE. MY BEST GUESS HE IS GRU. REQUEST PERMISSION TO ELIMINATE. HAVE LEAD ON PLANS.

TORNGREN (S. #14547)

It was, he decided, perfect—especially in light of the recent field troubles between GRU and KGB operatives. In the last seven months, three men had died quite mysteriously—two GRU agents, one from the KGB. The Torngren message would fit right into recent events and the GRU representative would have mighty little patience with it.

167

Borsilov again left his office. This time, he walked down the hallway, past the teletypes and the offices of the other section chiefs. He knocked on the door of the GRU representative.

"Yes?"

"It's Yevgeny Borsilov."

"Ah. Come in."

Borsilov entered the office of Vassily Leonovitch, chief representative of the GRU. The GRU mainly coordinated military intelligence, through its field operatives in many Western and most Communist-bloc countries. Leonovitch was a tall blond man with alert blue eyes and a ready wit.

"Hello, Vassily," Borsilov said.

"How are you, Yevgeny? How are things in Scandinavia? You wish you were in Copenhagen, yes?"

For a moment, Borsilov was startled. Then he realized the man was joking. "No, Stockholm I think. My taste runs more toward blondes."

"Ah yes. I had forgotten you were married to a blonde girl. What can I do for you, Yevgeny?"

"Vassily, you have a man at that Copenhagen conference, don't you?"

Leonovitch's eyebrows went up slightly. "So? Do you have some comment to make about the conference?"

It was not the sort of firm confirmation that Borsilov would have liked, but he decided to go ahead anyway. "Perhaps you'd better look at this." He handed the phony decoded telegram to Leonovitch.

The GRU representative took it casually, with a polite nod. He read it. Borsilov watched. As Leonovitch read, his face began to turn red. By the time he had finished, his blue eyes were flint-hard.

"This is your man, this Torngren?"

"That is his cover name."

"But is he KGB?"

"Yes."

"Scandinavian section?"

"Yes."

"Do you know this man? Is he experienced?"

"I understand he is an experienced operative. Something of a nuclear specialist. I do not know him well."

Leonovitch read through the telegram once more. When he looked up, his anger was fresh again. "Just what do you think we should do with this man, Borsilov?"

"Call him back and question him thoroughly. It's probably just a case of mistaken identity."

His words had their intended effect.

"Call him back?" Leonovitch asked, incredulous. "He's asking for permission to assassinate one of my men—and a very valuable man indeed, I can tell you, someone we've worked years to place in exactly the right spot, a man who is right now carrying out his most important assignment—and you want merely to bawl Torngren out?"

Borsilov shrugged. "What would you suggest?"

"We must eliminate these troublemakers, Yevgeny. Sometimes I think they are more dangerous to us than our foreign enemies."

"You mean you want to bring him back and put him on trial—and then execute him?"

"That's not what I meant and you know it. He has to be eliminated now."

"How?"

Leonovitch glanced at his watch. The day was nearly over. "I want the job finished before midnight tonight."

"But—"

"Yevgeny, you're not going to argue with me on this, are you? You're not a troublemaker, are you? No, of course you're not—you brought the telegram to my attention. And I thank you for that. But do you disagree with my solution?"

"It's not that, Vassily," Borsilov said, very pleased but not about to show it. "It's just that I don't think we can get a man there that quickly."

"Well, I can, Yevgeny," Leonovitch said. "I have a man just across the sound, in Malmö. That's 11 miles from Copenhagen. About a half hour by hydrofoil."

"I know the geography, Vassily."

"Yes. Of course. I'm sorry. Do you agree that we should handle this problem the way I have suggested?"

"If you insist, Vassily."

"Good. Now I need some details about this man Torngren—where he stays in Copenhagen, his safe house, other things."

"Fine," Borsilov said. "I'll have to get that information back at my office. I'll be back with it in a moment."

Chapter Fifteen

The little green Saab searched for a parking place on Peter Hvifeldts Straede, found it and pulled in. Miriam Shazar got out and walked briskly to the Svenska Quality Porno Shop, about half a block away. Inside, she found Ben-Ezra sitting at his desk, going through some airline schedules.

"Well," he said, "any luck?"

"Some," she replied. "We found out that the cable terminates somewhere in the Tivoli."

"The Tivoli? That's crazy."

"Maybe so, but the information we have seems pretty reliable."

Ben-Ezra paused before speaking. "You know, of course, that the Tivoli is a fairly large place," he said at last.

"Yes. Twenty acres, I believe."

"And coaxial cables are about an inch thick, aren't they?"

Miriam groaned. "Yaakov, I do not intend to look for the cables by digging around in the ground. A few questions, discreetly asked, and we should have some idea where it goes."

"Time is getting short, Miriam." Ben-Ezra leaned back in his chair and put his feet up on the desk. Both of his shoes had holes in the soles.

"So it is. But we are making progress. What Frederick finds out tonight from his friend Dahlgaard may be crucial. He's headed there now."

"We cannot count on him, Miriam. Dahlgaard may

know nothing. Your investigation at the Tivoli seems to be our best hope for finding the plans." He examined the holes in his shoes, with a frown.

"Perhaps things would go faster if you joined me, Yaakov."

Ben-Ezra looked at his daughter angrily. Was she actually telling him that he wasn't doing enough, that he was asking more of her than he was willing to deliver himself? He put his feet down and sat erect.

"No—I didn't mean that," she said, realizing what he was thinking. "I know you're busy dealing with the opposition."

"And making sure that we can get out of here when the time comes," he reminded his daughter petulantly.

"Yes." She was subdued now.

"Besides Tivoli, I want you to follow up on any information Frederick may get from Dahlgaard," Ben-Ezra said.

"I plan to call him at the hotel tonight. His conference doesn't begin until eleven tomorrow morning. If he has no leads, I may ask him to join me at Tivoli, at least until the conference starts."

"That sounds like a good idea to me, Miriam."

"I'm glad you approve, Yaakov."

Ben-Ezra tilted back in his chair, reflectively. "Miriam, must there be this constant sniping between us, this continual antagonism? I respect you and I hope you respect me."

"Yaakov, I meant nothing—"

"It isn't your words, Miriam, it's your tone of voice. If you remember, I didn't want to work with you on this assignment, for reasons I am sure you understand. But you wanted it and others insisted. Now we must cooperate. I'm trying to make it as pleasant as possible, and I feel you should do the same. Don't we owe at least that much to each other?"

Miriam winced as he spoke. "We owe more than that, Father," she said, when he finished, her eyes downcast. "You've made your point."

"And one more thing, while we're at it," Ben-Ezra went on. "There's a fair chance you've been spotted and described by the opposition. A change of costume might confuse our enemies."

"Maybe you're right. I forgot to tell you that we were followed by Abdul Amer when we left here, on the way to the TV repair shop."

"Amer?" Ben-Ezra had been taken off guard. "He followed you from this office?"

"Yes."

"In what kind of car?"

"A grey Fiat."

"Then the Arabs know where we are."

"I'm afraid so. But no one is outside now."

"You're sure?"

"Yes. I drove the street three times before parking and coming in." She watched her father's face, hoping he would approve.

"What about Amer? Did you manage to lose him?" Ben-Ezra was clearly worried.

"Yes. It took about twenty minutes and a minor car accident, but I shook him off."

Ben-Ezra was silent now, evidently putting the pieces together in his mind. "First the man who shot at me —then Amer. I'd say our presence at this place is pretty well known."

"Perhaps we should set up another headquarters," Miriam suggested.

"No time," Ben-Ezra said. "The best that we can do is to *use* the fact that our whereabouts is known. But that is my affair. You must worry about finding the plans."

"All right, Father."

"I only pray that Frederick has information for us. We have only two days left and there are so many complications," Ben-Ezra said.

Miriam felt a rush of sympathy for the man. He was tired and troubled. The usual self-confidence—often so annoying—was muted. She promised herself to do everything she could to help. She wondered whether it would be enough.

Chapter Sixteen

Ostap Kirov walked up to the ticket window at the hydrofoil dock in Malmö. Tall, dressed in a grey flannel suit from Saville Row, carrying a silver-tipped cane, with his salt-and-pepper hair carefully combed and his meticulously trimmed pencil moustache, he cut a very elegant figure.

"Round trip," he said.

"Ten Swedish *kroner*," the girl said, her tone respectful.

Kirov handed her a bill and received tickets in return. "When does the next boat leave?"

"In approximately twenty minutes, sir," she told him.

"Thank you."

Kirov walked into the glassed-in waiting room and sat down. If the boat was on time, he would be in Copenhagen by about nine-thirty. That gave him two and a half hours to do his job—enough, if the man was where he was supposed to be. If he wasn't, this assignment might be very difficult.

Kirov hated these hurry-up jobs. There was no time to plan, no time to consider techniques. He considered himself to be a skilled man, an artist of a sort. Now he was being asked to act as a blunt instrument. It offended his aesthetic sensibilities. He hadn't even had time to choose a weapon. Of course, that really didn't matter in the end. He had the two weapons he always carried with him.

To Kirov's surprise and pleasure, the hydrofoil arrived early. He took a window seat in the airplanelike cabin. A few other passengers—mostly business types —joined him. He'd made the ride often enough, but never at night. As they became visible, the lights of Copenhagen should be a very beautiful sight indeed.

At exactly the appointed moment, the ship's engines roared into life and the vessel glided out of the docking area. Soon Kirov felt a lifting sensation as the ship gathered speed and rose out of the water on its widespread legs. It was, he thought, much like taxiing in an airplane, a pleasant, light, floating feeling, totally unobjectionable, if you could ignore the noise.

Less than a half hour later, the lights of Copenhagen came into view, like a distant forest of lighted Christmas trees.

Kirov checked his watch as the hydrofoil docked in Copenhagen. It was 9:23. Plenty of time, if things were right. He walked quickly to the cab stand and got into the first taxi in the line.

"Radhuspladsen," he said.

"*Ja.*"

In the interest of self-protection, he'd decided not to go directly to the man's hotel, but to Town Hall Square. It would be just as well if the police could not easily connect a visitor from Malmö with what was about to take place. The hotel was only a few blocks from the square, anyway.

The cab ride was short and silent. Danish cabdrivers seem always to sense when conversation is not desired. The cab let Kirov off near a bus stop.

There was no need to ask directions since he knew Copenhagen well. He walked down Vesterbrogade, past the Tivoli, towards Colbjørnsensgade. It was a balmy night and many young people were wandering in and out of the amusement park. One young couple, especially, caught his eye. Or, at least, he took note of the female half of the couple. She was one of those statuesque dark-haired Danish girls with a perfect figure—huge uplifted breasts, buttocks so perfectly rounded that it was actually painful to resist the impulse to touch them. He slowed his pace so that the couple could pass him, then he followed at a discreet distance, watching the girl from behind. Her skirt was short. At home such things would be illegal. Once more he praised his luck for having been stationed abroad, particularly here in Scandinavia.

Unfortunately, the couple entered a small restaurant. Kirov's mind slowly returned to present business. He turned at Bernstorffsgade, between Tivoli and the Copenhagen Central Railroad Station. About halfway down the block he entered the station. As usual, it was bustling. It would be a good place to lose anyone who might be following him, either now or after his errand. He made a mental note of that.

Kirov sauntered through the high-ceilinged main corridor, watching the passing parade. The tourists were starting to arrive already. The building was filled with them—mostly scruffy-looking college kids from Germany, England, and the United States. He found nothing attractive about them. They were a kind of plague that infected Europe when the weather began to warm up, like mosquitoes.

He continued straight through the railroad terminal, out the other door, and onto Istedgade. This was not the prettiest part of Copenhagen. It was just like the KGB to order its man to take a room in this section. It would not do to expose him to the luxury of, say the d'Angleterre, the Royal or the Palace. If Kirov had been staying overnight, he might have chosen the first, the Grand Old Dame of Copenhagen hotels. After all, he thought, I am nothing if not a civilized man.

Colbjørnsensgade was only a block further down the street. Kirov turned right, looking for number nine. And there it was, a tidy five-floor brick building trimmed in white paint—Hotel Cuba. He walked in and approached the front desk.

"Yes, sir," the clerk said, bowing and scraping with his voice. "How can we help you?"

"You can help me by telling me the room number of Dr. Arne Torngren, a guest of this establishment, I believe."

"Of course."

The clerk flipped through a small card file. "He's in 412."

"Thank you," Kirov said and turned on his heel, toward the elevators.

"Sir, sir—" the clerk said anxiously, "are you going upstairs to see Dr. Torngren?"

Kirov paused. "No," he said, "I'm about to inspect your elevators for operating safety."

"What?"

"Of course I'm going to see Dr. Torngren," Kirov said sharply. "Didn't I just ask you his room number?"

"But you can't go up to the room unannounced."

"I am expected," Kirov said, continuing toward the elevator.

"Stop," the clerk called after him. Kirov ignored the voice. The clerk watched, helpless. For an instant, he looked at the house phone on his desk. Then he gave a small shrug, having thought better of it.

The elevator stopped on the fourth floor and Kirov got off. He reached beneath his jacket and withdrew his Walther P-38 automatic pistol. From another pocket he took a short black metal silencer, which he screwed onto the barrel of his pistol.

Kirov put the pistol in a side pocket and walked down the hall. Shortly, he came to room 412. He paused in front of the door for a moment, in thought. Then, he pressed an ear against the door and smiled. At least the man was in there. Getting him to the door might not be so easy, though. Then an idea occurred to him.

He banged loudly on the door with his closed fist. "Inga," he said angrily, "are you in there?" He waited a moment. There was no response. "Inga, I know you're in there. If you don't open the door, I'll break it down." He pounded again several times.

"There's no one named Inga in here," came the voice from within.

"Inga," Kirov shouted, "open this door at once." He banged some more.

"I tell you she's not here. You have the wrong room."

177

Kirov kept banging. "I know you're in there, Inga. Don't try to pretend you're not."

"Listen, you idiot, there's no one in here named Inga. You have the wrong room. If you keep pounding on the door, I'm going to have to call the management."

"You do just that. And I'll call the police. Then we'll see what happens." Kirov banged a few more times, then listened at the door. Finally he smiled. Footsteps. He reached into his pocket. The Walther felt cold and deadly.

There was the sound of the door being unlocked and the chain being slipped out of its moorings. The door swung open. The man who'd opened it was about six feet one inch tall, somewhat stocky, balding but with a light reddish fringe circling his head. His skin was very fair and profusely freckled. He was wearing a cheap brown bathrobe with some darkish stains on it. He gazed at Kirov in defiance. He held the door wide open, permitting Kirov a full view of the shabby little room.

"So. You see, your Inga is not here. Never was."

Kirov looked confused. "But you're not Karl Swenson."

"Of course not. I am Dr. Arne Torngren."

Kirov looked at Torngren in feigned surprise. "Who did you say you were?"

"Torngren. Dr. Arne Torngren."

"Oh," Kirov said, calmly regarding the man. He fit the description perfectly. "Well, in that case—" he withdrew the pistol from his pocket— "I have something for you." He fired twice, point-blank. The pistol made two little popping noises, nothing more than the sound of bubble gum cracking. Torngren looked at him with pure astonishment, then slipped to the floor lifeless, an arm flopping out into the hallway.

With an elegantly polished Bally black wing-tipped shoe, Kirov pushed the arm back inside the door. "Sorry to have disturbed you," he said. He pulled the door shut and sauntered down the hall, removing the silencer from his pistol and pocketing both. At the ele-

178

vators, he pressed the down button with the tip of his cane and checked his watch. It was 10:15. His evening meal had been a hurried snack, and hunger was with him again. There was plenty of time for a proper dinner. And Au Coq d'Or was only a short walk away. He would phone in later, when all his appetites were satiated.

Borgmann was exhausted by the time the cab dropped him off at the Hafnia. He walked through the lobby without so much as a sideways glance and found an empty elevator. He unlocked his door without even checking the hair he'd placed there earlier—as if it would have mattered. Evidently, anyone who cared knew exactly where he was at all times.

He undressed, hung up his clothes more or less, then sat on his bed, thinking. Borgmann's mind was aswirl with emotions and memories—not only of Bent and Maj, but also of Ruth. It was natural, on seeing the first love of his life, to think of the second. If only she were here now . . . .

The pain of Ruthie's death might have been eased had there been children to fill the void. There were none. At first, they wanted to wait, to live life unencumbered. Then, when they were ready, something was wrong. Ruthie couldn't get pregnant. There were doctors and hospitals and tests, all the while Frederick bearing the guilt, certain his years of nuclear research were responsible. But it turned out that the problem was with Ruthie and it was uncorrectable. For a while they talked of adopting, though neither had much enthusiasm for that. Anyhow, it wasn't that they needed a child to keep the marriage sound. The relationship seemed strong enough to go on forever. Forever came much too soon.

In a bad mood now, Borgmann let other unhappy memories surface. He thought of Niels Bohr. His work at Los Alamos finished in 1945, Bohr decided to return to Denmark. Borgmann could have returned with him. The elder scientist spent long hours trying to convince his student to do exactly that. Bohr said he'd worked

179

on the bomb only because he was convinced that if the Nazis got it first, civilization would be endangered. Now that the war was over, his conscience prevented him from spending any more time on weapons, and he sought to rouse Borgmann's conscience too.

In those days, Borgmann remembered, he was just a boy, interested in the game of war and weapons. Though his roots were in Denmark, he felt that his future was in America. To Bohr's great disappointment, he stayed at Los Alamos, helping to perfect the ultimate weapon. He also became an American citizen.

From the vantage point of the 1970s, Borgmann himself had trouble understanding why he had so willingly become a cold warrior, how he had so easily shifted his hatred and fear from the Nazis to the Russians. True, he was not alone, though that did not relieve him of responsibility in his own eyes. When Teller had proposed building the hydrogen bomb in 1948, Borgmann was beside him, an eager assistant. Just as the Russians had replaced the Nazis in his mind, so had Teller replaced Bohr. Looking back, he did not know which substitution was less admirable.

The beginning of the end of his association with nuclear weapons came on November 1, 1952. On that day, Elugelab Island, part of Eniwetok Atoll, disappeared from the face of the earth. Borgmann witnessed the detonation that destroyed it, the first thermonuclear test, and he realized—for the first time—that mankind possessed the seeds of its own destruction.

Yet for a while, he continued to work on the hydrogen bomb. To quit then would have been disrespectful to his new mentor. There was a camaraderie to the work and a challenge that any scientist would have found exciting, a sense of involvement that overrode the small naggings of his conscience. Besides, the U.S. H-bomb, he felt, was an excellent deterrent to Soviet expansionism. Some of Borgmann's colleagues did quit, nonetheless. Some had quit earlier, before the bomb was built.

In August 1953, the Russians detonated a hydrogen bomb of their own. The deterrent value of the American weapon all but vanished. And the mood of the country turned dark. Joseph R. McCarthy's power grew, and with it, Borgmann felt, the likelihood of a war in which there would be no survivors. His conscience no longer let him be.

In October 1953, he resigned. He tried to do it quietly, but that turned out to be impossible. His colleagues—those who remained with the H-bomb project—turned against him angrily. Those who had resigned earlier accepted him, though not without chiding him for his tardiness. Somehow the newspapers got hold of his letter of resignation, in which he spoke of "the danger to mankind, East *or* West," and "the conscience of a scientist who must first be a citizen of the world."

There were editorials, most of them condemning him. Though he'd been a U.S. citizen for six years, that question was reopened. An investigator for the Senate Permanent Investigations Subcommittee—McCarthy's committee—interviewed him and ominously promised, "We'll have more to say to you shortly." In April 1954, however, McCarthy turned his sights toward the army. Shortly after, Frederick received a letter from Yaakov Ben-Ezra, inviting him to Israel. Nothing could have been more welcome.

Borgmann was almost asleep when the phone rang. He instantly remembered that Miriam had agreed to call him at about this hour, to find out how his conversation with Dahlgaard had gone.

"Hello."

"Hello, Frederick." Her voice had a soft, whispery quality he hadn't noticed before, a very pleasing sound. "You had a nice dinner, I hope."

"Very."

"The meal was tasty?"

Frederick caught on. "It was a kind of appetizer. The chef inquired about my favorite dishes and intends to go shopping for them tomorrow morning. It should be a splendid lunch."

"I see. Any difficulties over the check?"

"None at all. The meal was on the house. And that

goes for tomorrow's lunch. The chef couldn't have been friendlier."

"I see. When will lunch be served?"

"Around the usual time. The chef said he'd begin preparing the meal about eleven, when all the other chefs get together. He's sure one of them will know how to prepare my favorite dish to my taste."

"That's good to hear," Miriam said, relieved.

"How will you be spending the day?"

"I'm going to see if I can tie up a loose end or two at the playground. Would you like to come?"

"Very much. What time?"

"I want to get an early start—how's nine?"

"Suits me fine."

"Meet you there, outside the front door."

"Good enough."

There was a click from the other end of the line. Miriam had hung up. Frederick had enjoyed the conversation. There was something intimate about the double entendres and the circumlocutions. He wished it could have gone on longer. But there would be more time for that tomorrow, at the playground—at the Tivoli.

MAY 14
DAY THREE

Chapter Seventeen

Borgmann's wake-up call came at seven-thirty, too early so far as his sense of fatigue was concerned, but exactly when he had ordered it. The Kong Frederik was a well-run establishment.

He pulled himself out of bed, showered, shaved and dressed. Downstairs in the hotel, he had a light breakfast, including some of the light, flaky Danish pastry that had been defamed by soggy, heavy American imitations.

By the time he finished, it was about twenty minutes to nine. There was no need to hurry. The Hafnia was within four blocks of the Tivoli. Borgmann stepped outside and glanced up at the old clock in the big red brick Town Hall tower to check his watch. He was just a minute slow—not bad, since the old clock was known to lose only one minute every century.

All around him, people were on their way to work. The number of bicyclists, especially, surprised him. The boxy yellow buses were lined up in front of the Town Hall like elephants. As soon as one moved out, it was replaced by another.

Borgmann looked across the huge cobblestone plaza in front of Town Hall to the building at the corner of Hans Christian Andersen Boulevard and Vesterbrogade—the one with the dark brick tower at the near corner, topped by a huge Irma Kaffee ad. He squinted up at the tower. Almost at the top, but below the coffee ad, was a copper-colored turntable that carried two life-sized bronze figures. When the weather was expected to be fair, he remembered, the figure of a girl riding a bicycle would be visible. When the forecast was for rain, the visible figure would be on foot, carrying an umbrella. Today he could see the girl on her bicycle.

Borgmann walked toward the Tivoli, which was just across the street from that building, feeling confident and buoyant. Today, he thought, would be the day. They'd discover where the plans were hidden in their search through the Tivoli this morning—or Dahlgaard would give them the necessary information this afternoon. After that, the plans would be on their way back to the Netherlands and forever lost to Israel, for all practical purposes.

There it was in front of him, the baroque, two-story entrance to the amusement park, with its massive stone arch and tiled roof. Already there were crowds in front of the place, even though it was not due to open for another ten minutes or so. There were also several police cars in view, some of them with dome lights flashing. Something was going on there, and Borgmann did not like the look of it.

Jack Salter stepped back, out of the crowd, but he made no attempt to run. That was one of the first things he'd learned at Foggy Bottom. People who run get chased. People who stand and watch are usually ignored. Besides, he was hardly anxious to get back to the Nyhavn office. Stabile would be waiting for him and, Salter was sure, would be mad as hell. He'd accuse him of exceeding his instructions this time. Damn it, he'd done just that—there was no way to deny it. However, if he'd done less, the girl would have been killed. In its way, that would have been exceeding his instructions, too. Yes—that was his defense, that was what he'd tell Stabile. If everything had worked out perfectly, it would have been a standoff. But the Arab had the drop on the Israeli girl. If Salter hadn't intervened—well, there was no use repeating it all to himself.

The police certainly hadn't wasted any time getting here. It was very impressive. In Amsterdam or London, the cops would take at least fifteen minutes to respond to even a fusillade of shots. He'd seen it happen.

Salter moved forward, into the curious but somewhat edgy crowd. Only he knew that the danger was entirely past. Now the police were beginning to tell the crowd to disperse. He intended to follow instructions, of course.

Despite police orders, Salter noted, one man continued to approach—a tall fellow, slender, dark-haired, wearing horn-rimmed glasses. He had strong, regular features. As the man approached, Salter realized that this was probably Dr. Frederick Borgmann. Here, he thought, was a fine opportunity to keep the ball rolling. And redeem himself in Stabile's eyes somewhat. He put himself in Borgmann's path.

"Excuse me," Borgmann said to Salter, in English, "do you know what's going on here?"

"I'm not sure," Salter replied. "Some shots were fired; then the police showed up. Whatever it was, it's over now."

Borgmann looked around the Tivoli entrance with increasing concern. There was no Miriam in sight. Could she have had some connection with the shots? At almost the same instant, he heard the odd, banshee siren of an approaching ambulance, alternating high and low notes, an ominous caricature of a child's whistle. The ambulance screeched to a stop at the Tivoli gate and three white-coated attendants hurried inside. Salter and Borgmann pushed forward, against the police lines.

Soon, the ambulance attendants came out of the park, carrying a stretcher which bore the motionless form of Abdul Amer. Borgmann felt his mouth go dry and his stomach turn to lead. If Amer was shot, what about Miriam? Had she shot him? Had he shot back? Where was she?

A few feet away, Borgmann watched a policeman questioning one of the ambulance attendants. The attendant shook his head. Amer was dead.

"My God," Borgmann said aloud.

"Looks as though the man is dead," Salter said coolly.

"Yes." Borgmann craned his neck to see if the ambulance attendants were going back in the park. Was there another body in there? The attendants slid Amer's body into the ambulance and slammed the door shut. Then the ambulance drove off, this time without the siren.

"Guess that does it," Salter said. The police also began to leave the scene. Salter watched Borgmann as Borgmann looked toward the gate. There was now no question in Salter's mind about the man. "You know," he said thoughtfully, "that man looked like an Arab. Didn't you think so?"

"Maybe so," Borgmann said. He wasn't interested in chitchat.

"What's the world coming to?" Salter asked rhetorically. "Arabs getting shot in the Tivoli."

"There's probably more to it than we can guess."

"I suspect so. Well, I have to be off. Have a nice day, Mr.—"

"Borgmann," Frederick said without thinking.

Salter smiled and drifted away.

Borgmann hardly realized he'd been talking with anyone. His eyes still searched the scene for Miriam, without success. He checked his watch—9:10. Surely she'd been there when the shooting took place. But where was she now? The more he thought about it, the more worried he got.

People were now starting to buy entrance tickets at the Tivoli gate. Borgmann joined them, went inside and continued to search for Miriam. There was no sign of the girl. What if she were hurt? Or just badly frightened? He realized he knew of only one other place to look for her—the porno shop.

Borgmann turned and strode out of Tivoli.

"Will you be coming back, sir?" asked a smiling female ticket taker. "We can give you a return check."

"No," Borgmann said. "I think not. Thank you anyway."

For a moment, he debated with himself about the fastest way to get to the porno shop from the Tivoli—by cab or on foot. It was about ten blocks away. His worry mounting, he quickly scanned the streets for an empty cab. There were none in view. He started walking in the direction of the porno shop. Borgmann had always been a fast walker, and now he was outdoing himself. His long, purposeful stride quickly transformed itself into nothing less than a heel-and-toe run—the fastest pace he could manage without attracting too much attention from the tourists, shoppers and working people through which he threaded his way.

About ten minutes later, half a block from the porno shop, Borgmann saw Miriam's Saab pulled off to the side of the street, more or less parked in a bus stop. He raced into the shop with hardly a nod to the salesgirl and rammed open the bookshelf-door leading to Ben-Ezra's office.

Suliman Ferrara was just about ready to pack it up. All of those conferences with Palestinian leaders had come to nothing. Nothing, that is, except Abdul Amer. Which still meant nothing. He'd waited here in the apartment for a full day past the appointed moment. Now it was time to see if one last promise had been kept. If the Palestinians had reneged on this one, there was nothing left to do but to go home and tell Amer to do the same himself. He pulled out his Copenhagen street map and located his destination—the central post office—then walked out the door.

The main post office was at 35 Tietgensgade, right beside the railroad station and cater-corner from the rear entrance to the Tivoli. It was only a couple of blocks away. Ferrara glanced at his watch. It was a few minutes till nine. He should be there by the time it opened.

Actually, he arrived a bit early. The guard was just

187

unlocking the door. Ferrara followed him in, then found the general delivery window. He was pleased to see there was no line.

"Any mail for Steven Furnal?" he asked.

The clerk went back to his cubbyholes. He returned with a letter and handed it to Ferrara. "Nothing more?" Ferrara asked, disturbed. "No package?"

"Packages are at window 18," The clerk told him.

"Thank you."

Ferrara found the proper window. Now there were two people ahead of him. He waited, quite impaiently. Then he remembered the letter. He examined the envelope, which bore a Czechoslovak postmark. Then his turn came. "My name is Steven Furnal," he said. "Any packages for me?"

The clerk searched a big bin behind him. As Ferrara watched, he came up with three separate packages, none of them larger than his palm. The clerk turned and placed them on the counter. "Identification, please."

Ferrara was staring at the trio of brown-wrapped boxes. He had expected one. What could be in the other two?

"Identification, please," the clerk repeated, his voice just as polite as before.

"Oh, sorry." Ferrara pulled out his wallet and showed the man an international driver's license. The clerk glanced at it and pushed the packages toward Ferrara, who took them and walked toward the post office door.

Well, he thought, with some satisfaction, feeling a trace of optimism again, maybe it will all work out. This time, they kept their promise. Maybe there were grounds for hope.

Ferrara walked back toward · his apartment as quickly as possible. He was anxious to see what was in the separate boxes and to read the letter. He needed privacy for both.

Inside, Ferrara ripped the letter open. It contained a single sheet of paper—a mimeographed set of instructions. He put it on the desk and opened the longest of the three boxes. Inside, packed in cotton, was a short, hollow, yellow-green plastic tube, open at both ends. Ferrara set it aside and opened another box. It contained a firing chamber, hammer and trigger assembly—also made from what appeared to be yellow-green plastic. The last box contained a combination handle and cartridge chamber—again, constructed of plastic. The cartridge chamber was loaded.

Now Ferrara once more turned to the instructions. They were in English. *"To the user:"* they began. *"These are your instructions for assembling the Topoliev nonradiographic hand weapon. Please note: this all-fiberglass weapon cannot be detected by any known X-ray or metal detection devices such as those now commonly in use in all international airports and most major United States airports. Any standard 9mm rounds may be used, however, the user is cautioned not to carry more than three on his person or in hand luggage when traveling by air, as more may trigger weapons detection devices. The Agency urges concealment of the weapon to prevent accidental discovery and requires its return upon completion of your present mission. Now please refer to the diagram below. Grasp part A with the thumb and forefinger of the left hand . . ."*

Fifteen minutes later, Suliman Ferrara held in his hand the completed pistol. It looked, he decided, exactly like a child's water gun.

Chapter Eighteen

Barging into Ben-Ezra's office, Borgmann found exactly what he had hoped to find—Miriam Shazar, alive and well, though obviously shaken. She'd been talking with Ben-Ezra, and Borgmann's rambunctious entrance had frightened both of them, bringing them to their feet.

"Good morning, Frederick," Ben-Ezra said, regaining his composure.

"Sorry I didn't knock," Borgmann apologized. He turned to Miriam. "I was worried about you. There was a shooting at the Tivoli and Abdul Amer was killed."

"I know," she said quietly, taking a deep breath. "I was there."

Once again, Borgmann remembered that there was a soft side to the girl, that her cool, invulnerable superwoman image was just that—an image.

"I was worried about you."

"I'm sorry I couldn't stay, Frederick. It didn't seem like a healthy thing to do."

"She was sure you'd come here, Frederick," Ben-Ezra put in. He sat down heavily in the chair behind the desk.

"Yes. You knew Amer was dead?"

"I thought he was." Miriam slumped back in the guest chair. For the moment, anyhow, her spirits were low.

"Then why did you have to leave so fast?"

Borgmann asked, perplexed. "Were you worried about the police?" He towered over her.

"Frederick, I didn't shoot Amer. He shot at *me*. I was about to fire back when someone else shot him."

"Someone else? Who?"

"I haven't any idea. I thought I might be his next target—that's why I ran."

Borgmann looked at Ben-Ezra. "Do you have any other assistants?"

The Israeli shook his head. "No. At least none that are known to me."

"Could someone be aiding you without your knowledge?"

"That's what we were talking about when you came in," Ben-Ezra said. "That and some other enemies."

"Other enemies?"

"Someone took a shot at me at about the same time Amer was shooting at Miriam this morning."

Borgmann was shocked. "You're not serious."

Ben-Ezra couldn't help smiling. "Would I joke about something like that?" He waited until Borgmann returned the grin. "Well, I'm not joking this time. Five shots were fired at me and if I hadn't been walking past a lamp post at the time, I might not be here now. This was no warning—whoever was shooting wanted me dead."

"Was it the man in the blue Volvo?" Borgmann asked.

Miriam looked at the floor. Evidently she and Ben-Ezra had just covered the same territory.

"No," she said. "Whoever it was was driving a light grey Mercedes."

There was silence in the room for a moment. Borgmann pulled himself up on the desk and sat. He was puzzled and depressed.

Ben-Ezra sensed his mood. "Listen, Frederick," he said, trying to reassure the man, "this isn't the first time I've been shot at seriously."

"I know," Borgmann said quietly.

"Even in Copenhagen. There have been three deliberate attempts on my life in the last four years."

"Have you been badly wounded?"

"In my book, you're badly wounded when you die from it."

"I mean, have you had to be hospitalized?"

"Once. It's all part of the business. I faced the same risks when I first came here—when we met."

Borgmann nodded. He hadn't been soothed at all. "I don't know about all of this, Yaakov. In the last two days you've been shot at twice, and Miriam's been the target once. You don't even know who your assailants were. What guarantee do we have that the shootings will stop? It's getting more and more dangerous."

"Frederick, I know you better than to think you're afraid. What disturbs you now?" Ben-Ezra's voice was calm and strong.

"I'm not afraid, Yaakov; you're right. Besides, no one has shot at me—yet. I'm just not sure the plans are worth your death—or Miriam's. Maybe we should take these warnings seriously."

"I can take care of myself," the girl said interrupting. The image was back in place, repaired as if it had been smeared makeup.

"The stakes are high, Frederick. I've already told you how important the centrifuge plans are to Israel. Consider something else: how would Israel fare if *Fatah* got hold of the plans? That's who Amer was working for, you know." It was a disquieting thought. Ben-Ezra went on with it, developing it. "Just imagine a Palestinian terrorist group destroying Tel Aviv with a nuclear weapon. Israel would have to respond in kind. And who could predict what would happen then? I have a feeling that even the citizens of Chicago, where you live, Frederick—even they would be affected."

"If you only knew how difficult it was for me to associate myself with this, Yaakov—"

"Believe me, I understand. But you are already more involved than you know."

Miriam glanced at her father, puzzled.

"What do you mean, Yaakov?" asked Borgmann.

"Something appears to have happened to your Dr. Torngren. Here, you know this language better than I do—tell us the details." Ben-Ezra handed Borgmann the morning newspaper, which he took with a furrowed brow.

Borgmann read aloud, translating as he went: "Dr. Arne Torngren, Finnish delegate to the current Conference of Nuclear Energy being held at Bohr Institute, was found shot to death early this morning in his room at the Hotel Cuba by a charwoman. There were no signs of a struggle, and since Dr. Torngren's wallet and personal possessions were intact, police have ruled out robbery as motive. Copenhagen Chief of Police Alf Landsberg has promised a full investigation of the murder. 'We will not rest until the perpetrator is found,' he told reporters.

"Meanwhile, the Danish Prime Minister has expressed his regrets to the Government of Finland and to Dr. Torngren's family. The scientist's body will be flown to Finland today at the request of relatives.

"According to the police report, two bullets were fired into Dr. Torngren at near point-blank range as he stood at his door, apparently responding to a knock. Since the occupants of nearby rooms say they heard no shots, nor any sounds of a commotion, police believe that a silencer was used. No motive for the killing is known and some officials believe it may have been a case of mistaken identity. . . ."

Borgmann looked up from what he'd been reading, his face ashen. "Yaakov—did you do this?"

Ben-Ezra snorted. "Me? Kill Torngren? No, my friend. In a way, you were responsible for his death."

"What do you mean by that?"

"When you unmasked him back at the conference, he evidently guessed that you were also not exactly what you seemed. He must have reported that back to his KGB superiors in Leningrad." Ben-Ezra stopped, as if that explained everything.

"I don't understand," Borgmann said, almost stammering. "So what if he did send a report on me to Leningrad. What did that have to do with his murder?"

Ben-Ezra and Miriam exchanged glances.

"I took steps to protect you, Frederick. When you

193

agreed to join us, I could not allow you to shoulder all the personal risks."

"You gave me a bodyguard?"

"Not exactly. I want you to know this is top secret—but we have men in the Soviet Union, in the KGB. They were asked to divert any suspicion or danger away from you."

Silence fell over the room again as Ben-Ezra waited for the information to sink in.

Ben-Ezra shrugged. "Another Russian, I believe. Perhaps a GRU man. I understand they and the KGB have been having their troubles lately." He tried to catch Borgmann's eye and failed. "Frederick, I did not mean for this to happen. But better he than you."

"Was that the choice, Yaakov?" Borgmann sounded glum.

"I think so, Frederick."

The silence returned.

"I know you were not prepared for this sort of thing, Frederick, but you can be sure that Torngren knew the risks," said Miriam compassionately.

Borgmann nodded. "And Abdul Amer?"

"He also knew the risks," Miriam said.

"But who killed him?"

"We don't know," said Ben-Ezra.

"Could it have been the same man who killed Torngren?"

Ben-Ezra thought a moment. "Unlikely. I don't think he would have had any way to know about Amer."

Ben-Ezra took a deep breath and winced. He attempted to make it look like a yawn. "I just hope that our anonymous helper keeps on helping us for awhile. We need him. And we need you, Frederick. According to your copy of the conference schedule, there will be two more closed sessions before the meeting ends —one this afternoon, one tomorrow afternoon. If we don't get the plans sometime during that period, they'll be beyond us forever."

"Frederick, you can't change your mind now," Miriam said, imploring him. "You must help us."

There was no way Borgmann could refuse her. His recent experience at the Tivoli had taught him how much he cared. "I gave my word, Miriam. I'm not about to beg off, not now. I'll go back to the conference and do my best to get Dahlgaard to tell me where the plans are."

"It's our best chance, Frederick," Ben-Ezra said. "It may be our only chance."

"Doesn't the conference begin at eleven?" Miriam asked Borgmann.

"My God" Borgmann said, jumping off the desk and looking at his watch. "I'd better get going."

"I'll take you," Miriam said.

"Fine," said Borgmann.

"Wait a minute," Ben-Ezra said, interrupting. "The less you two are seen together, the better."

"Yaakov, we've already been seen together over half of Copenhagen," Miriam said flatly. "Our enemies, whoever they are, must already know Frederick is with us."

For a moment, Ben-Ezra seemed about to reply, to argue. He reconsidered, though, as if he didn't want to make more trouble than there already was.

Then Borgmann and Miriam hurried out of the office.

Chapter Nineteen

Yaakov Ben-Ezra watched his daughter leave the room. She seemed so sure of herself, so blunt, so much a creature of the present, so contemptuous of him and his generation. Only he knew how much of this was an act, an almost reflexive pretense.

He leaned back in his chair and closed his eyes, remembering better days. It had not been easy for him to bring up a daughter. Miriam had been just a toddler in 1948, when her mother was killed in the initial Arab onslaught against the new nation of Israel. He'd brought her up with the help of friends in Tel Aviv.

He could picture her, at age ten, a brash youngster with much more energy than her father, who knew everything and wasn't afraid to tell anyone who asked. They were friends. They were more than that. Ben-Ezra hadn't particularly wanted a son, but their relationship was more father-and-son than father-and-daughter, probably because Miriam was so much a tomboy. More than that, though, there was a tenderness between them, for, despite her brashness, there was an underlying layer of sentiment.

She's started to retreat into her shell when she was in high school. It started when she followed her friends into GADNA (Regiments of Youth). Ben-Ezra didn't like the organization. He didn't like seeing high school students adopt a Spartan regimen, watching them emphasize endurance, physical strength, and discipline. He didn't like having Miriam participate in any organization with military overtones—but he never considered forbidding her.

He was home one day when she returned from a GADNA meeting, bubbling over with enthusiasm. "We're learning to be strong and courageous," she said. "It's never too early to learn that."

"Perhaps," he replied, doubtful. "But in my opinion, a person's strength must come from the inside. The greatest strength comes from a belief in the dignity of man."

"Yuli would say that you are soft."

"Yuli? Who is this Yuli?"

To his astonishment, Miriam had blushed. That explained a great deal.

A few months later Yuli was replaced by Daniel, a true believer in the present, a prophet of Israel's national destiny.

"We have a history, Miriam," Ben-Ezra told her. "We have not just suddenly materialized in Israel at this moment. There are reasons for the existence of our country. You know some of them, I am sure. I think it would be good if you learned the rest."

It was a dangerous business, pitting himself against Miriam's boyfriend this way, but Ben-Ezra was never one to keep his feelings or opinions to himself. Fortunately, Daniel, too, moved on. For a time, Miriam walked her own path, which, Ben-Ezra felt, was just as well.

Then, another interest entered her life. To Yaakov's initial pleasure and approval, Miriam decided to spend her vacations as an unpaid archaeological volunteer. She worked with Dr. Yigael Yadin, an old friend. Dr. Yadin was excavating a huge brown rock twelve hundred feet above the desert, with almost vertical sides, two and a half miles from the Dead Sea—Masada.

During most of this time—in the early 1960s—Ben-Ezra was at home. *Mossad* had given him a desk job, which he hated. Every night, Miriam would come home and tell him more about Masada.

The story was known well enough. In the years just before the birth of Jesus Christ, Herod, the Jewish

King (and Roman puppet), had built himself a palace on top of Masada, full of pseudo-Roman splendor, mosaic floors, baths and frescoes. The main entrance was cut into the face of the rock. Long underground tunnels—"the snake path"—led up to the palace.

Herod died in 4 B.C., not a moment too soon for his subjects. Masada became a Roman garrison. In 66 A.D., the Jews began a fight to rid themselves of their Roman overlords. For a year or so, it seemed as though they might win. But Emperor Nero sent his best legions and his best general, Vespasian, to put down the revolt. The Jews had long since captured Masada. A desperate band of Essenes, Zealots, and commandos the Romans called *Sicarii* (Jewish dagger-men) had killed the Roman garrison, then brought their wives and children to Masada. They numbered nearly a thousand.

Finally, in the fourth year of the rebellion, one complete Roman legion, ten thousand men in this case, commanded by Flavius Silva, was given the task of taking Masada, the last remaining Jewish stronghold. Flavius Silva threw up a wall around the fortress to make escape impossible. Twelve hundred feet above the desert floor, where the Roman general and his men encamped, one thousand Jews lived on a plateau about half a mile across.

Masada held out for three years. Even then, only a stupendous engineering feat sealed the fate of the defenders. Flavius Silva selected a rocky ledge 450 feet below the level of the fortress and built a solid earthen base on that 300 feet high. A stone pier raised the level another 75 feet. On this, the Romans somehow managed to place heavy siege guns and a 90-foot ironclad tower, which was topped with light artillery. Eventually, with additions, the Roman tower stood higher than the walls of Masada itself. The next step was a battering ram. It was hauled up the man-made mountain and its huge stone ball began to swing against Masada's masonry walls.

Still the Jews resisted. They built an inner wall of wood and packed it with earth. Each time the ball of the battering ram hit the old wall, it compressed the new earthen wall, making it stronger. Now Flavius Silva ordered burning torches catapulted into Masada. Soon one of the new wooden walls was aflame. It crashed with a roar, and Masada was exposed.

Flavius Silva planned to enter the fortress the next morning and take prisoner what defenders remained alive. But he did not reckon with Masada's commander, Eleazar Ben Yair. With what must have been remarkable eloquence and persuasion, Ben Yair convinced the entire population of the fortress to submit to suicide, rather than die at the hands of the Romans or be enslaved. In the end, 960 bodies—men, women and children—were found by the Romans. Only two old women and five children—all somehow hidden—survived.

Bit by bit, the excavations of Yigael Yadin confirmed this story, which had come down through history in the works of the Jewish historian Josephus, himself a Roman soldier in that war. Miriam told Ben-Ezra, wrote him, sometimes called him in her excitement to announce one discovery or another. It was a thrilling time for both of them. But even then, Ben-Ezra sensed that this was not the Jewish history he would have wished Miriam to rediscover.

"There is a lesson in Masada," she told him.

"What is that?"

"First, there must be strength—absolute, incorruptible strength."

It was a tempting thought. And this was not the first time in his life he'd been tempted by it. "No," he told her. "Strength is important, but it is not first. The first goal of life must be to live, not to be strong. That's when Ben Yair went wrong. If I hadn't felt that way, you wouldn't exist. You are the evidence of the joy your mother and I had together—the only evidence, except for my memories."

He never forgot what Miriam said to him then. "Joy is a risk," she said. "It invites tragedy."

"It is worth the risk."

"You say that now, with my mother—your wife—dead at the hands of the Arabs?"

"Yes."

It was not that he felt Miriam and her generation should choose weakness—far from it. But Israel was meant to be an expression of the best of Judaism, a country where people of hope and joy could flourish, if only their enemies would let them be.

There was something too uncommitted about Miriam for Ben-Ezra's taste. She allowed herself pleasure, but only the pleasure of the moment. Her attachments were fleeting, superficial. She seemed either unable or too frightened to love. Her youthful sentiment apparently had taken refuge somewhere deep inside. Sixteen-year-old girls shouldn't be that way, Ben-Ezra felt. After some thought, he believed he'd come up with a way to bring her out of her shell, to give her a feeling of continuity so that she would seek more on her own. He would take her to Yad Mordechai.

One bright day, the two of them drove South from Tel Aviv in Ben-Ezra's boxy brown Israeli-built Susita, along the winding coastal road, past the orange groves, the cotton fields, the vineyards and the banana plantations on the left, with the startlingly blue Mediterranean on the right. They drove through the gleaming white city of Ashkelon, reborn from the days of the Philistines, past canning factories and *kibbutzim*. They could see the cowsheds, chicken coops, orchards and vegetable beds from the road, likewise the arenas, theaters, schools and movie houses.

There are about twenty-five *kibbutzim* between Ashkelon and the Gaza Strip, the old Egyptian-Israeli border. On that day in 1965, he and his daughter were heading for Yad Mordechai, the southernmost of the Israeli *kibbutzim*. It wasn't the first time that father and daughter had made this pilgrimage. It was here that Karen Ben-Ezra had died. The trip wasn't intended as another visit to the grave, however.

Yad Mordechai had been founded in August 1943, and, before Ben-Ezra had parachuted into Denmark, he'd had a hand in that, along with about two hundred others, mostly Poles. The *kibbutz* was named after Mordechai Anlevicz, the commander of the desperate, futile Jewish uprising in the Warsaw ghetto in February 1943.

Here in Yad Mordechai, Jacob Kaplan—now Yaakov Ben-Ezra—had lived for three reasonably peaceful years, with his wife Karen and his baby daughter, born just before they'd left Copenhagen. In that period Ben-Ezra was a farmer, not a secret agent.

The end of that peace came in November 1947, when the United Nations agreed to partition Palestine into two countries, one consisting of 650,000 Jews, the other of about 1,200,000 Arabs—with the Jews holding most of the best land and the largest cities.

Ben-Ezra left his farm and went back to *Haganah* headquarters to offer his services. It was clear to every Jewish settler when the British surrendered control of the area, that the Arabs wouldn't simply accept the partition without argument. The *Haganah* found a use for him. They sent him to Czechoslovakia, to buy arms from Jan Masaryk. Then, he went to Italy, in search of the *Lino*.

When he returned from his missions, the *Haganah* sent him back to Yad Mordechai. Men were needed for its defense. Local bands of Arabs were sure to attack, but if the *kibbutzim* were prepared, the attacks could be beaten off.

As the deadline for British withdrawal approached, the war between the Arabs and the Israelis began in earnest, even though the British were just beginning to pack their bags. Ben-Ezra and about eighty others—the total fighting force of the *kibbutz*—strung barbed wire, dug trenches, built what bunkers they could. Despite their proximity to Egypt, they felt they could hold their own against any marauding Arabs.

On May 14, 1948, the State of Israel was born—and was immediately recognized by the United States. On May 15, the British pulled out the last of their troops. And an estimated 23,500 Arabs, well equipped with British and French tanks, airplanes, artillery and plenty of rifles and ammunition, attacked the new nation from all sides. Against them were 3,000 Israeli *Palmach* regulars and 14,000 *Haganah* militiamen, who had 10,-

000 rifles (and 50 bullets for each), 3,600 machine guns, 4 rusty Mexican cannons, a few Piper Cubs and no tanks.

Among the first Israeli settlements to face the full fury of the Arabs was Yad Mordechai. Instead of being attacked by Arab guerillas, the *kibbutz* was hit by a full Egyptian brigade, well armed, equipped with tanks and armored vehicles. To stop them, the men of Yad Mordechai had a few rifles, a few machine guns, 400 hand grenades and a couple of mortars.

The attack began on May 19. On May 21, Karen Ben-Ezra was killed by fragments from an Egyptian mortar shell. On May 23, Yaakov was wounded in the shoulder. That night, the last machine gun overheated and the barrel burned out. The game was up. Of the eighty defenders, twenty-four were dead and thirty wounded. Twenty-six men could not stop a brigade. The next morning, Yad Mordechai was abandoned.

It was this Yad Mordechai Ben-Ezra wanted to show his daughter. He wanted her to see not only the remnants of the battle, but the Yad Mordechai that had been recaptured and rebuilt from the rubble in 1949. Now, perhaps, she was old enough to understand.

"I'd be just as happy if we turned back now," Miriam said as their car approached the *kibbutz*. "I don't like seeing her grave."

"We'll skip the grave this time, Miriam. I thought you might want to see the town where you spent the first few years of your life."

It wasn't the whole reason, and both of them knew it.

He drove past the *kibbutz* itself, to a nearby park. Together they walked around it for a while, Ben-Ezra showing Miriam the bronze statue of Mordechai Anlevicz, for whom the *kibbutz* was named. She'd nodded without comment. Then he brought her into the center of the park. The water tower lay here. It had fallen to its side on May 20, 1948, a punctured mass of concrete and steel reinforcing wires, riddled by Egyptian cannons. Now it served as a memorial to the men who had died guarding the *kibbutz*. Ben-Ezra told Miriam its story.

"Is there a sufficient water supply now?" she asked truculently, angry that he was putting her through this.

"Now? I suppose so. There must be five-hundred people living in Yad Mordechai now. The farms are well irrigated."

"Then this is really useless junk."

"It is a memorial," said Ben-Ezra.

"I see no purpose to it."

"And what about Masada—was there no purpose to excavating that?"

"That's different."

Then they walked through a small forest, a grove of trees that had not existed in 1948, to a small museum.

"I do not much like museums," Miriam had said.

"Consider it a family album."

They walked slowly through the museum exhibits. In them, Yad Mordechai came to life again, as did its first settlers. Ben-Ezra was in the pictures, as was Karen—and Miriam, for that matter. For a time, tension eased as father and daughter made identifications. Then they were past the *kibbutz* exhibits, into the section that commemorated life in the Warsaw ghetto, life—if that's what it was—in the concentration camps. Seeing the photographs of Warsaw was, for Ben-Ezra, like being flung backward in time. He had not seen these pictures before. They brought back memories of such power that he had to struggle to hold onto the present. He turned to Miriam in search of contact, even support. But she was fighting battles of her own.

They walked out of the museum into the bright sunlight and the oppressive hold of the memories eased somewhat. Soon, they were in the heart of the *kibbutz* itself, among well-kept wooden houses and concrete-block public buildings.

As they walked past, the men watched Miriam appreciatively—which pleased Ben-Ezra. He wanted her to see that other things mattered here besides strength, though the border was only yards away.

Down the street a way, Miriam stopped to watch a

young man pulling a ladder onto the roof of a small house. He was struggling with it, still he managed to smile at her.

"Want some help?" she asked.

"Glad to have it. Why don't you come up to the roof? There's a stairway inside. I'll push the ladder up to you."

Miriam did as instructed. Soon she was tugging on the ladder as the young man pushed it skyward. Ben-Ezra gave the young man a hand. Shortly the ladder was on the roof, and so was the young man. Miriam, however, did not come down. She stood looking out toward the sand dune, shielding her eyes with her hand.

"Over there—" she called down to her father—"is that an Arab refugee camp?"

"Yes. It's just on the other side of the sand dune."

She gazed at it for a while, her expression one of disbelief. Then she turned to street level again. "You know how they're living there?"

Ben-Ezra shrugged. "I suppose so."

"It's horrible. They're jammed together in tents and huts. Dogs live better. I wonder how the *kibbutzniks* can stand it, knowing of the poverty just over the sand dune."

"Stand it? They cannot be concerned with it. They must build their own lives."

Miriam's face bore a thoughtful look. "I wonder," she said, "just how I would feel if I were there instead of here, living as an Arab, not a Jew."

Ben-Ezra felt his anger rising. "Listen, Miriam, we're not responsible for their poverty. It's a circumstance of war."

"Doesn't Yad Mordechai now cultivate lands that were once owned by the Arabs?"

"Yes, but it isn't the way it sounds. When we first came here, we bought the lands. The Arabs were happy to sell them to us. Those who did not sell lived with us as good neighbors."

"Where are they now?"

"What would you have us do, Miriam? Should we have surrendered to them? Should we not have attempted to recapture the *kibbutz?* Should we have gone back to Poland?"

"I don't know. I haven't any answer. But this one seems unjust."

"And so it did to us, Miriam. The men of Yad Mordechai were of the Mapam Party. From the first, we had wanted a binational state. We wanted the Arabs to live with us, to be part of Israel. It was not possible."

"So you say."

"The Arabs rejected the peace, not the Israelis. And the pattern was set long before the 1948 war. If you'll remember your history, you'll recall that in 1919, by the terms of the Balfour Declaration, the British offered the Jews a tiny homeland within Palestine that almost certainly would have become part of an Arab Palestine. If the Arabs had gone along with this, Arabs and Jews could now be living in Palestine in harmony, much as Arabs and Maronite Christians live in harmony in Lebanon. But the Arabs refused. There were many more British proposals in the late nineteen-thirties. All were rejected by the Arabs. The Jews were willing to accept nearly anything, so long as it was official and recognized. Two years before the war, the British offered their last plan, for a sort of city-state for the Jews, along with immigration limited to one hundred thousand persons. The Arabs refused again."

"The Arabs were stubborn," Miriam said. "They remind me of the Jews at Masada."

Ben-Ezra was horrified. "How can you say that?"

"They were fighting for what they believed was right, and they were not willing to give up an inch. Now, they've lost, but still they do not give up."

"Must I doubt your sympathies?"

She ignored his insult. "Have you ever imagined yourself an Arab, Father? If you were an Arab, wouldn't you fight to regain your homeland with all you had? Wouldn't you be willing to die? You cannot tell me you wouldn't—you did no less, either at Yad Mordechai or a dozen other times."

"They are our enemies, Miriam. It isn't the same."

"I agree with you. They are our enemies. But we must understand them."

He seized on that. "Won't the understanding weaken you?"

"No. Because we understand the Arabs, we are more dangerous opponents than you were."

They rode back to Tel Aviv nearly in silence. Perhaps the time was over when father and daughter could still make contact. Was it this way with all fathers and daughters, Ben-Ezra wondered? Or was the barrier between himself and Miriam somehow the result of Karen's death? Had he built it himself, by spending so much time away from her? And was it only a barrier between himself and his daughter, or between his daughter and anyone else?

There was no way to answer the question. And there seemed no way to destroy the barrier. Love, evidently, was not enough. But that didn't mean he would stop trying.

Chapter Twenty

Gary Stabile was sitting behind the big desk at the Nyhavn house, feet up, reading a copy of the *Manchester Guardian* when Jack Salter arrived. He dropped the magazine slightly.

"Well, well. What does the boy genius have to report?" There was no condescension intended.

"I have some good news and I have some bad news," Salter said brightly.

Stabile pulled his feet off the desk and fixed Salter with a hostile gaze. "I don't like that way of talking," he said. "You sound like some kind of comic strip. Tell me what I need to know."

"Yes, sir. What you need to know is that I followed both Miriam Shazar and Abdul Amer to the front gate of the Tivoli. They sneaked in and so did I. Then, they spotted each other and Amer fired a shot at the girl. He missed. She pulled out her gun while he was aiming again. I shot Amer before he had a chance to fire again and I killed him."

"You did what?"

"I shot Amer and killed him."

Stabile looked at Salter as if he were examining an insect just before swatting it. "And just why did you do that, Salter?" he asked, his voice low and even.

"I had to, Gary," Salter pleaded. "He would have killed the girl if I hadn't."

"Did I instruct you to kill Amer?"

"No, but I had to make a judgment on the spot. It was either him or the girl."

"You're a good shot, aren't you, Salter?" Stabile was now completely alert. He stood and moved toward his younger colleague, circling around the man, his eyes little more than slits.

"Yes," Salter admitted, almost reluctantly.

"Couldn't you have wounded Amer? Better yet, couldn't you have missed entirely, throwing him off his aim? Couldn't you have simply shouted 'Police!' and fired your gun into the air?"

Salter took a deep breath before answering. "I suppose so," he said finally. "There wasn't time to consider all the alternatives."

Stabile smiled. It was not a pleasant expression. "Did I at any time instruct you to shoot any of the principals in this case?"

"No, but . . ."

"What did I instruct you?"

"To see what they were doing, to make sure they saw each other, if possible. To not reveal myself at any cost."

"At least you have a good memory, Salter. I wonder if you know how much damage you did." Stabile was now standing next to the younger man, who was slightly taller than he. "You may sit."

Salter sat down. He'd known he was in for a tongue-lashing and he was prepared for it. But there was a coldness to Stabile that was beyond his expectations, even beyond his comprehension.

"First, you directly interfered in the case, against my specific instructions, possibly jeopardizing our goals. Second, you prevented those you were trailing from leading you wherever it was they were going. Third, by taking direct action, you announced your presence and possibly compromised me. I suppose the girl saw you."

"No," Salter said, gulping. "She just ran. I was behind a post. That's how I got the drop on the Arab. Besides, I did pick up one piece of information that may be valuable."

"What's that?" Stabile seemed doubtful.

"I saw Dr. Borgmann outside the Tivoli immediately after the shooting. I even talked to him."

"You talked to him?" Stabile was incredulous, his question an accusation.

"Yes. But just as one bystander to another. It was obvious that he had gone to the Tivoli to meet Miriam Shazar."

"How did you know it was Borgmann?"

"I said good-bye to him as the crowd dispersed—I said 'Mr.' and let him fill in the name, which he did without even thinking about it. I don't think he looked at me for more than half a second. He couldn't take his eyes off the crowd. Looking for the girl, I figure."

"Do you have anything else to report, anything about what either of them did at the Tivoli?"

"The girl seemed to be looking for something."

"Did she head in any particular direction?" Stabile asked, trying to squeeze more blood from the turnip.

"No. She seemed to be starting a systematic search."

"I see. Is that it?"

"Yes."

"You're sure."

"Absolutely."

"Fine. Now pick up the phone and book yourself on a flight out of Copenhagen for New York by tomorrow night. Twenty-four hours is enough to clean up your affairs here, I trust." It was all said almost completely without expression.

"You're taking me off the assignment, Gary?"

"That's right. You blew it, Salter. Oh, you're a smart fellow; I can't take that away from you. But you're a washout as a field man. You flunked the only test there is—choosing the right alternative with only an instant to make up your mind. Agents have to have an instinct about such things, and you don't have it."

"I don't believe what you're telling me, Stabile."

"You're under no obligation to believe, Salter. What I'm telling you comes from years of experience and from a pretty healthy instinct of my own. I have the feeling that if I let you stay on assignment for another minute, you'll mess things up beyond repair. As it is, I have my work cut out for me."

Salter searched for a reply. He felt the fury rising

within him, but there was no way he could let it out without looking like a fool. Besides, if Stabile pursued this matter, Salter knew he could end up in the States permanently, or maybe even out of the organization. "If only I had another chance to prove myself . . ." he began.

"Jack," Stabile said, kindly, "if you were me, would you associate yourself with a man you felt sure could get you killed?"

"Is that what you think?"

"I'm afraid so. Nothing personal, you understand. You're a likable fellow and eager, too. There's just no room for mistakes in the field."

"Your decision is final?"

"Yes." Stabile took his pipe from his jacket pocket and began filling it.

"What are you going to say on your report?"

"I'm going to report the incident as accurately as I can," Stabile told him without altering his tone of voice. He lit his pipe and took a few puffs to start it.

"I see."

"Tell you what, Salter. Take forty-eight hours. See Copenhagen. Enjoy yourself."

There was one last chance and Salter took it. "Stabile, aren't you going to need help here? This is an awfully complicated situation."

The older man chuckled, and that sound alone was enough to convince Salter he needn't have bothered to raise the point. "Now, Jack, I think I can manage by myself. You'd be surprised what one man can accomplish, if he has the instincts for the work."

Chapter Twenty-One

Suliman Ferrara was fitting a bullet into the chamber of his new pistol when there was a knock on his door. Amer, he thought—back already. Maybe he's found something important. Or maybe some help has arrived, tardy but very welcome. He put the gun on the desk and moved toward the door. There was another knock.

"Yes," Ferrara said, "I'm coming."

"Abne døren," came the voice from the outside. *"Politi."*

Ferrara stopped in midstep. The police! Why were they here? What could they know about him? Had Amer done something really stupid? The answers came almost as quickly as the questions, though they were tentative: they were here on some routine matter—after all, he'd done nothing wrong, yet. They knew nothing about him, since there was nothing to know until he acted. On the other hand, Amer might very well have done something stupid. Perhaps the fool is in jail somewhere and he's given them my name for some reason. If that were the case, Ferrara decided, he would wring the man's neck.

"Politi," said the voice, more insistent this time. *"Abne døren."*

"Yes, of course," Ferrara said. "I was just putting on my pants." He opened the door.

In front of him stood a uniformed policeman and a plainclothesman, a chubby man in his middle forties with very red cheeks and a shiny bald head.

"God morgen," the plainclothesman said with a reassuring smile. *"Herr Ferrara?"*

"Yes."

"Taler de Dansk?"

Ferrara looked at the man blankly. If he didn't reveal that he spoke a little Danish, he might have a tremendous advantage in the conversation that followed.

"Forstar De?" the plainclothesman asked.

"I don't understand," Ferrara said. "I don't speak Danish."

"Ah, you speak English," the plainclothesman said. "Fortunately, so do I."

"And you are—"

"Detective Lieutenant Poul Hansen, Homicide Branch, National Security."

Ferrara's eyes opened wide in spite of his attempt to control himself. "Homicide? National Security? I don't understand. Why are you here?"

"May we enter, Mr. Ferrara?"

"Of course."

Ferrara opened the door wide and stepped aside. He used the respite to regain some of his lost composure. Something was seriously wrong. Had Amer killed someone? Even if he had—the idiot—how had the police gotten his name and address?

"May we look at your lodgings, Mr. Ferrara?" the plainclothesman asked politely.

"Of course," Ferrara said. His voice was steady now. How different these Danes were from the police he had always known. They asked politely; they treated you with at least a show of respect. If this had been the Middle East, the uniformed man would have attacked him by now, while the dectective was ripping the apartment to shreds, looking for whatever it was he sought.

Ferrara suddenly remembered the fiberglass gun. He took a step toward the desk, but it was too late. Lieutenant Hansen had already noticed it. He picked it up.

"A water pistol, Mr. Ferrara?" he questioned, still smiling. "Have you any children?" The plainclothesman playfully pointed the weapon at Ferrara, his finger on the trigger.

"Oh, no," Ferrara said. *My God,* he thought, *there's a bullet in that gun!* "I found it under a couch. Must have belonged to a previous occupant. It's empty, of course. I was just going to throw it into the wastebasket."

The plainclothesman looked at the pistol curiously. "Pity," he said. "They're making these rather better than they did when I was young." He located the wastebasket beside the desk and dropped the pistol into it.

"Lieutenant Hansen," Ferrara asked, taking a deep breath, "could you tell me why you are here?"

"Of course, Mr. Ferrara. I was momentarily distracted. I am in charge of the investigation of the death of a certain Mr. Abdul Amer." He paused and looked directly at Ferrara.

Ferrara was flabbergasted and couldn't hide it. "The death! Amer is dead?"

"Yes, Mr. Ferrara, I'm afraid so. I see you did know him."

All at once, Ferrara remembered that he was being interrogated by a police officer. So far, the talk had the trappings of a polite conversation between acquaintances. That, no doubt, was why he'd dropped his guard. Despite the trappings, though, he realized that he was being questioned by a very intelligent, very perceptive policeman.

"Yes," Ferrara said. "He works for the family, in Beirut. A servant." He paused a moment. "But you say he is dead. How can you know that? Why would the Danish National Security Agency be interested in the death of a servant in Beirut?"

Hansen looked at the uniformed policeman, who had been giving the apartment a quick once-over. *"Hvad hedder finde?"*

The cop shook his head. *"Intet."*

This much Danish Ferrara knew. The cop was looking for something and hadn't found it. Perhaps he didn't even know what he was searching for.

Hansen nodded and turned back toward Ferrara.

213

"As a matter of fact, Mr. Ferrara, he died this morning at the Tivoli amusement park."

Ferrara managed to look shocked—and, indeed, he was—but not because Amer was in Copenhagen. Evidently Amer had found something—something important enough to get himself killed, something at the Tivoli. But who had killed him—and why, exactly?

"Abdul was here, in Copenhagen?"

"Indeed he was, Mr. Ferrara. He had your address in his pocket. You were unaware of that?"

"Totally."

"Did you know if he had any plans to visit Copenhagen?"

"He'd talked about it, but I had no idea that he was serious."

"Hvad onsker tror?" Hansen asked the cop.

Did they believe him? Ferrara waited for the cop's answer. It was slow in coming.

"Han er udmaerket," the cop said.

Ferrara puzzled over the expression for a moment, then managed to translate it for himself: he's all right. Good. They believed.

"When did you last see Mr. Amer?" Lieutenant Hansen asked blandly.

"Just before I went to Copenhagen."

"When was that?"

"About ten days ago," Ferrara said.

"And why are you in Copenhagen, Mr. Ferrara?"

"I am a tourist."

Hansen nodded noncommittally. "I see. Well, thank you, Mr. Ferrara. I have no further questions at this time. Except one: when do you plan to leave Denmark?"

"I have no specific plans, Lieutenant Hansen," Ferrara replied. "I might stay as long as six weeks."

"Yes. Well, would you mind giving me a ring before you leave?" Hansen opened his wallet, took out a card and handed it to Ferrara.

"Of course."

"Thank you for being so cooperative, Mr. Ferrara," Lieutenant Hansen said. He started toward the door.

"Wait, I have a question."

"Yes?"

"How did Abdul die?"

Hansen and the uniformed policeman glanced at each other as if seeking agreement. Then Hansen spoke. "He was shot, Mr. Ferrara. There was something of a gun battle."

"I really don't understand," Ferrara said. "Why would anyone want to shoot at Abdul?"

"Well," Hansen said casually, "he was carrying a gun of his own."

"He was?" Ferrara did his best to appear incredulous. He felt he succeeded.

"I think I've already told you more than I should, sir," Hansen said. "We're proceeding with our investigation. You are not suspect, but we may have more questions for you."

"Of course," Ferrara said. "I'll be happy to cooperate in any way you wish."

"You understand we must hold onto the body for a while."

"Yes. I understand."

"Good." Hansen extended his hand and Ferrara took it. They shook, in a carefully polite manner. "Thank you, Mr. Ferrara."

Hansen and the cop left and Ferrara closed the door behind them.

Now he was altogether alone. Possibly it was just as well. There were no illusions now. He must depend entirely upon his own resources. He remembered the gun in the wastebasket, fished it out and put it into his jacket pocket. Then, he left the apartment and headed toward the Tivoli. It was as good a starting place as any.

Chapter Twenty-Two

The ride from the porno shop to Bohr Institute was much tamer than the one Miriam and Frederick had taken the day before, when they had driven to the TV repairman.

"You're sure no one's following us?" Borgmann asked. "Yaakov *did* have a point, you know."

"I've been watching carefully," Miriam said. "There's no one on our tail this time."

"Good."

"To tell you the truth, Frederick, I wanted to go along to, well, ah . . ."

"To protect me?" Borgmann was amused.

"I have had some experience in these matters."

"Yes. I know you have. I appreciate it. I'm just not used to women who can handle themselves so well in dangerous situations. Most women——"

"Are weak and frightened. You're right. In Israel, it is different. We train, almost from our earliest days. We learn to handle weapons, we learn to defend ourselves. I have been shot at several times in my life and, as you can see, I have survived."

"You certainly have."

She smiled. "Don't make fun, Frederick."

The Institute loomed up in front of them. It was almost exactly 11:00.

"What are you going to do now, Miriam?"

"I was thinking of waiting here. Maybe you'll get quick news from your friend Dahlgaard."

"Okay. I'll find him and I'll get back to you within

twenty minutes at the latest. I don't know if he'll have any information for me yet, but if he does, we can act on it right away. If he doesn't . . ."

"Then I'll go back to the Tivoli and resume my search. And we'll arrange to meet when you know more from Dahlgaard. But I'll stay here for twenty minutes."

"Miriam—keep an eye out, will you? I don't think that Yaakov and I can manage this by ourselves."

"Don't worry, Frederick."

Borgmann walked up the steps to the Institute. Half-way up, he looked back at the little green Saab to make sure everything was all right. It was an odd thing, to have his protective instincts aroused by a woman and find that he aroused similar instincts in her.

Miriam watched Borgmann disappear into the Institute. There was nothing to do now but wait and watch for any unwelcome guests. That last glimpse of Frederick as he walked up the steps had stirred memories in her mind, old memories.

This was the second time in her life that Miriam had spent time with Frederick Borgmann. The first was back in the spring of 1954, in Tel Aviv. She had just turned ten; he was about twenty-six.

She'd been hearing of Borgmann's impending visit for weeks. Her father had been conferring with various officials from the government about the young scientist. They'd all thought she was in bed, asleep—but Miriam always eavesdropped whenever adults were talking downstairs in the living room.

From what she gathered before Borgmann's visit, the government was going to offer him some sort of very important job. He knew nothing of this. He was coming, so he thought, on the invitation of an old friend—Ben-Ezra. The job offer would come as a surprise. Night after night, her father and the government officials talked about how Borgmann should be approached, how he should be handled during his stay in Israel. They were most concerned, she recalled, that he feel relaxed and at home, that Borgmann have some sort of social life while he was here.

To Miriam's surprise, this most important guest

wasn't welcomed at Lod Airport by David Ben-Gurion and leading members of the *Knesset*. Instead, she and her father were the only ones to meet him.

Almost before she got a good look at him, Borgmann and her father had embraced warmly, the hug of two men who had faced much together and whose friendship had been born in the midst of a life-and-death struggle. And then, suddenly, she was being hugged too, and swept off her feet, flung to the sky. In a way, Miriam reflected, she'd never come all the way back down to earth from that moment of exultation.

To a ten-year-old girl, Frederick Borgmann was more than just an old friend of her father's. He was handsome, young, strong, a man highly respected by the government and sought after for an important job. He was brilliant, yet full of fun, serious yet charming, full of vitality yet pensive at times. He was tall, dark-haired, strong-jawed and clear-eyed. He was, in short, Prince Charming. Miriam developed an instantaneous crush on him. At age ten, it was her first.

To her surprise, Borgmann had a gift for her—not a doll, thank God. She would have rejected that with disdain. Instead, he bought her a tiny pocket chess set and an instruction book for "beginning and intermediate players," a phrase she still remembered. It was the first time in her life that she had been taken so seriously by an adult.

That night, Frederick and her father talked long past her bedtime. She listened as long as possible, then drifted off to sleep. At breakfast—a breakfast she cooked for both her father and his guest—Frederick said he'd like to see something of Tel Aviv.

Like the child she was, Miriam volunteered eagerly. Her father couldn't be with his guest today—he had urgent business at his office. Rather than letting Borgmann fend for himself, Miriam wanted—more than anything—to accompany him. She knew Tel Aviv and Jaffa as well as anyone. Her father wasn't so sure, but Frederick thought the idea a splendid one.

And so they went off, Frederick and Miriam, the young man and the little girl. Especially since Miriam had been in school, Yaakov Ben-Ezra had taken more and more frequent assignments abroad, leaving her with relatives or friends during his absence. That, she thought, is where her strong feelings of independence originated. She was very much on her own in those days, shopping for herself, getting herself to school and back, eating in restaurants at times, learning that she had good reason to feel self-confident.

Like every big city, Tel Aviv had its street urchins, but Miriam was not one of them. She was smarter than they, better able to handle herself in difficult situations, blessed with a sense of security for which her father was largely responsible. All of these qualities would stand her in good stead in the years to come.

"How shall we tour the city, Miriam?" Frederick had asked the girl. "Shall we rent a car, take buses or do it on foot?"

"Once we get downtown, we go on foot," Miriam said. "Everything else is too fast. If we need to go far, we can always hop on the bus. It's cheaper, you know."

"Don't worry about that, Miriam. The whole tour is on me, meals included." He smiled at her and she felt her insides go warm. "Where do we go first?"

"We catch a bus to Dizengoff Circle. From there we can go anywhere."

Miriam remembered the look that had drawn from Borgmann—amused but respectful. "Do you often go downtown by yourself?"

"All the time."

It was a short ride from Ramat Gan, the "Garden Suburb" where Ben-Ezra had his apartment, to downtown Tel Aviv—perhaps fifteen minutes. "Does every youngster—every young lady—in Tel Aviv speak English?" Borgmann asked.

"A lot of *sabras* do," Miriam said. "We believe in education in Israel, you know." It was such a supercilious remark. Even then, she had regretted it. But Frederick didn't seem disturbed.

"Is there a lot to see in Tel Aviv?" he asked. "I was

hoping to visit some historical sites, perhaps a museum or two, possibly an archaeological excavation."

"The excavation won't be hard," Miriam said, as the bus headed toward the center of the city. "Neither will the museums. But there aren't many historical sites in Tel Aviv. It's a brand-new city, you know."

"As a matter of fact, I don't know much about Tel Aviv."

"Well," Miriam began, remembering her classroom history, "until 1909, there was nothing here but desert. Then a man named Meir Dizengoff and some others founded a place they called Ahuzal Bayit. It was the Jewish suburb of Jaffa. As it grew, they changed the name to Tel Aviv. It means 'Hill of Spring,' in Hebrew."

Frederick pursed his lips appreciatively. "It looks," he said, "as if I've picked the perfect guide."

She beamed.

Miriam looked out of the bus window. "We're here," she said, rising, taking Frederick by the hand and pulling him toward the door. The bus stopped and Frederick and Miriam got off at *Kikar* (Circle) Zina Dizengoff, which was filled with tourists strolling aimlessly and locals on the way to work.

"You'll notice," she went on, "that six streets meet here."

"So they do," Frederick said, bantering with her. "And it looks like every one of them has a movie house. Do you come here often?"

"Father sometimes takes me to the Esther Cinema. But he always complains about the parking—especially at night. There are all sorts of restaurants and nightclubs in the neighborhood."

"Let's sit over there by the fountain, Miriam," Borgmann suggested.

"No, no. We'll come back here. Let's walk—I want to show you the city, you know."

He smiled at her. "Of course. Which way do we go?"

"Up the hill," she said. "I want to show you the Habimah Theater."

They trudged upward a little way. To the left, Borgmann noticed a small cluster of dilapidated wooden huts. "What in the world are those?"

"Those are the slums," Miriam replied. "Poor people live there, or new immigrants. Father told me that the slums will be torn down soon and replaced by new apartment buildings."

"I'm sure they will," Frederick said, still smiling.

"I have the feeling you're not taking me seriously," Miriam said petulantly.

"Of course I am," Frederick protested. "The only reason I'm smiling is that I'm surprised that someone, ah, as young as you are knows so much."

"I see," Miriam said, not entirely satisfied.

"Tell me more."

"Well, you know that Tel Aviv is a very young city," she went on. "It's also changing all the time. They're always building new buildings and tearing down old ones. Look up there and you'll see what I mean."

Ahead of them, between Sderot Tarsat and Huberman, an entire block of older buildings had been ripped down and workmen were putting up the framework of a huge new structure.

"What's that going to be?" Frederick asked.

"A new cultural center," Miriam answered promptly. "It is being named after the lady who donated most of the money to build it—a cosmetic lady, I think."

Borgmann thought a moment. "Jewish?"

"I'm sure."

"Helena Rubenstein?"

"That's it."

They watched the construction workers for a while, then ambled on, toward the foot of Dizengoff. There, where Dizengoff was joined by Rehov Ibn Gvirol and Rehov Haqirya, they were surrounded on all sides by a group of modern public buildings.

"Do you see that building with the trees all around it, the one next to the garden?"

"Ahead of us?"

"Yes. That's the main government building."

"Where Mr. Ben-Gurion works?"

"No, I don't think so. He has an office in another building. I'll show you."

They walked toward a large grey office block on the northeast corner of Haqirya. A small sign indicated that it was the Ministry of Defense.

"Mr. Ben-Gurion works over there," Miriam said, pointing to a smaller building next to the Defense Ministry headquarters. "His office is up there, overlooking the lawn and rose garden."

Borgmann gazed up toward Ben-Gurion's office. "Do you know him, Miriam?"

"Ben-Gurion? Yes. Father took me to see him once. And he visited our apartment another time."

"Your father and Mr. Ben-Gurion make quite a pair," Frederick said.

Miriam laughed. "They joked a lot, like old friends."

Frederick studied the building. "When your father is away, do you miss him a great deal?" he asked finally.

"No," Miriam said perhaps too quickly. "Friends or relatives take care of me."

They walked back toward the buildings under construction. "Let's sit a bit," Frederick suggested. There was a small park near them, Gan Yaakov.

"Father used to tell me they named this park for him," Miriam said, smiling. "Of course, they didn't."

"No."

"There is a story about the park, though. It's supposed to be the place that the city's founders brought their camels on the Sabbath to rest and feed them. They stood under the shade of those trees there and their water came from the well."

"Your father is quite a man, Miriam. Do you know how we met?"

"In Denmark. He told me. Before he met my mother."

"That's right. He saved many lives then, you know. Mine, for example. He took all sorts of risks then. From what I gather, that wasn't the last time."

"You're right, I guess."

To Miriam, that was a peculiar moment—a near-stranger telling her how brave her father was. Of all his

222

qualities, this one she knew least. When he was home, Ben-Ezra was a warm and loving father to his child, a man who left no doubt about what he thought and felt, who always had an extra moment for her—when he was in the country. But too often, when he was gone, off on some mission somewhere, then Miriam waited anxiously for his return, more angry at his absence than worried for his safety. She could never tell him this, however.

"Well," Frederick said, "I've had enough of a rest. Where to now? I'm tired of buildings, I think—how about some fun?"

"Hmm," Miriam said, thinking hard. "Well, the zoo isn't far."

"Would you like to go there?"

"I'd love to," Miriam said. "I haven't been there since I was a little girl."

"That long, huh?"

She punched him in the arm, playfully.

They spent the rest of the morning in the small zoo, off Sderot Karen Kayemet. Miriam discoursed about the birds and animals, gravely serious as she nibbled at a cone of wispy cotton candy. Frederick had bought one for each of them, "so you won't get mad at me if I eat too much of yours."

Then they walked along Karen Kayemet. "Look up the road," Miriam said at one point. "That's where the Ben-Gurions live when they're in Tel Aviv."

Frederick looked in the direction she was pointing. The head of the Israeli government lived in a pleasant but modest home, near a movie house.

They turned at the intersection of Karen Kayemet and Dizengoff, down toward a seemingly endless row of restaurants, shops and cafes. The streets were jammed with tourists and fashionably dressed Israelis. Teen-age girls, especially, abounded, some of them in truly outlandish outfits.

"It's a hangout," Miriam explained.

"Is this where you want to spend your time when you're a little older?"

"Don't be silly. There are lots more important things

to do. There's the army, politics, unions. Father says I shouldn't make my choice until I'm sure."

"You're pretty serious for a ten-year-old."

"Would you rather I were just an empty-headed child?"

Frederick looked at Miriam in surprise, an expression she still cherished without understanding it. "Oh," he said, "I'd much rather you were serious."

"What time is it now?" she asked.

Frederick looked at his watch. "Nearly twelve-thirty."

"Then it's time for lunch," she pronounced.

"I have a feeling you planned it that way, Miriam. It's time for lunch just as we find ourselves on Restaurant Row."

She giggled, once more the little girl.

"I'll bet you even have a particular place in mind," he suggested.

"We could go to the Rowal. But it mostly has cake and ice cream." It was clear from the way that she said it that Miriam didn't expect Frederick to agree. He did, though.

"You know, young lady, I haven't had an ice cream and cake lunch in quite a while. Too long, as a matter of fact. Where is this place you have in mind?"

"There." She pointed down the street. The Rowal was less than half a block away.

Miriam vividly remembered the lunch they'd had together. They'd carefully discussed which flavor ice cream to order and which types of cakes. Then, when they were served, they gleefully traded bites, to the amusement of some of the other patrons and the horror of others. Most of the Rowal's customers were older people, people from the old country—and the old days. It was hardly the spot for a little girl. But that had made it seem all the more like a date.

After lunch, she and Frederick strolled down the street, back to Dizengoff Circle. "What next?" he asked, recognizing the spot. "Want to take in a movie?"

"No," Miriam said, scolding. "There's a lot to see yet. Wouldn't you like to go to the Carmel Market?"

Frederick shrugged. "You know better than I do. Would I?"

"Sure," Miriam said.

They headed down Rehov Pinsker, past a few hotels and some shops, finally ending up at Rehov Allenby, Tel Aviv's main shopping street. Then they turned left, past the Mograbi movie house, and strolled by three blocks of stores and shops, toward Sderot Geula. There, to the left, was the Carmel Market, a hodgepodge of open-air stands, from which came a mixture of Oriental food odors that ranged from mouthwatering to repulsive. It was the most primitive, cheapest and most crowded open air market in Tel Aviv.

Miriam and Frederick entered the market, meandering down narrow alleys, past buyers and sellers squabbling over prices in at least six different languages.

"I want to buy you something, Miriam," Borgmann said. "A souvenir of the day. What would you like?"

Suddenly, Miriam was a little girl again, confronted with temptations at every turn—jewelry, music boxes, bible covers, gold and silver filigree work handmade by the Yemenites who lived near the market, olivewood chess sets and figurines, embroidered clothing, towels and blankets made by the Yemenites, brass and copper ashtrays, candle holders and jewelry boxes, dolls dressed in native attire, glassware, carpets, coins and a dozen other sorts of goods.

She stopped at a small, shabby stall covered by a threadbare tent that had once been green and gold. A bearded Yemenite stood behind a table covered with Bedouin jewelry.

"Go ahead," Frederick urged. "Whatever you like."

Miriam picked up a beautiful beaded leather bracelet.

"Ah," said the stall's proprietor, mistaking her for an American, "that is a beautiful item, handmade in the Sinai desert. Think of the stories you'll be able to tell your friends back in America."

"How much?" Borgmann asked.

"For you, sir, since I like children so much, only twenty-one pounds."

Frederick turned to Miriam. "How much is that in dollars?"

She calculated for a moment, mentally. "About five dollars American."

Borgmann picked up the bracelet and examined it carefully. "Five dollars," he said. "That doesn't seem too . . ."

"Ten pounds," Miriam told the peddler, bargaining.

The old man gaped in well-practiced shock. "Do you know how long it takes a Bedouin to make such a bracelet?" he asked. "More than a week," he said, answering his own question. "This is worth only ten pounds to you? I suppose I could sacrifice some of my profit, but I cannot go lower than eighteen pounds."

"Twelve is the best we can do," Miriam replied. Frederick watched her in awe, barely managing to suppress a smile.

The peddler blew his nose loudly in a disreputable handkerchief. "Then I am sorry, young lady. I cannot sell it to you at that price. I have to feed my children, you know. And the Bedouin who made this has to feed his. And our children have children. Would you take food from my grandson's mouth?"

"Wait a minute," Frederick began.

"It's all right," Miriam interrupted, pulling him away from the stall. "We'll find it cheaper somewhere else."

"But that isn't too much . . . ."

"Come on," said Miriam, tugging at his hand.

"You were never serious about buying," the peddler called after them. "Even if I said sixteen pounds, you would not take it. And at that price, I would lose money."

The young girl turned back toward the stall. "Make it fifteen and you have a deal."

"Oh, no," the peddler protested. "That's too low. Do you expect me to starve? Do you wish to steal from me?"

Miriam just shook her head no and pulled Frederick away from the stall again.

"All right," the peddler said quickly. "Fifteen pounds. Cash."

Miriam caught Frederick's eye. "That's a little more than three-fifty," she told him. "Is that all right?"

"Of course."

The peddler fit the bracelet to the girl's arm while Frederick paid. "You're quite a bargainer for an American. And such a little girl."

"I'm not an American," Miriam said.

"No?" said the peddler, with mild interest, taking the money from Frederick. "English? Canadian?"

"No. I'm Israeli."

There was a brief flash of anger in the old man's eyes, quickly replaced by a look of malicious cunning. "You think you're very smart, don't you? Well, I would have taken thirteen pounds."

"Really?" Miriam said coolly. "We would have paid seventeen."

She turned away from the booth, pulling Frederick with her. "That's a beautiful present, Frederick," she said, holding out her arm so they could both admire the bracelet. "Thank you very much."

She threw her arms around his neck, pulling him down at the same moment, so she could kiss him on the cheek. Borgmann accepted the gesture awkwardly, though he showed his pleasure.

"You're a tough little bargainer," he said, with respect.

Miriam smiled. She wanted nothing more than to impress Frederick.

They came out of the Carmel Market at *Kikar* Magen David and walked slowly down Allenby, past the Hamashbir Lazarchan department store, airport ticket offices, banks, clothing shops and restaurants.

"You wanted to see historical sights and museums," Miriam reminded Frederick.

"Yes."

"I have one of each to show you."

The young man and much younger lady turned right at Sderot Rothschild, crossed Rehov Nahlat Benyamin and walked over to the other side of the boulevard.

"That's the Dizengoff House," Miriam said, pointing. "It's the Tel Aviv Museum now."

"What kind of museum?"

"Mostly art. But there are concerts in the main hall every weekend."

They walked in, wandered among the Chagall Bible illustrations, looked at works by Rodin, Degas, Utrillo, Modigliani, Epstein and others. In the main hall, there was a small bronze plaque. "In this hall, the State of Israel was proclaimed on May 14, 1948."

It was late mid-afternoon when they left the museum.

"What about the historical monument?" Frederick asked.

"Don't be so impatient," Miriam said, imitating some adult she'd heard. She led him back across Rehov Nahlet Benyamin, to the Jubilee Monument, on which the names of Tel Aviv's sixty founders were inscribed and the development of the city depicted pictorially.

"Remember," Miriam warned, as Frederick studied the monument. "Tel Aviv is a young city. If you're really interested in historical sites, you'll have to go to Jerusalem."

"Maybe we can do that tomorrow," Frederick said.

"I'd love to."

They walked back to Allenby, by way of the Great Synagogue, a large, square stone building with a domed roof and a colonnaded portico.

Miriam never did take Frederick to Jerusalem and they never did visit any archaeological sites—alone, at least. That night Yaakov took his guest to a relative's house for a party. And Borgmann met Ruth Ben-Zvi.

Ruth Ben-Zvi was the daughter of one of Yaakov Ben-Ezra's sisters, a willowy dark-haired girl in her early twenties with an infectious laugh. She was also Miriam's favorite cousin.

The way Miriam's father described it to her a couple of days later, Frederick and Ruth had spent the entire evening talking to each other. The party had broken up, and still they talked.

Miriam saw Frederick and Ruth often in the weeks that followed—always together. Sometimes, they took her along when they went to a movie or a concert.

Once, she accompanied the couple when they visited the Tel El Quassila excavations north of Tel Aviv, where they studied an Israelite casement wall that had apparently been built over the ruins of an earlier Philistine city wall. But only Miriam was interested in the excavation. Frederick and Ruth were interested mainly in each other.

Surprisingly, perhaps, she didn't resent this. In fact, she felt somehow a part of it. She had a monumental crush on Frederick, certainly, but it seemed right that he chose her favorite cousin Ruth.

When Frederick wasn't occupied courting Ruth, he and Yaakov were debating about whether he would remain in Israel and take the job the government was offering. Several times Miriam listened to their discussions when they thought she was asleep. Now she thought of those talks.

"I'm through working on bombs," Frederick had told Ben-Ezra. "I've been working on weaponry for almost ten years now, and I think the weapons I've helped build have brought us closer and closer to war, not farther from it."

"But Israel is so vulnerable . . ."

"I know, Yaakov, I know. But more is at stake here than Israel. Adding A-bombs to the Middle East situation could set the whole thing off. That's why I must refuse even you."

There had been no appeal from her father, and yet the same argument was repeated night after night.

Even before Frederick had been in Israel for a full month, he and Ruth announced their engagement. For a while, Miriam thought that meant Frederick would stay in Israel after all. But from eavesdropping on his talks with Ben-Ezra, she soon realized she'd be losing a cousin, not gaining a cousin-in-law.

On June 26, 1954, Frederick Borgmann and Ruth Ben-Zvi were married in Tel Aviv. Miriam remembered it vividly. It was a lovely, flower-filled wedding in a beautiful old synagogue. Miriam stood up for the bride, at her cousin's request. She and her father picked out a handsome set of embroidered linens for the new-lyweds.

And then, the young man and his wife flew back to Chicago and out of her life—forever, she'd thought.

Borgmann entered the main conference hall just as Professor Kampmann was gaveling the proceedings to order. It was several minutes before he spotted Dahlgaard and even longer before he managed to gain his attention. He slid through the rows of seats—most of the delegates were still finding their way into the au-ditorium—toward Dahlgaard.

"Bent—"

"Good morning, Frederick. You slept well?"

"Yes. Fine. I don't want to appear blunt or rude, Bent, but were you able to get any information about the matter we discussed last night?"

"As a matter of fact, I was, Frederick. But we can-not discuss it here. Are you in a hurry?"

"I'm afraid so."

"Then let's go into the hall."

Dahlgaard led the way. Together, they plowed through a crowd of delegates heading the other way. Back of the auditorium, they found a small empty classroom, went inside and closed the door.

"What have you learned—do you know where the plans are?"

"I am not certain, Frederick. My sources are not willing to tell me exactly. But from what I gather, they are hidden within one of our small experimental nu-clear reactors. They'll be broadcast to the closed ses-sions via TV."

"Hidden in a reactor?" Borgmann asked, puzzled. "But why?"

Dahlgaard stuck his hands in his pockets. "I believe they thought it would be advantageous to use a security setup already in force. And they felt that hiding the plans within a reactor would discourage any espionage agents who somehow found out where the plans were."

"An impressive plan," Borgmann said sincerely.

"I'm afraid I've brought you bad news, Frederick."

Borgmann agreed. "Is that all you know, Bent?" he asked.

"I can offer you nothing more, Frederick. If I ask any more questions, it might attract the wrong kind of attention."

"Thank you, Bent. I know you've done your best for me."

The door of the classroom suddenly opened and a man carrying a box of fluorescent light bulbs walked in. Both Borgmann and Dahlgaard were startled into silence.

"Undskyld," the man said apologetically, seeing he'd interrupted them. He backed out of the room. *"Undskyld."*

Dahlgaard got up and closed the door behind the janitor. "Will I be seeing you again soon, Frederick?" It was a simple enough question, but Dahlgaard managed to load it up with all sorts of subtle meanings.

Borgmann had been lost in thought but Dahlgaard's words roused him. "What?"

"Will I be seeing you again, Frederick? Would you like to come out to dinner once more?"

Borgmann got to his feet. "I just don't know. I don't know how long I'm going to be in Copenhagen. I would like to see you and Maj and the kids again but—well—I'll try to call you."

"Will you return to the conference?"

"I don't think so."

Borgmann held out his hand and Dahlgaard shook it warmly. "It was good seeing you after all these years, Frederick. Good luck with whatever you do."

"Thank you Bent. I appreciate your help—and your friendship."

Dahlgaard left the room first, Borgmann followed a few moments later. To his surprise, not ten feet from the door, he saw the chubby, bald figure of Dr. Bertel Lindeborg. The man was making notes on the back of a pad, either unaware that he was being observed, or pretending to be unaware—Borgmann couldn't tell which.

"Good morning, Lindeborg," Borgmann said firmly.

He knew that if he were to discover anything, he had to confront the man directly.

"Oh, hello, Borgmann. Enjoying the conference?"

"Very much. And you?"

"For me it is merely a social occasion. I'm already quite familiar with the technical details of the centrifuge—in a general way, of course."

"Of course. Tell me, Lindeborg, how do you expect the conference to turn out?"

"My guess is that the Scandinavian countries will join the project, Borgmann," Lindeborg said. He removed a carefully folded white handkerchief from his pocket, wiped his hairless dome, glanced at the handkerchief to see if it had collected dirt or grease, then pocketed it once more. "And when that happens, Europe will give you Americans quite a run for your money."

"I imagine so. That wouldn't bother me. I was born in Denmark. But then, you must know that."

"As a matter of fact . . ." Lindeborg began.

"I know, you read it someplace—you can't remember where." Borgmann said it with a smile, but there was no mistaking the hostility of his tone.

Lindeborg looked at him curiously for several moments before answering. "Yes," he said finally, "I did read it someplace."

Borgmann smiled again, managing to turn the expression into something truly nasty. "Well," he said, as if something had been settled, "see you later, Lindeborg."

A few moments later Borgmann bounded down the long flight of stairs leading from the Institute to the street. The green Saab was still there. To his relief, Miriam waved again.

Chapter Twenty-Three

Lieutenant Colonel Yevgeny Borsilov walked slowly through the park, waiting for the inevitable collision with his contact. Though he'd talked about it all night with his wife, he still wasn't happy about his decision. Already, he'd taken extraordinary risks. Now he was about to take another.

That's what he'd told Marina, again and again. "You know how they punish men for failure," he'd reminded her. "Imagine what they do to those they believe disloyal. Is that what you want for me?"

"Of course not, my dearest. But there are ways to do these things discreetly, aren't there?"

"I suppose," he said, grudgingly. "But . . ."

"I remember your sister, Yevgeny, even if you don't."

Those were harsh words. Yevgeny could never forget his sister, even though he'd been only thirteen when she died. Her screams of terror still rang through his ears in nightmares, like the screeching of tires before a crash.

"You know I remember her, Marina."

"And still your loyalty to Mother Russia is without limit?"

"It's not my loyalty to Russia that makes me hesitate," Borsilov said. "It's my fear for you and the children."

"You're afraid?"

"Yes." It was not an easy admission.

"It's fear that caused the pogroms in the first place,"

Marina said. "It was fear that made the Jews docile as they were led to the concentration camps. If they'd fought with all their might against both, from the beginning—not with words, but with weapons—the outcome might have been different."

"I'm not sure I believe that. Besides, Israel *is* fighting—and with everything it has."

"Do you feel no obligation to help?"

"I have already helped."

"But there is more you can do."

The argument went on for hours, with Borsilov yielding bit by bit. Finally, he agreed to forward what information he had. In the early morning hours, he struggled to compress the message into as few words as possible.

"Warning: High-level deep-cover GRU agent at Conference—not Torngren nor his assassin. Motives, details unknown."

Before he left for work, he called the code telephone number, letting it ring twice. Then he hung up, dialed again and let it ring eight times, the signal for the time of meeting. Sixty seconds later, his own phone rang once and was silent. His message had been acknowledged.

Later that morning, in the park, Borsilov walked along a paved path, toward the clump of trees near where he'd bumped into his contact the previous day, his note hidden in his palm. Suddenly, an eight-year-old girl on a red scooter came careening around the corner, running directly into him. He caught the girl in his strong hands, preventing her from falling, though the scooter hit the pavement with a clatter.

"Oh, excuse me, sir," the girl said.

"Are you all right?" Borsilov asked. She was an adorable child.

"Oh yes, I'm fine. My scooter may be dented, though."

They both bent down to examine the little vehicle. "Seems okay to me," Borsilov said.

"Yes," the girl said happily. "It has just a little scratch." She pointed and Borsilov looked. A small but unmistakable Hebrew letter *heh* had been scratched into the scooter's faded red paint. He looked up at the girl sharply. She was smiling.

"So it is," Borsilov said. "But this should cover repairs." He reached into his pocket, withdrew a coin, and handed it to the girl, together with his tightly folded little note. Even if a witness had been standing within three feet of the scene, there would have been no cause for suspicion.

The little girl smiled, curtsied, and said, "I thank you, sir. My mother thanks you. My father thanks you. We all thank you."

For the casual observer, it would have been only a funny, charming, polite little speech. For Borsilov, it meant a great deal more.

"Glad to be of help, little girl," he said.

Ben-Ezra sat in the backroom office, waiting for Miriam, or Frederick, or both of them. He glanced at his watch: nearly noon. They were fast running out of time. In about thirty-six hours, Herman Wedke and Joseph de Block, the EURATOM security force in charge of protecting the centrifuge plans, would be packing them up for shipment back to the Netherlands. No doubt the director of EURATOM security, Eduard Jelle, would also be on the scene. He knew all three men. Jelle was a retired police chief inspector from Brussels. During the war, he'd been very active in the underground, a no-nonsense sort with inexhaustible courage. Wedke and de Block had both been recruited from Interpol, where they'd operated as a team. Ben-Ezra had worked with them briefly in the early 1950s, tracing down a lead on Martin Bormann. The lead proved to be a dead end but he'd been enormously impressed by the thoroughness and diligence of the two men from Interpol. Once these three regained the centrifuge plans, Israel's chance of "obtaining" them was over.

Distantly, through the walls of books, Ben-Ezra heard the phone ring. He resisted the impulse to pick up his extension. Then there was a knock on the door and a whispered, "It's for you."

Ben-Ezra picked up the phone. "Hello, Kaplan," came the voice, shrouded with static.

"Hello, Jacob," Ben-Ezra said, a bit loudly, giving the password. The code words were really unnecessary this time. He recognized Nachman's voice, and he was sure that Nachman recognized his.

"I have some news for you. Can you hear me well?"

"Yes. Go ahead."

"Mr. Bear tells me that the General Railroad Utensils Company has an important branch office in your area. Staffed by a very experienced man—I don't know if you know him—he's apparently never told anyone who he's working for. Am I coming through?"

"Very clearly." Ben-Ezra thought quickly. "You're not referring to Mr. ah—Elk—are you?"

"Oh, no, definitely not. And I don't mean Mr. Lugar, either."

"What are their corporate plans?"

"That's all Mr. Bear could tell us."

"I see. Do you have any suggestions?"

"Not really. Except that when you go calling on clients, it would be best to meet with them before they see this man from General Railroad. I imagine he wants to make a sale, too."

"Nothing new about that."

"No. I suppose not. Offer whatever discount you have to. We're hoping for a big sale in your territory."

"If I make one, can we renegotiate my pension?"

"Possibly. Look, I have to run. When will I be hearing from you?"

"Sometime tomorrow night, I hope."

"Have you made your presentation yet?"

"Not yet. I'm having a hell of a time finding the man's office. Sent my secretary out for a map, though, and she should be back momentarily."

"I see. Say, did you hire that assistant we talked about?"

"As a matter of fact, I did. He's working out quite

236

well. Should be a big help. If we can't do it with him, we'll never do it at all."

"Yes. Well, keep in touch."

"Of course. Goodbye."

Ben-Ezra hung up. He always enjoyed these conversations with Nachman. There was always something to laugh about—General Railroad Utensils, for example. Nachman was an imaginative fellow. Ben-Ezra reviewed the information he had received: there was a high-level GRU agent on the scene, a deep-cover man, probably planted years back. And this was neither Torngren—Mr. Elk—nor his assassin—Mr. Lugar. The information had come directly from an Israeli agent in the Soviet Union—Mr. Bear.

There wasn't much he could do about this, except to exercise caution. Perhaps the GRU man wasn't even involved with the centrifuge matter. On the other hand, perhaps it was this agent who had fired at him this morning, or even killed Amer. The pieces hadn't quite fit together yet, but possible patterns were emerging.

Ben-Ezra was toying with various combinations when there was another muffled knock on the bookshelf-door and it opened. Miriam and Frederick were back and they seemed excited.

"We think we know—" Miriam started.

"The plans must be—" Borgmann began, simultaneously.

"One at a time," Ben-Ezra said.

Borgmann nodded to Miriam. She took a deep breath and started off.

In a few minutes, Ben-Ezra knew everything they did, including their conclusion: this secret reactor Dahlgaard had referred to was located somewhere beneath the Tivoli Gardens amusement park. As for Lindeborg, Borgmann continued to keep his suspicions to himself.

"What if the plans are actually inside the reactor, Frederick?" Ben-Ezra asked. "Will you be able to remove them?"

"I think so. There will be some risk, but I have a

237

good working knowledge of most types of nuclear reactors," Borgmann answered.

Ben-Ezra felt a tickle at the back of his throat. He coughed to remove it. "If we can get hold of a Geiger counter," said Borgmann, "we should have no problem."

Miriam snorted. "No problem? The Geiger counter will tell us where the reactor is buried, but will it show us the door?"

"Miriam," Borgmann said patiently, "do I tell you how to spy? There's bound to be a low-level radiation leakage at the entrance. The Geiger counter will spot it for us."

Ben-Ezra got up and began to pace. They were finally on the trail now, and he was getting excited. "Wait a minute," he said, suddenly worried. "Where the devil do we find a Geiger counter?"

"In any good instrument supply house," Borgmann replied smoothly.

It took eight minutes and three telephone calls to locate the instrument. All at once, the sense of purpose was back. There were two possibilities again.

Chapter Twenty-Four

"Okay," Ben-Ezra told his charges, "let's do it this way: you two pick up the Geiger counter and go to the Tivoli. Find the entrance as soon as possible, then come back here."

Miriam was both surprised and disturbed. "You're not coming with us, Yaakov?"

"I have things to do here, Miriam—important arrangements to be made."

"What?"

"Nothing for you to worry about."

The girl groaned in exasperation.

"But we might need you, Yaakov," Borgmann said. He was as concerned as Miriam. "I'm sure there'll be guards and locks to deal with. I won't be much help there. Do you think Miriam can handle that part by herself?"

"She could, if necessary. She has before. But that's not what I had in mind. All I want the two of you to do now is find the entrance to the reactor. We can't look for the plans this afternoon, anyhow."

"Why not?" Miriam asked. It was a challenge.

Ben-Ezra regarded her with a nasty glare. "What's happening at the conference this afternoon, Miriam?"

"Oh."

" 'Oh' is right. They're holding the closed sessions. If we're right, the reactor room will be crawling with TV technicians. We'll have to swipe the plans tomorrow morning—before the final closed sessions in the afternoon." Ben-Ezra turned toward Borgmann, who'd been leaning against an old grey filing cabinet and listening without comment. "Don't you agree, Frederick?"

Borgmann didn't respond immediately. "I guess you're right," he said at last. "But how do you know we'll be able to get into the reactor area tomorrow morning? What if security is just too tight? And how can we know if I'll be able to get the plans out of the reactor? That might take a while—assuming I can figure out which plans are genuine."

Ben-Ezra took a fingernail clipper from his pocket, with maddening nonchalance. "How long will all that take, do you think?" he asked.

"I can't be sure—two or three hours, maybe," said Borgmann.

"Two hours," Ben-Ezra repeated. "Well, there are two possibilities. Either we can give you two hours to do your work, or we can't." He started clipping his nails.

"There are three possibilities, Yaakov," Borgmann said bluntly. "The third one is that I'll fail."

Ben-Ezra yawned. "There was always that possibility."

"And what about the question of entry?" Borgmann went on, pressing the point.

"I think Miriam and I can handle that," Ben-Ezra replied easily. He finished with his right hand and started on his left.

"Why do you make it sound so simple, Yaakov?" Miriam was annoyed. "We're all risking our lives, and you know it. Besides, we may be entirely wrong about the location of the plans."

"It all seems to fit," Ben-Ezra reminded her.

"We can't be sure until we find the reactor," she snapped back.

"That's true." He pocketed the clipper, undismayed.

"And what about the competition, Yaakov?" Miriam went on, trying to rouse him. "What makes you so sure they won't give us any trouble?"

"I've planned for that, Miriam," he said pleasantly.

Borgmann realized the discussion might soon turn into an argument. He decided to intervene on the side of harmony. "Listen," he said, his voice calm, "it was clear from the start that this would be difficult, if not impossible. That hasn't changed. We'll just have to do the best we can. And maybe we'd better get going." The last remark was directed at Miriam.

A moment earlier she seemed ready for combat. Borgmann's words put the priorities back in line. "You're right, Frederick," she agreed, "we have a lot of work to do this afternoon."

"The Tivoli covers twenty acres," Borgmann reminded her. "Unless we're really very lucky, we could be there until it closes at midnight."

"I want you to let me know the instant you find something," Ben-Ezra said. "And no risks—not today. Take special care not to be followed. Is that clear?"

Miriam made a mock salute.

"You'll hear from us—soon, I hope," Borgmann said.

Miriam looked through the peephole to make sure the outer store was empty, then pushed open the bookshelf-door. Outside, they got into her Saab.

"Sometimes Yaakov worries me," Borgmann said. "He seems so casual about everything."

"I know," Miriam replied. "It bothers me too. I have the feeling he knows something we don't."

"Yes," Borgmann said, thoughtfully, "that's it exactly. But if that's true, why won't he tell us?"

Miriam shrugged. "We'll know that eventually, I suppose." She started the car and they drove off.

Ben-Ezra waited until the door was closed, then he got up, unlocked the file cabinet Borgmann had been leaning against, reached deep into the top drawer and came out with three silvery cylinders, each about the size of a cigar. The time for killing was over, he hoped. From now on, the only violence associated with this mission would be violent sleep. He took out three refill cartridges, then slammed the cabinet shut and relocked it.

Then, with the cylinders and their refills in his
241

pocket, he looked up a telephone number in the Copenhagen phone book and dialed.

"Gunnar Neilborg, please." He waited for the connection. "Gunnar? This is a voice from the past—Yaakov Ben-Ezra."

"Yaakov? Yaakov! How are you, old friend? It's been a long time."

"Nearly three years, I think. I'm about as well as can be expected, Gunnar. And you?"

"Very well."

"Still in the same job?"

"Yes. They gave me a couple of assistants, though."

"I'm glad to hear it. A pay raise, too, I hope."

"Yes, a little. But I suspect you did not call to exchange pleasantries, Yaakov. Am I right?"

"I'm afraid so, Gunnar. I need a favor . . ."

"Whatever you want, Yaakov—reservations, freight pickup, itineraries, a seat on a plane that's already full—you name it."

"Well, Gunnar, the favor I need is a bit more complex than that, something rather special. You see . . ."

Gary Stabile stood outside the Tivoli main gate, scrutinizing the picture that had come over the office teleprinter less than half an hour ago. He cursed once more. A school yearbook photo more than ten years old—that was the best photo of Suliman Ferrara the agency was able to find. What are they doing with all those billions, anyhow? Fortunately, this was Denmark, where most of the population was blond and blue-eyed or dark-haired and fair-skinned. Ferrara should be easy to spot.

He was a good-looking fellow, at least in this picture, Stabile granted. Straight, sandy hair, a swarthy complexion, strong, regular features, a shade over six feet tall, with greyish green eyes. That might be a helpful detail. He quickly reread the typed description that had come along with the photo, keeping one eye on the gate:

Subject graduated Yale June 1962, then returned to Beirut, where he now follows underworld career on a high level. May have been involved in local espionage, but not thought to have undertaken international project until he contacted several Palestinian leaders approximately four months ago. Weapons and language proficiency unknown.

Stabile knew all about such reports. He'd written dozens of them himself. Mostly they were extractions from more general information gathered from field agents. They were accurate enough, as far as they went, but they rarely went far enough. In this case, one important question about the man remained glaringly unanswered: Was Ferrara in touch with any other intelligence outfits—the Russians, for example? Well, Stabile thought, I guess I'll just have to discover that myself. Now, the main thing is to spot Ferrara as he enters the amusement park. Surely he'll be here soon, either to find out why his man Amer was shot, or trailing one of the Israeli group.

Stabile walked toward the entrance, paid his two *kroner* entrance fee and took up a position just inside the gate, near a refreshment stand. He pulled a pair of sunglasses out of his pocket, bought some cotton candy and sat down on a low stone wall, an exact copy of a resting American tourist.

Suliman Ferrara strode purposefully toward the Tivoli, his mind buzzing with plans and ideas. At least Amer had given him a first-rate description of Borgmann. The girl, from what Amer had told him, was obviously the same one he'd seen at the train when the plans were unloaded. He was quite sure he'd be able to recognize her, and probably Borgmann, especially if they were together. If not, he could always go back to the porno shop and pick up the trail there. But time was slipping away rather quickly now. Surely the Israelis would be here at the Tivoli—if his guess was right, if that's where the plans were hidden.

Ferrara knew he had to be careful. He didn't think the Israelis knew about him, but there was no way to be sure. If the girl recognized him, as she had recognized Amer, they'd never let down their guard. A moment's suspicion and his plan was worthless. The thieves had to feel—at least for a moment—that they were beyond danger. That's when he planned to strike. And Ferrara fervently hoped that the Israelis would be successful thieves. If there was any way to give them a helping hand without arousing suspicion, he would be more than willing.

He approached the Tivoli ticket office, purchased a ticket and entered the amusement park. Its beauty touched him. He wasn't used to such a profusion of flowers, trees and grass. And then there were the Danish girls. Someday, he'd come back here—with nothing on his mind but pleasure. He glanced around the park, at the restaurants and rides. Then, he spotted a blonde girl in a very collegiate attire—was it the Israeli agent? He felt his heart pounding as he waited for her to turn around. No. Just another American tourist. He reprimanded himself. I have to be more alert, he thought. I've been a boss too long. Maybe I've lost the edge. If so, I have to concentrate that much harder.

The stop at the instrument house, fortunately, took only a few minutes. It stocked about a dozen different kinds of Geiger counters, ranging from monsters of the size of TV consoles with separate gauges for each major type of radiation, machines that could be equipped with a wide variety of remote sensors, down to tiny gadgets about the size of a transistor radio.

"I'd like that one," Borgmann told the salesman, pointing to the smallest instrument in the shop.

"To buy, lease or rent? We have a very attractive lease-purchase plan."

"Rent," Borgmann said.

The salesman nodded, took out a form and began filling it out. Miriam supplied the cash and the proper identification. "Do you prefer direct readout or earphone?" the salesman asked.

"Earphone," said Borgmann.

"Fine. Would you like one of our technical people to instruct you how to use the device properly?"

"That won't be necessary."

The salesman pushed the form toward Miriam for her signature. "Would you like the device delivered, or do you wish to take it with you?"

"We'll take it," Borgmann said.

"Fine. You know," the salesman said, "I think that's the fastest instrument rental I've ever made."

"Glad to hear it," Borgmann said. He turned to Miriam. "Shall we go?"

"Why not?"

Borgmann put the instrument in his pocket and he and Miriam hurried out to her car. This whole trip had been a series of mixed emotions, a different set of them every day. Now, he was struggling to reconcile feelings of excitement, fear, and—he might as well face it—a growing attachment to Miriam.

"I never thought he'd stop talking," Miriam said.

"Me neither." Borgmann looked at her and wondered if her thoughts were similar to his.

They got into her car and drove off toward Tivoli.

Stabile took another mouthful of cotton candy. Why did kids like this stuff anyway? It was sticky, granular, and much too sweet. Though he did his best to stay neat, wisps of it stuck to his fingers and he found himself licking them. Underneath the cotton candy was the taste of pipe tobacco, which he much preferred.

Ever since he'd sat down, there'd been a steady stream of people entering the Tivoli. He sorted them out as they entered—tourist, native, tourist. By far the greatest number were under twenty. A few were upwards of sixty. It was the middle-agers who were missing, Stabile concluded—the working people who didn't have time for this kind of nonsense, unless, of course, they were dragged here by their kids. Stabile savored the wave of contempt that rose up in him. He hadn't married and he was glad—no wife to plague him, no kids to dictate how he spent his money or his life. The only person he had to answer to was himself, which was no problem, since he easily met his own standards.

Had he gotten here too late? He looked at his watch. Just about two-thirty. He'd been sitting on the wall for about half an hour. Before that, he'd watched the gate from the outside for nearly an hour. If Washington hadn't taken so long to transmit Ferrara's picture, he might have been here by noon, perhaps slightly earlier. Then he could have been positive. Even now, the odds were in his favor. Borgmann had probably gone to the conference this morning. Ferrara couldn't have discovered that his helper had been killed, or when it had happened, much before noon. Maybe he still didn't know. But Stabile dismissed that thought. It wouldn't do to underestimate the man.

For the first time since he'd dismissed Salter, Stabile thought a few moments reviewing his assignment. It was a very complex task, full of subtleties, the espionage version of "let's you and him fight." His assignment was to make sure everyone lost, preferably with each of them knocking off the other. It was easy enough to state the idea in a single sentence, but making it happen on schedule took finesse—of the sort Stabile had several times demonstrated over the years. If he had been in a position to do so, he would have chosen himself for the job.

The American was basking in such pleasant thoughts when his eye settled on a tall figure who had just entered the main gate. There was a determination in his gait that contrasted sharply with the ambling aimlessness of those who'd come for fun. This man wanted something. Once more, Stabile pulled the picture out of his jacket pocket. He glanced from man to picture and back again. His eyes twinkled.

What I need, thought Suliman Ferrara, is a spot where I can observe without being observed. With any luck, I have beaten the Israelis back to the park. They'd certainly had to regroup after the shooting incident this morning.

To his left was the Peacock Theater, a large, open-air stage. A small audience was clustered around it, watching a costumed pantomime show. The characters on the stage seemed vaguely familiar. Ferrara briefly searched his memory. It came to him from a surprising

246

source—his college course in Renaissance literature and art. He was watching Harlequin, Columbine and Pierrot. He joined the audience, standing around at the side so that he could see anyone entering the main gate. His own presence, he was sure, would be masked by the other spectators. To his right, on the stage, the pantomime went on with the slapstick exaggeration common to that theatrical form. The antics of the characters brought repeated cries of laughter from the audience, at least half of whom were rather young children.

Ferrara paid it no heed. His eyes were riveted to the entrance. They darted from one face to the next, examining, then dismissing. With each passing moment, his fears rose that he'd either arrived too late and the Israelis were already somewhere within the Tivoli or that Amer's death here was not materially related to the centrifuge plans. He'd made one guess on top of another, and if any were wrong, he was lost, his mission a failure.

At about 2:45, the play came to an end. The audience in which he'd hidden himself began to applaud, then drift away from the open-air theater. Still, there were no Israelis in view. Ferrara kept gazing at the entrance gate.

Then he saw them—an attractive blonde girl and a tall American, clean-cut, wearing horn-rimmed glasses. This time the girl was dressed in a blue pants suit. But there was no mistaking her. She was the girl he'd seen at the train, the one Amer had told him was named Miriam Shazar. Keeping an eye on them, Ferrara moved away, following members of the pantomime theater audience as it headed for other attractions. He circled around behind the pair, until he was directly in back of them. To his surprise, Ferrara noted that the man—Borgmann—was wearing a hearing aid—no, he slowly realized, it wasn't a hearing aid at all. He was listening to a transistor radio. Now that didn't make any sense.

Ferrara followed the couple at a safe distance. They paid no attention whatever to any of the attractions. Instead, they methodically started at one corner of the amusement park and began to work their way down. Every once in a while, Borgmann would stop, cock his head as if listening more closely to the transistor radio and say a few words to the girl. Then they'd walk on a dozen yards or so and repeat the procedure. They frequently looked around the park, as if they worried that someone might be following. Ferrara had no trouble evading their glance.

What could Borgmann be listening to? Ferrara was thoroughly mystified. If Borgmann was getting some sort of instructions by radio, just what could they be? How could they help him search the place better? And exactly what was he looking for? Then it dawned on him. Borgmann wasn't listening to a radio at all. That earphone was attached to some sort of instrument. The instrument was picking up—Ferrara had an inspiration—radiation of some sort. That's it, he was certain. Borgmann was listening to a Geiger counter. But why? What, in this place of flowers and trees, could be a source of radiation? He couldn't imagine the Danes subjecting any Tivoli visitors to dangerous radiation of any sort. Besides, what Borgmann should have been looking for was some sort of hiding place, not a radiation source.

Suliman Ferrara let his thoughts tumble over each other as he followed the Israeli girl and her scientific friend. He considered the facts, as best he knew them: Borgmann was here, at least in part, to help the Israelis get the centrifuge plans. Getting the plans was clearly Miriam Shazar's prime mission. The plans, if one had to depend on logic alone, were very probably at the Bohr Institute. Yet here were they both, deadly serious, carefully tracing some kind of radiation. The plans must be here, at the amusement park, Ferrara told himself. No other conclusion made any sense. And somehow their hiding place was connected to radiation. It was bizarre, but it fit. Well, he reflected, one way or another, I'll know soon enough if my guess is right.

Behind Ferrara perhaps twenty feet, and also wary of Borgmann's field of view, was Gary Stabile. He was

248

hiding behind still another paper cone loaded to over-flowing with pink cotton candy and nibbling without enthusiasm, sauntering along as if he had just begun his retirement, his eyes as alert as a rattlesnake's.

Chapter Twenty-Five

"Hear anything yet?" Miriam asked anxiously.

"Just background radiation—and children screaming," Borgmann replied. He shifted his body slightly, so that the Geiger counter's probe hidden in his jacket pocket had a new area to examine.

A group of young boys aged nine to twelve came running by, one of them pushing between Miriam and Frederick.

"I'll bet they're playing hooky," Borgmann said. "Just like I used to do."

"Frederick," Miriam said, teasing, "you played hooky? I thought you spent your entire boyhood studying nuclear physics."

"We just called it physics in those days, Miriam. As a matter of fact, I didn't study much at all. Eidetic imagery did the job for me."

"Eidetic imagery?"

They approached a small snack bar. Miriam's eyes combed the place, searching for any familiar—and unwelcome—faces. She saw none.

"Yes. Photographic memory. All I had to do was read something once, carefully, or examine a diagram, looking at every detail, and I could reproduce it at will in my mind's eye."

"I thought there was no such thing as a photographic memory, that it was just an exaggerated term for very good recall."

"Not at all," Borgmann said. He cocked his head for a moment, listening carefully to the earphone. Then he shrugged—nothing. "It's a well-documented phenomenon, a kind of freak visual capacity."

Miriam grinned mischievously. "You seem entirely normal to me, Frederick."

He shared the fun. "Listen," he said, as they came up to the snack bar, "would you like something?"

She thought a moment about how events repeat themselves. "Yes," she decided, "an ice cream cone—so long as you have one too."

Borgmann bought them both double-scoop cones of soft chocolate ice cream, then they resumed their stroll through the park, looking to any unsuspecting spectators as if they were a couple on a date, not two people on a mission of vital importance. Suddenly, Borgmann stopped in mid-stride and swung his body slowly to the left.

"Hear something?"

"No. Only a slight increase in background radiation, probably a natural variation."

He resumed his walk.

"Tell me more about—what did you call it, your memory?"

"Eidetic imagery. Well, it's very rare, for one thing." They walked on, toward what appeared to be an Arabian palace, a fantasy of towers, arches and strings of colored lights. "A lot of people say they have photographic memories, but they're usually just talking about excellent—but ordinary—powers of recollection."

"What's the difference?" Miriam asked, licking her chocolate ice cream. She looked around, making sure they weren't being followed.

Frederick took a lick of his own ice cream. For the moment, anyhow, Miriam seemed open and vulnerable. He liked her this way. "The difference is that those people with eidetic imagery actually store pictures in their minds and retrieve them at will. Their recall is exact."

Suddenly, Borgmann stopped dead and stared. Ahead of them was the beautiful, delicate *Glassalen*—the Glass Hall.

"What's the matter, Frederick? Do you hear something?"

"No," he said softly, "it's that building."

"Which?"

"The Glass Hall, there. It was destroyed in the occupation. The Nazis tore it down for some reason. But there it is again, exactly as it was. I don't understand."

They both gazed at the structure for a moment. Sounds of a band concert could be heard drifting through the open doors.

"It was rebuilt, Frederick," Miriam said gently. "The Danes probably took the original plans and made it again, as it was."

"That must be it, Miriam," Borgmann said. "It was just a bit of a shock to see it standing there, like suddenly running into someone you thought had died."

The girl nodded sympathetically. They walked on for a while in silence, nibbling at their ice cream cones, Borgmann occasionally pausing to listen more closely to the earphone.

"It was your photographic memory, wasn't it?"

"What?"

"The business with the Glass Hall, I mean."

"Oh. I guess so. I remember going there, when I was young."

They cut back now, through the flower beds around the Nimb and Wivex restaurants, Borgmann swinging his body from side to side, as if he were stepping through a series of puddles. They stopped at the statue of H.C. Lumbye, the Danish composer who had conducted the Tivoli orchestra when the park had first opened.

"Hear anything yet?" Miriam asked, glancing behind them, determined to spot anyone who might be trailing them.

"Just an occasional click—background radiation, nothing more."

"I hope we're right about this, Frederick."

"So do I. But there's no reason to be concerned yet. We've only covered about ten percent of the place."

They sat on a low bench and looked toward the middle of the park, toward the *Muslingeskallen*, the platform where circus performers traditionally displayed their skills. Today, it was tightrope walkers. Far above them, an athletically slim man in tights teetered on a wire, holding a long pole across his chest. He took three fast, mincing steps forward, then two back, then three forward again. Below him, the crowd—mostly children—gasped and buzzed with excitement.

Finally, having finished their ice cream cones, Frederick and Miriam rose and continued their apparently aimless stroll, heading past the *Muslingeskallen* and the Glass Hall toward the lake.

"The longer we go without finding something, the more nervous I get," Miriam said. "I'd hate to have to go back to Yaakov and tell him we found nothing."

"So would I," said Borgmann. "That's why I'm walking toward the lake now. If there is a reactor somewhere beneath the Tivoli, that would be a likely place for it. Water is an excellent radiation shield."

"But how could something be underneath a lake, Frederick?"

"It would be unlikely if we were talking about a natural lake," Borgmann agreed. "But the Tivoli lake is man-made. Back in the early eighteen hundreds, it was a moat. In fact, all of Tivoli Gardens was once an old fort that guarded the southern side of old Copenhagen. Some of the ramparts still exist, beneath us. That's why I wasn't so surprised at the suggestion of an underground reactor here. There are old stone walls eight feet thick beneath us, and they'd be fine insulation for a nuclear facility."

"But what about construction, Frederick? Wouldn't someone have gotten suspicious while the reactor was being built?"

"Not really. Remember Miriam, Tivoli is closed from September to May. Furthermore, there's always something being built here—a new ride or a new restaurant or something. Construction is perfectly natural. In the case of the reactor, most of it would have been underground, anyhow, out of sight."

They were approaching the lake now, a roughly kidney-shaped body of blue water perhaps two city blocks long. It was filled with tourist-packed rowboats. Borgmann stopped frequently, listening carefully to the earphone. Miriam was quiet. They circled the northern end of the lake, passing the boat rental dock and a small cafeteria, near a playground designed for small children.

"Anything?" Miriam finally asked.

"Not a click."

"Maybe if we looked for a possible entrance," she suggested.

"That's a good idea," Borgmann replied. "If there's an underground installation, there has to be a way to get down there."

By now, they were within a few feet of Faergekroen, an old, salmon-colored, half-timbered inn perched at the edge of the lake. They looked at each other, nodded and walked in, meandering through the inside dining room, a traditional place with a high old fireplace on a raised hearth and windows looking out on the lake. Then they went out on the dining terrace.

Frederick glanced at Miriam, his head cocked as he listened to the Geiger counter. He shook his head. There was nothing to report.

"What was that wonderful smell?" Miriam asked, as they walked out of the restaurant, back onto the path around the lake.

"They call it *lobscouse*," Frederick told her. "It's a meat and potatoes dish spiced with butter, bay leaf and pepper. Make you hungry?"

"Very."

"Me too. But it's only four-thirty. We'd better hold off dinner until we've found something—or until we're sure we're not going to find anything."

Behind them, perhaps twenty yards, walked Suliman Ferrara, apparently unconcerned, relaxed, seemingly enjoying a stroll. A close observer, however, would have noticed that he was sweating profusely, even though the temperature wasn't quite seventy. He'd followed the pair into the restaurant, then, when they

254

turned and started out, he'd had to duck into the men's room to avoid being seen. Later, when he came out, they were gone. For the next ten minutes, he searched the area frantically, certain he'd lost them. Then, all at once, there they were, walking along the path, with no more urgency than before, obviously unaware of him, for all the girl's backward glances. Ferrara took a deep breath and dropped back. This time, he told himself, he'd been lucky. Once more he swore at his rusty skills and vowed to be more careful.

Another twenty yards behind Ferrara, Gary Stabile stopped for a moment and lit his pipe. He was finding this all very entertaining. Ferrara either didn't know or had forgotten some of the elementary rules of trailing a person. As a result, he'd almost lost his prey. Stabile had seen the whole thing while relaxing on a bench in front of the restaurant. Of course, it wouldn't have been so amusing if Ferrara had turned the wrong way when he finally came out of the place. Then Stabile would somehow have had to arrange for him to come across Borgmann and the girl once more, somewhere else in the park. That might not have been easy.

Borgmann pulled the earphone out of his ear, stuck his finger in and wiggled it around.

"Something wrong?" Miriam asked.

"No. It was just starting to hurt."

"Why not try the other ear?"

"Exactly my thought," Frederick said, reinstalling the earphone.

They were now directly across from the Krudthuset, a restaurant that attracted a teen-age crowd and echoed with the beat of rock and roll music.

"Can you still hear?" Miriam asked, raising her voice over the noise.

"Barely," Frederick said. "But there's nothing to report."

Soon they approached the Tivoli entrance at Tietgensgade and Hans Christian Andersen Boulevard.

They'd covered about a third of the park and it was nearly five o'clock already.

"Tell me," Miriam asked, "in that photographic memory of yours, is there anything like a diagram of the old fortifications beneath us—something you might have seen in a history book at one time or another?"

"I thought of that," Borgmann replied. "I seem to remember some ramparts along what is now Tietgensgade Street, and a V-shaped bastion over by present-day Bernstorffsgade. I was hoping to remember where the powder magazine was. Magazines were usually built below ground, a likely spot for the reactor we're looking for. But I can't come up with a location."

Miriam listened with respect. There was a great deal about Frederick that impressed her. She saw in him enormous strength—fierce determination, masked by gentleness and humor. She liked being with him.

They rounded the corner and headed toward the liveliest spot in Tivoli, the sideshows and the rides. Though it was now nearly dinner time, the air was filled with the near-hysterical screams of happy children, blending with rock and roll music, a band concert and, off in the distance, a calliope, in a raucous cacophony of happiness.

"Now there"—Borgmann said, pointing—"there is a building I've never seen."

"The Concert Hall," said Miriam. "Yes. It's new." She looked at him and shook her head. Sometimes that memory of his was spooky, almost superhuman. Had others felt this way about him?

"Frederick," she said thoughtfully, "how can you tell if you have a photographic memory—I mean, as opposed to a very good ordinary memory."

Borgmann smiled. "When I was a youngster, they just took my word for it—and that was good enough, since I usually got a hundred percent on my examinations and never lost anything, not even a mitten or a pair of rubbers. When I was about twelve, a psychologist named Klüver tested me. He showed me a piece of paper with part of a number on it, printed in the same kind of colored dots used in color blindness tests. Then he took it away and showed me another piece of paper with the rest of the number. If a person is an eidetiker, he can merge the two images in his mind and come up with the number—and I could—easily. Klüver said it was one of the most classic cases he'd ever seen. I wouldn't do as well today, though."

"Oh? Why not?"

"Well, Eidetic imagery usually fades with age. The early memories remain, but the later ones are held for a shorter and shorter period."

Borgmann stopped abruptly and stood stock-still. He held a hand over his ear to eliminate any outside noises. Then he pulled the earphone out of his ear and held it up to Miriam's.

"Listen," he said, excited.

She did. What she heard resembled the sound of a fast-beating metronome. "Does that mean we've found something?"

"It sure does, What you're hearing indicates definite radiation leakage—nowhere near enough to be dangerous to anyone, but enough to convince me there's some sort of atomic installation within two hundred yards of here."

Not far away, Suliman Ferrara, sipping a glass of chocolate milk at the Maelkeriet—the Milk Bar—was watching the couple carefully. It was obvious to him that they'd found at least some indication of what they were looking for. They were grinning at each other like children, and passing the earphone back and forth. They couldn't know it, of course, but whatever they discovered he also discovered.

At that moment, Gary Stabile was painstakingly scraping a wad of gum from the sole of his shoe with his pipe tool, cursing the child who'd dropped it on the sidewalk. But he was also watching Ferrara and, up the path a bit, Borgmann and his *sabra* companion. Like the Arab, the American agent had long ago figured out that Borgmann's transistor radio was something more than that and that the two of them definitely were not—however it might look—sharing listening time to a local radio station. He'd spent enough time around scientists in years past to guess Borgmann was listening to a Geiger counter. It was clear enough Borgmann believed that he'd find the plans here in Tivoli, connected in some way with radiation. All Stabile had to do now was to keep his eyes open and lend a hand, if necessary. With luck, it would all work out.

Frederick and Miriam at first started out directly north, heading around the other side of the lake. The Geiger counter clicks dropped off immediately. Then they returned to the spot from which they'd started and went directly south, toward the Restaurant Bix'en, a small, self-service beer garden. Again, the counter grew quiet. There was only one direction left—aside from the one from which they'd come—due east, toward the sideshows, the shooting galleries, the Ferris wheel and the other rides. They walked slowly in that direction. In the excitement, Miriam had grabbed Frederick's hand.

"It's getting stronger," Borgmann said, almost inaudibly. On they walked, for a few yards more, Frederick's face grim with concentration, Miriam smiling nervously, trying to look like a tourist. "Even stronger," Borgmann said. They kept going. Finally, they stopped just outside of the huge fun house.

"From the radiation signal I'm getting, I'd say the entrance has to be very close now," Borgmann told Miriam. They looked around in every direction. It was just about the busiest spot in the entire park. The paths were jammed with happy children, weary parents and shouting teen-agers. The only structure in the area, the only place an entrance to an underground installation might have been hidden was the House of Mirrors, part of the large sun-house complex—unless there were a grassy trapdoor somewhere in the vicinity.

Miriam and Frederick made eye contact. They'd come to the same decision. "In there?" Miriam asked.

"Looks that way," Frederick replied. He bought a pair of tickets at the kiosk and the two of them entered the building, after first carefully checking out the area, to be sure they weren't being followed.

The Tivoli House of Mirrors is a maze composed of full-length floor-to-ceiling mirrors and mirrored panels on the ceiling. Once you enter, you are almost instantly lost in a jumble of conflicting images. You see visions of yourself no matter which way you look. Finding the path that leads through the mirrors is not impossible, but to do it with any speed you must have an unusual sense of depth perception. As a result, it's the rare individual who can walk through the House of Mirrors, from entrance to exit, without bumping his nose against more mirrors than one, and pretty hard at that. Large families can manage the course with speed only if they hold hands.

Frederick and Miriam had two advantages over the usual visitor to the House of Mirrors. First, they had a Geiger counter which would lead them unerringly in the direction of increasing radiation—and no doubt at least partway through the maze. Second, they weren't interested in laughing when they collided with a mirrored wall mistaken for a doorway. They had an urgent purpose in mind.

Clutching Miriam's hand tightly now, Frederick plunged forward, leading them both through the maze, toward they knew not what. "Watch the floor," he whispered back to her. "It's worn where the real path is and not so worn on the dead ends."

"Good idea," she whispered. "Also, look for fingerprints on the mirrors. Those at the end of a trail have plenty of fingerprints on them, but not the others."

"Wait a minute," Borgmann said, head cocked, listening to the Geiger counter. "This way," he said, pointing.

At that moment, a hoard of Oriental children—perhaps half a dozen—came running around a corner, laughing, giggling and screaming, running headlong into mirrors, punching and tickling each other. They were followed by a pair of grim-faced parents. Frederick and Miriam plastered themselves against the mirror-covered walls and the children came rumbling, tumbling by.

Given the excitement he'd seen on Borgmann's face, Suliman Ferrara felt that he had to follow the pair into the House of Mirrors, despite the risk. They were getting close, he was certain. If he lay back now, he might miss the crucial moment of discovery. Ferrara paid his money at the kiosk and entered the House of Mirrors as carefully and cautiously as he knew how. He held a handkerchief in one hand, ready to "blow his nose" or otherwise disguise his face if that's what had to be done.

Behind Ferrara, Gary Stabile made the same decision, and for the same reason. Fun and games were just about at an end, he sensed. The next ten or fifteen minutes might tell the tale. But uppermost in his mind was the thought that if Borgmann saw him now—before the plans were located—the entire mission might be blown.

Stabile bought a ticket and waited. He needed a camouflage of some sort. Three hulking teen-age boys, loud and obnoxious—probably drunk, Stabile thought—soon sauntered up to the ticket booth, shoved their money through the window and headed toward the House of Mirrors as if they were about to essay the Atlantic in a sailboat. Stabile entered with them, staying as close as his nose and sensibilities would permit.

Frederick and Miriam walked slowly along the mirrored halls, Frederick leading the way, his head cocked as he listened carefully to the Geiger counter. He paused and swayed his body from right to left.

"Can't be far from the door now. I'm sure it's here—the counter shows a definite increase."

"Frederick, let's start looking for hinges or locks or anything that might indicate a door."

Borgmann nodded, concentrating fully on what he was hearing through his earphone.

The pair turned a corner, choosing against an obvious dead end, and proceeded forward through the mirrored hall. The shouts of teen-agers could be heard far behind them. "Wait a minute, Miriam," Borgmann said. "The level is dropping."

"I don't understand—"

"We must have passed the entrance," Borgmann said, worried now.

They backtracked, several times bumping into people following the maze in the proper direction. Soon, they found themselves at an intersection. In one direction, they saw, lay a dead end. The other led through the maze, in the direction from which they'd come. This time, they headed toward the dead end, Miriam looking nervously behind her. She saw no one suspicious.

"My God," Borgmann said softly, listening to the earphone. "It must be within a few feet of where we're standing."

They walked slowly along the mirrors, studying the cracks between each of the full-length pieces of plate glass, examining the floorboards and checking out the mirrored ceiling panels. Behind them, the crowd flowed through the maze, laughing and stumbling as usual.

"Frederick, look at the floor here," Miriam urged. "Doesn't it seem darker at this point?"

Borgmann knelt down and, for the first time, removed the small Geiger counter from his jacket pocket. He held it at floor level, as close as possible to the mirror. Then he looked up at Miriam and nodded once, gravely. He rose, peering at the crack between the mirror directly in front of him and the one to the right. There was nothing. At the same time, Miriam examined the separation between that mirror and the one to the left. She glanced at Borgmann and shook her head no.

Then Borgmann looked up at the ceiling. There was a slight gap between the mirrored ceiling panels and the wall mirrors. He stretched to his full height. Unable to see as high as he wanted to, he reached up and felt around.

Suddenly he pulled his hand away. "Feel this," he

told Miriam. He took her arm and guided her fingers along the top edge of the wall mirror.

"Buttons," she said in surprise. "Three buttons."

"A combination lock, I'll bet," said Borgmann. "But what does it open?"

Miriam thought a moment. Then, she swiveled around. The hallway was narrow—perhaps two or two and a half feet wide—so she immediately confronted a mirror directly opposite to the one they'd been studying. As Frederick watched, slightly puzzled, the girl ran her fingers down the separation between the plate-glass mirrors, first on the edge to her right, then on the edge to her left. "Look!"

Frederick bent forward. Only on the closest examination could he see it—a floor-to-ceiling hinge, carefully recessed and painted black, to merge with the narrow separation between the mirror panels.

"It must open left to right," Miriam observed.

"But how? There's no handle."

"Well, I imagine that whoever wanted to enter would press the three buttons in the proper order, then the door would spring open by itself," Miriam said.

"But maybe there is something to press—another button, possibly," Frederick theorized. He reached up to the top edge of the wall mirror that hid the door. Nothing. "Or maybe there's something to kick or press with the foot." He knelt down and studied the floor once more. One floorboard, he noticed, was perhaps a quarter of an inch higher than the others. He drew Miriam's attention to it and she knelt beside him.

At that moment, a four-year-old girl wandered into the dead end. She watched them for several moments before they noticed her.

"What are you looking for?" she said, in a loud open voice of a child who knew nothing of being embarrassed.

Frederick stood up suddenly, like a little boy who'd been caught with his hand in the cookie jar.

Miriam remained kneeling. She calmly turned to the child and smiled. "I dropped my earring," she said, without a moment's hesitation.

"Oh," said the little girl, evidently an American, "can I help you look for it?"

"No," Miriam said sweetly. "Don't you think you'd better run along? Your mother will be worried about you."

"No she won't," the child replied. "She's waiting outside on the bench, resting. She doesn't care when I come out."

"To tell you the truth, little girl," Frederick put in, "the lady really didn't lose an earring. We stopped here because we heard some kind of ferocious animal behind the wall."

"That's right," Miriam said, picking it up. "A lion or a tiger, I think. We're trying to figure some way to let it out. Will you help us?"

The girl backed away, wide-eyed. "No," she said uncertainly, "no, I don't think so. I have to go." She turned and ran down the hallway.

"I hope we didn't scare her too much," Frederick said. Miriam just laughed. They returned to their examination of the floor. Borgmann pressed on the protruding floorboard and it clicked. He released it and it popped up. He pressed once more and it clicked again. "It's spring-loaded," he told Miriam. "It could easily be a latch of some sort. Probably won't work unless those locking buttons are pressed in the proper order. I'm certain this is the entrance to the reactor."

"So am I," Miriam said. They both got to their feet.

"What do we do now?"

"We go back to Yaakov. As he instructed us. He has something cooked up."

Frederick agreed reluctantly, as if he wanted to press further.

"Shouldn't we mark this deadend in some way, so that we can find it quickly tomorrow? I assume we'll be coming back."

"I'm sure we will. That's a good idea."

"Why don't you put a lipstick mark on the floor?"

"I haven't worn lipstick since I was fourteen," Miriam said.

Borgmann couldn't help smiling. He took out his

Swiss Army knife and quickly carved a small "F" on the floor just inside the intersection where the deadend met the main hallway.

Suliman Ferrara walked carefully down the mirrored hallway, handkerchief in hand. The reflections worried him. What if his image bounced around a corner and ended up directly in front of the Israeli girl? Would she recognize him? He lingered behind others, looking ahead as far as he could. Finally, he caught a glimpse of them, up ahead, crouched in a hallway, examining the floor. He took one step backward and stopped. Now, he could see only the tip of Borgmann's shoe. Hopefully, they could see no more of him.

Ferrara gathered that the pair was looking for some sort of door, possibly a trap door. Maybe they'd already found it. Either way, he was sure they'd make no attempt to enter without Ben-Ezra. They'd have to go back for him. When they did, he could examine the floor himself and find out exactly what they'd discovered.

Following a person on a street—or even in a car— was child's play compared to this, Gary Stabile thought. All of these angles and mirrors made concealment nearly impossible. The only thing to do was to stay back, to keep others between yourself and those you were trailing and to be ready to duck almost as a reflex action. The one thing that wouldn't work was the trick amateurs were sure to try—the handkerchief-in-front-of-the-nose gambit. He'd used that technique himself in his younger days, with disastrous results. The boys at Foggy Bottom had later done a study on "clandestine reconnoitering of individuals in variable environments" and found that a handkerchief to the nose will "invariably attract attention, precipitating discovery, rather than providing concealment." But everything else in that study was useless in this situation. In fact, "surveillance personnel" were specifically warned to avoid brightly lit or sharply limited areas. The House of Mirrors was not only both of these, but it also sent images all over the place, even around corners.

The best thing he could do—the only thing, in fact—was to blend in with the crowd. For a while, it was no problem keeping Ferrara in sight—he was just up the hallway. Then, suddenly, Ferrara stopped. Stabile stopped too, and bent down to tie a shoelace, in the approved manner. The boys moved on and he was left without much cover. The next group coming through was made up mainly of small children. There was no way he could blend with them.

"I think we'd better get back to Yaakov as soon as we can," Mariam said.

"Let's go, then," Frederick said. He started toward the front entrance of the House of Mirrors, evidently not interested in following the maze through to its end. Miriam took three steps with him, then stopped abruptly.

"We have to go the other way, Frederick, to the exit." She said it softly, but with surprising urgency.

"But this way is faster."

Miriam pulled on Frederick's hand. He went along without understanding.

"Don't look back," she whispered, "but we're being followed."

"Followed? By whom?"

"An agent—come on, just act like we're here for fun."

Frederick caught on quickly—stumbling against mirrors, trying obvious deadends, then backing out, running into his own image. They laughed and giggled and did a pretty good job of imitating a young couple on a date, which, in an odd way, is exactly what they were.

All at once, they were through the exit door and out into the light. Miriam quickly pulled Frederick away from the door, behind the building where they could watch people as they came out—without being spotted themselves.

"Who was it?" Borgmann asked.

"Suliman Ferrara," Miriam told him, "a Palestinian agent."

"Are you sure he was following us?"

"Absolutely. I saw him earlier at the train station, when the centrifuge plans were coming into Copenhagen. No doubt he was working with Amer."

"And he's probably after the plans too."

"I'm sure of it," Miriam said.

"Is there any doubt in your mind it was Ferrara?"

"Well, he had his handkerchief up to his face. I guess there is some possibility I was wrong. Let's wait here to see who comes out, just to be sure."

Inside, Ferrara, totally unaware he'd been spotted, briefly examined Borgmann's small carved "F" and walked on, making no attempt to find or force the door. There'd be time for that later. He was followed a few seconds later by Gary Stabile, who did just the same thing. Their conclusions were identical: Borgmann and the girl had found what they were looking for—some kind of door—and were going back for help. The attempt to enter probably wouldn't be made that night, since the evening crowds at Tivoli wouldn't permit it. Tomorrow morning was the likely time.

Ferrara now hurried through the maze, Stabile only a few yards behind him. He knew what Ferrara was thinking—that the time for caution was over. But Stabile didn't agree. The time for caution was never over. Ferrara might be a skilled thief, Stabile thought, but he wasn't much of an espionage agent. Perhaps he'd spent too much time supervising lately—and too little in combat. He cursed the Arab under his breath, though he had no choice but to keep up with him.

"There," Miriam said, nodding her head toward Ferrara, who had just walked out of the House of Mirrors exit. "That's him. Stay back so that he doesn't see you."

Borgmann watched from almost around the corner. Ferrara never looked around. Instead, he walked directly toward the exit. Before Borgmann could turn back to discuss the matter with Miriam, Gary Stabile strolled out of the House of Mirrors. He stopped, let the crowd pass, pulled out his pipe and looked around, directly into Borgmann's eyes. They both experienced the shock of recognition. Stabile was the first to recover.

"Well, well," Stabile said, his eyes twinkling, "imagine seeing you here. Having a good time?"

"Why are you following me, Stabile?" Borgmann demanded.

"Following you? What nonsense. I'm just here to enjoy myself."

Borgmann moved threateningly toward Stabile. "Stop playing games, Stabile. I want to know why you've been tailing me and I want to know now. I don't like being followed. This isn't the United States, you know. You have no special powers here. If you keep it up, I'll go to the police."

Stabile shrugged. "What would you tell the police, Dr. Borgmann—that you found me sitting next to you on the plane and that you met me here in the Tivoli? I don't think anyone could find anything illegal in that."

"You and I both know you're following me, Stabile. And if the police won't do anything about it, I will."

"Violence? And from the pacifist scientist? My, my! How unexpected. Especially in the presence of a young lady. I'm surprised at you, Dr. Borgmann. Calm down. Count to ten. Introduce me to your charming lady friend. Then we'll all shake hands and I'll fade away into the woodwork, never to be seen again."

"I'm Miriam Shazar," Miriam said directly. "And just who are you?"

"My name is Stabile, Gary Stabile. I'm with the U.S. Government."

"CIA," Borgmann added, still angry.

"You have an enormous amount of nerve, Mr. Stabile, coming up to us this way."

"I know. No harm done though, eh?"

"That remains to be seen," Miriam said coldly.

Borgmann slowly recovered his self-control. His eyes were now on Miriam. He hadn't been thinking of her as an espionage agent. And, to a degree, she'd stopped acting like one. Now she was incredibly alert again, a coiled cobra ready to strike.

"Well," Stabile said, "you two have yourselves a good time at the Tivoli. I'm sorry if I disturbed you. I don't expect we'll be running into each other again."

"We'd better not," Borgmann said, his tone low and angry.

Stabile gave a small, slightly embarrassed wave and walked off, puffing on his pipe. Both Miriam and Frederick waited until he was well out of earshot. Ferrara had long since disappeared.

"This gets more complicated every moment," Miriam said as she watched Stabile shrink in the distance. "Are you certain he was trailing us?"

"I'm certain of it. We had a long talk on the plane. He's definitely interested in the plans, though I'll be damned if I know why. The only other possibility is that he's following Ferrara."

Miriam nodded. "Maybe. But Ferrara was following *us*."

"There's no doubt of that, I guess," Borgmann admitted. "Do you think they saw us mark the dead-end?"

"We have to assume they did, Frederick. And if they did, then they must suspect that the centrifuge plans are nearby. We have to get back to Yaakov—and quickly."

A few minutes later, in the back office of the porno shop, Yaakov Ben-Ezra listened calmly to all the revelations. He seemed to care only that they'd found the entrance to the reactor.

"I suppose there are some complications," Ben-Ezra said, "but, all in all, things seem to be going well."

"How can you say that, Yaakov?" Borgmann asked, incredulous. "The CIA and the Arabs know our move. I'm not sure we have any information they don't also have. What's to prevent one of them from beating us to the plans?"

"Think about it logically, Frederick," Ben-Ezra told him. "Can you imagine your friend Stabile operating the reactor? Or Suliman Ferrara? Neither one of them knows an atom from a molecule. Besides, I think they both have something else in mind."

"But what, Yaakov?" Miriam asked.

"It's only theory now, not worth discussing." He wouldn't elaborate.

Borgmann was exasperated. "I can't understand your optimism," he said, shaking his head.

"Well, my friend, there are always two possibilities—"

"Cut it out, Yaakov," Miriam said angrily. "It's obvious you know something we don't, or you think you do. Are you going to tell us, or leave us dangling?"

Ben-Ezra leaned back in his chair and inhaled deeply. In a flash, the pain was back. He held his breath for a moment, hoping it would subside. When it didn't, he exhaled slowly. Still, the pain remained. He got up from his chair and went to his jacket, which was hanging from a nearby hook. He took another breath. It was a sharp pain, as if he had inhaled a needle or a pin. Finally it began to fade.

"Yaakov?" Miriam was puzzled at his silence.

"I can tell you this," Yaakov said, as if he'd intended to pause all along, "we'll be well able to take care of ourselves, no matter what the opposition."

He withdrew the silver cylinders from his inside jacket pocket.

"What are those, Yaakov?" Borgmann asked.

"Gas guns," Miriam said. "One squirt, and whoever they're aimed at is out like a light."

"Would you mind if *I* told him about them, Miriam?" Yaakov said testily.

Miriam made a mock gesture of servility and bade Ben-Ezra continue.

"What these are," Ben-Ezra said, addressing Borgmann, "is gas guns. Point them at someone within ten feet, push this red button, and they'll fall asleep instantly. One shot keeps them out for about five hours. The things load with a cartridge. This other button, the blue one, opens the gun for reloading. Each cartridge is good for five squirts."

Borgmann took one of the cylinders from Ben-Ezra's

269

hand and hefted it in his own. He examined it closely, studying the two buttons. He tentatively pressed the blue button and the back end of the cylinder flipped open. After looking in, he pushed it closed until it clicked shut. Then he aimed it at Ben-Ezra.

"Hey," Ben-Ezra said, "no practicing."

"Take my word for it, Frederick," Miriam added, "it works."

"You've used one of these things, Miriam?"

"Well, yes, on occasion."

Borgmann slipped the cylinder and its refill into his jacket pocket. "So now we're armed. What next?"

"Let's meet here at about nine. I'd like us to be inside the Tivoli around nine-thirty."

"Why not earlier, Yaakov?" Miriam asked, puzzled. "We could be the first people through the gate. We could even sneak in before the place opened. That would give Frederick more time."

"No. I don't think we should get there before nine-thirty," Ben-Ezra insisted.

Frederick and Miriam exchanged there-he-goes-again looks.

"By the way, I want you both to bring your luggage and your passports. There may not be time to pack later," Ben-Ezra continued.

"This makes no sense at all, Yaakov," Miriam said. "Every moment counts, yet you're making plans as if you were going sightseeing. We're surrounded by enemies; yet you assure us that a squirt of sleeping gas will provide us with perfect safety. And you're all the time hinting that you know something we don't."

Ben-Ezra sat out her anger before he spoke, like a man waiting under an awning for the rainstorm to end. "And you, Frederick—do you feel the same way?"

Borgmann had been listening to the argument in growing confusion. He had no answer for his old friend.

"Frederick?"

"I don't know, Yaakov. What Miriam says makes sense. But I've trusted you in the past and you've never disappointed me."

270

"Ah," Ben-Ezra said. He'd found the word he'd been looking for. "Trust. That's what I want from both of you—one more time. Get a good night's sleep and meet me here at nine."

"Aren't you even going to eat dinner, Yaakov?" Miriam asked.

Yaakov considered the question momentarily, glancing at Miriam and Frederick. "No," he said, at last, "I don't think so—at least not now. I have some thinking to do. But why don't the two of you go ahead without me?"

Borgmann caught Miriam's eye. "Still hungry?"

"Sure am."

"I know a good place."

"Then let's go."

They bade Yaakov good night. Soon, they were back in Miriam's Saab. She started the engine. "Where to?"

"You like fish?"

"Of course."

"Then head up Gammel Strand. There's a place there that's been around so long my parents went there when they were children."

"You must mean Krog's," Miriam said.

"Ah," Frederick said. "You've eaten there?"

"No. But I've heard about it."

Ten minutes later, they were seated in the old Danish fish house, which was located in a building dating back to 1798. A polite but weary waiter took their order—two portions of filet of sole, steamed in hock, garnished with shrimps, salmon, peas and lobster, and served with shrimp sauce. It was the specialty of the house, a meal Frederick had eaten there many times.

Then they were left to themselves, or, rather, to each other.

"I don't understand what's going on with Yaakov," Miriam said.

"Me neither." Frederick admitted. "But we have to go along with him."

"I suppose." It was agreement of the most reluctant sort.

The waiter returned with a cold bottle of white wine.

Borgmann reached across the table and put his hand over Miriam's. "Listen," he said, "I have a suggestion: let's try to spend the evening without worrying or talking about this centrifuge business."

Miriam glanced at his hand. It covered hers almost completely. "That's fine with me," she said with a twinkle. "But what shall we talk about instead?"

Frederick pondered the question, as if it were the knottiest problem he'd ever faced. "I'm not sure," he said slowly. "We could discuss the weather, or the food, or politics or sports or cars or clothing. You choose."

"We could discuss why an attractive man like you is unattached," she suggested, her expression mischievous.

"Or why the same is true of a beautiful girl like you," Frederick proposed, returning her volley.

"There must be better things to talk about," Miriam said, still smiling.

"Certainly," replied her companion. "We could discuss the stock market, where we went on our last vacation, or the inequities of income tax."

Their eyes met and held. "Yes," she said. "We could."

The feeling that flooded through Borgmann's consciousness in no way resembled the intense tenderness he'd once felt for Maj, nor the sense of oneness he'd had with Ruth. Instead, he felt he was with an equal, a woman with whom he might share whatever adventures came along, a companion who had the strength and vitality to be an adversary when necessary. He was powerfully drawn to her. He wanted to touch her as deeply as possible. He wanted to make love to her, and not just because she was a damned attractive girl.

Miriam recognized his gaze for what it was—or at least part of what it was. They'd been playing with each other and teasing each other for days now. It was inevitable that the moment would come when he wanted something more from her. She knew the pattern well. It had repeated itself with most of the men she'd known since college. There were good times and intimacies; then each went his own way.

She smiled at him. He smiled back, awkward now, for the first time. She'd been anticipating this moment, but now that it was here, she felt oddly ambivalent. When both parties played by the rules, things always went well, even ended well. Miriam wasn't sure that Frederick would play by the rules. She wasn't even certain that he knew them.

"Is there no one in your life, Miriam?"

"You mean, do I have any emotional attachments?"

"I guess that's what I mean."

"No—none. They never work for me. How about you?"

"They're all in my past."

They were both silent, each trying to think of the right thing to say next.

The waiter came, just before the silence turned awkward. He served the meal, refilled the wine glasses, removed the salad plates, restocked the butter dish, then departed.

"What were you saying, Frederick?"

"I wasn't saying anything."

"About your past emotional attachments."

"Oh. Well, I was married, but my wife died in a car accident some years ago."

"Yaakov told me."

"Since then—well, I just haven't had time for relationships. I've been married to a breeder reactor."

"Frederick, you'll have to forgive me. I don't know anything about breeder reactors."

"Well, it's a nuclear power plant that makes its own fuel—when it works. Kind of like perpetual motion. Anyhow, I've been working with the team that's trying to debug the thing."

"And so you'll return to your work, when we've finished here?"

"I'm not sure," Borgmann answered. "We solved the last big problem just before I left. I guess I'll be looking for a new project when I return to the lab."

"I see."

"What about you, Miriam? Will you be going on another assignment as soon as you get home?" Both of them knew this wasn't the casual inquiry it seemed on the surface.

"I'm not sure. They can't always find a spot for me."

Frederick started to eat and motioned to Miriam to begin.

Somehow, the food lubricated the conversation. They talked about their favorite restaurants, about what they did when they weren't working, about how much they loved to play tennis and how quickly their game deteriorated when they didn't play, about which season they liked best, about their favorite music, about the books they'd read. Before long, they were pelting each other with information about themselves, both of them in a rush to tell the other who they were and why.

When they finished dinner, Borgmann paid the check and they rose from the table, heading toward the door.

"Now what?" asked Miriam.

"Would you like to walk for a while?"

"For a while."

"Toward my hotel."

They walked holding hands, down the Stroget. The talk continued. It was a romantic moment for Frederick, though he did his best to hide it. It was not a romantic moment for Miriam, and she did her best to hide that.

They stopped at the hotel newsstand briefly. Frederick bought a paper.

"Now what?" Miriam asked again.

"My room's on the tenth floor."

"Oh."

He led her into the elevator. It filled up with the usual conglomeration of tourists, bellhops and small children. They were briefly separated. Miriam looked at him, wondering just what it was he wanted of her, what he thought she wanted of him. She felt no need to ask herself that question.

He opened his hotel room door and they stepped inside.

"Now what?" she asked, teasing.

"Now this," he said. He put his arms around her and

274

pulled her to him and simply held her. She thought about pulling away, about saying something witty that would keep the moment free of cloying sentiment. In the end, she just let him hold her. It felt good.

When he bent to kiss her, she closed her eyes and joined in enthusiastically. It was a long kiss, a gentle kiss, with distinct erotic overtones. When they finally parted, she was short of breath.

"Now what?"

He lifted her off the floor in one smooth motion, so suddenly she thought the teasing question had angered him. Then, in four strides, they were beside the bed. He set her down, not in anger, but as an answer.

They undressed each other quickly, playing and poking, too excited to be romantic about it, enjoying themselves and each other like eight-year-olds rolling in the hay.

He expertly undid her bra and slid it over her shoulders. "Well, well," he said, looking at her appreciatively. "So that's what's under the bulky sweaters."

She unzipped his trousers and tugged on the cuffs. "My," she said, "so that's what's under—"

He was on top of her then, quickly, his lips against hers, his tongue prying her mouth open. She seemed to yield reluctantly, but she was just trying to make it more intense for both of them.

In the midst of the kiss, Frederick reached down to tickle her. She broke out in a near fit of giggling, but he didn't let up. When he had her breathless, red-faced and protesting, he suddenly changed tactics, caressing and fondling, exploring. She welcomed the change, matched his actions with caresses of her own.

There was no time for talk now, nor any need for it.

He lay on top of her for awhile, luxuriating in the warm softness of her body. Then the time for foreplay was over for both of them. Miriam linked her arms around his back and pulled him to her, tightly, at the same time arching to meet him.

They made love artfully, passionately, imaginatively, first in one position, then another. It was as much discovery (or self-revelation) as sex. Then they were quiet, lying in bed together.

"You're full of surprises, Miriam."

"Why do you say that?"

"Well, I just didn't expect—"

"What? That I was a match for you?" She pretended to be insulted. "I'm no baby, you know."

"I know. Believe me, I know."

"That's more like it."

Miriam got up, restless, and turned on the radio. She disappeared into the bathroom for a few minutes.

"What's the matter?" Frederick asked, when she returned.

"I don't know. Nothing."

"Thinking about tomorrow?"

"What? No. I was thinking of going back to my place."

Frederick looked away from Miriam, suddenly interested in a picture hanging on the wall. "No." He said.

"What do you mean, no? I do what I want."

He turned back to her. "What is it you want, Miriam?"

She wasn't shaken by the question. "Good times. Closeness. No obligations on either side."

"I don't believe it."

"I won't try to convince you. But that's the way it is."

"You're self-sufficient, aren't you? You don't need anybody."

Miriam didn't answer.

"Right, Miriam?"

"Right."

"Come here."

"Just like that?"

"Just like that."

He put his arms around her once more and pulled her close. "I felt that way for a long time. Maybe I'm just beginning to realize I'm wrong."

"What way?"

"You're avoiding the issue, Miriam."

"It's your issue, not mine."

"So you say."

Frederick kissed her again, softly this time. He knew that she was in pain, that she'd been in pain for a long time. Holding her, he tried to draw it from her.

They made love again, with much less passion than before, their moment of discovery past, their needs more modest. It was better this time—less exciting, more real. Then they lay together for a long time.

"I have to go, Frederick," Miriam said.

"Why?"

"I always have to go."

"That's just smart talk, Miriam. Or not-so-smart talk."

"You sound so fatherly, Frederick. It doesn't fit—not after how we've spent the evening."

"You're right. I take it all back. If you have to go, go."

She glanced at him and he caught just a glint of fear in her eyes. "Do you really want me to?"

"Do you think I do?"

"I guess not." Her voice was almost inaudible.

He put his arms around her again. This time she cried.

Chapter Twenty-Six

Gary Stabile hadn't exactly been overjoyed with the confrontation he'd had with Borgmann and Miriam Shazar, but there'd been no way to avoid it. He'd handled it as well as possible, under the circumstances.

But what would Ben-Ezra think when he found out there was a CIA man on the scene? Stabile answered his own question. The old man wouldn't even raise an eyebrow. He might even guess my plan, Stabile thought with a sly smile. Perhaps he'll even conclude he can outwit me. And Ferrara, too. That should be amusing.

After running into Borgmann and the girl, Stabile had circled around the Tivoli, reentered the House of Mirrors and thoroughly explored the door they'd found. The three-button locking system was exactly where he expected it to be and the floorboard latch was in the right place too. He'd seen plenty of similar security devices at secret laboratories or high security areas in the United States.

Stabile wondered how the professor and his female friend had reacted when they found the lock. Did they think Ben-Ezra could open it, at will? No doubt they did. Stabile knew better. Button-locks triggered an alarm when the buttons weren't pressed in the proper order. And, in the United States anyhow, the combination was changed at least once every twenty-four hours, to make sure that proper order didn't become too widely known. There were no tumblers, no clicks. The devices had time and time again survived the best efforts of the most talented safecrackers the Superintendent of the Federal Prisons could find. No, Ben-Ezra would be beyond his depth here. He would need the help Stabile intended to provide.

He spent most of that evening at the Nyhavn office. It took nearly a half hour of rummaging through file cabinets, safes and equipment storage containers to find what he wanted—a small brown plastic box with seven holes in it. The holes were on the back of the box. On the front were corresponding "nixie" tubes—those electronic tubes often used in calculators to display any number from zero to nine. On top of the box, there was a rocker switch for each hole-nixie tube combination.

Stabile hadn't worked a device like this for years, so he fervently hoped he could find the instructions. CIA procedures dictate that equipment instructions and actual equipment be stored separately, for the sake of security. As a result, Stabile was forced to spend the next half hour searching through the instruction file folder. He admitted it would have been easier if Salter had been there, but some things couldn't be helped.

Just as Stabile was about to give up on the instructions and try to remember how the gadget worked, he found the sheet he'd been looking for. It was entitled: "Operating Instructions, A153 Electronic Closure Safeguard Decoder." He read through it quickly:

"The A153 Electronic Closure Safeguard Decoder operates on four AA Alkaline Cells. These are installed in compartment '1' (see diagram), which is opened by slide latch 'A' . . ."

Stabile opened the battery compartment. It was empty. He swore under his breath and started tearing apart the drawers and cabinets again. To his infinite disgust, there wasn't a battery in the place. On second thought, he told himself, it was better that Salter wasn't here. If he had been, there would have been another tongue-lashing to give. Stabile didn't exactly dislike giving tongue-lashings, but he disliked giving more than one to a single individual—it smacked of inefficiency. Well, he decided, he could buy batteries easily enough tomorrow morning. Fortunately, the gadget used a common variety and size.

Stabile continued to read the instructions to himself, aloud:

"Battery viability should be checked by pressing test switch 'B' on left side of decoder (with holes at back) (See diagram). Caution: battery failure will render this device inoperative."

He looked up from the instructions and pushed the little recessed battery test switch. There was a small window beside the switch and a needle gauge divided into red and green. At his push, the needle remained in deepest red. He continued reading.

"Upon locating Closure Safeguard device, carefully hold decoder over lock buttons. Caution: decoder is not designed for lock buttons exceeding ⅝th inch in diameter or half-an-inch from front to back. Its use on Closure Safeguards with lock buttons larger than this could trigger any associated alert system. Caution: decoder cannot be used on Closure Safeguards with more than six buttons. Use may trigger any associated alert system . . ."

Stabile looked at the holes on the back of the box and tried to remember the buttons he'd felt in the House of Mirrors. There were three buttons, so there was no problem there. And he thought they were within the size limitations. He continued reading.

"When decoder is in position, depress rocker switches on top of the device (See diagram) from right to left. Depress all rocker switches, no matter how many buttons (up to six) on the Closure Safeguard lock. The proper combination sequence will then appear on the nixie tubes on the front of the decoder (see diagram). Closure Safeguard devices built before 1970 operate in simple serial sequence. This will be revealed on the nixie tubes. Closure Safeguard devices built since that date may have more complex patterns, such as, in the case of a four-button lock, 4321-2314-4321-3214. These patterns will also be revealed on the nixie tubes. When dealing with Closure Safeguards of a vintage more recent than 1970, it may be helpful to have a notepad handy when operating the decoder."

Stabile opened a desk drawer and withdrew a small pocket notebook. He never failed to be impressed with the instructions for these devices. They considered every possibility. A five-year-old could operate them, if he knew how to read. He put the notebook in his jacket pocket and went back to the instructions.

"Caution: Before operating Closure Safeguard, conceal decoder A153 at least 100 yards from the scene. Both the existence of the A153 and the technology behind it are currently unknown to the opposition and the company wishes to maintain this status. If secure concealment is impossible it is recommended that the decoder be buried at least five inches below the ground. The case is made of Lexan, a synthetic plastic, and is immune to metal detector search. Experience has shown that the burial spots most likely to escape visual identification are at the edges of corners of buildings, under stair landings, beside drywells, etc. In extremis, smash the decoder by striking vigorously with the heel of the shoe as many times as necessary to shatter the case."

Stabile allowed himself a smile. By tomorrow afternoon, he was entirely certain, the decoder would be back in the equipment cabinet, safe and sound—and with working batteries installed. In twenty-two years of field operation, he had never lost or even damaged any nonexpendable equipment and he wasn't about to start now. He had his pride.

At the same moment, across town, in the dingy flat behind the railroad station, Suliman Ferrara paced nervously back and forth. He had the distinct impression that he'd been hanging on to the Israelis by his fingernails. One slip, one instant of inattention, and they'd be out of his grasp forever, along with the centrifuge plans.

Once more he cursed all the Palestinian splinter groups who'd promised to send help, then reneged. If he'd had men, he could now be keeping tabs on Borgmann, Ben-Ezra and the girl, whether they stayed together or separated. He could have a man at the

Tivoli. Whenever the Israelis made their move, he could be ready. As it was, he had to guess.

He'd been guessing ever since he got to Copenhagen, and so far he'd been right. Now, he had to make one last correct guess: he had to figure out how and when the Israelis intended to get the plans out of Denmark.

Ferrara had one "given," or he thought he had: the theft attempt must come tomorrow morning. Otherwise, the plans would be packed sometime in the next afternoon, then sent back to the Netherlands.

He sat down in one of the room's two pale green plastic-covered lounge chairs. Though the weather was cool, the chair was sticky. So the Israelis would take the plans tomorrow morning, if they could. What then? The answer followed logically. They'd hustle them out of the country as quickly as possible, to the safety of Tel Aviv. Once the theft was discovered, the Danes would seal off their borders and close down the airports. So the Israelis had to get out before anyone knew the plans were gone.

Ferrara had an idea. He picked up the telephone and called El Al.

"Do you have a flight to Tel Aviv tomorrow?"

"Yes, sir. To Lod Airport. Flight 42. It leaves at two o'clock in the afternoon. Would you care to book a reservation?"

"Ah—well—yes, why not? My name is Steven Furnal."

"Yes, Mr. Furnal. Coach or first class?"

"Coach."

"Round trip or one way?"

"One way."

"And will you be picking up your ticket in Copenhagen or at Kastrup Airport?"

"At the airport."

"Then we'd like to request that you arrive no later than forty-five minutes before flight time."

"Certainly. I guess it takes time for security processing."

"Yes. How will you be paying for your ticket, Mr. Furnal?"

"Cash."

"That will be fine. Thank you for calling El Al."

Ferrara hung up and sat at the desk while he reflected on the situation. He now had a reservation on El Al Flight 42. If he were still guessing right, so did Yaakov Ben-Ezra, Miriam Shazar and Professor Borgmann. It all seemed to fit.

The question now was would the Israelis succeed in lifting the plans? Ferrara desperately hoped they were good thieves. But he intended to do more than hope. Tomorrow morning, he intended to be at the Tivoli when it opened. He wasn't at all sure that Ben-Ezra, Borgmann and the girl could break into the House of Mirrors hiding place, overpower the guards who must be there, steal the plans and make a clean getaway. Israeli agents depended too heavily on finesse and wit. Ferrara made a rational decision: he would supply the necessary brute force.

If there'd been any way he could have sped the passage of the night, Ferrara would have done it. He was in a holding pattern until morning, plans made, goals set. And yet his mind would not rest. He dwelt not on today's events or tomorrow's, or on what the future might bring. He thought, instead, of the past. He thought of his parents.

His father had died without knowing just what his son did for a living, which was just as well. The old man wouldn't have been pleased to learn that his offspring controlled much of Beirut, the same way the Mafia controlled much of New York. He wouldn't have approved of his son's association with gambling, liquor and sleazy hotels. Fortunately, the elder Ferrara, a retired agricultural official, concerned himself more with his garden than anything else. His innocence protected him.

His mother knew the truth. Her connections among the Moslems were widespread, her ear for gossip sharp, her intelligence acute. She was not pleased with her son. It wasn't so much that she disapproved of the criminal life—though she did—it was that she felt Ferrara was wasting his talents. She wanted him not at the top of the Beirut underworld, but at the forefront of her own cause—the Palestinian Liberation Movement.

Until his father's death, Ferrara treated his father's innocence and his mother's politics with equal forbearance. Like many a son who believes his education and experience have lifted him above his background, he felt that his parents were to be honored and cared for—but not otherwise taken seriously.

With his father's death, that changed. Riska Sarami Ferrara, a slender, vigorous woman who was not yet fifty, unexpectedly turned out to be a force in her own right, after years of obeying Moslem customs and taking a back seat to her husband. More and more, Ferrara found himself listening to her—and agreeing with her.

He no longer remembered exact words or phrases, though the message was vivid enough. It concerned the Palestinian refugees. His mother wasn't one of them, but she shared their sense of outrage. Years ago, her own family had lived in Jerusalem. She still had relatives there. Other relatives, however, had been forced out by the Israelis back in 1948. They'd fled before the Zionist troops, the hordes of European Jews—"colonists, no more, no less"—who'd overrun the Arab land of Palestine. Now they lived in hovels, some near Gaza, others on the Jordan's West Bank. They raised their children in hovels, grew old in hovels, and in these hovels, nurtured the dream of return.

And that was the mother's message to her son: sooner or later, the Palestinians must return to their homes, to the lands that had been illegally expropriated by the Zionists. Decades might pass before they gathered sufficient strength, possibly even generations, but some day they *would* return. Hopefully, there would be no bloodshed—but if blood had to be shed, so be it.

The firmer Ferrara's hold on his underworld organization, the more interested he became in his mother's ideas. Through her tutelage, he became involved in Pan-Arab politics. One day, for example, when he visited his mother, there was a guest in the villa—Wadi Rahman, his mother's uncle, a Palestinian refugee who had lived in Jordan since the 1948 war.

After dinner, they talked late into the evening about the plight of the Palestinians.

"What I cannot understand, Rahman," Ferrara said, "is why the refugees cannot settle their differences. As it is, they have little political power, except where they reside."

"There are two reasons," said Rahman. He was a tall, dignified man who wore the long white robe and white headcloth of a sheik, for that is what he had been. "First, we do not have geographical unity. We are scattered over a half dozen Arab nations, most of which consider us beggars. Second, we are divided—as is the rest of the world—into parties that occupy the full political spectrum, from left to right. If we were not dispossessed, these parties would be contending for the leadership of the Palestinian nation, and properly so. Since we have no homeland, they are only a symbol of our disunity."

"Will the time ever come when the Palestinians act together?" Ferrara asked.

Rahman took his time answering. "Yes, I think it will happen someday. But only when we are guided by rationality instead of emotion."

Ferrara was skeptical. "It sounds to me that you expect a whole culture to change its character. I don't think that will happen within your lifetime or mine."

Now his mother spoke, looking directly at her son. "If the leaders are rational men, that will be enough."

For all the talk, Ferrara was not ready to actively join the cause. It was already clear that another confrontation between Israel and the Arabs was coming. Nasser's words were growing more and more strident. Only the UN observers, it seemed, stood between Israel and its opponents. Ferrara warned the Lebanese government.

On Monday, June 5, 1967, the storm finally broke.

Once the war broke out, Suliman Ferrara's sources were no better than those of his countrymen—the various Middle Eastern radio stations. He sat in the grill at St. George's Hotel, eating European food and listening to a transistor radio, like everyone else.

"Oh, Arabs," cried Radio Cairo, "prepare to die as martyrs, for martyrdom is the way to paradise. . . . We stand ready. Oh, Nasser, you have shown the way. . . . Aqaba is ours, we shall surely take it . . . and let the Sixth Fleet go to hell! . . . We know the name of the beast that is against us: Oh, America, we are coming to slay you! . . ."

Radio Baghdad—removed from the battle—shouted, "Kill the Jews!"

Radio Damascus told its listeners that the enemy was already collapsing and that Arabs would spend their summer holidays in Haifa and Jaffa.

Radio Beirut announced that the Lebanese Army was already in the thick of battle and the country stood united for war. Ferrara laughed bitterly.

Radio Amman repeated King Hussein's words, that Jordan would fight to the death.

The vituperation was shortly replaced by statistics.

At first, the Egyptians claimed they'd shot down twenty-three Israeli aircraft. Before the day was over, the number was changed to forty-two. There was no word of Egyptian strikes against Tel Aviv.

Ferrara ordered coffee. Business in Beirut had come to a stop. The only reality was the radio announcer's voice and there was no way of knowing how much truth he spoke.

As he listened, a small demonstration passed the hotel. Perhaps a thousand youths carried flags and Nasser portraits toward the American Embassy. The police met them and they scattered, most of them ending up in juice bars, eating meaty *charwarma* sandwiches.

From the BBC, Ferrara heard that a tank battle was raging in the Sinai desert. It was a disquieting thought. He imagined the *fellahin* maneuvering Russian-made tanks in the sand, trying to stop the hardened Israelis. The Arabs were like children here, and these were not children's games.

One of his chief lieutenants, Ahmed Majali, found him in the grill, pulled up a chair and sat down.

"So?" Ferrara asked.

Majali made a nervous, dissatisfied gesture with his shoulders. "The Israelis are attacking from Gaza. Hussein means to counterattack from Jordan. I think we have a disaster in the making."

"*Insha'llah*," Ferrara said. "We'll survive."

Ferrara spent the evening at his mother's house. It was not pleasant. She worried about her relatives still in Israel. "There'll be reprisals, you can be sure." She feared for the Egyptians and the Jordanians. "Hussein is the best of them," she said. "And he is not good enough."

By Tuesday, June 6, the cries of war had turned into cries of hatred. Ferrara rose late. He took a taxi to the Chinese Restaurant, on Corniche Mazraa, passing a corner cafe on which was mounted a loudspeaker that screamed in anger. Young thugs eyed his cab with interest, trying to decide if he were European. Happily, they judged him Lebanese.

Outside the Chinese Restaurant, the street hawkers clustered around a bootblack, who had a transistor radio tuned to Radio Damascus. Inside, the wealthy patrons did the same . .

"What's the news?" Ferrara asked the maitre d'.

"Radio Amman quotes Hussein as saying that American warplanes actively assisted the Zionists."

"Do you believe that?"

"No. But it is a brilliant lie, isn't it?"

Further news was hard to come by that day. Military censorship was in full effect. That evening, though, it seemed to break down. Ferrara listened with Christine, his girlfriend of the moment. Radio Beirut talked of food shortages, army call-ups, and minor attacks on both the British and American embassies. Radio Amman revealed that Jenin and Ramallah were in Israeli hands and Nablus was in danger. So much for the West Bank. A Jordanian soldier, interviewed in an Amman hospital, told the radio audience, "We did not see our adversary.... There was no man to fire our guns at.... This liquid fire came from the sky."

"Liquid fire?" asked Christine in her whisper-soft voice.

"Napalm," Ferrara told her. "From Israeli airplanes."

"Oh."

On Wednesday, Ferrara spent some time at his office, then he walked over to the American University, on Rue Bliss. He had good relations with several professors there. Besides, he loved the atmosphere. He enjoyed nothing more than sitting in one of the parks, with the mountains to the back and the sea to the front, debating politics with a friend. But today the place was closed. If he hadn't known the guard, he wouldn't have gotten in. He soon spotted some friends walking down one of the peaceful lanes and joined them.

"The Egyptians are just bluffing," said Abu Ghazali, an old man, but still the most militant professor in the group. "They aim to lure the Israelis as close to the canal as possible; then the rockets will start falling on Tel Aviv. When the Israelis retreat, they'll be pursued by Egyptian troops. When they arrive back in Israel, they'll be met by Jordanians."

"What Jordanians?" asked Robert Kahled, another professor, also a Moslem. "They've already been beaten."

"What rockets?" asked Vincent Coates, a British history professor.

"If they wait much longer with the rockets," Ferrara put in, "they'll have to drop them on Cairo."

"What I want to know," said Ghazali, "is where are the Saudis, the Kuwaitis, the Iraqis, the Libyans, the Moroccans, and the Algerians?"

"At least we know where the Palestinians are," Ferrara said. "General Murtagi made sure they were in the vanguard of the Syrian army."

"Somehow that doesn't seem fair," Kaled said, only half-seriously.

Ferrara lunched with his friends in the faculty cafeteria. The ever-present radios blared out the news: the

Russians and the Americans were both demanding a cease-fire, an ominous sign.

Before the day had ended, the Israelis were at the canal. Radio Jerusalem, now Israeli-held, announced that the buses would be running on schedule on Thursday, that schools would reopen on Friday and that the concert set for Sunday would take place on schedule.

Ferrara spent the night by himself. When he opened his apartment door the next morning, the newspaper was there as usual. Front-page editorials screamed defiance. "We refuse to accept the cease-fire," one said. "We say, 'Fight on!' to the Arab armies . . . on to Tel Aviv. . . . We say to the West, we withhold our oil, we withhold the Canal. . . . We threaten you with a total boycott. Then let the Texan gangster talk!"

By Friday, the Arab radio stations broadcast mostly patriotic songs. The only news was from Syria, where the Israelis were driving Arabs from the Golan Heights. That night, a haggard, hesitant Gamel Abdel Nasser appeared on television and resigned. The despair that followed could not have been more effective if it had been staged by Hollywood. Beirut was filled with demonstrations, riots and disturbances. Europeans, especially, were subject to attack, and the Jewish quarter had to be guarded by crack Lebanese troops. Wherever Ferrara went, he heard shouts of "Nasser, Nasser."

On June 10, it was over. Arab passion had been broken on the anvil of Israeli intellect. His mother summed it up for him: "We shall never win, not until we are more rational than they."

"And when will that be, Mother?"

Her gaze held his. "Perhaps in your lifetime. Perhaps not."

It had come sooner than anyone expected—not really a victory, but a revenge. The 1973 war turned the tables on the Israelis, puncturing the myth of invincibility that had grown up around them, showing the world how precarious their position was.

Once again Arab voices were raised, crying for Israeli blood. Some hysterically screamed for Israel's total destruction. The more moderate voices asked for a multinational state, on a West Bank Palestine. The cowards feared that Israel would strike again, on her own.

At first Ferrara had great hopes. With the Arab nations acting in unaccustomed unison, wielding the oil weapon like a scimitar, the West backed down. Israel was brought to negotiations with Western industry, the hostage.

The Arab nations proclaimed that nothing—not even Israel's complete surrender of all lands taken during the 1967 war—would satisfy them, if Israel did not let the refugees establish a Palestinian state.

But even this war, a victory of sorts, brought nothing to the Palestinians in the end. Those who had been forced from Palestine remained exiles. Israel remained a nation of Jews, a nation of colonists.

"The Arabs have won their victory, Mother," Ferrara said to her. "But what good has it done the Palestinians?"

His mother thought a long time before answering. "It has taught us a lesson," she said. "It has taught us that no one will look out for us. We must take care of ourselves. Though we are in exile, we must become a nation. We must arm ourselves. We—and no one else—must retake Palestine and free ourselves from Israel."

"But how can we do that, Mother? Even the unity the Arab nations mustered against Israel has collapsed. How can the Palestinians, scattered as they are, become one "

"That I do not know. Perhaps it is for you to find the answer."

It was midnight at the Tivoli. The last patrons were drifting out of the exits and the strings of colored lights scattered around the park were winking off.

In a large dimly lit room below the House of Mirrors, Eduard Jelle checked the large wall clock.

"It's midnight, Hans," he called to a uniformed policeman who was sitting at a small wooden table. "The relief shift should be here momentarily."

"I'll be glad when it comes," the cop said. "I get nervous down here with that—" He pointed toward a massive concrete door decorated with a triangular radiation warning symbol.

"If you're referring to the reactor," Jelle said coolly, "there's nothing to worry about. It's been here seventeen years without incident. What worries me is what's inside."

"The plans, you mean."

"I'm surprised at you, Hans." Jelle chided the policeman. "First, you shouldn't have any idea what I'm talking about. Second, you should have the good sense to keep quiet about what you know."

"Mr. Jelle, I've been with you and these plans for almost nine months now. You can't expect me not to have some idea of what I've been guarding."

Jelle chuckled. "That's what I get for asking for intelligent guards."

A white bulb mounted above the policeman's table suddenly lit up. "That'll be the relief shift." He stood up, drew his service revolver, and stationed himself behind a pillar. Jelle watched, approvingly, then turned to the reactor room door. He pushed a nearby buzzer and called into a speaking tube. "Mr. Vondeling and Mr. Von Mierlo, we can go up now," he said. "Same goes for the reactor operators."

The huge door rumbled open and two nervous young TV technicians walked out, a tall, red-faced man in his thirties and a shorter fellow who looked to be about twenty-two or twenty-three. They weren't happy. Two older men followed, both white-coated scientific types. They began removing their uniforms and hanging them up in lockers.

"I don't see why we have to wait down here so long," the red-faced technician whined. "We stopped broadcasting nearly four hours ago."

Jelle impaled him with a cool stare. "That was all settled in your contract, wasn't it? You knew you would have to stay in here until closing time, and you knew it before you were retained."

"Yes," said the younger technician, "but it's getting on my nerves. Three days now, from eight-thirty to midnight. And with all this radiation around. I'm a young man, you know. I plan to have children."

The two scientists smiled at each other. "Then you have nothing to worry about, Mr. Von Mierlo—except your own natural capacity. I assure you you're in no danger," Jelle said.

"That's just it, Mr. Jelle," said the red-faced technician, Vondeling. "We're broadcast men, not nuclear physicists." He pointed to the scientists who were changing into street clothes. "It's unfair to subject us to these conditions."

Jelle heard him out. "Well, then, you'll be pleased with what I have to tell you now. Though the contract calls for four days' work, your services won't be required tomorrow morning. You can report here at one-thirty. You can expect to leave by four at the latest, and that will wind up the job. How does that sound?"

Both men were pleased and said so.

At one end of the room, two uniformed policemen came down a long flight of stairs that curled down from ground level and had four separate landings. They were accompanied by two scientists who came on shift to take charge of the reactor. The uniformed policeman downstairs watched them, gun drawn, until he saw familiar faces. Then he stuck his gun in its holster, picked up a newspaper and a paperback book from the guard table, and headed up the stairs, followed by Jelle and the two technicians.

"Have a good evening," the departing policeman told the two entering policemen and the scientists as they came down the stairs.

"And no sleeping," warned Jelle, with a twinkle. "The relief shift will be here by eight tomorrow morning, along with Mr. Groot, and you know how he feels about snoozers."

The arriving policemen laughed. They'd heard Jelle talk like this before and they knew he was joking—but heaven help them if Groot really caught them napping. Jelle was a gentle, considerate man. His deputy was neither.

The scientists paid no attention to Jelle. They calmly changed into white uniforms, entered the reactor room, and closed the gigantic concrete door behind them.

As they had for the last two nights, the reactor guards spent a quiet evening. They did sleep—but only one at a time. By the next morning, they were more than ready for the relief shift. All the books and newspapers on the guard table had been read, all the small talk exhausted.

MAY 15
DAY FOUR

Chapter Twenty-Seven

At almost exactly 8:00 A.M., the light bulb above the reactor room guard table flashed on. While the night shift watched, Claude Groot, a thin blond man with watery grey eyes, came down the stairs, accompanied by a stocky, swarthy uniformed policeman and a pair of scientists.

"Anything to report?" he asked one of the night guards.

"No, sir."

"Everything is in order?" he inquired of the departing scientists.

"Of course."

Groot frowned. He didn't care for flip answers. This was serious business. However the Danes felt about their antiquated reactor, there were the plans to worry about.

Groot and the uniformed guard watched while the night shift trudged up the stairs. Shortly, the warning light blinked out.

"Sergeant Von Hahn," said Groot, his high voice echoing through the large underground chamber, "I want you to stay here at the table. I'll be in the reactor room—watching the experiments. Please don't disturb me, except in the event of emergency."

"Yes, sir," said Von Hahn. He kept his voice strictly neutral. Von Hahn didn't like Groot at all. The man was arbitrary and overbearing. Watching the experiments—hah! Von Hahn knew better. Groot was going in there to take a nap. God help EURATOM Security if that man ever succeeded Jelle. If he'd have been in command when the Chinese attacked, back in Amsterdam, the plans would have been in Peking already.

By now the new shift of scientists had changed into their white coats. They pressed the button that opened the reactor room door and disappeared inside, Groot on their heels. Then the door slid closed.

Von Hahn put his feet up on the guard table, pulled a paperback novel out of his pocket and began to read. At least Groot's absence allowed him to relax a bit instead of spending every instant staring at the entry warning light.

At 8:59 Gary Stabile arrived at the Tivoli main gate, the decoder resting comfortably in a side pocket. Inside, he headed directly toward the House of Mirrors. What he had to do wouldn't take long, he thought. But he had to beat both Ferrara and the Israelis to that secret door.

As he approached the House of Mirrors, Stabile saw the ticket agent unlocking her window and opening her cash drawer. An enormous feeling of relief swept over him. Now he was sure he was the first to arrive. Ferrara and the Israelis would never break into the Tivoli. The chance of attracting police attention was too great.

Stabile bought his ticket and entered the House of Mirrors. Inside, he wasted no time, going directly to the deadend marked with the small "F." He felt around until he'd located the button lock. Then he took the decoder out of his pocket, put it in place, and started pushing the rocker switches. As the numbers flashed on the nixie tubes, he scribbled them down on his note pad. The numbers stopped appearing after about ten seconds or so, at which point Stabile pulled the decoder from the buttons and pocketed it. Then he carefully punched the lock buttons in the indicated pattern: 322–213–333–132–111–311. For a moment, he almost walked away, and left it at that. Then, he realized he'd better test out the decoder's work. He knelt down and pressed the single protruding floorboard. Instantly a mirror panel opened up behind him.

Stabile reacted with admirable speed, considering his age. He shoved the door shut almost the moment it opened. Somewhere down there, he knew, a guard was watching some kind of entry indicator. With luck, it would flash only briefly and the guard would consider the indication a momentary malfunction. At worst, he'd come running. Stabile backed away, into the main hallway. He'd give it five seconds.

Down below, the entry warning light flashed for less than a second. Von Hahn, immersed in his book, glanced up for a moment. Something bright had attracted his attention. But by the time he looked up at the entry light, it was dark again. He shrugged and went back to his book.

The five seconds up, Stabile counted his blessings and stepped back into the deadend. Once more, he punched out the code on the lock buttons. The next person to step on that protruding floorboard would open the door. And unless Stabile was wildly in error, that person would be Suliman Ferrara. Satisfied, he headed out of the maze. It was 9:04. Stabile bought a roll and some coffee at a refreshment stand, then sat down to watch and wait.

At 9:04, Suliman Ferrara was striding urgently toward the House of Mirrors. It was a threatening grey morning and the amusement park, he noticed, was nearly empty. So much the better. When he got to the House of Mirrors ticket kiosk, the old lady attendant was hanging up her coat. Evidently, Ferrara decided, he was her first customer.

"Good morning," he said.

"God morgen."

"One, please."

He pushed his money through the window and she pushed a ticket back at him. For a moment he thought of asking the woman if anyone had preceded him into the House of Mirrors, but he didn't want to contend with more Danish.

Inside, to his great pleasure, he found the place empty. No screaming children, no angry parents and, evidently, no Israelis. The mirrored maze had confused him at first, but now he had no trouble finding his way to the deadend Borgmann had marked.

Ferrara felt around the mirror cracks and soon located the door hinges and the door itself. There was a brief moment of triumph, followed quickly by a sense of frustration. He found no visible locks, handles, knobs, or latches. Yet somehow, he was sure, this panel opened up. Behind it was some sort of secret room. And the plans were there—if all his guesses were right.

The young Lebanese got down on his hands and knees, looking for some sort of trigger that would open the mirrored door—and found nothing. How long would he have until the Israelis arrived? Four or five minutes? Ferrara had to find a way to get into that secret room, and fast.

One floorboard was slightly higher than the rest. Could that be the key? He bent down for a closer look. Then he ran his eyes along the corridor leading out of the deadend. Every other floorboard was perfectly level. He put his hand on the one that stuck up and let his full weight press down on it. There was a slight click and, behind him, the mirrored door swung smoothly open.

Ferrara leaped to his feet, astonished, adrenalin flowing into his veins. What he saw was a long, twisting stairway leading downward, he had no idea to what.

At the guard table, Von Hahn's attention was finally attracted by the entry warning light. He glanced at his watch—9:06. Probably the TV technicians, late as usual. They'd been told to be here by 8:30, before the crowds started arriving. But yesterday morning, they hadn't arrived until 8:50. And on the day before that, it was 8:45. Now, Von Hahn guessed, on their last day, they were even less concerned about punctuality than before. He waited to hear their footsteps on the stairs. And kept on reading.

Ferrara took one tentative step into the stairwell. Nothing happened. He walked carefully down the first three steps. Still nothing. There must be guards, he thought suddenly. He pulled his fiberglass gun from his pocket and held it at the ready. He took a few more steps down. And still no one challenged him. Now he was at the first landing, perhaps a dozen steps down from the entrance door. He peered over the wooden railing into a huge underground room. There at a table was a single guard, reading a book. In front of him, a white bulb burned steadily. There was a door to the rear, with a radiation warning painted on it.

At that moment, Von Hahn started to worry. He looked up and saw that the entry light was still on—and yet no one was coming down the stairs. He pulled his feet off the desk and stood up, withdrawing his service revolver. Something strange was happening here.

Ferrara ducked back and retreated up the stairs. The guard would soon be coming after him, he realized. Or rather, he'd be coming up the stairs to see exactly what or who was causing that light to stay lit. Ferrara had about thirty seconds to set up an ambush—or to run. If his plan was to work, it would have to be the former.

At the top of the stairs—but still inside the underground chamber—Ferrara now looked around anxiously for some spot to hide, some spot he could conceal himself so that the guard would approach without suspicion. There was no such place, not on the stairway anyhow. But outside the door—that was a definite possibility, Ferrara thought, his mind working at lightning speed. He would leave the mirrored door ajar and hide behind it. When the guard came up the steps, he would see that the door was ajar, open it and step out into the mirrored hall, to discover how that could have happened.

Ferrara took up his position, pressing his ear to the

wall, hoping to hear the guard's footsteps. And, sure enough, he did.

Von Hahn walked up the stairs, his gun drawn, puzzled. The light was on, and yet there were no TV technicians on the steps. Had they opened the door, then stood there chatting about the weather? Was something wrong with the warning light? It was probably something simple like that. In all his years as a security officer, nothing very exciting had ever happened at an installation like this. To be sure, there'd been unauthorized entries, but usually by workmen or persons authorized to enter at other times who'd simply forgotten to get authorization on a single occasion. There was no reason to be worried. Especially, there was no reason to notify Groot. Von Hahn could just imagine the man's reaction if he was disturbed (and probably embarrassed, since he was no doubt asleep) for a short circuit or other similar breakdown.

When he reached the top of the stairs, Von Hahn found, to his surprise, that the door was slightly ajar. He could see a crack of light through it. But no one was in view—no TV technicians, no unauthorized visitors, no EURATOM personnel, no one. The stairs were empty. Could the door have opened by itself? The Danes were careful people... It was unlikely they would have allowed a malfunction such as this to occur. Von Hahn stood on the stairway side of the door, trying to figure it out. Perhaps something was stuck under the door, he reasoned—a candy wrapper or a wad of gum. He bent down and looked at the sill. Nothing.

Von Hahn slowly pushed the door open, stepping out into the mirrored hallway. As he stuck his head out, Ferrara clubbed him with the gun. The first blow only stunned the guard. But a second, then a third, and, finally, a fourth put him under but good.

Now Ferrara found himself with an unconscious guard on his hands. Fortunately, the House of Mirrors was devoid of patrons. But it was 9:25 already. Soon—certainly within a few minutes—the Israelis would be here. The Lebanese dragged Von Hahn through the maze as quickly as he could. He was a strong man, but Von Hahn was large and heavy.

At the exit, Ferrara somehow pulled Von Hahn erect and slipped an arm around him. Once again, he thanked God that it was a grey day and that the park was nearly empty. A few feet from the House of Mirrors, Ferrara found a men's room. He pulled Von Hahn into it, opened a stall and seated the guard on the toilet. Then he closed the stall with both of them inside and locked the door. After making sure it was secure, he pulled himself over the top of the door and walked out.

The mirrored door, he remembered, was open. How would the Israelis react to that? With suspicion, at least. Well, there was no helping it. He didn't dare go back into the House of Mirrors. Surely Borgmann, Ben-Ezra and the girl would be there by now.

Ferrara felt a certain sense of satisfaction. He had done exactly what he had hoped to do—opened the secret door and eliminated a guard. Hopefully, the Israelis would be able to handle it from here on. All that was left to do was wait. Ferrara found a bench some distance from the House of Mirrors with a view commanding both the entrance and the exit. He sat.

Gary Stabile bit into his pastry and took a sip of coffee. Ferrara had appeared exactly as expected. The American felt a lovely warm, pleasant emotion—an unfamiliar one. The conductor of an orchestra must feel this way, he decided. Then he corrected himself. He felt more like the director of a play, moving men around at his whim, putting them through a series of actions that they might not understand, though he did, in complete command of all the trappings, from scenery to lighting. He glanced at his watch and frowned slightly. It was nearly 9:30. The Israelis were a bit late. Would they need prompting?

Chapter Twenty-Eight

Despite the fact that Ben-Ezra had told him to stay away from the porno shop until 9:00, Frederick Borgmann arrived there at 8:45. He was anxious to get going. It was always this way when decisions were at hand. He wanted the issue settled, whichever way it was going, and he wanted it settled fast. For three days now, the three of them had been searching for the plans. Step by step, they had discovered the hiding place. Now it was time for the attempt.

Even though he'd spent most of the night talking with—or making love to—Miriam, Borgmann was alert and awake, almost tingling with nervous energy. According to Dahlgaard, the plans were somehow within the reactor. But that phrase made no sense. Reactors aren't boxes in which things can be placed. Most are solid—or liquid. Except for heavy-water reactors, the only openings into the core are for control rods, and such openings are always filled. Well, there was no figuring out in advance. He'd just have to see when he got there. If he got there.

When Borgmann arrived at the porno shop, the shade was still drawn on the front door. He tried the handle. It opened. From the outside room, he could hear conversation from within Ben-Ezra's office. No, not conversation. Argument. Borgmann knocked at the door, then pushed it open. Ben-Ezra, who was sitting at his desk, looked up at him and nodded a curt hello, then turned his attention back to Miriam. They'd agreed to arrive separately, for propriety's sake; she'd preceded him by about ten minutes.

Whatever anger there was in this room—and apparently there was plenty—was Miriam's. Her face was tight with it. Even Frederick's appearance didn't end the argument.

"I say we should leave now, Yaakov," she said obviously repeating a remark she'd made several times.

"We have to wait."

"For what? For our last chance to slip away? You and I both know getting that door open may be next to impossible. And neither of us have the faintest idea of what lies beyond it. The place could be guarded by a regiment—armed with more than gas guns, you can be sure."

"Miriam, Miriam," the older man said, "just take my word for it—we must wait until at least nine-thirty."

Miriam looked at Borgmann. "Say something to him, Frederick. We only have a few hours left, and he wants to play."

Borgmann sighed—and complied. "What worries me, Yaakov, is the reactor. Dahlgaard told me the plans were within the reactor. I don't know exactly what he means by that, but I expect I'll have to cool it down before the plans can be extracted. I don't know if I'll be able to do that—certainly I'll need time."

Ben-Ezra gazed at Borgmann with a quiet, confident little smile. "Ah, Frederick, your modesty becomes you. You saw the first reactors in the world being designed, and you've worked on dozens since. Do you really think this machine will puzzle you?"

"Well, I suppose not. But it could take time to figure out. That's what we're talking about—time."

"Would fifteen minutes really make that much difference?" Ben-Ezra asked, still smiling.

Borgmann shrugged. "Who knows? There's another problem, you know—identifying the genuine set of plans. Time is essential *there*. I have to look at every part of every set of diagrams and those diagrams are very complicated."

"Well, you'll do your best."

"Of course I will, but some extra time . . ."

"We're in the endgame now, Frederick. Every move must be carefully contemplated. If we rush, our perfect checkmate could turn into a stalemate."

"Here we go with the chess analogies again," Miriam said sarcastically. "Perhaps this is all a bit too much for you, Yaakov. Perhaps you'd like to stay here while Frederick and I go on. Perhaps we have not paid proper respect to your age."

At these words, Yaakov Ben-Ezra's calm evaporated and his face turned red with anger. "Sometimes you go too far, Miriam. *Then* you do not pay proper respect to my age—and to my experience. You—you, of all people—you know what I have done in the past. Yet you still doubt. Do you have any idea how painful it is for me to hear your doubts?"

Borgmann followed the argument like a man watching a tennis match. Miriam opened her mouth to reply, but no sounds came out. She seemed embarrassed, Borgmann thought—perhaps even ashamed. He looked back at Ben-Ezra.

"Will there ever come a time when I have finally proved myself to you, Miriam? Will you continue to judge me all your life?" They were hot words, private thoughts spoken aloud only in extremis. Ben-Ezra threw them at Miriam like daggers. Borgmann looked back at Miriam. There were two arguments going on here—only one of them concerned the time. The other? Borgmann could not guess its genesis, but he sensed it had been going on for years.

Miriam was now looking at Ben-Ezra, her eyes softer than Borgmann had ever before seen them. There was a depth of tenderness that before last night, he would have doubted was within her capacity.

"I do not mean to judge you, Yaakov," she said very quietly. "How can I judge you?"

And now Yaakov was returning that tender look. Only once before had Borgmann seen that expression on Ben-Ezra's face, years ago, in Israel. He reached for the memory, but it flew from his grasp.

Ben-Ezra looked at his watch. "It's nine-twenty—time to get going. Is your luggage outside, Frederick?"

"Yes, in the other room."

"Let's get it into the car."

Now Borgmann began to feel just as he had thirty years ago, when the two of them helped the Jews escape to Sweden. There was excitement then, and fear. The Storm Troopers marched through the streets searching for the very prize Kaplan concealed. Their patrol boats swept the harbor, their searchlights darting from point to point like cats' eyes looking for mice, seeking fishing boats filled with refugees. Again and again, Borgmann had watched the boats pull away from the quay packed with the descendants of Moses, heading for yet arother promised land. Again and again, the signal light had flashed on the far shore of the sound and he and Kaplan knew another group had arrived safety.

Not every boat arrived safely, though. Routes, departure times, quays and even types of boats were varied in a random pattern and Danish skippers knew the waters far better than their Nazi "guests"—but sometimes the refugee boats failed to evade patrols, perhaps through bad luck, perhaps because of something more sinister.

Borgmann's parents were in one such boat and, except for a last-minute switch, he would have been with them. There were signals for the boats that didn't make it too—not lights on the opposite shore, but the distant gruesome rattle of machine guns. That was the signal he'd heard, standing on the dock with Jacob Kaplan, a half hour after saying what was to be a final good-bye to his mother and father. He and Kaplan both hoped it involved some other vessel.

Now they were together again, risking their lives not so much for the existing generation but for the future of an entire country. He closed his mind to the political arguments before they came flooding in, accompanied by confusion. There were more immediate questions anyhow. The main one was simple enough: which signal would prevail, when all was done? Would the boat

305

arrive safely? Would it be intercepted and mercilessly sent to the bottom? One never knew in advance.

Copenhagen glided by as Miriam drove toward the Tivoli, not the Copenhagen of 1943, but the Copenhagen of the atomic age. There was silence in the car, nothing to be said now, everyone absorbed by his own thoughts. Borgmann glanced at Miriam. Her knuckles were white as they gripped the steering wheel. But he knew she would be ready. He turned back to catch Ben-Ezra's eye. No chance. Yaakov was looking out of the other window. There was a bond between them all whether they spoke of it or not. Frederick felt it strongly. Would it persevere into the future?

At almost exactly 9:30, the little green Saab pulled up at the Tietgensgade entrance to Tivoli Gardens and parked. The gates were open but the crowd was thin. The grey weekday was not the sort that encouraged pleasure-seekers to satisfy their desires out of doors.

Frederick and Miriam got out of the car in a hurry and Ben-Ezra attempted to do the same. Pain prevented him. It came on suddenly, with a breath—needles and pins in his lungs. He could neither exhale nor inhale.

A few steps from the car, Miriam realized Ben-Ezra was not following. She went back, Borgmann beside her. Yaakov was in the rear seat, leaning back, his face pasty white. He smiled at them wanly.

"Father?" Miriam asked, sticking her head into the car, her voice not much more than a whisper.

Ben-Ezra took a breath. "It's all right, Miriam. It's passing now. You two go on—I'll be there in a moment."

"It's the pain again, Father?"

"Yes, But I feel better now—really."

"Are you sure?"

Ben-Ezra sat up, erect now and breathing normally. "Yes, yes I'm fine now. Let me rest a minute. I'll catch up with you."

Miriam pulled her head out of the car. "He wants to rest a minute. Says he'll catch up with us," she told Borgmann.

"Okay."

They walked toward the gate.

"I heard what you said to him, Miriam," Frederick said.

"What's that?"

"You called him 'Father.' "

Miriam hesitated. "Yes," she said. "Yes I did."

"You're his daughter?" Borgmann asked. For some reason, he couldn't grasp it.

"It usually works out that way for a girl when a man's her father."

Borgmann squinted at her. "Yes," he finally said, as if he remembered something that would explain it all, "that accounts for it."

Miriam smiled. "For what?"

"For the bickering. And for the nagging memory."

"The memory?" She laughed. "Don't tell me you remember me."

"Well," Borgmann admitted with a grin, "no. Not as you are now. But I seem to recall a skinny little ten-year-old who took an American tourist on a marvelous tour of Tel Aviv."

He paused at the ticket kiosk and bought two tickets. They entered the park together and headed directly for the House of Mirrors, a short walk from the Tietgensgade entrance.

"And you think I'm that girl?" Miriam inquired, teasing.

"Well, aren't you?"

"All this chitchat," Miriam said. "Don't we have some serious business to do?"

The House of Mirrors was directly ahead of them now. "Just like a woman," Borgmann said, "always changing the subject. We'll get back to it—you'll see."

"I know," Miriam said, bantering. "You never forget anything."

Once more, they bought tickets. This time, they entered the House of Mirrors.

From his vantage point, Suliman Ferrara had no trouble spotting Borgmann and the girl as they went into the House of Mirrors. So far, he thought, so good. They were a bit late, but they were there, except for Ben-Ezra. He had no idea how long it would be until he knew if they'd succeeded—an hour, perhaps two, possibly even longer. Well, there was nothing else on his schedule—except that El Al flight at 2:00.

Gary Stabile watched with annoyance. The curtain was up and the supporting players had taken their places. Now where the hell was the star? He peered impatiently toward the entrance—and was rewarded with a view of Yaakov Ben-Ezra slowly sauntering toward the House of Mirrors.

So this, thought Stabile, this was the legendary Ben-Ezra. He'd been hearing about him for nearly twenty years, on and off. The company always held him up as an example, an agent to emulate. Stabile looked at the man with interest. He was old, he was a bit flabby around the middle, there was no spring in his step. And yet there was an intelligence in those eyes. Ben-Ezra glanced casually at his surroundings, visually vacuuming the area for every detail of interest. Inevitably his eyes fell on Stabile, and the American was certain he saw the briefest flicker of interest, possibly even the beginnings of a smile. Could he have recognized me, Stabile asked himself. Not a chance. Borgmann couldn't have described me that well—and I'm sure the Israelis don't have my picture.

Oddly, Ben-Ezra gave him a distinctly uncomfortable feeling, as if Stabile were the student and the Israeli the teacher. What was it about the man that disturbed him so? Stabile studied him as he bought his ticket and walked into the House of Mirrors, with no more urgency than if he were about to visit his mother-in-law.

What disturbed him was Ben-Ezra's confidence. It showed in his every action. Stabile would have called it arrogance, but he reserved that term for those who merely feigned confidence. No, this man gave the impression of knowing both his limitations and his abilities. He also gave the impression of being able to handle

308

anything that might happen except, perhaps, the apocalypse. Stabile had half a mind to interfere, to take sides, to deflate that confidence. But that wouldn't have been at all well received by the Company.

Chapter Twenty-Nine

Frederick and Miriam had no trouble finding the little carved "F." But when they saw the secret door, they stopped short. It was perhaps a quarter of an inch ajar.

"Has someone beat us to the punch?" Borgmann asked, his heart pounding.

"It's possible," Miriam said grimly. "There's only one way to be sure."

Borgmann raised an eyebrow.

"Don't you think we'd better wait for Yaakov?"

"Yes," Miriam said quickly. "Of course."

She reached into her small brown suede bag and pulled out her gas gun. Borgmann did the same. Moments later, Ben-Ezra came around the corner, feeling his way through the mirrors. "Quite a place," he said. "Might be fun—some other time."

"Yaakov," Miriam said, her voice low, "the door is ajar."

Ben-Ezra pursed his lips and pondered, almost too seriously. "Well, there are two possibilities: either someone has been here before us, or the EURATOM Security has suddenly come down with a bad case of carelessness."

"What do we do if someone has beat us to the plans?" Borgmann asked, now thoroughly upset.

"We have two choices," Ben-Ezra said, unperturbed. "We can go in and interrupt them, or wait until they come out. But it's my opinion that we have nothing more here than an open door."

"Come on, Yaakov," Miriam said, the argumentative tone back again, "we can't be that lucky."

"Who said anything about luck?" Ben-Ezra inquired slyly. "That open door is no accident. Someone is giving us a helping hand—someone with ulterior motives, of course."

"What are you talking about?" Borgmann asked, confused. "Who could be helping us?"

"That's why you insisted we wait until nine-thirty," Miriam said, almost simultaneously. "You wanted to give our helper time to ease our way."

Ben-Ezra nodded. "Now you know."

"So? Why the secret. You didn't trust us?" Miriam said, challenging.

"I wasn't really certain myself," Ben-Ezra explained. "Besides, a man wants to feel useful."

"But who is it?" Borgmann repeated, bewildered.

"Your friend Stabile—Ferrara—the Russians—I'm not sure yet."

"Why would they help *us*?"

"Look, Frederick," Miriam interrupted, not very gently, "we can stand around here all day theorizing, or we can get to work. We can't do both."

"She's right, Frederick," Ben-Ezra said. "Let's get the plans; then we can discuss it for a week, if we like."

It was Ben-Ezra who stepped into the stairwell first, leaving Frederick and Miriam in the mirrored hall. After a moment, his arm appeared in the doorway and waved them in.

The Israeli team crept down the stairs, Ben-Ezra leading the way, deeper and deeper, down into the cavernous room beneath the House of Mirrors. At about the halfway point, Ben-Ezra leaned over the railing, then motioned the others to take a look.

"The guard post," he whispered, pointing. "It's abandoned."

"Our helper?" Miriam asked.

"Quite likely."

By the time they reached the bottom, it was clear that the room was empty. What wasn't so clear was whether or not there were guards in the reactor room itself.

"Notice the light," Ben-Ezra said to Miriam, pointing. "I'm sure it goes on when the door above opens."

"A warning."

"Yes. The guard probably sits at that table and watches it."

Borgmann continued through the room to the giant concrete door.

"The reactor is in here," he said. "What now?"

Ben-Ezra scratched his head. "We find out if the inside room is guarded, I guess." He went to the door, gas gun in hand, pressed the buzzer and listened at the speaking tube. There was no response. He buzzed again.

"What is it?" came the voice from within, sleepy and annoyed. "I thought I told you not to disturb me, Von Hahn."

"Visitors," Ben-Ezra said.

"Oh, okay Von Hahn. I'll be right out. I was watching an experiment."

The door rolled open and Claude Groot stepped into the anteroom. A single squirt from Ben-Ezra's gas gun put him out before he had time to do anything more than raise his eyebrows.

Borgmann started through the reactor room door.

"Wait," Miriam said, running ahead. "There might be more."

"Hey," Borgmann said as Miriam passed by, "there are scientists in there running the reactor. Don't put them to sleep, or the whole place may blow up."

"Don't worry." Miriam stuck her head inside the reactor room and peered around. "You were right," she told Frederick, retreating a step. "There's a scientist working at an instrument console on the balcony. What do we do with him?"

"We let him keep working. Once he knows why we're here, we'll have no trouble from him. His only worry is to keep the pile simmering.

"Help me with this fellow, will you, Frederick?" Ben-Ezra asked. He and Borgmann dragged Groot over

312

to a small cot in one corner of the anteroom and dumped him, with reasonable care.

"Will he remember anything when he wakes up?" Borgmann asked.

"Oh, yes," said Ben-Ezra with a smirk. He'll have a very clear memory of my gas gun squirting on his face. I imagine he'll be quite upset."

"Well, Yaakov," Borgmann said, "now it's my turn."

"Yes. Unfortunately, I must leave you both for a while. I have to make some arrangements."

Borgmann was incredulous. "You're leaving us?"

"What would I do down here? I don't know an atom from a molecule, remember?" Ben-Ezra said. "Miriam can handle any emergencies that might come up—other than technical problems. Am I right, Miriam?"

"I suppose so, Yaakov."

"I'm going to close that door upstairs," he told her. "You keep your eye on the light. If it goes on, you have unwelcome company. If you want to leave before I get back, there's an inside latch on the door that shouldn't give you any trouble."

"But where will we meet you—and when?" Borgmann asked, still slightly panicked.

"Don't get so excited," Ben-Ezra said gently. "I'll be only a half hour or so. After that, I'll wait upstairs, just to make sure you're not interrupted."

Borgmann was still worried ."It might take me quite awhile," he warned.

Ben-Ezra checked his watch. "It's nearly ten now, Frederick. We have to be out of here by one at the latest."

"Three hours, huh? Well, if I can do it at all, that should be time enough."

"Good. See you both later."

Miriam touched her father's shoulder, the first physical contact Borgmann had seen between them. "Take care, Yaakov."

"Of course. But there's nothing to worry about." He gave a small wave, climbed the long stairway and disappeared through the door at the top.

Upstairs, Ben-Ezra was relieved to see that there was

no one in sight—except two seven-year-old boys, who fortunately hadn't noticed his sudden, inexplicable appearance. Ben-Ezra pushed the mirrored door shut. He was puffing from the climb. An old man shouldn't have to do things like this, he thought. An old man shouldn't be working this hard. He should be loafing, reading, studying, sleeping and eating—especially eating. Well, it wouldn't be long now.

Chapter Thirty

Miriam and Frederick watched Ben-Ezra vanish through the door at the top of the stairs. A second later, the light at the guard table winked out.

"Let's get started," Borgmann said, in a businesslike voice.

They walked into the reactor room, a huge, domed chamber with thick concrete walls devoid of openings—except for the door. In the center stood a hexagonal concrete structure about fifteen feet in diameter and ten feet high, dotted with glass-covered ports and openings. A railing ran around the top. The wall of the chamber was lined with a spiral catwalk that, at one point, arched through the room and connected with the top of the hexagonal structure. At another point, the catwalk broadened into a kind of balcony, the site of a large control console with hundreds of dials, gauges and buttons. A white-coated scientist leaned over at the console, making adjustments. So far, he hadn't noticed Frederick and Miriam.

"Maybe we'd better say hello," Borgmann said. "I'd hate to surprise the man."

"Are there others, do you think?"

"At least one more," Borgmann answered. "Probably down below."

"Below?"

"That's right. What you see is only the tip of the iceberg. Underneath the floor—right where you're standing, as a matter of fact—is a jungle of pipes and tanks. That's the heavy-water handling system."

"Water?"

"Yes. It keeps the reactor from running wild. In the old days, we used graphite. The guy below manages the plumbing. Let's get acquainted with the man at the console."

Miriam swallowed hard. She was over her head here and she knew it. She was frightened. Not about guards or security men—it was the reactor that made her nervous. If something went wrong, hundreds of thousands could be killed, not to mention Frederick—and herself. "Okay," she agreed, her voice cool and well controlled.

"Hey, up there," Borgmann said. "You speak English?"

The console operator's head jerked around. He was clearly flabbergasted at being addressed this way—at being addressed at all. Seeing Frederick and Miriam, he nearly went into shock.

"Do you speak English?" Borgmann repeated.

"Yes," the technician said finally, his voice a whisper. "Who are you? What are you doing in here? Don't you know this is a radiation area?"

"I know all about it," Borgmann said. "We're here to get something. You're in no danger at all. You won't be hurt."

"Who are you?" He'd recovered his voice and was demanding an answer.

Miriam pointed the gas gun at him. "You don't need to know that. You do what that man says or I'll shoot."

The technician gazed at Miriam for a moment, then grinned nervously. "You'll shoot? Then what will you do? Do you realize what would happen with no one at the console? You'd end up obliterating half of Copenhagen, yourselves included."

"The lady has no intention of harming you," Borgmann assured the technician, "not unless you do something foolish. But I could handle the reactor if necessary. Now—how many men are there below?"

"What do you mean you could handle the reactor?" The technician sneered. "This isn't a child's toy, you know."

"I know. It's a heavy-water moderated reactor fueled

316

with enriched uranium alloy and cooled by heavy water. You do beam work with vertical 'thimbles,' horizontal beam holes, test holes, pneumatic tubes, and thermal columns. From what I can see, the machine is a nearly exact copy of the CP-5 at Argonne National Laboratory. I'd guess it was built in the late nineteen-fifties."

The technician looked at Borgmann, open-mouthed. "Who are you?" he asked once more, this time with respect.

"That doesn't matter," Frederick said. He was in complete command of the situation, Miriam noted with pleasure. "I'm the one who's asking the questions. How many below?"

"One."

"One? How long has he been down?"

"About an hour. He isn't scheduled to come up until shift change, at four."

"Fine. Let's leave it that way. There are some foreign objects in the reactor tank," Borgmann said. "You know about them, don't you?"

"Yes."

"Well, we want to look at them. Do I operate the crane, or do you?"

The technician seemed to be having trouble making up his mind. "I'll do it," he said at last. He kept glancing at Miriam's gas gun.

"Good," Borgmann said.

"What's happening?" Miriam asked, under her breath.

Borgmann pointed toward the top of the dome. "You see the crane and winch up there?"

"Yes."

"Well, it drops experimental materials into the reactor tank and pulls them out when the experiment is finished. I'm sure that's where the plans are. Hey! Up there on the balcony. That's TV broadcast equipment, isn't it?"

Miriam looked where he was pointing. A complete broadcast unit, including camera, monitor and lighting equipment, was set up near the control console. The

317

camera aimed across the room, its field of view passing directly over the center of the hexagon.

"Where are the TV people?" Borgmann asked.

"Not here this morning," the man said. "Supposed to be back around two."

"Fine."

"This is it," Miriam said excitedly. "They're here."

"No question of it. They're in the tank. When the crane lifts them, while they're hanging in midair, the TV camera zooms in on them, and broadcasts them."

Miriam stared upward at the crane. "Won't the water in the reactor tank ruin the blueprints?"

"Delicate materials are usually embedded in Plexiglas," Borgmann said. "I imagine there's one plastic-encased blueprint in each experimental thimble. Only problem is, which one do we want?"

"Correction," said the console operator. He'd gradually wheeled his chair about three feet along the balcony to a bank of electric switches. "There are several problems. First, how do you get the plans off the crane? Remember, they've been soaking up radioactivity for days. Second, how do you carry them anywhere without frying yourself and the girl?"

Miriam gulped. The more she heard, the less likely it seemed they'd succeed.

"He's bluffing, Miriam," Borgmann assured her. "There has to be a case around here somewhere. I'll bet the plans are kept in a reactor at The Hague, too. All we have to do is find the carrying case and drop the plans into it."

"There's a case, all right," the console technician said defiantly, "but they don't keep it here. They don't want to make it easy for thieves—like you."

"Then I'll have to be inventive, won't I? I'll find some way to shield the blueprints; don't you worry."

"Maybe you will. But I'm about to give you a problem you can't solve. I'm going to pull the master fuse and smash it. Everything will shut down for at least twenty-four hours and—"

skill had come back to him quickly. "It takes years of practice to operate the crane," he said. "It's like threading a needle with twine."

"Well, then, you do it. I'll sit at the reactor control."

Borgmann was now relaxed enough to turn and look at her. "Why, certainly," he said. "We'll compress ten years of reactor experience into ten seconds and you can take over."

"You don't have to be sarcastic," Miriam said. "Why can't I sit here while you work the crane and tell you what's happening on the control board? If something goes wrong, you can tell me what buttons to push."

"That's silly," Borgmann said. He turned back to the control panel and made a small adjustment.

They argued for several minutes. And the more they talked, the more sense it made to him. After all, the crane controls were only about a dozen feet from the reactor console. In any real emergency, he could be there in a few seconds. And teaching Miriam what to look for wouldn't be all that difficult. The reactor gauges and dials were set so that when all was well, every needle pointed straight up. Alarm lights covered other problems. He couldn't teach her what to do in the event of an emergency, but he could either leave the crane controls when there was trouble at the reactor console or call over instructions to Miriam.

"All right," he said. "I give up."

"You mean it? You'll let me do it?" She could hardly contain herself.

"Anything to make you happy."

"Frederick. Sometimes—"

Borgmann got up from the chair at the console. "Here," he said. "Sit."

Miriam eagerly took the chair. Then she looked more closely at the myriad of dials and gauges on the control panel. Her pleasure began to fade.

Frederick hovered over her, his hand on her shoulder protectively. "Take a look at this," he instructed, pointing out a small button near the bottom of the panel. "It's called the scram button. It slams the control

Ben-Ezra quickly found a pay phone not far from the House of Mirrors and made his call.

"Gunnar Neilborg, please."

He waited until his friend came to the phone.

"Hello, Neilborg here."

"Gunnar—Yaakov."

"Ah, Yaakov, my friend. Today is the day?"

"Yes. This afternoon. We should be there by two. What can you do for me?"

"There's a one-twenty to London—would that do?"

"That would be perfect, Gunnar. But can you hold it that long? I don't want you to get into trouble."

"Are you kidding? I never get into any trouble. Besides, what's forty minutes? But don't make it any later than two, okay?"

"Don't hold it a minute longer than that. We'll be there by two or not at all."

"Right."

"And Gunnar—thanks."

"I owe you one, Yaakov. We Swedes have long memories."

"I know. Thank God for that, Gunnar. See you later."

Ben-Ezra walked back to the House of Mirrors as quickly as possible.

The luggage handler outfit was a bit tight, the man thought to himself, not that it mattered. He had no choice but to wear it. His employers required it. He had no choice but to use the equipment they had provided him with. He had no choice but to play his role, not that he would have done differently if he had.

The luggage handler closed the valise, opened the trunk of his Mercedes and dropped it in. It occurred to him to wonder if his employers had all the details right. They'd erred in the past—though not often. Perhaps this time was just another false alarm. He hoped not.

Borgmann was faintly conscious of a quick movement on his left, and of a brief hissing sound. As he watched, the technician crumpled over. His hand—

which had been about to grasp the fuse case—fell short of its goal. He was asleep. By the time Borgmann looked back at Miriam, the gas gun was in her purse once more.

Without a word, Frederick vaulted up the stairway leading to the balcony. He raced to the control console and looked feverishly at the guages and dials, touching a lever here, moving a dial there.

"I had to do it, Frederick," Miriam said from below. There was doubt in her voice. She badly needed his approval.

Borgmann understood the plea, but for the moment he was too occupied with the reactor to respond. It had been years since he'd sat at a reactor console. Now, without an instant's warning, he had to take control of this atomic monster and keep it in line. He stared at the gauges and dials, fighting to remember what each meant, struggling to recall exactly what must be done. It was as though he'd unexpectedly fallen into a swimming pool, eyes open. Everything blurred in front of him momentarily. He was in immediate danger of drowning.

Then, slowly, his vision began to clear. The unfamiliar control board in front of him began to merge with his memories. Pictures flashed into his thoughts from old, unused corners of his mind. He was back at Stagg Field, at the controls of the world's first nuclear reactor; then he was at Los Alamos, working with the small research reactor set up during World War II; then he was at Argonne National Laboratory, in the Chicago suburbs, handling the CP-5. He stared again at the Tivoli reactor control console. The dials, gauges, buttons and levers were marked in Danish and some of the terms were unfamiliar to him. That was the least of his problems. He could replace the Danish nameplates at will with English ones, in his mind at least. He took a breath.

"Frederick?" Miriam said. He hadn't responded to her last remark. In fact, she had the distinct feeling that he hardly knew she was there. "I had to put him out."

"What?" He was back. "Yes, I know. Good thing too. He meant what he said."

He'd said all this without once glancing in her direction. The control panel was commanding all of his attention. For once, Miriam felt helpless.

"Are you doing okay?" she asked uncertainly. "Can you handle this thing?"

Borgmann once more swept the dials with his eyes. All was in order. He slowly began to relax, for the first time realizing just how much tension he felt.

"Can I do anything to help?" Miriam asked meekly.

Borgmann permitted himself a glance in her direction—but only a glance. "Yes. You can get out of here, close the door, and watch that warning light." He turned back to the console. Everything was running perfectly.

"I'm not leaving you," Miriam said, her voice retaining its power. "Yaakov is upstairs, anyhow. No one will get by him. I'm coming up to the balcony to help."

Borgmann moved a dial slightly. A misbehaving needle gauge obeyed his touch. "I wish you wouldn't. Frankly, I wish you'd get out of here and take Yaakov with you."

Miriam paid no attention to him. She climbed the metal grating stairs leading to the balcony, her footsteps echoing loudy in the huge concrete dome. Frederick watched her out of the corner of one eye, his main attention still on the control console. She edged along the catwalk.

"I'm not worried about myself or Yaakov," she said. "I'm worried about the mission."

"The mission?" It was more of a laugh than a question. "Im afraid we'll have to forget about that." A light flashed on the panel and Borgmann stabbed a button. The light went out.

"Well, I'll have to work the crane, I guess," she said matter-of-factly.

"You? Operate the crane?"

"What's so amazing about that?"

Borgmann was starting to feel at home at the reactor. Like an expert typist or a good pianist who'd returned to his machine after a long

rods back into place and stops any wild reaction. If anything goes wrong, you hit that button."

"Why don't we press it now?" She no longer sounded ready for anything.

"If we hit the scram button now, we'd shut down all the power to the reactor and lock the experimental thimbles. The crane would be useless. We'd never even get a glimpse of the plans. That's why."

"Oh."

"Now look up here, at these rows of indicator lights. They go on when something needs adjusting. You should expect one or two to wink on from time to time. Don't worry—just call me. If five or more light up, well . . ."

"Press the scram button," Miriam said, finishing Borgmann's sentence.

"Exactly."

A light blinked on and Frederick turned a dial. The light dimmed, then went black.

"Okay," she said, "let's get on with it."

"Whatever you say," he said. He kissed her briefly on the cheek, then he walked toward the crane controls.

Miriam stared at the console instruments. She felt as though she was in the pilot's seat of a 747, coming in for a landing in impenetrable fog, one engine out, the co-pilot dead of a heart attack. She cautiously put a hand on the panel surface. It was cold and hard. In the left corner, a needle wavered momentarily, then steadied—but even this small variation sent her pulse racing. Miriam fought an almost irresistible impulse to twist every dial, push every button, move every lever. The scram button beckoned to her, magnetically.

"We're right about the TV setup," Borgmann called to her, his voice breaking the tension. "I'll have to figure out how to work it. How are you doing?"

"So far, so good," Miriam said, flippantly.

Now Borgmann studied the broadcasting unit. He'd seen one rather similar to it at Los Alamos, where dangerous experiments were conducted by remote control, performed not by human hands, but by mechanical ones. Operators watching television directed the mechanical hands in their delicate tasks. But this was a commercial television broadcast setup, with provisions for multiple cameras, tape pickups, remote location shots, and such.

He did his best to put Miriam and the reactor console out of his mind and studied the television switches. Finally, he found the one he was looking for—the *on* button. Next to it was *remote broadcast*. He pushed the first and made sure the second was off. Soon the monitor screen was filled with dancing confetti. Okay, he thought, so much for the monitor. Now I have to get that camera running. Without disturbing any of the contrast, brightness or focus settings on the TV camera, he managed to turn it on. On the monitor, there slowly materialized a blurry picture of the opposite side of the room.

"Frederick!" Miriam cried out. "A light just went on."

Borgmann was at the console in three long steps. "It's only one," he said calmly. "No sweat." He jabbed a control-rod motor button a few times and the light blinked off. "But I'm glad you told me."

"How are you doing with the television setup?" She was slightly breathless.

"Very well. It's operating now. The next problem is lifting the plans out of the reactor and identifying the genuine set."

"Frederick, I don't want to hurry you, but, well—the reactor . . ."

Borgmann grinned. "Why, Miriam," he said, "I have the distinct impression that you're uncomfortable sitting in that chair. I would think you'd enjoy operating a nuclear reactor."

Miriam wasn't in the mood for banter. "Frederick," she said, "couldn't we just get on with it?"

"Of course. You just relax."

He moved back down the balcony, this time past the broadcasting equipment to the crane control panel. For an instant, he was back in the dark again. The panel was totally unfamiliar to him. All the confidence he'd gained mastering the reactor once more drained away. He stared at the crane controls as if he'd never seen such a thing before in his entire life.

Borgmann fought his way back into his memories. He had never actually operated a crane himself, though he'd watched it being done countless times. He'd always had the upmost respect for the technicians who did the job. It required a rock-steady hand, a pulse rate of no more than fifty. A name and face sprang into his mind—Harry Wagner. Harry Wagner was the day-shift crane operator at the CP-5. He could pluck experimental thimbles from the reactor as though they were fish in a barrel. Borgmann pictured Harry at the controls, smiling, chewing tobacco, cursing constantly. In his mind's eyes, he watched the man manipulating the control levers.

He shook loose from the memories and gazed once more at the crane panel. Then he pulled out a long metal lever. Above him, the ceiling-mounted crane clanked along its tracks toward the reactor tank. Borgmann watched it, tense as a drumhead. When it was exactly above the reactor tank, he pushed the lever back in. Though the lever was shaped to conform to his hand, no object could have felt more foreign—or so Borgmann thought.

Now, he knew, he must find the control that lowered the crane head. He studied the panel for a while, then took hold of a slide switch. For some reason, the crane controls weren't labeled. It made sense, Borgmann thought. The operators knew which control did what—even if *he* didn't. He pulled down on the slide switch, hoping his memory was right. The crane head began to sink slowly toward the tank, its chain playing out link by link. From his spot on the balcony, Frederick could see seven thimbles—experiment holders—deep in the tank, their hooks barely visible above the surface of the heavy-water pool.

What he'd done so far, he knew, was the easy part. Now, he had to maneuver the crane hook so that it engaged one of the thimble hooks—and he might have to do it seven times. That required the sort of physical

325

dexterity and hand-to-eye coordination that came only with practice and more practice. Borgmann hoped he'd find the genuine plans quickly. Just hooking seven of those thimbles might take him hours.

Borgmann glanced at the TV monitor. There it was, the crane cable, in perfect focus. With luck, there'd soon be a set of centrifuge plans on that screen. With good luck, it would be the right set. With exceptional luck, he'd find a way to jerry-build a shield for it and they'd be off. He lowered the crane head until it was even with the thimble hook. Then he hit the other lever, the one that moved the crane back and forth, from wall to wall. The crane hook banged against the thimble hook and bounced away. Damn, Borgmann said to himself. He tried again, from the opposite direction. This time the crane hook missed the thimble entirely. He tried once more. The two hooks were perfectly lined up now, parallel to each other. But no matter how he jiggled the levers, the hooks wouldn't engage. He pulled the lever back, then advanced the hook once more, every fragment of his attention focused on his task. The sweat was gathering along the line of his forehead and on his palms. Once more, the hook touched. The crane hook started to twist . . .

"Frederick! More lights!"

Borgmann nearly hit the ceiling. He'd jumped a mile at the sound of Miriam's voice, having forgotten that she was sitting there at the reactor console, having forgotten even where he was, having forgotten everything but the task of getting those two hooks to mate.

He ran to the console. This time, three lights were on—one of them a blinker. "It's the shim-safety rods," he told Miriam, turning a dial. "They function automatically, down there below the floor. But every once in a while, they need adjustments." One by one, the lights went dark. "It's nothing to worry about if you're an experienced reactor operator—just routine."

"Routine? For you, maybe. Not for me."

Borgmann smiled. "I understand, believe me."

"How are you doing with the plans?"

"Well, I'm trying to hook a set so I can study it. You could do me a favor, though."

"I'll try. Just tell me what you want me to do."

"When more lights come on, call me just like you did before—but try not to shout. I'm having a hell of a time over there. I've already wasted fifteen minutes."

"I'll whisper, okay?" There was a trace of sarcasm in her voice.

Borgmann ignored it. "Anything, so long as I can hear you," he said.

He walked back to the crane control panel, his mind returning to the problem. Perhaps both the up-and-down and the back-and-forth controls should be manipulated simultaneously, he thought.

He took his position at the control panel, glancing at the television monitor. At first, what he saw made no impression whatever. Then he realized that something impossible had happened. The two hooks were engaged. Had someone else linked them together? Could they have joined accidentally—and if so, how?

Borgmann remembered Miriam's terrified shout when the alarm lights flashed on. His hands had jerked—that was the only explanation. He'd linked the hooks totally without knowing it. It was an accident against all the odds. With luck that good, the plans he'd hooked would be the ones he wanted.

He slowly raised the crane, pulling the thimble out of the reactor tank. Just as Borgmann had guessed, a flat rectangle of acrylic plastic came up with it. He peeked at the monitor. It was covered with plans. Were they genuine? Borgmann locked the crane in position and started to examine the televised blueprints. It was 10:40 now.

Studying the prints, he was once again impressed by the centrifuge concept. The problem was to separate the rare kind of uranium useful in bombs or power plants—U-235—from the relatively common kind that wasn't—U-238. In nature, the two were inextricably mixed. The United States—and Britain, Russia, France and China—did the job by "gaseous diffusion." That involved changing uranium into uranium hexafluoride gas, then pumping it through thousands of filters, one after another, each one of which held back more and more of the undesirable U-238. The final product was "enriched" uranium—mostly U-235.

Centrifuges did the same thing, but in a different, simpler way. The uranium hexafluoride gas was piped into a rapidly spinning hollow top. The centrifugal forces of the top threw the heavier U-238 out to the sides, while the precious U-235 was drawn off at the bottom. Not only did the centrifuges cost much less than those multibillion dollar gaseous diffusion plants, but they also used only ten percent as much electricity— another major saving.

The centrifuge idea dated back to 1919, but not until the late 1930s did a German physicist, Gernot Zippe, figure out how to make them practical. The large early centrifuges quickly burned out bearings at their tips, since they were suspended from a sort of holder. Zippe's smaller, lighter machine sat on a steel needle and were kept upright by magnets. That allowed them to spin so fast that the gas within was subjected to a million times the force of gravity. Zippe further developed his ideas while he was a Russian prisoner after World War II. Then he went to work for the United States Atomic Energy Commission. Finally he ended up at EURATOM, where his work was fully appreciated. And Zippe—astonishingly—had been the name Torngren hadn't known, Borgmann recalled.

The principles behind the centrifuge were known well enough to most nuclear physicists. Borgmann had been reading about them for years. But only EURATOM had been able to make the principles work. The secrets involved the shape of the container and the materials used in its construction—and which type of material was used where.

As Borgmann studied the plan on the television screen, he began to suspect that it was a phony. Two centrifuges were shown operating in tandem, their product drawn off and stored. It couldn't be that way, he was sure. The gas had to be subjected to repeated centrifugings. Sadly, he lowered the plans back into the reactor pool and disengaged the crane hook. Fortunately, that was easy. Then he started the delicate job of hooking another thimble.

At that instant, the reactor room siren sounded, a piercing wail that God might have chosen to announce Armageddon. Borgmann dropped the crane controls and ran back to the reactor console. Four control rod limit lights were on and blinking. Miriam was in a state of near shock.

"My God," Borgmann said, when he saw the control board. "What have you been doing?"

"Nothing," Miriam said, truly innocent. "I may have brushed a dial with my hand and not noticed it, though."

"You might have brushed a dial?" Borgmann shot back at her. "You know what you've done here—this thing is well on the way to going critical!" He pushed between Miriam and the console and started turning dials and pushing buttons. "Look at that gauge!" he said, more to himself than her. "And the period meter. We're practically sitting on a bomb, Miriam!"

"Can't you stop it?" Her voice trembled.

"I don't know. I'm sure as hell trying."

Miriam gaped at Frederick. His knuckles were white with tension. He was staring at the board with such total concentration that she felt he'd be able to see right through her hand if she tried to block his view.

"What about the scram button?"

"If we hit it now, we could lose our last bit of control over the reaction. We'd fuse the core at least. Or the whole thing might blow. You watch that gauge— the period meter. When—or if—that needle gets back into the green, we're all right."

There was nothing reassuring to be seen on the period meter. While Miriam watched, the needle crept further and further into the red area. Borgmann looked like an organ virtuoso, pushing buttons and twisting dials in various combinations, making careful, precise corrections.

After several minutes, the needle stopped climbing. "Are you making progress?" Miriam asked. She was astonished to hear her voice quivering. How could she have gotten herself into such a situation? She and Frederick should be . . . well, somewhere else.

Borgmann leaned back from the control panel. "I think we have it now," he said. He mopped his forehead with a handkerchief. The needle began to fall back, into the green section.

"Is everything all right now?"

Borgmann took a very deep breath. "Yes. God, for a moment, I thought we were going critical. I've never seen a reactor so far gone."

"I don't know why a reactor would be so dangerous, Frederick. A bomb I can understand. But aren't reactors designed to be safe?"

"Reactors are built to produce chain reactions. So are bombs. The difference is that, in reactors, you can control the chain reaction, keep it down to the useful level. What just happened is that we nearly lost control. It wouldn't have been a big explosion. The radius of destruction probably wouldn't have been more than a few blocks. But that would have been bad enough."

"I can't understand why the Danes built such a device here in the Tivoli, with so many people around," Miriam said.

"Hah! A reactor isn't dangerous. Not with a reasonably competent operator at the controls."

"Was that a dig?" Miriam's confidence was returning.

"I guess so. But I take it back. I can't expect you to be a nuclear physicist."

"I should hope not." Both of them were smiling now.

Borgmann got up and turned the control panel chair over to Miriam. "Just don't brush against any knobs or push any buttons. That episode cost us another ten minutes. It's ten-fifty now."

"Don't worry. I won't even breathe hard."

Chapter Thirty-One

More than fifty feet above Frederick and Miriam, Ben-Ezra waited patiently by the hidden door. The House of Mirrors was fairly empty today, probably since it was a school day. Very few adults came down the halls, and those who appeared were accompanied by children. That was as it should be, Ben-Ezra reflected. He smiled at them and they smiled back. No one made anything of the fact that he didn't move through the maze. Men of his age were allowed to stop and rest from time to time, without attracting any suspicious glances. So there were a few advantages to age, even for an agent.

Watching the young Danes, Ben-Ezra was slowly drawn back to thoughts of his own youth. Certainly it had been nothing like this. Until he was fifteen he'd lived in Plonsk, a Polish *shtetl*, population three thousand—the same settlement from which David Ben-Gurion (then David Grien) had emigrated in 1906 to go to Palestine.

Life in Plonsk had been both bucolic and religious. It was a time of *hallah* cooking in the oven; of kosher chickens; of the *shammes* calling through the streets on *Erev Shaabes*, "Jews to the bathhouse!"; of women weeping as they prayed over the Sabbath candles; of the *shul* and *besmedresh,* where, draped in his *talis,* he prayed; of the teeming marketplace, unpaved streets, rotting wooden buildings; of summer dust and mud in the streets.

Many families, Ben-Ezra remembered, had chicken, geese, possibly a goat or a cow. Pigs roamed the streets, eating garbage, immune because of Jewish law. The open market was surrounded by the house of the "rich"—men who in any other society would be judged poor. Often these houses had stores in them. On market day, the owners would stand in front of their stores, calling out news of their goods, greeting friends and neighbors, convincing them to come in and buy. In one section, vendors sold dairy goods—sweet butter wrapped in cool leaves, sour cream in earthenware pots, milk in huge vats. In another section, vendors sold fish, in still another, farm produce.

How unlike Copenhagen it all was. The bargaining was loud and vigorous, at least at midday. His mother had always sent him to the market early in the morning, when the stalls were relatively quiet and the day's prices hadn't been set. Bargains could be had then, or at the end of the day, when merchants were eager to get rid of the leftovers.

And at home, there was study, always study. Ben-Ezra had learned Hebrew before the age of seven. From the first, he had been a *masmid,* one who is always bending over his books. Before he was ten, the old men of Plonsk called him a *iluy*, a *chochem*, a *gaon*—a genius. It was then, in his youth, that he had learned there are always two possibilities, and if the worst one comes to pass, there are still two possibilities, and if the worst of these happens, well, there were still more—ad infinitum.

As he grew older, Ben-Ezra was swept up in the *Haskala*, the Enlightenment, the revolt against dogma and legalism. With other boys, he read Schiller's poetry —translated into Hebrew—and popularizations of Darwin's theory. In the woods and in their attics, he and his friends read Mapu's novels. He saw the Jews as proud, fiery and independent people—a different vision from that ordinarily perpetuated in the *shtetl,* where Jews were resigned to their fate, unwilling or unable to fight for themselves.

On the surface, his father disapproved of him, for

being a "fence breaker." But even then, Ben-Ezra sensed a certain satisfaction beneath the surface. Only true scholars, it was said, could join the *Haskala*.

Ben-Ezra had lived in a *shtetl* at a time when it was a disintegrating institution. Some residents were drifting toward Palestine, where they found life even harder than it had been in Poland. Others had gone to America and many of these had sent for relatives. But most had headed toward the cities—Warsaw, Lodz, Cracow, Wroclaw, Poznan, Gdansk. The Kaplan family chose Warsaw.

When he arrived there in 1931, a fifteen-year-old boy, he felt like he was taking up residence at the center of the world, for Warsaw was nothing less than that if you were a Polish Jew, no matter how the Poles despised the Jews. In September 1939, it became something less than that. Within a few months, Poland was no longer Polish—it was German, it was Nazi. The ghetto—which had disappeared less than a generation ago—was not only reestablished, it was bricked in—a tiny, crowded slum twelve blocks long, ringed with barbed wire.

Ben-Ezra hadn't lived through the Nazi holocaust himself. Just before the Germans had attacked, he'd left his home in Warsaw against his father's express wishes (and his father stayed, against his own express wishes) and found his way, with a few others, through Romania, Bulgaria and Turkey and finally by sea to Palestine. Three million Polish Jews did not make that trip, or any other, except to Treblinka, with its thirteen gas chambers, or Chelmo, Auschwitz, Belzec, Maidenek, and Sobibor. They were not heard from again.

Among the missing were his mother and father, two brothers in their teens, a twenty-three-year-old sister and an eleven-year-old sister, several aunts and uncles with their children and almost all of his boyhood friends and friends of his parents. The Rabbi and the *chazan* of the synagogue to which he belonged also vanished, along with the tailor, the butcher, the schoolteacher, the neighbors who'd lived on either side—they all had names and he could remember them. But if he remembered the names, then he'd remember the faces —and he'd rather not remember the faces.

In Palestine, Jacob Kaplan joined the *Haganah,* the moderate, disciplined militia of Jewish Palestine. It had been a small, relatively inactive force until 1939, when the Arabs had attacked the Jews in practically every Palestinian city. Then the *Haganah* grew. So did its bloodier, more violent shadow, the *Irgun Zvai Leumi,* the organization of Jewish terrorists.

For a while, the British seemed to be the main enemy. It was they who controlled Palestine. It was their navy which blockaded Palestinian shores, preventing all but 75,000 of the hundreds of thousands of European Jewish refugees from entering the country. It was the British who stopped the Arabs from selling land to Jews and prohibited any new Jewish settlements, unless the Arabs approved. And this while the ovens of Nazi Germany worked on three shifts. It was the British who, in April 1939, turned back "to their ports of origin," the *Assando,* the *Assimi* and the *Pangia Konstario,* three ships laden with Jewish refugees who had somehow escaped from Germany and Romania. In 1940, the British turned back the *Salvador,* with 350 Bulgarian Jewish refugees. Some 231 of them died when the *Salvador* hit a violent storm on the Mediterranean; the rest were sent back to Bulgaria—and the Nazis. The *Pacific* and the *Milos,* which carried 1,800 Jews, many of whom already had relatives in Palestine, met similar fates. A British warship stopped the two tramp steamers in the Haifa harbor, transferred their passengers to the steamer *Patria,* and the British authorities announced their intention to inter the Jews on the Island of Mauritius for the rest of the war. On November 25, 1940, the *Patria* exploded and more than 200 refugees were blown to bits or drowned, within sight of their chosen homeland.

Jacob Kaplan, standing on Mount Carmel with some of his new friends, saw that explosion. Looking down on the lovely panorama of Haifa, he could see the harbor clearly. He could see the thrashing bodies drowning and the women and children without heads or arms or legs, being dragged into patrol vessels by boathooks. Among his companions that day was a fourteen-year-old boy named Eliahu Ben-Hakim. In 1944 that same boy murdered Lord Moyne, Britain's highest Middle East official, a crime for which he was hanged. This was the same Lord Moyne, who, when informed of a Jewish plan to trade one million trucks to Hitler in return for one million Jews said, "My dear fellow, whatever shall I do with a million Jews?"

And so he joined the *Haganah*. Many of his friends joined the *Irgun* instead, but, despite it all, he could not stomach the *Irgun*'s senseless murdering. Besides, the Nazis were really the main enemy. When the British began their life-and-death battle against the Nazis, the *Haganah* and *Irgun*—except for the bloodthirsty Stern gang—decided to make a truce. Even the sinking of the *Struma* did not break this truce. The *Struma*, a 180-ton cattleboat, never made it to the shores of Palestine. Instead, it waited for five months in the Istanbul harbor, its 769 Jewish passengers living in deck-mounted cages measuring sixty by twenty feet, while Jewish leaders in Jerusalem pleaded with the British to give them visas. On February 24, 1940, Turkish officials got tired of waiting. They sent the vessel to the Black Sea. There the *Struma* sank, with one survivor.

Nevertheless, the *Haganah* cooperated with the British when the British fought against the Nazis. In 1941, for example, *Haganah* commandos—Kaplan among them—entered Vichy-held Syria to blow up bridges and destroy communication lines. One of Kaplan's companions was a young *sabra* from the settlement of Nahalal, Moshe Dayan. Later, Kaplan, along with thirty thousand other Palestinian Jews, donned British uniforms to fight Nazis in Egypt. Meanwhile, terror against the British continued. Many *Haganah* leaders spent months in jail, only to be released, allowed to fight the Nazis, then imprisoned again.

Though Kaplan's *Haganah* specialty was information, not terrorism, he was arrested in summer, 1942. He served four months in a Jerusalem jail. When he got out, he petitioned both the British and the *Haganah* to go to Europe, where he could fight the Nazis directly. In the end, he was one of just thirty-nine men the British permitted to be parachuted into various European countries. He landed not far from Copenhagen. There his next adventure began.

There was a danger in daydreaming about the past, Ben-Ezra knew. It made the horrors seem fresh and once more threatening. Such horrors, he knew all too well, could paralyze. And there was another task at hand. Once more, it was a question of survival.

Ben-Ezra glanced at his watch. They still had slightly more than two hours. How were they doing down there? Had Frederick mastered the reactor? Had he identified the genuine plans? That might pose more of a problem. The agent breathed deeply and was pleased to feel no pain. Well, there were always two possibilities. . . .

Chapter Thirty-Two

It took Borgmann fifteen minutes to hook the second thimble. Unfortunately, the plan that hung below it also turned out to be a ringer. He hooked the third thimble in just ten minutes, but he spent another twenty to find these blueprints were also fake. Hooking the fourth was easy enough. This time, a thorough study of the plans revealed no obvious flaws. But, Borgmann realized, that didn't guarantee these were the genuine plans. To be certain, he had to look at the other three also, whether or not there was time. It was now 11:45—an hour and fifteen minutes to go.

At least Miriam wasn't giving him trouble. She was quickly catching on to her duties and now rarely called him when a light flashed. Usually she knew which dial to twist or which lever to pull.

He continued hooking sets of plans, bringing them up in front of the television camera and studying them. By noon, he'd seen them all. Four were obvious ringers. Another was probably false also. But he could find nothing wrong with either of the others. He shared his problem with Miriam.

"Why don't we just take both blueprints with us, then?" she asked.

"I'm not sure how we're going to shield one set, much less two," he replied. "There's enough radiation soaked into that Plexiglas to sterilize a regiment of Cossacks. Besides, each set of plans must weigh nearly ninety pounds. I may be able to carry one, but certainly not two."

"How *are* we going to shield the plans?" Miriam asked, stuck on that problem. "You know we're going to be flying them back to Israel. Couldn't the radiation endanger everyone on the plane?"

"It could, unless we find a shield. But leave that to me. I'll come up with something."

Miriam gazed at him evenly, unconvinced. "I do have a suggestion for figuring out which is the genuine set of plans," she said, at length.

Borgmann snorted.

"Don't reject it before you've heard it," Miriam said petulantly.

"Okay," he said, giving in to her, "what's your idea?"

"Why not examine the hooks on the thimbles? One of them must be scratched more than the others by the crane hook, and that will be the genuine one—the one that's been pulled out of the pool most often."

"Won't work," Borgmann said. "The thimble hooks are as old as the reactor itself. The only new objects are the plans themselves." Suddenly he lifted his head. "But that does give me an idea," he said, his voice tight with excitement. "The genuine set of plans has spent less time immersed in the pool than the rest, so it should have absorbed less radioactivity. The difference will be slight, but we should be able to measure it."

Borgmann dunked the plan he'd been studying back into the reactor tank and went down to the main floor. Instruments and gauges dotted the outside of the large hexagonal structure. It was a simple matter to measure the radioactivity levels of the experimental materials within. One by one, he checked each set of plans. By 12:15, he had finished.

"I've got it, Miriam," he said. "It has to be plan number five."

"One of the plans you thought was likely?"

"Yes."

Borgmann vaulted up the metal stairway, to the crane controls. He lowered the hook, engaged the hook from thimble number five, lifted the plans from the reactor and then locked the crane in the up position.

"Okay, Miriam," he called. "Hit the scram button now."

With her whole fist, Miriam hit the big red button on the console. For an instant, every alert light on the board flashed on, then almost as quickly, the entire board went dark. Within the hexagonal concrete structure, the sound of control rods slamming into their holes could be heard. One by one, the control panel dials dropped to zero.

"Frederick," Miriam called, "a blue light just went on!"

"Good. That means the reactor has shut down." He came down to the main floor. "We can forget about it. After we're gone, the Danes will have no trouble starting it up again. Now we have to figure out how to carry the plans safely. And we have"—he looked at his watch—"exactly forty-five minutes to do it."

Miriam left her post at the reactor console, the relief evident on her face. She joined Frederick on the main floor. "How can I help now?" she asked.

"Well," Borgmann replied, appearing to consider the matter seriously, "you could go out and buy some lead sheets and bring them back down here."

"Buy some lead sheets? You can't be serious!"

"As a matter of fact, I'm not. It would take days to get lead sheets of the required thickness. We have to find a substitute somehow."

Borgmann walked around the huge reactor room, looking in equipment cabinets and tool lockers. Then he walked around the hexagonal structure, studying. One part interested him, a large, lead-shielded porthole. He took a tape measure from the tool locker and held it up to the lead plates. "Two and a half feet by three feet," he announced. "That should be more than enough. But we'd better make sure." He rummaged through the tool locker and came up with a yardstick, then ran up the stairs. With an extending caliper, he measured the height and width of the Plexiglas block in which the centrifuge plans were imbedded. "Twenty inches by thirty inches," he said, his voice ringing with excitement. "We can do it. I'm sure we can do it."

"What? What can we do?"

"We can build some sort of briefcase, I think—a briefcase of lead plates?"

"Frederick, you've lost me. How can we build a briefcase of lead plates?"

"Bend down here and take a look at this with me. You see the way these lead plates are screwed into position around this beam hole?"

"Yes," Miriam said, uncertainly.

"The screw holes are quite close together. About an inch between them, I'd guess."

"You're right," Miriam said. "But so what?"

"Well, there's some heavy electrical wire in the tool chest over there, and a roll of lead foil about an inch wide." Borgmann paused, as if the explanation was over.

"I still don't understand, exactly," Miriam said.

"We unscrew two of the lead plates and lay them one on top of the other. Then we wire them together —like a braided wallet—and lay a strip of lead foil over the wire, on the longest edge. We leave a loop of wire sticking up. Then with the crane, I drop the plans on top of one lead plate, and catch hold of the loop on the second, flipping it over, on top of the first plate. The wire will hold the plates together and the lead foil will fill any gaps. Once we have the plates on top of each other, we wire the other edges together and line them with lead foil too. Now do you understand?"

"Now I understand," said Miriam. "What still puzzles me, though . . ."

"Yes?"

"Is how you or any ten people are going to carry the package anywhere."

Borgmann grinned. "I can carry it. Up the stairs and to the car. We may have to make a stop on the way to the airport for a hernia operation, though. Besides, there isn't any other way."

"Then let's get to it. What do I do?" Miriam was all business again.

"You get the screwdriver and start unscrewing those reactor plates. I'll measure the wire and the lead foil."

"One thing bothers me, Frederick," Miriam said,

brow wrinkled. "Without those plates, won't there be radiation leakage from the reactor?"

"Not while it's shut down. And they'll notice the problem before they start up, believe me. Let them find a place to buy lead plates. We don't have time for that sort of thing."

It took them nearly twenty minutes to strip two lead plates from the reactor, lay them out, lace them up and line the lacework with lead foil. Then Borgmann once more raced up the stairs to the crane controls and began the delicate task of dropping the Plexiglas package between the lead plates.

"Miriam, I want you on the other side of the reactor," he said sternly. "If this thing slips off its hook, it could bounce—maybe shatter. Then we'd have to run, if we wanted to avoid serious radiation burns." Despite his effort to hide it, there was fear in his voice.

Miriam retreated as ordered.

Under Borgmann's guidance, the crane slowly swung back from the reactor pool. He rotated the crane housing, then worked the lever that started the hook moving.

"It's swaying, Frederick, it's swaying."

Borgmann brought the crane to a stop, his heart pounding loudly in his chest. The plans, which had been swaying dangerously, like a pendulum threatening to break loose from a clock, finally stopped moving. Then, sweating again, the lever slippery in his grasp, Borgmann started the crane again. The thing slid along its tracks so slowly that a quick glance might not have revealed any movement at all. Time stretched to cover its movement. What took little more than a minute seemed to take half an hour.

Finally the crane was directly over the spread-out plates. Borgmann locked it in place, ran down to the plates and looked up. "Right on target," he said, puffing. He hurried back up the stairs to the crane controls, his gait awkward, his tension obvious.

With Borgmann slowly pulling on the lever, his hand so taut that it was nearly in spasm, the hook dropped toward the floor, its pulleys and chains clanking. Below dangled a Plexiglas rectangle about the size of a desk blotter and an inch thick or so. About ten feet above the lead plates, for no particular reason, the rectangle began to spin, as if it were tied to a twisted telephone cord instead of a heavy metal hook on a chain. Borgmann tensed his whole body, as if he could influence what was happening at the end of the hook, like a prize-fight spectator bracing for a punch thrown at his favorite.

"It's swinging, Frederick," Miriam called out, terrified.

"I know, I know. The crane wasn't meant to operate this low. I think the cable may be unwinding. It'll stop—I think." His fingers were so slippery that he was having trouble holding onto the crane controls.

But it didn't stop. It twisted around in one direction, revolving perhaps a dozen times, then twisted an equal number of times in the other. Nervous and irritable, Borgmann lost patience. "You stand back, Miriam. I'm going to lower it until it's touching the plates. I think that'll stop the spin. Then I'll drop it in place."

Leaning forward against the catwalk railing, his right hand straining backward, his sweaty thumb and forefinger grasping the crane lever as if to crush it, Borgmann peered at the crane head and the plastic package twisting and dangling beneath it. He pulled the lever slowly, trying to draw on a confidence born of nearly two hours of continuous practice. The Plexiglas rectangle hit the lead plates gently, without coming off the hook, but at a crazy angle.

Borgmann breathed deeply, raised it no more than an inch, let it twist some more, then lowered it once again, his heart pounding furiously. The angle was still wrong. For an instant, his fingers slipped off the lever. He grabbed backward, panicked, then took the lever firmly once more. He raised the crane again and lowered it again. This time, the long edge of the Plexiglas rectangle was square with the long edge of the lead plates. Borgmann exhaled. So far, so good.

He pulled the crane lever once more and the hook descended about three inches. Dammit—the rectangle was falling properly, but on the wrong plate, the one with the wire loop, the one that was supposed to go on top.

Once more, he raised the crane. The package wavered. Sweat dripped down his sides. It's not going to work, he thought. I won't be able to do it. The package came upright, but maintained contact with the lead plate on the floor. Now Borgmann glanced back at the crane control panel, wiped the sweat from his other hand on his pants and took hold of a second lever. He was shocked by its cool dryness.

Frederick Borgmann had worked with radioactive materials before—for all of his adult life, for that matter. Many times he'd been in situations far more dangerous than this. But he'd never been more shaken. He was very nearly submerged in fear. Slowly he realized that it wasn't so much the danger that had shaken him this time. It was the fear he wouldn't succeed. It was Miriam. He tried to steady himself with another deep breath.

Once more Borgmann lowered the crane hook. The plastic rectangle gradually sank to the floor, against the proper lead plate this time. Then it was down. The match was as perfect as if it had been put into position by human hands. He exhaled. The tension seemed to drain away.

Borgmann dropped the crane hook another few inches and it detached itself from the plans. With an expert touch that surprised even himself, he caught the second plate's wire loop with the crane hook, lifted it and neatly dropped it on the top of the plastic-embedded centrifuge. The big clock on the wall read 12:42.

"That's it," Miriam said, exultant. "You did it."

"So I did," Borgmann said, surprised. "I didn't think I could." His suit hung limply on his body, drenched in sweat.

"I wasn't worried," Miriam said nonchalantly. "At least, not very."

Together, Miriam and Frederick spread the lead foil around the edges and tucked it in. Then, they laced up the rest of the "briefcase," quickly pushing the wire through the screw holes. Borgmann ended up fastening a handle he made from heavy plastic-insulated cable. Then he checked out the whole package with his Geiger counter.

"Well," Miriam said, "is it dangerous?"

"You sound concerned," Frederick said, teasing.

"Worried. But not concerned." She tossed it right back.

"I wouldn't want to use it for a bedboard," he said, "but an hour's contact shouldn't hurt."

Miriam looked up at the wall clock. It was nearly five minutes to one.

"Hey, we'd better get going. Yaakov will be wondering if we made it after all."

"My God—Yaakov! I almost forgot about him."

Borgmann took hold of the makeshift handle and pulled the "briefcase" off the floor. The strain showed in his face.

"Can you carry it up the stairs?" Miriam asked.

"We'll know that in a minute or two," he answered, trying not to sound flippant.

Borgmann dragged the package through the reactor room door, past the cot where Groot was sleeping and up to the first landing of the stairway. "You go on up and tell Yaakov I'm coming. Wouldn't want to be greeted up there by some unexpected strangers."

"Right," Miriam said, taking the stairs two at a time.

Behind her, Frederick tugged on the case, dragging it up the stairs, thumping along, gouging chunks out of the stair treads and the railing. Sweat was dripping off of him now. He could feel it running down the small of his back. He stopped every few steps, but that didn't help much. Borgmann was in his forties and he usually thought of himself as a young man, middle age indeterminately distant. Today he was getting an unwelcome lesson concerning the facts of life. He could have done without it.

He was about three-quarters of the way up the stairs when Ben-Ezra came down to meet him. "Can I help you carry that thing?" he said. "I heard all about it."

"Damn case only has one handle," Borgmann said. "I didn't quite think of everything."

"We're going to make it, do you know that?" said Ben-Ezra. "All we have to do is catch a plane and we've done it. But we have to get on the plane before the Danish police figure out what's happened."

Borgmann pulled the case up to the last landing before they reached the door, grunting. He felt like the wire handle was making a permanent groove in his hand. Finally they reached the door. Ben-Ezra stepped out, then motioned Frederick to follow, quickly.

Out in the mirrored hallway, the few children who were wandering through took little or no notice of the trio and the strange package one of them carried.

At the airport, the luggage handler looked up at the digital clock in the main hallway. It was well past one now. If they ever were going to do it, they'd have done it by now. He stepped into a phone booth, put a coin in the slot and dialed. The number rang—and rang —and rang. He hung up. Perhaps there was a malfunction in the line. His instructions said to try three times. The luggage handler dialed the number once more. And once more, there was no answer. He watched the crowds of tourists flowing through the airport. They couldn't have been less interested in him. No doubt, they were thinking of spending an evening in the Tivoli, or visiting the home of Hans Christian Andersen, or eating at some fine restaurant. He marveled at their innocence. He tried to recall if he had ever been innocent. Unlike some others he knew, his memory simply wasn't good enough. Once more, he dialed the number and once more, there was no answer. It was certain now. There was no one alive—or, at least, no one conscious—at the Tivoli reactor. The Israelis had apparently succeeded in stealing the plans. Now the luggage handler had to prepare to receive them.

Chapter Thirty-Three

Anyone watching the exit to the House of Mirrors on that overcast day in May would have seen a strange sight: two men and a woman leaving together, the taller of the two men half carrying, half dragging what seemed to be a thin rectangular piece of metal about the size and shape of one of those briefcases fashion models carry around from job to job filled with photographs and clippings.

Two observers, however, had been hoping to see exactly this—a burr-headed American named Gary Stabile, and a suave, good-looking Lebanese, Suliman Ferrara.

Stabile was best situated to see the Israeli team as it left the House of Mirrors.

I'll be damned, he thought to himself. They did it. He glanced at his watch. It was a couple of minutes past one. Took 'em long enough, though. And they wouldn't have managed it at all without my help. Now they were hurrying—to the airport, of course. To El Al Flight 42, no doubt. In some ways, the Jews were such subtle people. In others, they were so obvious, even innocent. That would be their undoing. Stabile shifted his gaze toward Suliman Ferrara, who'd been patiently sitting on a bench on the other side of the House of Mirrors. The bench was empty. The American chuckled. Opening night was going beautifully, even though there had never been a dress rehearsal. It would all be over soon now, Stabile thought. He rose from his bench, dusted himself off, and strolled toward the main gate. It wouldn't do to hurry, he cautioned himself. He wanted to arrive just in time to pick up the pieces, to mark his scorecard, so to speak.

Suliman Ferrara's eyes widened as he saw Borgmann struggle out of the House of Mirrors exit, accompanied by Ben-Ezra and the girl. He'd nearly given up hope. What problems they'd faced down there he had no way of knowing, but there was no doubt in his mind that they'd been difficult ones. What Ferrara could not understand—at first—was the nature of the object Borgmann was carrying. It seemed to be nothing more than a large leather briefcase. But from the way Borgmann was struggling with it, it evidently weighed at least 150 pounds. What could weigh so much and still fit inside a briefcase? Certainly blueprints weren't heavy. Gradually Ferrara realized that the contents of the briefcase weren't so heavy—that the great weight was the briefcase itself, and that it wasn't made of leather, but of metal. He couldn't piece it all together in his mind, but he was certain Borgmann had the blueprints. There'd be plenty of time to ponder the details of the briefcase. Now there was other work to do, perhaps the most important work of his life. He walked quickly toward the nearest gate and hailed a cab. "Kastrup Airport, please," he told the driver.

Miriam unlocked the small trunk of the green Saab and lifted the lid. Then, with a grunt, Borgmann picked up the lead briefcase and dropped it heavily into the opening. The trunk was wide enough to accommodate the package, but it wasn't deep enough. With the trunk lid closed, nearly four inches of the lead plate stuck out, protruding over the little car's back bumper.

"What do you think?" Ben-Ezra asked. "Can we drive with it this way?"

"We can't take the chance, Yaakov," Frederick replied. "One good bump and we'll scatter radioactive blueprint chunks all over the highway."

"The rear seat folds down," Miriam said. "That should give us plenty of room."

"Yes, but how would we all get into the car?"

"You drive," Miriam said, "and I'll sit on top of the plans."

"Well," Frederick said, considering the problem, "it's only a forty-minute ride to the airport. There's no significant danger, I suppose. Okay."

The back seat was folded down, the plans shoved forward and the trunk lid locked. Then the trio piled into the car, Borgmann at the driver's seat. In a few moments, they were out of the center of the city, on their way, and at a good clip.

"You know," Borgmann said, grinning now, "I think we've done it."

"It does look that way," Miriam said, trying to suppress a growing sense of triumph.

"This isn't the time for overconfidence," Ben-Ezra said, warning them both. "First, we have to get out of Copenhagen before the police catch on. And we still have to deal with our anonymous helper. Don't you think he'll want some payment for his favors?"

"What do you mean 'payment,' Yaakov?" Borgmann asked. He expertly steered the car around a trailer truck.

"Whoever opened the door for us and took care of the anteroom guard almost certainly knows we have the plans. He probably was watching the House of Mirrors from a discreet distance. There can only be one explanation for his actions: he wants those blueprints."

"Ferrara?" Miriam asked.

"Stabile?" Borgmann inquired.

Ben-Ezra shrugged. "Either," he said. "Or both. I think I'm ready for them, whatever they have in mind. But let's wait until we get to Tel Aviv to start celebrating."

"You know, Yaakov," Borgmann said, slightly annoyed, "I'm not sure I like the way you just assume I'm coming with you to Tel Aviv. I have a return ticket back to Chicago, you know. I've done what you asked of me and not without serious doubt. I've had to cash in an old friendship, enter a nuclear installation illegally, steal secret documents and, in the process, risk not only my life and yours and Miriam's, but also the lives of half the citizens of Copenhagen. That reactor almost got away from us, you know."

"Ah, Frederick," Ben-Ezra began, his tone one of gentle understanding. "Your conscience bothers you. It shouldn't. Think of the result. The whole world will know that Israel has the centrifuge plans. Even without building the machines, our most powerful enemies will be sufficiently afraid of us to leave us alone. That's all we want, to be left alone."

Borgmann glanced into the rear view mirror, his eyes meeting Miriam's. She gave a little shrug and smiled. He smiled back. "Fathers and daughters often disagree, Yaakov," Borgmann said.

"You told him?" Ben-Ezra asked Miriam, unbelieving. "I thought we agreed it could only complicate things."

"I didn't tell him, Father. He overheard me when you were in the car, before we entered Tivoli this morning."

"Oh." Ben-Ezra was silent for a moment. "She's been in the service for nearly eight years now, Frederick—since soon after college. They tell me she's first-rate. Even so, I didn't want her with me here. Nachman insisted."

"I understand," Frederick said softly. He overtook a brown Volvo, then eased back into the right-hand lane.

"They said she was perfect, what with her blonde hair and blue eyes," Ben-Ezra added.

"Perfect?" said Borgmann. "Well, that's a bit of an exaggeration. But close enough, I guess."

Miriam reached forward and slapped Frederick playfully on the shoulder. The gesture wasn't lost on her father. He glanced at her, then at Borgmann, then back again. "Well, well," he said under his breath, both surprised and pleased.

"Now listen here," Miriam said, her playful mood instantly replaced with anger. "Don't you go drawing any conclusions—"

Ben-Ezra held up his hand. The Saab was approaching an emergency pulloff on the main highway shoulder. "Turn off here, Frederick," he instructed. "I have to make a telephone call. It will take only a second."

Borgmann guided the Saab off the road onto the widened shoulder and pulled up to the outdoor pay phone. Ben-Ezra hopped out of the car and placed a call. Try as they might, neither Frederick nor Miriam could hear a word he said. All in all, the conversation took less than a minute. Soon Ben-Ezra was back in the car and they were once more underway, Borgmann's foot heavy on the accelerator.

"Whom did you call, Father?" Miriam asked.

"The airport. I wanted to check the schedule."

"Really?" Miriam asked, suspicious. "I can't believe you didn't check it out in advance."

"I wanted to be sure our plane was on time."

"I still don't believe you."

Ben-Ezra groaned. "Sometimes I think you are lucky, Frederick—having no children. They don't always provide their parents with joy and satisfaction, you know."

"Why did you make that call, Yaakov?" Borgmann asked, not about to be sidetracked from the main issue.

"What I don't understand, Father," Miriam added, "is why you need to keep secrets from us. It seems to me that the more we know, the more helpful we can be."

Ben-Ezra was silent for some time. When he finally spoke, he seemed oddly subdued. "I have worked alone so much in the past," he said. "I've rarely had anyone to share my secrets with, so it has become habit to keep them to myself. And then there's the matter of affection. I care for both of you deeply—I'm sure you both know that. Sometimes to share the secrets is to increase the danger to others."

"But does that apply now, Yaakov?" Miriam asked gently. "The mission is nearly complete. Shouldn't we both know what you're planning?"

Ben-Ezra took a deep breath. "I called the airport and spoke to the El Al reservations desk," he said, his voice low. "I told them that Flight number 42 would be bombed or hijacked by a well-disguised team of saboteurs."

Borgmann felt his mouth drop open. "Good God, Yaakov—why? Isn't that the flight we're taking?"

"No. We won't be on that plane. But I hope Ferrara or Stabile or whoever it was who's been helping us thinks we are. I believe that's what they'll conclude, seeing us leave the Tivoli as we did."

"How can you be sure they saw us leave?" Miriam asked.

"We were rather conspicuous, you know," Ben-Ezra answered. "And I can't imagine our helper leaving the scene after opening the reactor door and disposing of a guard—can you?"

"No," Miriam said, from her position on top of the lead briefcase, "I guess not."

"I still don't understand why you told El Al that Flight 42 will be bombed or hijacked, especially if we're not going to be on it," Frederick put in.

"*We* know we're not going to be on the flight, Frederick," Ben-Ezra explained. "Stabile or Ferrara—or whoever it was—doesn't. So there's a good chance the plane *will* be hijacked or bombed, even without us on it. I called to protect the passengers. I had to do that, though it increases the danger to us."

"How could it do that?" Borgmann asked, thoroughly confused by now.

Miriam understood. "Yaakov's warning gives our helper some vital information, if he's smart enough to see it. There'll be extra security precautions that could tell him we're onto him."

"I see," Borgmann said thoughtfully.

They stopped momentarily for a red light.

"I've tried to place some obstacles in his path, of course," Ben-Ezra said. "All we need is about fifteen minutes of confusion and we're home free. If my plan works out, we'll get the time we need."

"What's the plan, Yaakov?" Miriam asked, prodding him.

"Oh. Yes. Well, I've arranged to fly to London, then to Tel Aviv. The flight to London will be aboard a plane that, so far as the public knows departed at one-thirty, according to the terminal signs. Actually, it's being held at the gate for what they're calling a tire change. The passengers are waiting in the lounge, which is right next to the El Al lounge. I have a friend who's agreed to hold them there until two."

"A friend from the file?" Miriam asked.

"No. There's nothing at all Jewish about this fellow. But I gave him a hand years ago and he remembers that."

"So we have about fifteen minutes to get ourselves and the briefcase aboard the plane," Borgmann observed.

"Not exactly, Frederick. I want you and Miriam to stay, at least till I'm safely in Tel Aviv. That should be sometime early tomorrow."

"But you had us bring our luggage—" Borgmann couldn't understand.

Ben-Ezra laughed. "Well, you'll have to come to Tel Aviv to retrieve it. I'm shipping it on Flight 42."

Borgmann accelerated slightly, passing an airport limousine.

"Why do you want us to stay, Father?"

"In case someone makes a last-minute attempt on the plans, outside help could be very useful. You still have your gas guns, don't you?"

"Yes," Borgmann answered.

Miriam just nodded.

"Good. I can't take mine on the plane. The metal detectors would spot it in a moment. And, incidentally, you'd better get rid of yours before you fly out of here tomorrow. That goes for that little pistol you carry around, Miriam."

"You know about that?"

"You didn't seriously think I wouldn't find out, did you?"

The girl shrugged. "You want us to stay here because you think there might be an attempt on your plane."

It was Ben-Ezra's turn to shrug. "Who knows? I

352

think I've thrown them off, but in the end-game, especially, you dare not underestimate your enemy."

"That's the airport up there, Yaakov," Borgmann pointed out.

"Thank God."

Borgmann wheeled the Saab through the increasing traffic as he entered the airport road system. Miriam and Ben-Ezra were both looking through the windows, watching for any sign of trouble or interference. Borgmann's thoughts were elsewhere. For some reason, he was thinking of Ruth.

In his mind's eye he saw her near Tel Aviv, walking through the orange groves, strong, tanned, vibrantly alive. She would have approved of this, he thought. No struggle, sacrifice or risk was too great when the fate of Israel was at stake, so far as she was concerned. Convincing her to leave her homeland for the United States had been the hardest task he'd ever had—and he'd succeeded only by promising they'd return someday, together. Well, tomorrow he would be returning, not with Ruth, but with some blueprints, with Yaakov Ben-Ezra—with Miriam.

Miriam watched her father out of the corner of her eye. He seemed well, free of pain for a time. More important, he seemed happy. Unless something unexpected happened, the mission would succeed gloriously. Years from now, Ben-Ezra would be remembered by it. Miriam wished nothing more than to be present when her father delivered the plans to General Nachman. She and Nachman had argued for days about whether or not Ben-Ezra could do the job. Somehow, Nachman knew all about his friend's health problem. He knew also, however, of Ben-Ezra's determination and resourcefulness. With the condition that she accompany him, Nachman approved the mission. Borgmann was part of the plan, though neither she nor Nachman were certain Yaakov could deliver him.

And now it was coming to an end. Yaakov would never know. There was no need to tell Frederick, either. He idolized Ben-Ezra, and Miriam didn't want to lessen that admiration in any way. Tomorrow they'd all be in Tel Aviv—and how different things would be then. Yaakov would be a hero. So would Frederick. As for herself, Miriam resolved to stay in the background and let her menfolk take the praise. The phrase caught in her mind—her menfolk. Was Frederick included? She glanced forward. Borgmann seemed entirely absorbed in piloting the car through traffic. Soon, they'd be in Tel Aviv again, together, as they had been years earlier. She would show him how the city had changed, how it had matured. Maybe what had begun last night would actually continue.

Yaakov Ben-Ezra's quick brown eyes darted around the airport parking lot. What he was searching for he didn't know—a man with a gun? A hijacker? A platoon of Arabs? If something was going to happen here, he knew he wouldn't see it until the action was right on top of him. Yet there was no way he could voluntarily turn off his alertness.

Try as he might, Ben-Ezra could not fit the attempts on his life into master plans designed either by Stabile or Ferrara. Could that mean that there were others interested in the plans? If so, who? At any rate, there was still plenty of reason for caution.

There was reason for hope too. Something was going on between Frederick and Miriam. Ben-Ezra could see it in Miriam's eyes. There was just a trace of sentiment there, a slight softness, a barely tangible desire to please. And since she certainly wasn't trying to please him, Frederick must be the subject of this tenderness. As for Frederick, the signs were just as obvious. He was more than polite to Miriam; he was protective, solicitous. He laughed too readily at her jokes, showed too much concern for her in times of danger.

Ben-Ezra projected himself forward in time for a moment—to Tel Aviv. They would relax there, the danger and urgency gone. Miriam and Frederick would come to know each other in different circumstances. What there was between them now could grow stronger. Of all the things that might have happened on this mission, this one Ben-Ezra least expected. He'd considered Borgmann a middle-aged widower, a researcher, a man so absorbed in his work that he had little time for people, especially women. A mature man, in his forties, in contrast to Miriam, who—it seemed to her father—was young for her age. Besides, she'd long shown herself disinterested in anything but superficial relationships. Perhaps both of them had changed. Maybe they had changed each other.

Chapter Thirty-Four

Gary Stabile pushed through the milling crowd surrounding the El Al lounge. What was going on here? Had he missed something? Had Ferrara already tangled with the Israelis? By this time, the passengers should be aboard Flight 42 and the purser should be processing any latecomers—Ben Ezra, for instance, who should be here shortly, according to Stabile's calculations. The American agent slipped between two plump ladies, past a young couple holding hands, around a well-dressed businessman and up to the front desk.

"Flight delayed?" Stabile asked the attendant.

"Yes, sir. Are you ticketed?"

"Yes I am. Going to visit my daughter. She's living on a *kibbutz,* can you imagine that?"

"Yes, sir."

"How come the delay, anyhow? Nothing wrong, is there?"

"No, sir," the attendant said, showing all his teeth. "Just a routine security check. Happens all the time. We should be leaving in a half hour or so."

"Oh, that's fine. Nothing to worry about. I've waited two years to visit Glenda, and another half hour or so won't make any difference."

Stabile found his way over to a corner and lit his pipe. He kept his eyes on the flight desk in the lounge. Ferrara would certainly show up shortly and he'd head directly for the desk to pick up his tickets. But he'd have one hell of a time getting on board the plane with any weapons. It was Ben-Ezra who had seen to that, with this extra "routine" security check. He must have called El Al. The Israeli agent was still a step ahead of the Arab, Stabile told himself.

On the other hand, Ferrara must know that the Israelis ran a very tight ship, security-wise. The chance of anyone getting on board an El Al jetliner with a gun, hand grenade or bomb was just about nil. Just what did he have in mind?

Possibly I'm underestimating Ferrara, Stabile thought. There are ways to smuggle weapons on board airplanes, even those craft guarded by metal detectors. Did the Palestinians know about them? Perhaps this trick of Ben-Ezra's, this extra security check, would do nothing more than warn Ferrara that the Israelis were watching for him.

Stabile puffed contemplatively on his pipe. His own weapon was in his shoulder holster, ready for use if needed. If one of the antagonists so completely outwitted the other and his victory seemed certain, Stabile would have to step in and even up the odds a bit. He recalled his instructions now that the climax approached: if possible, see that the plans are destroyed, with plenty of publicity (none of it mentioning the CIA). Also, make sure the antagonists fight and embarrass each other as publicly as possible.

The Company always couched its instructions in two steps like that. In truth, though, there was only one instruction—the first. Stabile was determined that the plans never reach the Mideast. Hopefully Ferrara and Ben-Ezra would save him the trouble of taking action himself. If not, he knew exactly what he would do. It would cause quite a mess, but that couldn't be helped. He left the lounge and strolled toward the observation desk.

At first Ferrara was completely thrown when he found the Israeli plane was not loaded yet, that the passengers were still in the lounge, that the flight was delayed for security reasons. Was it just a coincidence, or had someone discovered his intention?

Ferrara pushed his way out onto the observation deck. Danish and Israeli security agents were going over the plane like ants. There must have been twenty of them, obviously looking for a bomb. If that's what they were worried about, he thought, he was home free. Then he noticed the luggage loading area. A team of men was going over the baggage with detectors of some sort. Another security man led some dogs through the stacked suitcases, evidently animals able to smell out explosives. No matter. The fiberglass gun would fool them all.

Then an ominous thought passed through Ferrara's mind. Suppose the Israelis had good reason to suspect someone had planted a bomb on board Flight 42— *someone else?* Could it be that others besides he and the Israeli team had designs on the blueprints? There was no way to know—not now. Anyhow, that security team out there was eliminating any competition. Or so he hoped. Ben-Ezra was problem enough. Ferrara left the observation deck, picked up the ticket he'd reserved and disappeared into a bathroom. Five minutes later he emerged, sporting a new headful of acrylic blond hair. He wasn't the perfect Nordic, perhaps, but he was sure he'd pass casual inspection. There was no way the Israeli girl would be able to identify him now.

Ferrara showed his ticket to the attendant and took a seat in the lounge. Now, all that remained was for the Israeli team to join him in the lounge, then on the plane. He'd see to it that Flight 42 landed not at Lod Airport, between Tel Aviv and Jerusalem, but at Beirut. That single act would change the fate of the entire Mideast—perhaps of the world.

On the tarmac, an Israeli 707—Flight 42—was parked about seventy-five yards from a BOAC VC-10. Security agents were finishing up a search of the Israeli plane while workmen were puttering around the landing gear of the British aircraft, apparently changing or inflating a tire.

A uniformed luggage handler sat in the cab of a forklift truck, looking first at one plane and then at the other. Something was wrong here, but he wasn't quite sure what. He'd been surprised by the security check on the Israeli plane—and worried. Yet only one person knew he was here, and she wouldn't dare say a word. She'd threatened from time to time—though not for years. His employers would go hard on her if she interfered with his work, and she knew it. The luggage handler shrugged away his few small doubts, opened his valise and began to assemble the equipment with which he had been provided.

Borgmann pulled the green Saab into the terminal area. They unloaded the lead briefcase as quickly as possible and Borgmann dragged it into the terminal building, Ben-Ezra leading the way, Miriam acting as rear guard.

The trio was met at BOAC by a tall blond man in a grey business suit, flanked by two porters and a luggage cart. He smiled broadly when he saw Ben-Ezra.

"Good afternoon, my friend," he said. "It's good to see you again."

"Good to see you too, Gunnar," Ben-Ezra said. "You haven't aged a bit."

"Neither have you—except for that belly."

Ben-Ezra chuckled. "Is everything ready?"

"Just as you requested, my friend. You're ten minutes early, you know."

"I wanted to get this package loaded in the cargo bay before you brought the passengers back—in case there's any trouble."

"Do you expect trouble? I swing some weight with airport security you know. We could have reinforcements here in a couple of minutes if you need them."

"No. I don't think that will be necessary. The less fuss, the better."

"Of course. I understand completely. You men take that package and wheel it out to the plane."

The porters lifted the lead case onto the cart. Frederick and Miriam watched without saying a word.

"Just a moment, porters," Ben-Ezra said. "I want to walk it out to the plane with you. But I have some good-byes to say. So would you first take the two bags from the car and put them on El Al Flight 42?"

He took Frederick and Miriam aside. "Why don't the two of you go up to the observation deck. You can see everything from up there."

"What if you need help?" Miriam asked.

"You'll be in a good place to give it to me."

"And we'll be out of the line of fire," Miriam observed coolly.

"There's not going to be any firing," Ben-Ezra retorted.

"We'll be up there," Frederick said. "And we'll keep our eyes open."

"Good. Now there's a flight out of here for Israel tomorrow morning. I want you both to be on it."

"Okay," Miriam said. "Whatever you say, Father."

"Listen to that, Frederick," Ben-Ezra said with a grin, "suddenly it's whatever you say, Father. How about you—will you be on that flight?"

"Whatever you say, Yaakov," Borgmann said.

They all laughed.

"There's one other problem I wanted to mention, Frederick. Come over here for a moment." Ben-Ezra led his friend a few feet away from Miriam.

"Yes, Yaakov—what can I do for you?"

"In case, well, in case anything goes wrong—ah—"

Borgmann looked steadily at his old friend. He had known the man thirty years and this was the first time Ben-Ezra had asked him for any personal favor—and even this wasn't a favor, it was a pleasure. "Take care of Miriam? Of course I will, Yaakov. You can depend on it."

"That's what I wanted to hear."

Miriam waited discreetly until the men had finished

talking. When they returned, she gave Yaakov a quick kiss on the cheek.

"We'd better get moving, Yaakov," Neilborg said.

The porters started wheeling the lead case toward the door. "Good-bye kids," Ben-Ezra said, with a bit more cheer than he felt. "I'll meet you at the airport tomorrow."

He turned and followed the porters out a door, onto the tarmac. Reluctantly, Miriam and Frederick watched him go; then they headed upstairs toward the observation deck.

Chapter Thirty-Five

Every person, no matter how meek, has a breaking point. The woman had reached hers. She'd lived with him and with the knowledge of his deeds without complaining, without even seeking a release. It had slowly drained her of her spirit, her energy, her desire for life. Even at home, she'd lived every moment as if on stage, pretending to herself, to her friends, to her parents, to her children. Only with her husband was there no pretense at all.

And now it was going to happen all over again. It hadn't taken much to figure out the cryptic message. Evidently they'd felt coding was unnecessary. They were that sure of her. It was their contempt that had stirred her anger. It was also the memory of a love long past, of two loves long past. She struggled with it all morning, slowly building her courage. Finally it had come.

Today she would seek redemption. If she were to be judged by the way she'd lived her life, she wanted this act to be included in the evidence. As she hurried to get into her Audi, she wasn't sure she had enough time. That would be the worst irony of all—that finally, after all these years, her gesture would come too late. If that cryptic message were right, she had only a half hour or so. The feelings of desperation welled up in her once more and she struggled to act despite them. . . .

The luggage handler finished assembling the equipment provided by his employers, made it ready for use and put it back in the valise. It wouldn't do to show the gadget around. People might get frightened.

He simply couldn't understand what was happening with that British plane over there. Technicians had been working on a tire for more than a half hour now. The luggage handler admitted to himself that he was no expert when it came to airplanes. But something was strange if it took four technicians more than a half hour to change a tire. He'd changed a tire on his Mercedes once and, though he was all thumbs when it came to things automotive or mechanical, it had taken no more than twenty minutes—without help.

The luggage handler placed his valise on the seat beside him and drove the forklift truck out toward the VC-10. He intended to make some inquiries.

"How are you doing, fellows?" He offered his best Oxford accent.

One of the repairmen looked at him curiously. "What the hell are you doing out here?" he asked. His Cockney tones were somewhat less than polite.

"Well," said the luggage handler, undaunted, "I was just watching from over there and I wondered what was going on here."

"You were watching, huh?" A second technician turned to regard the luggage handler, his contempt evident. "Suitcases getting you down?"

"I only drove out here for a friendly chat," said the luggage handler. "Thought maybe I could lend a hand."

The third technician, a tall, swarthy man, laughed aloud, a very unpleasant sound. "Why don't you take that Erector Set toy you're driving and park on runway seven for a while," he suggested, smiling ominously.

"Okay," the luggage handler said, taking one last look at the landing gear. "I can take a hint." He turned the forklift truck around and headed back to the baggage collection area.

His employers had made a mistake, he reflected. They should have provided a technician's uniform.

That would have given me free entry to any section of the airport. Oh well, it shouldn't matter just this once.

Anyhow, he'd seen enough to confirm his doubts. The tire wasn't flat at all. Yet the airhose was lying next to it. From a distance, it might have seemed attached. Those technicians were simply stalling. But why?

The luggage handler hopped down from his forklift truck and walked over to the intercom phone on the baggage collection area wall.

"Hello," he said, when the operator answered. "Could you connect me with BOAC ticket desk?"

"Certainly, sir."

There were a few clicks on the line. "BOAC," said a female voice.

"Hello," said the luggage handler. "The VC-10 at gate four—could you tell me its scheduled departure time?"

"Oh, that plane has already left sir. The gate closed at one-thirty."

"Thank you." He hung up and turned toward the VC-10. It hadn't moved an inch. So it's already left, he said to himself. Of course. Who would suspect a plane that's already left? Now that was a very clever idea.

But was it fact or theory? Suddenly the luggage handler was filled with doubts. The Israeli 707 was also on its pad, in the last stages of a very careful search by a large mixed team of Israeli and Danish security agents. Was this a serious search or a diversion? Now he was confused. His employers hadn't instructed him on situations such as these. Their orders were simple and direct and did not admit of complications. He could have backed away from the job at this point, probably with nothing less than a mild reprimand. In fact, that would have been standard procedure. His employers had always told him: when in doubt, don't. Well, he was in doubt. But he would take the initiative this time. He had a personal stake in the matter.

He was standing at the telephone when another luggage handler walked over to his forklift truck and started the engine. With a shock, he realized his valise was still aboard. He ran after the truck, shouting. Finally, the other luggage handler stopped long enough for him to retrieve his valise. He was now standing on the other side of the Israeli airliner. The British plane was more than a hundred yards away.

The luggage handler found a small stool near the hangar entrance and sat down. He was winded and sweating. That wouldn't do. He needed to be cool, in complete possession of himself. He removed his uniform cap, and mopped his sweaty forehead.

Now he had an occasion to study the Israeli airliner. The security men seemed to be winding up their search. From what he could tell, they hadn't found a thing. They didn't seem terribly disturbed by this. It was the rule, no doubt.

What the luggage handler needed to know was why they had conducted a search in the first place. This one had gone far beyond normal precautions. Were the Israelis taking special care because there would be special cargo aboard this flight? Or was this just a bluff, designed to fool him or any others like him?

He glanced over at the VC-10 again. The damn plane was still there. The technicians continued to fiddle with the landing gear. There was no reasonable explanation for it. Except one.

The luggage handler took his valise and walked toward the British plane. He would set up housekeeping midway between the two aircraft. Whichever one it was, he would be ready. How was it, he wondered, that the Israelis could be so clever—with decoys, phony searches, planes delayed beyond departure times, other tricks—and yet so stupid, parking the decoy and the real thing next to each other, so that both could be covered by a single man?

The luggage handler carried the stool with him, placing it directly between the two planes, against the outside wall of the baggage collection department. He unzipped his valise and checked his equipment one last time. Everything was in order. There was only one matter left to be considered—his own exit. Then he remembered just what sort of device he had there in that valise. People would soon be preoccupied with other matters. After what was about to happen, who would take any interest in a lowly luggage handler? Now, if he were a technician, that might be a different matter. His employers were right after all.

He looked at his watch. It was 1:56—exactly.

The luggage handler looked back at the terminal. They should be here by now—but there was no sign of them. Could there be *another* decoy? Had they taken a private plane? Were they planning to wait a few hours, then sneak out of Copenhagen by car? His employers had been certain they'd leave by plane as soon as possible. He hoped they were right. If not, he would be deprived of the pleasure of carrying out his instructions.

Carrying out his instructions hadn't always been a pleasure. In the early days, he'd thought of rebelling— of fighting them. There was a time—when he was very young, in his twenties—that he'd told them to cross him off their list, that he wasn't going to follow any more orders, that he owned himself. They took it very calmly. They reminded him of a few facts. They showed him a brown file folder with a swastika on it and his name written at the top. After that, he followed instructions. It would have been silly not to, since they rarely asked for anything difficult or unreasonable. Most of the time, they left him alone. He lived the good life.

Chapter Thirty-Six

One story below, Frederick and Miriam could see the planes lined up on the tarmac. They were directly above the BOAC gate. To their right was the El Al gate.

"What will we do in Tel Aviv?" Borgmann asked.

Miriam smiled. "It's changed a lot since you were there last, Frederick."

"So. You admit you were the little girl who showed me the city back in 1954?"

"Admit? I don't consider it a confession of any great crime."

"On the contrary, you were a delightful host," Borgmann said graciously.

"You have me at a disadvantage, Frederick. You remember me at that age better than I remember myself."

"Ah, yes, my memory. But that would be true even if my memory was ordinary. I was an adult, you know."

"Are you trying to tell me that you're the wise grownup and that I'm . . ."

"The inexperienced youngster? No. Haven't we been through all that? Maybe that was so back in 1954, but that was a long time ago."

Miriam dropped her eyes. "I do remember the wedding," she said.

"So do I, Miriam. Come on now, there's nothing to

367

be sad about. Ruth and I had a happy time together, and I'll never forget it."

The girl looked at him. His hand was gripping the railing. She put hers on top of it. There was nothing more to be said at the moment, so they both looked down at the BOAC jetliner, trying to spot Ben-Ezra.

"Look," Miriam said at last, "he's walking up to the plane now."

"I wonder what took him so long."

"Maybe there were tickets to buy," Miriam said. "I'm quite sure the Danish police don't know the plans are gone—yet. We should have until four, when the shift changes at the reactor."

"That means we still have two hours before the commotion begins," Borgmann said. "Maybe we'd better get on El Al Flight 42. Do you want to be around when the Danish police start searching for the plans?"

Miriam considered his suggestion. "Father was right about you," she said. "You do think like a spy. Let's see if there's any space available."

They took one last look at the BOAC jetliner. The porters had opened a baggage compartment door, and, together, were heaving the lead briefcase into it. Even from a distance, strain was visible on their faces. Ben-Ezra was watching their every move.

Downstairs, the El Al ticket office turned out to be right across from the lounge.

"Are there any seats left for Flight 42?" Borgmann asked the pretty dark-haired Israeli girl behind the counter.

Her eyebrows went up slightly and she looked at Frederick and Miriam with badly disguised suspicion. "That flight is due to depart in five minutes, sir. There's no chance that you can be boarded—even if there are seats."

"I understand the plane is being held and that the passengers have not been boarded," Borgmann said.

"Where did you hear that?" the ticket agent said, her suspicion open now.

"I was watching from the observation deck," said Borgmann. "But what difference does that make? You haven't answered my question—are there seats available?"

The girl consulted a list. "We have one seat in first class and two in coach," she said. She seemed to be looking around, as if for help.

"We'll take the coach seats," Borgmann said.

"Yes, sir," said the girl. She took out two ticket forms and began filling them in. "Do you have your passports with you?"

"Of course."

And how will you pay for this, sir, by cash, credit card or check?"

Miriam stepped forward. She'd taken something out of her purse—some sort of small ID wallet. She showed it to the ticket agent. "Charge it to this account," she told the girl.

The ticket agent's eyes widened slightly. "Oh, yes, ma'am," she said, her suspicion instantly transforming itself to awe. "Certainly. Is there anything I can get you? Would you like me to make connecting flight arrangements?"

"That won't be necessary," Miriam said briskly.

The girl handed over the tickets and smiled nervously. "I'm sorry I didn't have two in first class," she said. "The tourist traffic is so heavy nowadays, you know."

"We know," Miriam said.

They walked toward the lounge, toward the crowd waiting to board the plane.

"Attention all passengers," said a low voice over the loudspeaker. "Technical adjustments on BOAC Flight three-ninety-two have been completed. Passengers should report to the departure lounge. Boarding will begin in ten minutes." The announcement was repeated in Danish.

"You know what that means?" Frederick said to Miriam. "It means we've done it."

"Let's hold off a minute on the self-congratulations,"

Miriam warned. "I'm not willing to consider the mission a success until the plans are delivered to Dinora."

"To Dinora?" Borgmann asked, surprised. "That's the nuclear reactor headquarters—where Israel is building the bomb!"

"Of course," Miriam said.

"But Yaakov promised me that—"

"You didn't think we were going to store the plans in a museum, beside the Dead Sea Scrolls or something, did you? They'll be kept in maximum security. And our best security network is at Dinora. Were you really that ready to believe the worst, Frederick?"

Borgmann was suddenly serious. "Miriam, I helped build the atomic bomb that destroyed Nagasaki. With my own two hands, I contributed to the development of the hydrogen bomb. I worked side by side with Edward Teller on the Eniwetok weapon. We gave mankind power to eradicate itself, Miriam. It took me a while to realize my own responsibility. But when I did, I quit weapons work forever. You know that I wouldn't have helped you and Yaakov if he hadn't given me assurances. Then, when you mentioned Dinora—"

"I understand," Miriam said gently.

"Yaakov was telling me the truth, wasn't he?" Borgmann asked. It was clear what answer he wanted.

"Of course he was. There'll probably be pressure to use the plans once we get them back, but we simply can't afford it. Besides, Yaakov will fight any pressure from the Right. He's a very respected man back home, you know."

"I imagined that he was," Borgmann said, smiling again.

Gary Stabile saw Borgmann and the girl buy their tickets. There was no doubt of it—they were taking El Al Flight 42. But where was Ben-Ezra? As usual, Stabile answered his own question. The agent was no doubt downstairs, loading the plans onto the aircraft. Soon, he would join Borgmann and the girl. Or perhaps he would just enter the plane from below, never passing through the lounge. At any rate, everything was going according to plan, so far. But the crucial moments were still to come. Stabile found a phone booth, dropped a coin in the slot and dialed.

"*Polito,*" a voice answered.

"Hello," Stabile said pleasantly. "I am a Weatherman. I am going to blow up an airplane at Kastrup Airport between two-thirty and three o'clock this afternoon. This is not a joke. It is a protest against Danish complicity in American imperialism."

"Who is this?" Who—"

Stabile hung up the phone and strolled out of the booth. Within a few minutes, Kastrup Airport should be swarming with airport security men, all planes grounded. Then the Danish police could recover the plans at their leisure.

Stabile paced the corridor and then checked his watch. He'd called the police the moment he'd seen Borgmann and the girl walk up to the El Al ticket counter. The security force should be running around like crazy by now. Maybe the police didn't believe him. Anyhow, they weren't hurrying. More than anything, Stabile wanted to stay out of this affair. But with each passing moment, that seemed less likely. In a few minutes, passengers would start boarding El Al Flight 42. What was necessary now was a delaying tactic, hopefully one that would cause the maximum confusion. Stabile glanced into the lounge and snorted. There was Ferrara in a ridiculous blond wig. Then he looked over at Borgmann and the girl—not fifteen yards away. He walked toward them. . . .

Suliman Ferrara was sweating. The blond wig was hot, but that wasn't the problem. He was impatient, almost nervous. Borgmann and the girl were only a few feet away from him, oblivious to his presence. No doubt, Ben-Ezra was also close by—possibly on the plane already. With the plans. Ferrara was anxious to be on the plane. He wanted it to be in the air, en route, to the Mideast.

All of his life, Ferrara had been terribly uncomfortable at moments like this—when the climax was approaching. He couldn't stand an undecided issue. At times he'd had to fight off forcing a decision that was bound to turn out against him, rather than waiting for the moment when the odds were in his favor. His urge now was to pull his gun on the flight attendant and force him to get the passengers on board and the plane airborne. Failing that, he wanted to attack Borgmann and the girl, here and now.

But, as usual, Ferrara forced himself to be the rational man, aware of his impulses, aware of the need to stifle them. He put his feet together very tightly, took a copy of *Time* magazine from a table and stared at the "People in the News" section. Leonid Brezhnev stared back, scowling under his beetle brows. According to the item, he'd just been given a new car by the British Prime Minister, a Jaguar with a V-12 engine. Well, Ferrara recalled, at least the Russians helped us. He patted the fiberglass pistol in his pocket. Its compact hardness settled him down, somewhat.

He turned the page, to the education section. So much at stake, he thought, so much to be decided in such a short time. His mind was a vortex—with pictures of his mother, of Yasir Arafat, of the Palestinian slums and hovels in Beirut, of his trip back and forth from *Fatah* headquarters racing through his thoughts in disordered succession.

With a great effort of will, he focused on what he must do. In a few short minutes, he and the Israeli team—plus the plans—would be aboard El Al Flight 42, on the way to Tel Aviv. In something less than four hours, the plane would land at its scheduled destination—unless he intervened.

His fiberglass pistol would give him an unexpected advantage over any security men who might be aboard. But he had to use it with perfect precision if he were to accomplish his mission. It wouldn't do, he thought, to

372

take command of the plane immediately after it was airborne. That would give the crew too much time to regain the initiative. No, Ferrara told himself, it would be best to show his hand a few minutes before the plane came into Israeli airspace after traversing the Mediterranean.

Even if he waited until just before landing there could be problems. Suppose the pilot had a chance to radio Lod Airport about the hijack? Surely the Israeli Defence Ministry would know of the plane's precious cargo. Would they send up interceptors to force the aircraft to land in Israel? Would the American-built Phantoms have orders to shoot down Flight 42, if forcing it to land proved impossible? Of course they would —Israel would do anything to prevent the plans from reaching Palestinian hands. It would be simple enough to blame Egypt or Syria for the airliner crash. And the world would be inclined to believe, as they usually believed, reports of Arab terrorism.

There was no question of it—Ferrara's first order of business must be to stop the plane from making radio contact with Israeli ground control, at least after his hijack attempt began. The Zionists must have as little warning as possible. Of course, that would mean he could not contact Beirut in advance. No matter. He knew, from bitter experience, that the Lebanese Air Force would be in no danger. It wouldn't know, until an hour after the event, that anything unusual had happened. He chuckled snidely, drawing the unwelcome attention of the matronly lady beside him. They exchanged hostile glances, then looked away.

So the radio must be his first target. How would he get to it? In his mind's eye, he pictured a typical jet flight. Coming over the Mediterranean, destination Beirut, passengers were always told to fasten their seat belts even before the coast was visible. Touchdown followed within fifteen minutes. It must be the same for the Lod Airport approach. After all, the two landing fields were within a half hour's flying time of each other, not that any planes made the trip. That was the moment, then, when the seat belt sign flashed on signaling the final approach.

Ferrara stood up. He paced for a few minutes back and forth in front of a row of waiting passengers. He was getting nervous now, but it was the kind of tension that improved his performance instead of destroying his efficiency. What he pondered now was a way to make a credible threat without bringing down on top of him not only the aircraft security man but Ben-Ezra, the girl, and Borgmann.

A stewardess—it was mundane, but effective. He'd pretend to be having trouble with his seat belt. She'd bend over to help—and find a gun in her face. Yes, that was it. A stewardess. Best of all, she'd have entry into the pilot's cabin. The only possible worry was if someone rushed him. And that thought didn't bother him much. His years of experience would give him the edge there. He could tell when people were going to move even before they knew it themselves.

Now he had a plan of attack. He found a chair and sat down. There was no way to plan everything, of course. He'd have to handle surprises as they presented themselves. Ferrara inhaled deeply. He was back in familiar territory, at least in his mind. No one was more at home in the unexpected than he. He leered at the matronly lady, who reacted as if he had made an obscene suggestion.

"I wish they'd let the passengers board," Borgmann said to Miriam. "The sooner we're in the air, the better I'll feel."

"Me too," Miriam agreed. "At least we don't have to worry about any bombs or hijackers. Israeli security is very thorough, Frederick. But I'm still concerned about Stabile. And Ferrara. They must be planning something."

Borgmann smiled at the girl. "Another few minutes and we'll be out of here. We won't have to worry about them."

"Do you really believe that?"

Borgmann shrugged. "I really want to believe it."

"So do I."

"We'd better keep our eyes open, and hold on to the gas guns until the last possible moment," Borgmann said, glancing nervously around the lounge. "Do you see your friend Ferrara?"

Miriam looked around the room, her eyes flicking over the faces one by one. She zipped by Ferrara without recognition. He didn't look up from his *Time* magazine.

Ben-Ezra watched Gunnar Neilborg lock the baggage compartment. The catch gave a satisfying click. Neilborg turned to follow the porters back to the terminal.

"Gunnar, do you mind if I stay out here? I'd rather—ah—"

"Keep an eye on the plane?"

"Yes."

"That's okay with me, Yaakov. I have to notify the crew and flight staff and get this beast into the air. You can board with them. They'll be out here in a couple of minutes, if I can wake them up."

"Fine."

Neilborg walked briskly toward the flight crew headquarters, leaving Ben-Ezra standing by himself next to the VC-10.

If ever there was going to be a right moment, the luggage handler told himself, this was it. It was between no one else but himself and Ben-Ezra. He unzipped his case and withdrew his equipment—a sawed-off grenade launcher. He blew off a dust mote that had somehow attached itself to the weapon, then raised it to his shoulder. It felt good there, like a surgeon's scalpel designed to conform to the hand. He steadied himself and took a deep breath, as instructed.

Chapter Thirty-Seven

The woman pulled up to the airline terminal curb, leaped out of her car, and ran into the building, her long sweep of auburn hair flying in the wind. She no longer knew whether she'd be in time. When she'd started toward the airport, she intended to be cautious—not to reveal herself unless there was no other choice. She'd imagined herself interceding if she could, staying back if she arrived too late. Now she was running up the long, modern airport corridor in reality, not in her mind's eye. She had only one act of rebellion in her and this was it.

As she ran, the woman began to realize that people were turning to stare at her. She felt like a freak for a moment, running while others were strolling casually through the corridor, browsing at shop windows, sitting at snack bars, leafing through magazines at newsstands. Then she realized what all of this attention meant. It meant that nothing else unusual was happening at the airport. It meant that she still had time.

In the El Al lounge, Flight 42 was announced and the passengers queued up at the gate. Frederick and Miriam lined up with the others. The way the queue formed, they would be among the last to board. Ferrara was near the front of the line, paying them no attention whatever.

Stabile gave up waiting. The police would just have to pick up the pieces when they arrived. He cursed them again and reached underneath his jacket for his weapon. It was then that he heard the shouting coming from down the corridor somewhere.

"Stop the plane!" the woman yelled, running toward the El Al lounge. "Stop the plane. He's going to blow it up!"

Throughout the terminal, people turned to stare.

Still, she kept running. "He's got hand grenades!" the woman shouted. "He's going to blow up the plane!"

Now there were people chasing her—security officers.

The woman's words had come ringing down the corridor, shocking passengers and their guests into silence. Frederick and Miriam looked at each other in bewilderment—and the beginning of panic.

About twenty yards away from them, across the hallway, Gary Stabile stepped back into the shadows, leaving his weapon in its holster. Suliman Ferrara cocked his head, confused.

The security guards had gotten a late start on the woman. She was still some distance ahead of them when she reached the El Al lounge, still shouting, "The plane, the plane—he's going to bomb the plane!"

As the woman reached the lounge, the flight attendant grabbed her.

"My God," Borgmann said involuntarily, "it's Maj!"

Maj Dahlgaard spotted Frederick Borgmann at exactly the same moment he saw her. "He's down there!" she screamed, trying to pull away from the flight attendant. "He has hand grenades and he's going to blow up the plane!"

Frederick and Miriam pushed toward her.

"Frederick," Miriam said, suddenly comprehending, "he's after Father!"

Borgmann now had himself under control. "I think you're right, Miriam," he said. "Is there a way down to the asphalt from here?" he asked the flight attendant, who was still struggling to hold Maj.

"Sir," he said, "you'll have to wait until the security guards come."

Borgmann pulled Maj from the flight attendant's arms, picked him up by his lapels and held him a foot off the floor. "Is there a way out there?" he demanded.

The attendant stared at Borgmann, bug-eyed.

"Well?"

"Th-there's a stairway over there. It goes right to the packing apron. But civilians aren't allowed—"

Borgmann let the man drop and he and Miriam bolted for the stairway. They ran down it, toward swinging doors marked "No passengers beyond this point," in both English and Danish.

Yaakov Ben-Ezra strolled up toward the VC-10's wing. It was a handsome thing, a jetliner. He admired the rivets, sunk flush with the plane's skin. Close up, the tires were surprisingly small—but there were a lot of them. Soon, Ben-Ezra thought, he'd be inside that thing, 35,000 feet in the air, on the way first to London, then to Israel. He smiled to himself.

Nachman would have very little to say—but he wouldn't be able to control the expression on his face. It would be a small, but quite satisfactory payment. And then there was Frederick and Miriam—another cause for satisfaction.

He wandered back, toward the aircraft's tail. Another few minutes and the crew would be coming out. Then the passengers. It had worked out perfectly—better than he had any right to hope, he admitted.

Ben-Ezra looked toward the terminal, getting a bit impatient now. How is it for a man who is about to begin his retirement? Is he sorry to leave the old life, full of nostaglia and feelings of disconnection? Or is he anxious to get on with it, to start something now—even though he knows it can't last long?

There was a man sitting near the terminal wall, almost leaning on it—a uniformed fellow, a luggage handler, perhaps. He was toying with some kind of tool. Ben-Ezra squinted. It looked like a large grease gun.

378

Suddenly Ben-Ezra realized that the tool wasn't a grease gun at all. He took two steps forward, then stopped. The luggage handler was pointing the thing at him. He turned to look for cover.

Out of the corner of his eye, he saw Miriam and Frederick burst through a door behind the luggage handler. The only cover around was the airplane landing gear. Ben-Ezra leaped for it. So it wasn't going to turn out so well after all, he thought.

Stabile watched with surprise as Borgmann and the girl vaulted down the stairway, disappearing from view. There was no doubt of it. Borgmann had definitely known the woman who'd come running down the hall, shouting. Now he and the Israeli girl were headed out to the planes for some reason. Whatever was happening, it was a first-class emergency. Perhaps it would all work out as he intended, anyhow. Down the hall, he could see a group of policemen running toward the El Al lounge. Their timing wasn't perfect, but it would do.

From Suliman Ferrara's standpoint, nothing that was happening now made any sense at all. Screaming women, Borgmann and the girl running down some stairs and out toward the planes, security men coming from all sides—he'd lost control of the situation, if, indeed, he'd ever had it.

Ferrara pressed forward, toward the wondow overlooking the parked airplanes. He gradually realized that others were after the plans too—but who? He sensed an enormous wave of confusion on the way and he sought to gauge it. With any luck, he thought, he might yet have his opportunity.

Borgmann punched open the door at the bottom of the stairs, with Miriam barely a half step behind him. In front of them, they saw a man wearing a luggage-handler's uniform, facing the BOAC VC-10. He was raising a sawed-off grenade launcher to his shoulder and taking aim. His weapon was pointed in the general

379

direction of Yaakov Ben-Ezra, who was running along beside the plane, past the engines mounted between tail and wing, toward the partial protection of the landing gear.

"Hey, you!" Borgmann shouted at the luggage handler.

The man turned slowly, momentarily distracted. He lowered his weapon slightly. It was Bent Dahlgaard. The hope he'd been nursing evaporated.

"Bent! It's too late! Drop the gun!"

Dahlgaard silently and without expression turned back toward Ben-Ezra and raised the grenade launcher again.

Suddenly and surprisingly, Borgmann heard the sharp crack of a gun, slightly behind him, from his right. He wheeled to see Miriam holding a pistol, her arm straight and steady, taking aim for a second shot.

He looked back at Dahlgaard. The man wavered for a moment and sank to one leg. For an instant, he appeared to lose his grip on the grenade launcher. Yaakov, meanwhile, had taken cover behind the plane's landing gear. Then, as if mustering his last strength, Dahlgaard put the grenade launcher to his shoulder again and fired. At the same instant, Borgmann heard a second gunshot behind him.

As Dahlgaard crumpled to the ground, the projectile from his gun smashed into the wing root of the big blue-and-white jetliner. It exploded ferociously, on impact, sending a shower of fragments in all directions. For a fleeting instant, Borgmann caught a glimpse of Ben-Ezra running away from the plane. A moment later, the grenade explosion was followed by an even larger secondary blast. Then there was a third explosion and a fourth.

Borgmann stopped viewing the matter logically. His mind filled with jumbled visions of exploding gas tanks, flaming fuselage sections being hurled hundreds of feet into the air, and a sensation of being suddenly hit by an immense gust of superheated air. Instinctively he threw himself to the ground, pulling Miriam down with him, covering her as much as possible with his body.

Then he looked back at the plane. It was nothing more than a single huge fireball now, from tail to cockpit, a mass of flame a hundred feet long and nearly as high. Borgmann had seen such a fireball before—on films taken during the first firing at Alamagordo test range in New Mexico. Yet this was no atomic blast. It was fifty thousand gallons of jet fuel, ignited by Dahlgaard's grenade. About fifty yards ahead of them, Borgmann could see Dahlgaard, lying motionless on the macadam. Closer to the plane, he knew, was Ben-Ezra. But Borgmann couldn't see him—he was evidently in the area enveloped by the fireball.

It was a scene from a blood-and-thunder exploitation movie, the sort of thing one always assumes is done on some studio backlot with miniatures, where the flames are the result of nothing more than a liberal dousing with barbecue fire starter. But this, Borgmann slowly realized, was real.

Chapter Thirty-Eight

Back in the lounge area, the panic was nearly total. People were pushing, shoving and stepping all over each other in a desperate, frightened effort to get as far from the explosion as possible.

Not everyone was running, though. Ferrara stayed at the window and watched for his opportunity. What he saw, instead, was a sequence of events that he was powerless to interrupt. Laid out in front of him now was a tableau of disaster—a burning BOAC jetliner, a luggage handler's motionless form, an El Al 707 slowly taxiing away from danger, and Borgmann and the girl lying on the asphalt near the door.

As Ferrara struggled to make sense of what had happened, one fact penetrated the confusion: the blueprints were gone. There was no question that they'd burned up in the explosion that wiped out the jetliner. And if the blueprints were gone, his dream for the Palestinians was over. Only a moment ago, it seemed, he'd been hopeful and alert, waiting for his opportunity. Now the hope had evaporated. Despair replaced it—and rage. The rational man had failed. The emotional man yearned for revenge.

Gary Stabile had waited for the passengers to abandon the El Al and BOAC lounges for the main hall, then casually strolled up to a boarding ramp. No one was paying the least attention to him. He opened the door, entered the ramp, and walked to the forward observation windows.

It was ironic, he thought. After all his careful work, someone else appeared on the scene and finished the job—and in fine style. He watched the BOAC jetliner, smoldering now. There wasn't a doubt in his mind that the blueprints were now no more than charred scraps of paper. Ben-Ezra, it seemed, had not survived the explosion. At any rate, he couldn't be seen. Borgmann and the girl were all right, though. Both were moving. The figure that puzzled Stabile was that of the uniformed luggage handler lying on the pavement, his weapon beside him. His role in recent events was clear enough. It was his identity that was a mystery.

Stabile tried to reason it through for a moment, then decided to drop it. The luggage handler, he told himself, could be anyone's lackey. He could be controlled by the Russians, the Chinese, or even—God help us—the Americans. But no matter. The mission was now a success. The only problem remaining was how to take credit within the organization for what happened. He'd have to go slowly on that until he was sure who had employed the luggage handler.

He glanced out at the parking apron once more. Security men were converging on the area from every direction now. In the distance, he could see the flashing lights of fire trucks. Soon the air was filled with the sound of reverberating sirens. Below him, Borgmann and the girl had gotten to their feet and were sprinting toward the smoldering wreck. Looking for Ben-Ezra, of course, Stabile told himself. And that woman who'd come screaming down the corridor, the one who'd seemed to start it all, she'd apparently torn free from the flight attendant. She too was running along the asphalt, toward the luggage handler. Still screaming, her cries were lost amidst the eerie wail of the fire trucks.

As Borgmann watched, the fireball seemed to collapse on itself, shrinking like a punctured balloon. Now the plane was clearly visible, a blackened wreck. It looked like a child's toy that had been stepped on by some careless adult, then charred in the incinerator.

Miriam wriggled out from under him, scrambled to her feet and started running toward the smoldering wreck. "Father! Father!" she shouted. Borgmann took off after her.

"Be careful, Miriam," he yelled, "there could be more explosions." The warning didn't slow her in the least.

They threaded their way through bits and pieces of airplane, along scorched runway. Grey smoke hung over the scene like fog. Parts of the fuselage were still glowing.

"Do you see him anywhere?" Borgmann asked.

"N-no," Miriam said. "I think he managed to get behind the landing gear. I'm praying he did."

"Miriam—the fireball—I don't know how anyone could have survived—"

He would have continued his sentence, but the pain he saw on her face made him stop.

Ahead now, on the other side of the fuselage, Borgmann suddenly saw someone lying on the pavement. "There—look!"

Miriam changed course slightly. Now she was heading directly for the fuselage, intending to run beneath it to her father.

"No," Borgmann said, grabbing her arm. "The body of the plane could collapse any moment."

"Yaakov—I have to get to him."

"I know. We have to go around—this way."

Together they circled around the nose of the plane, still running, Frederick in the lead, clutching Miriam by the hand. There was no doubt of it—the man on the ground was Ben-Ezra.

"Father!" Miriam cried out, breaking loose from Borgmann and running ahead. She knelt down beside the man. "Father—are you all right?"

Ben-Ezra looked up at his daughter, trying to prop himself up on an elbow. "Miriam . . ." he said. It was little more than a whisper. "The man with the grenade launcher—be careful—"

"I shot him, Father. We don't have to worry about him any more."

Ben-Ezra managed to nod. His face was blackened by the smoke, his clothing was charred. "Good," he said, almost inaudibly. "The plans. What about the plans?"

Miriam shook her head.

"Damn," Ben-Ezra whispered. "Frederick. Is Frederick okay?"

"I'm here, Yaakov," Borgmann said. "You're going to be all right. I can see the fire trucks and ambulances on the way."

"Thank God," Ben-Ezra said hoarsely. "Thank God you're all right." He started coughing. At first it seemed almost as if he were trying to clear his throat. Slowly, though, his coughing turned into a fit, a hacking, choking series of paroxysms that shook him time and time again.

"Breathe slowly," Frederick said. "Take a shallow breath."

The old man nodded, his face pale under the soot, his eyes bloodshot.

"Does it hurt, Father?" Miriam asked gently.

"Only when I—" he coughed again several times, wincing each time "—laugh," he finished weakly, trying to smile.

"You're going to be okay, Yaakov," Borgmann said. "Just take it easy."

"I'm not going to be okay. You both know it and so do I. I breathed the flames."

"Oh, God," Miriam said.

"Come on, haven't we had enough dramatics?" Yaakov whispered, his head cradled in his daughter's lap. "I've just had a somewhat shorter retirement than I figured."

"Father—how can you?"

"The main thing is that Frederick is all right," Ben-Ezra murmured. "And you. That means we've won."

"I don't understand, Father," Miriam said.

"His memory," Ben-Ezra gasped. "It's as good as having the blueprints. You studied the plans, Frederick. When you get back, you can re-create them, can't you?"

"Of course, Yaakov. You know that memory of mine."

"We know all about his memory, Yaakov," Miriam said, "but what about the Russians and the Arabs? Do they know?"

Ben-Ezra appeared to think for a moment. "Make sure they do, Miriam," he whispered. "It'll be the same as if we got the plans."

The piercing cry of the sirens grew louder as the ambulances and fire trucks closed in on the still-smoking wreck. Borgmann jumped up and waved frantically. "Here!" he shouted at an ambulance, "over here!" He bent down to Ben-Ezra once more. "They're coming, Yaakov. They'll be here in a minute."

Ben-Ezra smiled. Then his expression fell slack. The ambulance attendant came running across the runway, spurred on by Borgmann's frantic waving. He knelt beside Ben-Ezra, took the Israeli's wrist, and tried to find a pulse. After a moment, he released the wrist and pushed his stethoscope beneath Ben-Ezra's shirt. Then he stood up, sighed, and shook his head.

"Are you sure?" Borgmann asked, his anguish evident. He bent down and tried to lift Ben-Ezra to his feet. "Yaakov, Yaakov—"

Miriam put a hand on Frederick's shoulder. Another ambulance attendant joined the first and they stood a short distance away, watching respectfully.

"It's over for him, Frederick," Miriam said.

Borgmann gently laid Ben-Ezra's body back on the runway. He rose, then put his arms around the girl. For several moments they held onto each other, sharing both grief and affection.

As they parted, a chubby, bald plainclothesman and a uniformed policeman came running toward them from the terminal building. "I don't believe it," the plainclothesman said, puffing as he approached the body, "it's Jacob Kaplan!"

"Yaakov Ben-Ezra," Miriam said firmly, correcting the man.

"Yes," the plainclothesman said. "I know him by that name also. And you must be—"

"She's Ben-Ezra's daughter," Borgmann put in.

"Yes," the plainclothesman said. "I know that, too. Miriam—Shazar, I believe you call yourself."

Miriam stared at him, amazed.

"And I—" Frederick began.

"You are the famous Professor Frederick Borgmann," the plainclothesman said. "My name is Poul Hansen, Detective Lieutenant, homicide branch, National Security." He extended his hand and Borgmann shook it. "I'm sorry about your father, Miss Shazar. I knew and respected him. We had hoped to prevent this from happening, but we simply hadn't enough information." He gestured toward the plane. "I assume the blueprints were in there."

"Yes, lieutenant," Borgmann said.

"Of use to no one now," Lieutenant Hansen said.

"That's right," Miriam said hastily.

"Such a waste," Lieutenant Hansen said, shaking his head sadly. "Kaplan, the plane, Dahlgaard—we haven't the faintest idea who shot him, you know," he said, looking directly at Miriam. "Evidently the shots came from within the building."

"You don't know who fired them?" Borgmann asked.

"No," the plainclothesman said. He had made it clear he wasn't interested in further conversation on that subject. "National Security has been watching Dahlgaard for some time now, you know. We believe he worked for the Russians."

"The Russians?" Borgmann said, incredulous. "I don't believe that."

"Well," Lieutenant Hansen said, "Let's ask him. I understand his wounds are serious, but he's still alive."

Frederick and Miriam took one last look at Yaakov

Ben-Ezra. The ambulance attendants were unfolding a stretcher and were about to slip it under his body. They paused to let the pair say their final farewell. When Borgmann and the girl turned back to Lieutenant Hansen, both were composed. Together, they slowly walked away from the burning wreck, Lieutenant Hansen and the uniformed policeman a step or so behind them. Ahead of them, between the plane and the terminal, Bent Dahlgaard, still in his luggage handler's uniform, lay on the pavement, surrounded by security men. His wife was huddled over him.

"Miriam—" Borgmann began, searching for some way to relieve his pain and hers.

"Don't, Frederick," she said, taking his hand. "It isn't necessary, for either of us. Yaakov had only another six months or so, at the most. And from what the doctors told me, it would not have been a pleasant time for him."

"Yaakov was ill?"

"Yes. Lung cancer. You saw it, in the car, back at the Tivoli."

"I thought he was just tired. Old and tired."

"The doctors never told him, Frederick. But he must have known. He must have expected a far more painful death than this."

"But the assignment—didn't your intelligence agency realize . . ."

"As a matter of fact, they did. Nachman originally gave the assignment to me. I was to contact you. I begged him to let Yaakov join me. I wanted so much for him to feel needed."

"Then why the constant arguments, the fighting?"

There were tears in Miriam's eyes now. "It was the only way we could talk to each other, Frederick. It wasn't really hostility."

Behind them, the fire trucks had started to hose down the ruined plane. The sirens had been switched off, but the red lights still flashed, illuminating the entire scene with a rosy, stroboscopic effect. Dahlgaard was just a few yards ahead now.

Borgmann struggled to find a way to express his feelings. "Then perhaps this was the best way for him to die, Miriam."

"He knew the mission had succeeded, Frederick. That was so important to him."

"You know," Borgmann said, reflecting, "you know what he wanted back there in the BOAC luggage area? He wanted me to take care of you."

Miriam glanced sharply at Frederick and smiled a bittersweet smile. "He never stopped planning, did he?"

Chapter Thirty-Nine

At a gesture from Lieutenant Hansen, the security men surrounding Dahlgaard parted as Frederick and Miriam approached. Dahlgaard was propped up against a stool. Beside him, Maj sobbed openly.

"Ah, the good Professor Borgmann," Dahlgaard said, his eyes unnaturally bright, his breathing shallow. "This time you have lost, eh?"

"Lost? You're lying here on the pavement, badly wounded, after having murdered someone and blown up an airplane while thousands watched—and you say *I've* lost?"

"Are the plans destroyed?" Dahlgaard asked quickly.

"Yes."

"Then I have won," Dahlgaard said, deciding the question. "For once, I have beaten you."

Miriam and Frederick exchanged glances. "Nothing you've done makes sense to me," Borgmann said. "Nothing you've said now even sounds sane. The police tell me you were working for the Russians. Can that be? Can my old friend have acted like this?"

"Your old friend?" Maj interrupted bitterly. "He was never your friend. He's only sorry that you weren't there next to Ben-Ezra when he fired the grenade. He's been jealous of you as long as I've known him."

"Is that true, Bent?" Frederick asked, hurt.

"I've always hated you, Frederick," Dahlgaard confided. "It's been the one true passion of my life. You've always beaten me at every turn. I never finished first in

390

any examination we took together, because of that trick memory of yours. I loved Maj before you ever noticed her, yet you were first with her too—you abandoned her to me or I wouldn't have had her. And when Professor Bohr asked you to accompany him to America—when he called you a prodigy and ignored me—that was the final insult."

Borgmann listened, silently, astonished.

"Once I almost had you," Dahlgaard went on, wild-eyed, still trying to hurt. "It was when Kaplan was trying to save all the dirty Jews from the Germans—"

Maj interrupted. "Bent—don't. He doesn't need to know that—"

"It seemed so easy then," Dahlgaard continued, ignoring his wife. "All I had to do was tell the proper people what boat you'd be on. The Nazis would take care of the rest. You simply wouldn't exist any more. Then Bohr would call for me. *I* would be the prodigy. Maj would love *me*."

Borgmann was horrified. "You considered telling the Nazis—"

"Considered?" Dahlgaard laughed horribly, almost choking. "I *did* tell them. Only you played hero—sent your parents on the boat and waited for the next one."

Borgmann stepped toward Dahlgaard, menacingly. "You killed them!" he said, his voice guttural with grief and anger. "You killed my parents!"

"It was the only harm I was able to do to you," Dahlgaard said, enjoying the expression on Borgmann's face. "I am pleased to see that the injury was deep."

Miriam put her hand lightly on Frederick's shoulder. Her touch restrained him. Borgmann took a moment to collect himself. "One thing I don't understand, Dahlgaard," he said. "Why did you help me find the plans? Why were you so nice to me when we met at the Conference?"

"You never doubted my friendship for a moment, did you?" Dahlgaard said, his face twisted into an ironic grin. "I was only following orders, professor. If

I'd acted as I truly felt, I would have ignored you. No— I would have *forgotten* you."

"Whose orders were you following, Dahlgaard?" It was Lieutenant Hansen's question.

"Ah," Dahlgaard said, his gaze shifting to the rotund plainclothesman. "The police. And on the wrong side, as usual. Only in Denmark does this happen. I was working for the Glavnoye Razvedyvatetnoye Upravlie-nie, the GRU, the Chief Intelligence Directorate of the Soviet Armed Forces. The Russians, Borgmann, the Russians." He said it almost with glee. "I've been working for them for years."

"But why, Bent?" Frederick asked. "Why would you turn against your country?"

"They forced him to work for them, Frederick," Maj said, interceding. "They captured Nazi records and found his name on a list of informers. They knew all the details of the boat incident. It was blackmail."

Dahlgaard nodded patiently, waiting for his wife to finish. "That's true—all of it."

"Why didn't you struggle, Dahlgaard?" Lieutenant Hansen asked, "Why didn't you come to us?"

"Come to you?" Dahlgaard laughed weakly. "How would you have dealt with a Nazi informer?"

The silence that greeted his question confirmed his assumption.

"Oh, I did try to get out a couple of times," Dahlgaard went on. "But they made it very difficult for me. Besides, they asked for very little—just a bit of information here and there. It did no harm. I lived a good life."

"You call what was between us a good life?" Maj asked accusingly.

Dahlgaard shrugged. "We must all make compromises."

"You killed a man today and blew up a British aircraft," Lieutenant Hansen said, challenging the wounded man. "I suppose you think that comes under the category of no harm done."

"Not enough harm done, lieutenant. Borgmann is still alive, isn't he?"

"You're despicable," Miriam said venomously. "You're a revenge-seeker, not a human being."

"You Jews are such moralists—for everyone but yourselves. Tell me, is not revenge a human emotion? Haven't you felt it yourself? Don't you and Borgmann feel the need for revenge right now—against me?"

"I did feel anger at first, Bent," Frederick said coolly responding. "Now I feel only contempt."

"I want to get this straight—for the record," said Lieutenant Hansen. "You have been a willing agent of the Soviet Union for many years."

"Sometimes willing, sometimes not so willing," Dahlgaard said. "But in this case, you could certainly say that I was willing. I was eager."

An ambulance pulled up to the group and a doctor jumped out. He examined Dahlgaard quickly. "There's been a tremendous loss of blood," he said. "It doesn't look good." He asked his assistant to get some blood plasma, then he rolled up Dahlgaard's sleeve and prepared to start the transfusion.

Maj's sobbing increased. "If only I'd found out sooner," she said through her tears.

"You were unaware of your husband's activities, Mrs. Dahlgaard?" Hansen inquired.

"No. I've known for years. It's been like poison in my heart. I meant if I'd found out earlier what he planned to do today—"

"You did come to the airport, Maj," Borgmann said gently. "Why?"

"I knew you were involved, Frederick. I knew there was danger—for both of you."

Dahlgaard nodded off for a moment, then revived when the doctor inserted the needle into his vein. "Maj?" he said. "Are you there, Maj?"

The woman looked at him with an almost visible mixture of hatred and love. Finally she bent down and took his hand. "I'm here, Bent."

"Dahlgaard," Borgmann said, "you were the one who shot at Ben-Ezra the other day, weren't you?"

"What?" Dahlgaard said blankly. "Oh. Yes. I would have hit him if it hadn't been for that lamp post."

"And you killed that Arab in the Tivoli Gardens, didn't you, Dahlgaard?" Hansen asked.

"Arab? What Arab?"

"Abdul Amer—didn't you shoot him?"

Dahlgaard's eyes fluttered, then closed.

"He's unconscious," the doctor pronounced.

"Will he live?" Hansen asked.

"Honestly, I don't think so," the doctor said. "One slug evidently nicked his aorta."

Maj's sobbing redoubled.

"Come," Hansen said to Frederick and Miriam. "There's nothing more to be done here." He stopped to confer with one of the security guards, evidently about Maj Dahlgaard. The guard looked at her, at any rate, then looked back at Hansen and nodded confidently. He would take care of matters here.

Now the trio headed back to the terminal building, toward the same stairway Frederick and Miriam had come down, less than fifteen minutes ago.

"There are a lot of unanswered question in this case," Hansen told them. "Like that Arab—Amer. We don't know who killed him or who he was working for. And then there was the Finnish delegate to the conference—Torngren, I think he called himself. We've done an identity check on him and it turns out that Torngren was a phony. The lab boys tell me that he was wearing Russian shoes. And no one wears Russian shoes unless he's a Russian. Maybe you have some information." Hansen was talking to Borgmann.

"Me? No, none at all. Never met the man."

"Thought not. What about you, miss? Any information you might give me?"

"None," Miriam said. "Maybe it was just a squabble between Russian agencies," she suggested. "The answer may lie with Dahlgaard."

"You're right," Hansen said, as if the idea hadn't occurred to him before. "I'll have to check that out—that is, if Dahlgaard lives."

They stood at the bottom of the stairs now. Above them, the terminal loudspeaker buzzed momentarily.

"Attention all passengers," came the voice over the loudspeaker. "The director of flight operations is pleased to announce that the emergency is over. Normal flight schedules will be resumed in approximately half an hour."

"Then there are other questions," Hansen said, after the announcement. "For example, did Ben-Ezra steal the plans by himself? When we got to the Tivoli installation, there were guards sleeping all over the place. Very odd."

"Was anyone hurt?" Borgmann asked.

"Hurt—no. One guard was slugged, though. We found him locked in a men's room. But when we gave him Ben-Ezra's description, he said that wasn't the man who'd knocked him out. You wouldn't know anything about that, would you, Professor Borgmann?"

"Nope. Never slugged a man in my life."

"Thought not."

"Will you be requiring any more from us, Lieutenant Hansen?" Miriam asked.

In front of them, the El Al 707 taxied back to its parking place and the extendable passenger ramp began to edge out from the terminal.

"Glad to see things are getting back to normal," Hansen said. "Just think, in a few hours, that plane will be landing in Tel Aviv, far away from our troubles here. Do I require anything more of you? Well, in cases such as this, the police usually request all material witnesses to hold themselves available for further questioning, if necessary. They're instructed not to leave town. You understand that it is my official duty to pass these instructions on to you. You do have your passports with you, do you not?"

"Yes," Borgmann said, smiling now.

"And you hold tickets on El Al Flight 42?"

"Yes," Miriam said, slowly understanding.

"Your luggage is aboard that aircraft?" Lieutenant Hansen asked, indicating the Israeli jetliner.

"Yes—if there's been no foul-up," Borgmann answered.

Hansen stuck his hand out and Borgmann shook it. "I wish you well," he said. Then he took Miriam's hand. "My condolences, Miss Shazar. I sincerely wish things could have turned out differently for you and your father."

"Thank you, Lieutenant Hansen."

"Remember now," he said, eyes twinkling, "keep yourselves available for further questioning."

He smiled, tipped his hat, turned and walked back toward Dahlgaard.

"I'll be damned," Miriam said.

"We'd better get on that plane," Frederick observed. "He may change his mind."

"Agreed."

They hurried up the stairs, stopping only to drop their weapons in a garbage can.

Chapter Forty

When Gary Stabile saw the El Al plane taxiing back into position, he knew it was time to get out of the extension ramp. He'd seen enough, anyhow. Ben-Ezra was dead, the plans destroyed. Whoever it was who had blown up the BOAC jetliner was dead or dying. The game was over now. He was a bit surprised when the stout plainclothesman apparently lost interest in Borgmann and the girl, but then, why not? Holding them wouldn't have accomplished anything.

The burr-headed American ambled out of the ramp door as if he'd had every right to be where he'd been. Ferrara, he noticed, was still standing at the window, still wearing that ridiculous blond wig. Stabile wondered if Ferrara realized that he'd lost—that everyone had lost, for that matter—except the CIA.

Stabile felt almost entirely satisfied. Neither the Israelis nor the Arabs had gotten the plans. The plane explosion would make headlines the world over, to the embarrassment of both parties. In the future, EURATOM would be much more careful with its blueprints. He had fulfilled every part of his instructions. The only thing that bothered him was the man who fired off the grenade, the fellow who'd made it all happen. Was he Russian? Chinese? Stabile didn't like sloppy endings. He'd have to find out. The fat plainclothesman—he'd know. He resolved to find the man tomorrow and ask a few questions, possibly through the offices of the American Embassy.

He'd barely had time to find his way out of the lounge when Borgmann and the Israeli girl appeared at the top of the stairs. This was not the time to exchange pleasantries. The American agent ducked into a nearby men's room.

Suliman Ferrara tried to control his rage. He knew that feeling would paralyze him, if it lasted. He tried to rationally figure out what he could do now. The main chance was gone—was there a lesser opportunity?

It was hard to think in the midst of this confusion—both external and internal. He forced himself to reason. He'd lost everything, but so had the Israelis. At least there was that consolation.

Then a thought occurred to him. The Palestinians might not be able to have the plans, but they could certainly take credit for keeping them out of Israel's grasp. And there might be further damage he could do.

Ferrara glanced out of the window again. The plain-clothesman had finished with Borgmann and the girl. In a moment, they'd be coming up that flight of steps to his left.

Once again, Ferrara touched the weapon in his pocket. He could still hijack the El Al flight. Maybe Borgmann and the girl would be aboard. Or he could teach the Israelis a lesson, by killing Borgmann. If that discouraged local Jews from helping Israeli agents, it would be worth the effort—and the risk. Anything that could be done to separate world Jewry from Israel would be a valuable contribution to the Palestinian cause.

The more Ferrara thought about it, the better the idea seemed. If he had the opportunity, he'd do away with Borgmann—the girl too, if possible. Failing that, he'd hijack the plane and land it at Beirut. And he'd call Reuters and say that Black September had blown up the BOAC plane. It wasn't as good as coming back with the blueprints—not by a long shot—but it was a lot better than wallowing in frustration.

Inside the men's room, Stabile found, to his delight, a shoeshine stand. He hopped up on a chair, leafed through a stack of magazines on the chair next to his until he found a copy of *Playboy*. The attendant went to work on his shoes. At least he could do something worthwhile while he waited for Borgmann and the Israeli girl to go their way.

At the top of the stairway, Frederick and Miriam met two airport security guards, who waved them on into the lounge after the briefest hesitation. Things were returning to normal within the terminal. Passengers, ticket agents, porters, flight attendants, newsstand clerks and all the rest were back where one expected to see them, a bit edgy, possibly, but anxious to resume the routine.

"I wish I could forget everything that's happened in the last half hour, Miriam," Borgmann said. "That's one of the penalties of a trick memory—the painful things remain as vivid, as well as the pleasurable ones."

"Yes," Miriam agreed. "There are a lot of things I'd like to forget too."

They walked into the El Al lounge and sat down. The place was rapidly filling up now. From time to time, a passenger would walk to the window overlooking the runways, take a look at what was left of BOAC Flight 392, gasp, shake his head in awe, then return to his seat.

While they waited, Miriam and Frederick heard an announcement over the terminal public-address system. According to airport officials, the accident was caused by a welder's torch that came into contact with a fuel tank. "Though no passengers were aboard," the voice told them, "one workman was killed and another badly injured." The accident explained, to the satisfaction of all except those who knew better, the field was deemed fit for normal operation.

"Didn't take long to come up with a cover story," Miriam said.

"It won't hold long. There were plenty of witnesses.

The newspapers are sure to have conflicting accounts."

"But we won't be here to read them."

"No," Frederick said. He took his glasses off and rubbed his eyes for a moment. He was fighting with his memories once more, thinking of another hasty departure from the country of his birth, of another time when he'd left Maj and Bent behind.

"Frederick?" Miriam gently nudged him out of the past.

"Sorry. I was somewhere else."

"I know. I wish you'd hold off on that until we get to Israel. It will all look different from there. I'll take you through Tel Aviv again—you can't imagine how it's changed. We'll visit Jerusalem. You can see all of it now, you know. There'll be so much to do."

The flight attendant, a tall, attractive, uniformed fellow with a slight Israeli accent, picked up a wall microphone. "Good afternoon again, ladies and gentlemen. Flight 42 will be ready for boarding in about ten minutes now."

Borgmann stood up. "I think I'll make a stop at the men's room," he said.

"I'll wait for you here."

"Okay."

Miriam watched Frederick walk across the hall, into a door marked *"herretoilettet."* That much Danish she understood.

At the back of the lounge, a blond-haired man—Suliman Ferrara—also got to his feet. His eyes followed Borgmann across the hall and into the men's room. Would he ever have a better opportunity?

Ferrara walked slowly toward the *herretoilettet.* There was nothing at all suspicious about him, he was sure. He stopped at the door, as if to make sure that this was the place he wanted to go. Then he remembered the girl. Was she watching him? Was his disguise holding? He glanced back into the lounge. She was sitting in the back, looking in his general direction, but not at him in particular. Ferrara pushed the door open and walked into the men's room, his hand in his pocket, clutching his pistol.

Miriam Shazar kept her eye on the men's room door. To her surprise, she felt lonely and exposed out here without Frederick. Especially now that Yaakov was . . . She pushed her thoughts forward, past the words she wanted neither to think nor to hear. For years now, she had acted on her own, seeing her father from time to time, but maintaining only tenuous links in between. Now, without him, with the possibility of seeing and talking with him—even in conflict—gone forever, she felt an almost overwhelming wave of loneliness. The thought of him lying on the asphalt out there was too painful to contemplate. Miriam knew she would recover her balance. She'd had friends and loved ones killed before, sometimes while she watched. She'd always found her way back.

Now, with Yaakov gone, there was no one else in her life that she cared about—except Frederick. Frederick would never run the risks Yaakov had faced almost daily. Unlike her other friends, Frederick would live a quiet, peaceful life, far from danger. There was reassurance in that, at least. She watched the men's room door. At this moment, she wanted to be as close to him as possible, to lean on him, to borrow his strength.

Something bothered her about the man now entering the men's room. He glanced her way in what she took to be a furtive manner. Then, he slipped into the men's room as if he was heading for an assignment. Miriam smiled to herself, sadly. She felt pity for these men. But her mind wouldn't let go of the picture. Something was wrong here, something she couldn't quite grasp. She ran through the scene again, in her mind's eye—the man pausing at the door, looking her way, then opening the door not an inch more than necessary and almost slithering inside. He was blond, dressed in a light-colored sport jacket and contrasting pants, wearing brown shoes. Nothing extraordinary here, and yet there was.

Something about his appearance nagged at her. There'd been a line at his collar—a dark line. From the back, at that distance, it seemed as though he was wearing a dark shirt underneath his sport jacket. But when he turned to look her way, Miriam had noticed that he was wearing a white shirt.

The realization came slowly, piece by piece. The dark patch of his collar hadn't been a shirt at all. It was hair. The man had dark hair. He was wearing a wig. His hair wasn't blond at all. Miriam shut her eyes and tried to imagine the man with dark hair. The harder she tried to hold onto the image, the fuzzier it got. And yet she felt, almost instinctively, that there was something familiar about the man. With a start she was on her feet, running toward the men's room. The pieces had abruptly come together . . .

Stabile looked down at his shoes. The little old man had finished with one and it was gleaming, blackly. He was slow, but his work was outstanding. He stooped, pulled a catsup bottle with a shaker cap from a small compartment under the seats and sprinkled Stabile's second shoe with water. The American's gaze returned to *Playboy*. Then the door opened. He looked toward it, out of habit. My God, he thought, astonished, it's Borgmann! Before he even had a chance to think about it, Stabile had the magazine fully in front of his face. His eyes followed Borgmann's feet, as the man walked past the shoeshine stand. There was, he noted, just the slightest pause. Possibly Borgmann had thought he recognized the man in the chair. Very likely, Stabile felt, he hadn't been recognized at all. He continued to read the *Playboy*. Now he was stuck in the chair until Borgmann had done whatever it was he had come to do, and left. The little old man put the catsup bottle away and started on the unpolished shoe.

Less than a minute later, the door opened once more. Once again, Stabile glanced at the man who had entered. He almost dropped the magazine. Jesus, he thought, that's Ferrara. Does he know that Borgmann is in here? If so, what does he have in mind? Stabile had the sinking feeling that the trouble wasn't over yet. He put the magazine aside and craned his neck as far to the right as possible, in an attempt to see into the washroom area. But that was impossible.

Stabile slipped out of the chair, to the distinct surprise of the man shining his shoes. *"Nej, nej,"* the old man protested. *"Og sid ned. Og sid ned."*

"Sorry, old fellow. I'll be back." Stabile pushed a dollar bill into the old man's hand. Then, he walked directly into the washroom area.

Borgmann was at the sink, his glasses on the little shelf just above the faucets. He'd apparently just finished washing his hands and face and was now rubbing both with a brown paper towel. Past him, against the wall, was a man standing at a urinal, his back to the door. One of the toilet stall doors was closed. Ferrara was two sinks down from Borgmann and looking toward him. He held a small yellow object in his hand. Stabile had taken in all of this in a glance. Now he had to figure out exactly what was happening and what, if anything, he should do about it.

This situation was simple enough, Ferrara thought. Borgmann would be dead before anyone else in the men's room knew what happened. He would be the first one out the door. If the noise had attracted any interest, he'd shout out that someone had been murdered inside the men's room by a man with a gun. The crowd in the terminal was still jittery from the plane explosion. This would send them running in all directions, terrified. He'd stop in the next men's room, get rid of his blond wig—and his tie and sport coat too, for good measure—then leave the terminal quietly. He'd take the hydrofoil to Malmö, call the Danish police and

403

take credit for both the destruction of the plane and Borgmann's death, in the name of Black September. The only thing Ferrara had to worry about, he told himself, was making that first shot effective.

Chapter Forty-One

"Hello, Ferrara," Stabile said casually, his gun in his hand.

The Lebanese stopped in mid-motion, as though he'd just received a shot of some paralyzing drug. Then he slowly turned toward Stabile, his fiberglass pistol drawn and ready.

"I have a feeling that isn't a toy you're holding," Stabile said pleasantly. "Drop it."

Ferrara very nearly squeezed the trigger. But there was something in this man's voice that told him he'd die if he made any quick movement. He relaxed his grip on his pistol and it clattered to the floor. "Who are you?" he asked, the rage and frustration welling up in him once again.

"Stabile," Borgmann said in disgust, answering Ferrara's question. He was standing behind Ferrara, ready to defend himself if necessary. "How long have you been following me, Stabile?"

"Would you believe me if I told you I just happened to be in here, getting a shoeshine?"

"No."

"I seem to have lost my credibility with you, professor. But at least you'll give me credit for being around when I'm needed."

"I suppose so," Borgmann admitted grudgingly.

"You're American," Ferrara said. It was an accusation.

Stabile shrugged and continued to smile. "I am a

405

man without a country, Mr. Ferrara, a citizen of the world."

"This was none of your business," Ferrara said angrily.

"To tell you the truth, Mr. Ferrara, I haven't any business of my own. If I didn't get involved in other people's business, I'd just have nothing to do, I guess."

Borgmann picked up Ferrara's gun. He looked at it curiously. "Plastic," he said to Stabile.

"Russian," Stabile said. "Their hijacking model. Only the firing pin and the bullets are metal. No detector in the world can spot it."

Ferrara looked nervously toward the door. Stabile blocked it effectively. He was trapped.

"What do I do with it?" Borgmann asked, turning the gun over in his hand.

"You could give it to me," Stabile suggested wryly.

"Any other ideas?"

"Give it to that Israeli girl you're with. She'll know what to do with it."

"What are you going to do with me?" Ferrara demanded.

"Do? Not a thing. I have no official power here. You can do whatever you want now."

"Except shoot your Professor Borgmann."

Stabile looked at Ferrara and shook his head sadly, as if the man was a student who hadn't done his homework. "Mr. Ferrara," he said gently, "you disappoint me. Ben-Ezra is dead; so is Amer. The plans are destroyed. Neither of you have won. Now you want to go one up by killing a nonprofessional? Haven't you any standards of behavior?"

The man at the urinal had turned now and was watching the little drama with open-mouthed surprise. He hadn't yet zipped his fly. Across from him, the locked stall door remained closed.

Miriam was now certain that the man who had followed Frederick into the men's room was Suliman Ferrara. There was the barest chance it had been a coinci-

406

dence, but Miriam couldn't take the risk. She hurried toward the men's room, fishing in her purse for her pistol, then remembered she had gotten rid of it. No matter. She didn't need a weapon, she told herself. Surprise would be enough.

She cut through a group of Oriental tourists, and, to their surprise, shoved open the men's room door and walked in.

"*Dame, dame!*" the shoeshine man protested. "*Herretoilettet*. Men's room."

"Watch out, Frederick," Miriam called, striding past the shoeshine stand into the washroom. "Ferrara's in here!"

She came around the corner to see the three of them—Stabile, Ferrara and Borgmann—confronting one another, and gazing at her with bemusement, shock and pleasure, in that order.

"Oh!" she said, seeing Stabile holding his gun on Ferrara.

"Nothing to worry about, Miriam," Frederick said.

"Hey," said a voice from within the locked stall. "What's going on out there?"

Seeing Miriam, the man at the urinal started to zip up. He looked around, desperately embarrassed, hoping to find a place to hide. He ended up jumping into a stall and slamming the door.

"May I suggest that we all leave?" Stabile said. "I'm afraid we may be calling attention to ourselves."

Ferrara gave Stabile one last furious look. "Someday—"

"—you'll get me," Stabile said, finishing his sentence for him. "I know. Someday everyone is going to get me."

"You ruined everything," Ferrara said bitterly.

"It's always my fault," Stabile agreed. "I admit it. But I have a suggestion for you. Why don't you call up the Danish police and claim credit for blowing up the plane. Tell them the PLO did it. Or Black September. Or *Fatah*."

"I don't need your help."

"No. Of course not."

Ferrara pushed past Stabile, out the men's room door.

"You're very brave, young lady," Stabile said. "Foolhardy, but brave. I think it will be safe out there for the two of you."

A passenger entered the men's room, looked at Miriam, hesitated a moment, then retreated.

"Thank you, Stabile," Borgmann said.

"It galls you, doesn't it?"

"You are an infuriating man," Miriam said.

Stabile smiled wickedly. "So I've been told." He hopped back up on the shoeshine chair.

"Why did you help?" Borgmann said, unwilling to let the whole thing drop.

"Why not?" Stabile answered. "I saw no sense of it. With the plans gone, the issue was already decided. You and Ferrara both lost. Bathroom murders are very messy, anyway. And they might have ended up questioning me."

"*Hvad?*" the shoeshine man said. "Murder?"

"I wasn't talking to you," Stabile said.

Another man entered the men's room, took one look at Miriam and backed out, apologizing. "We'd better get out of here, Frederick," Miriam said, taking his hand.

"You're right. Good-bye, Stabile."

"Good-bye, professor. See you around."

"I think not," Miriam said.

Ferrara hurried blindly down Kastrup's main corridor, out of control, overcome by frustration and rage, not caring where he was going, not knowing what he'd do. The mission was a total failure now—the thought repeated itself in his brain again and again. Oh, he'd call the Danish police and say *Fatah* was responsible for the destruction of the BOAC plane. Then he'd contact the Danish newspapers and perhaps the British and American news services and talk about how Palestinian agents had prevented the Israelis from stealing nuclear secrets from the Danes, despite American complicity.

For a while, there would be a splash in the newspapers. Ferrara knew, however, that the Danes, the Israelis and the Americans would deny everything. BOAC would certainly stick with its original story—the one about the errant technician and his acetylene torch. For lack of evidence, the story would die.

The rage and frustration was now almost entirely replaced by despair. His cause was just; Ferrara was just as certain of that as he'd been a week ago. Despite his failure, he felt no less strongly that the Palestinians had the right of return and that this right must be exercised, whether or not it meant further conflict and bloodshed.

Through the despair, there came a single dim light. There would come a time, Ferrara told himself, when the Palestinians were no longer a backward, relatively uneducated, technologically naïve people. They would build their own universities and research labs. They would develop their own weaponry. And with education would come political sophistication. When that day arrived, the Palestinian armed forces would be a match for Israel's. Then they would march triumphantly back into the lands they'd owned for centuries, carried on the wings of passion and justice.

But was all this a fantasy? And, if not, would he live to see it?

The despair closed in again.

Borgmann opened the door and walked out with the girl. Outside the two men who had attempted to enter earlier were waiting—arguing. They fell silent when Miriam came out, both gazing at her in astonishment. Only when she was well away from the door did they enter.

Ferrara was nowhere in sight.

"Do you think we're rid of Ferrara?" Miriam asked.

"Yes," Frederick told her. "I have his gun." He handed it to her.

Miriam examined the fiberglass pistol in confusion. "It looks like a toy," she said, puzzled.

"It's plastic—fiberglass, I'd say. It's designed to foil the metal detectors at airplane departure gates."

"Did Stabile see this?" she asked.

"As a matter of fact," Frederick said, "he told me to give it to you. He said you'd know what to do with it."

Miriam laughed aloud. "Well, someone back at *Mossad* will. The thing could be very useful."

"Attention all passengers," a voice on the terminal loudspeaker system said, "El Al Flight 42 is ready for boarding. Will all passengers on El Al Flight 42 please report to the boarding lounge?"

Miriam and Frederick slowly walked across the hall, toward the El Al lounge. The passengers were lined up in front of the flight attendant's desk. He was checking the tickets and taking seat reservations. They joined the line.

"Have we accounted for all of them, Miriam?"

"I think so. I hope so. Still, I'm glad to have this— this thing—in my purse."

"I can't get over Dahlgaard," Borgmann said. "He was my friend—my best friend. But I'm being callous—you've suffered more from this than I have."

"The important thing is that we won, Frederick. We did it. Even Stabile didn't realize that. Wait until he hears the rumors about your memory. We Israelis are very efficient gossips, you'll see."

Borgmann started to say something, then changed his mind.

The flight attendant checked their tickets. There'd been a vacancy in the first-class section, so they were able to reserve seats there together. As they left the seat reservation line, another flight attendant—a girl— guided them to still another line.

"Just pass slowly through the arch," she said politely, "and slip your hand luggage over this counter. We're sorry for any inconvenience, but this checking is necessary for the protection of us all."

Miriam glanced at Frederick with a raised eyebrow. Then she walked through the arch. Nothing happened. Borgmann passed through and joined her on the other side. Together, they walked down the entry ramp, into the waiting aircraft and found their seats, which were near the front.

Shortly after, El Al Flight 42 took off, an hour and twenty minutes late. Frederick and Miriam gazed out the window as Copenhagen faded away beneath them.

"Do you think you'll ever be back?" Miriam asked.

"No way to know. I don't think so, though. There's nothing there for me anymore."

"Nothing but memories," Miriam observed.

"I think I've come to terms with most of those," said Frederick.

"I'm glad to hear that."

The plane leveled off and the engines shifted to a slower speed.

"I haven't been completely honest with you. I have to tell you something about my memory, Miriam," Frederick said.

Miriam was startled. "What do you mean?"

"Well, an eidetiker's powers always fade with age. I can still remember the old things vividly, but I can no longer absorb new material—at least not much better than anyone else."

"But the centrifuge plans—"

Borgmann shook his head. "I can't remember them. The genuine blueprints and the phony ones are all mixed up in my mind. No hope of straightening them out."

Miriam made no comment. At last she said, "Why didn't you tell me earlier?"

"There wasn't really any opportunity, Miriam. Besides, after Yaakov died—well, I wasn't eager to add another disappointment."

"I see." She was hardly listening to his words now.

"I only told you now because I knew what you'd be expecting—" his voice faded.

"Frederick," she said excitedly. "There's still a way! Does anyone know your memory has faded?"

"Just you. Not that it matters."

"Then we can still bluff! We'll start the rumors, just as we planned. Is there proof of your memory somewhere?"

"I guess so. In school records."

"Where?"

Borgmann gazed at her, trying to figure out why she was excited. "In Denmark, in the United States. The records are there to see for anyone who's interested. But I don't remember the plans. I won't be able to re-create them, no matter how long I'm given."

"You and I know that, Frederick. But the Russians don't. Neither do the Egyptians, the Syrians, or the Palestinians. After they hear about your memory, they'll think we have the plans and that we're building the centrifuge. That's what Nachman intended all along."

The stewardess wheeled a tray of drinks down the aisle. "Would you like something?"

"No, thank you," Miriam said.

Frederick waved her off. He was thinking.

For a time, neither of them spoke. Then Borgmann began to laugh. It started as a chuckle and ended up a belly laugh.

"Frederick—what in the world is so funny?"

He did his best to control himself. "Now it *has* to be a bluff—don't you see that? It can't be anything else. No plans, no centrifuges, no bombs." He started laughing again.

Soon, Miriam was laughing too.

Less than four hours later, the jetliner touched down at Lod Airport, making such a gentle landing that its occupants were scarcely jostled. It was dinnertime in Tel Aviv.

"What now?" Miriam asked.

Frederick didn't reply immediately. He was thinking. "That restaurant in Tel Aviv, Miriam—"

412

"Which one?"

"Believe it or not, I can't remember the name. We ate there."

"Oh. The Rowal," she said.

"Yes. Does it still serve ice cream and cake?"

"Well," she said. "There are two possibilities. . . ."

NATIONWIDE BESTSELLER!

THE RIVETING TRUE STORY OF
A HARDNOSED NEW YORK DETECTIVE WHO SOLVED
SOME OF THE MOST DARING CRIMES OF OUR TIME!

AVON
24307
$2.25

ALBERT A. SEEDMAN AND PETER HELLMAN

CHIEF!

Al Seedman . . . hard-boiled, city-wise, smart as a whip, and as tough as they come. As Chief of Detectives in the biggest, roughest American city, he cracked the notorious Kitty Genovese stabbing, the Black Liberation Army cop-killings, the "Crazy Joe" Gallo murder, and many others. Cases that thrilled and horrified millions of newspaper readers . . . cases that baffled everyone but Al Seedman.

Now he tells it like it was—giving all the facts, and all the details, plus sixteen pages of photos.

"THE BOOK'S GUTS HAVE A .38 CALIBER KICK!"
Publishers Weekly

"I WAS ENTHRALLED! TRULY A GREAT COP STORY ABOUT ONE OF THE GREATEST DETECTIVES IN THE WORLD'S GREATEST CITY!"
Robin Moore, Author of
THE FRENCH CONNECTION

CC6-75